In the Shadow of a Hoax

A Fareview Fairytale

Book 2

By Maci Aurora

Maci Aurora Books

In the Shadow of a Wish, book 1
In the Shadow of a Hoax, book 2

Coming Soon

In the Shadow of a Dream, book 3

CL Walters Books

The Messy Truth About Love

In the Echo of this Ghost Town
When the Echo Answers
The Stories Stars Tell

The Letters She Left Behind

In the Shadow of a Hoax

A Fareview Fairytale
Book 2

By Maci Aurora

Mixed Plate Press
Honolulu, Hawaii
www.MixedPlatePress.com

In the Shadow of a Hoax
Fareview Fairytale Book 2
©2023 Maci Aurora w/ Mixed Plate Press
Honolulu, Hawaii

cover art: Sara Oliver Designs

ISBN: 979-8-9850325-5-0 (eBook)
ISBN: 979-9850325-4-3 (paperback)

About this book: *In the Shadow of a Hoax* was inspired by the Grimm's Fairytale, "King Thrushbeard". It contains explicit sexual situations and is intended for mature audiences (18+).

For

Those who might feel lost,
Those who might need a guide,
Those who need a champion,

There is always a way out of the woods.

Author's Note

In the Shadow of a Hoax is a reimagined fairytale with mistaken identities, royalty, and mysterious characters. Even fairytales traverse dark roads and face scary monsters, however. Tarley's story—while a romance—does focus on that happily-ever-after, but doesn't preclude her, and thereby the reader, from facing some very real and possibly disturbing obstacles. I felt it was important to share what could possibly be triggering for those who wish to know. *If you don't, please stop reading here and begin the story.*

Tarley Fareview and her sisters live in a land dominated by men, where women are subjugated to them. There are several instances when agency is taken from Tarley by way of physical assault (no rape). None of these situations are graphically glorified. I have done my utmost to care for Tarley (and my readers) and hope any scenes are presented with that caution in mind. Please note, that given the fantasy elements, there are some dark creatures and a battle in the final act, depicting violence.

Thank you so much for being willing to take a chance on *In the Shadow of a Hoax*. I hope you love this story as much as I enjoyed writing it, and that in all your endeavors, you are able to strive to present your true and authentic self.

Once upon a time . . . .

Kaloma Law of Means

As decreed by King Asher Hollis, fifth of the Holy Hollis Line on this day in Kaloma Year 767:

As written by church law and sanctioned by the state under the reign of King Asher, fifth of the Holy Hollis Line on this day in Kaloma Year 767, provisions must be made in the care of and continued welfare of the gentler and weaker female sex of all ages upon loss of male guardianship in order to protect said parties from behaviors of a predatory nature upon their means and their person. Therefore all holdings–coin, land, and/or material assets—will pass to the nearest male relative, who is in turn responsible for the care of the well-being of the female(s) under his guardianship. All females left without a male custodian, will thereby defer all holdings to the Kaloma church for the proper guardianship.

Tarley

arley, second daughter of Scarlett and Tomas Fareview, wasn't sure if she liked the man sitting across from her youngest sister Aurielle. As Tarley stood at the barrel of ale, waiting for the last of the four tankards to fill, her eyes drifted to Auri, ensconced at a table in a darkened corner of the inn with her suitor. It may have been the middle of the day, but the inn was shrouded in the dark ambiance of too much stone and wood and not enough light. Despite that, Tarley still attempted to assess what was happening between her sister and the stranger in their dark corner. Tarley was protective of her little sister, and she didn't trust easily—especially men.

It had been a little less than an hour ago that Auri had shown up at the back door to the kitchen of The Copper Pot Inn, asking for Tarley to cover for her.

"Auri, Mother is going to kill you." Tarley had lowered her voice so that the words sounded like air escaping from her throat.

"Tarley, please?" Auri had clasped her hands between her breasts and begged Tarley with her gray eyes. "It's just an outing, which Mother makes impossible."

Tarley had rolled her own eyes.

Auri wasn't supposed to be beyond the hedge where they lived with their parents. Since Auri's *Great Nap Escapade*—falling asleep in the woods and losing her red ribbon, a gift from their mother—she'd been relegated to "around the cottage duties."

"Do you think I want to cross Mother?" Tarley had glanced over her shoulder into the kitchen, thinking their mother might materialize, but it was empty. Instead, the dinner was steaming in a pot roasting over the heavy iron stove. Herbs and empty pots hung along the open wooden beams of the ceiling. Open shelves defined spaces holding dishes, utensils, jars, and supplies. The large square woodblock workstation held several loaves of fresh bread, still cooling, the aroma hanging in the air. Tarley had turned back to Auri. "Don't be daft! She'll have me as your second in tincture making, relegated to remaining behind the hedge." Tarley had shuddered. "No thank you."

Auri had stepped through the doorway and straightened her emerald skirts as if Tarley had already said 'yes.' "Mother was called to Denneby and took Jessamine with her. They'll be gone, two days at least. And Brinna won't tell. Besides, she and Papa and Mattias are out in the woods today."

Tarley hadn't liked the chicanery, but she also understood. Auri was a grown woman. How could she blame Auri for needing to get out? She did the same— her trips into the woods kept her sane. Tarley was sure Auri felt a bit like a prisoner. She would.

"Are you meeting the mysterious stranger you've mentioned?" Tarley had asked, recalling Auri's giddiness a few nights prior. The only question in her mind as Auri had regaled them with minor and evasive tidbits was *How?* How could her sister have met anyone? And in Sevens!

Auri had nodded, a smile lighting up her face. "Yes!" She'd grabbed Tarley's forearms and shaken her with excitement. "You'll get to meet him. And I'm safe. Nothing bad will happen. I promise."

"Famous last words." Tarley had arched an eyebrow. "How did you meet him again?"

"Oh—" Auri had looked away and fussed with her skirts again. "On a trip to town."

Recognizing her sister was lying, Tarley had narrowed her eyes. "That you never make anymore." Tarley had grabbed at her own wrist, finding comfort in the ribbon still tied there.

Her sister had begged Tarley with her look to acquiesce, which Tarley had done with a nod. "Fine."

Auri had flown into Tarley's arms, wrapping her in a hug. "Thank you. I will owe you."

"Just so we're clear, I don't trust any man."

"This one, you can." Auri had stepped away and backed out of the kitchen.

"I'll believe it when I see it."

"He's wooing me." Auri had grinned, a becoming blush brightening her cheeks.

Tarley had given Auri a look of disbelief, but now, nearly an hour later, Tarley watched as the dark-haired man across from her sister smiled, leaning forward across the table to touch Auri's cheek. His touch lingered, his thumb so near Auri's mouth. It was such a familiar gesture, Tarley felt the need to look away due to the intimacy of it, but she didn't. Worried her sister was being duped by this handsome newcomer to Sevens, Tarley struggled to piece together Auri's timeline. None of it made sense, especially because that touch suggested they knew one another. Perhaps better than Auri was letting on. Unless she was a bigger fool than Tarley took her for.

Goodness, he was handsome, to be sure. He could probably sway a blind woman, before opening his mouth and ensnaring the deaf woman too. More handsome than a man had the right to be, with that bronze skin dusted with a day-old beard, dark eyes, head of dark, unruly curls, and those unconventional dark clothes. It all added to his mystique.

Tarley watched her sister smile, her eyes flickering to the tabletop, then back up to the suitor she'd introduced to Tarley as Nixus Uraiahs. His appearance alone made it difficult to trust he had Auri's interests at heart, but Tarley had never met a man who had anyone's interests at heart other than his own. Add to it all this man, Nixus, was named after the old-world mythology's god of night and darkness. Who named their child after an evil god?

To be fair, Tarley only tolerated most men. She loved her father and brother, and she accepted Mr. Cobble, a sweet old man from the marketplace, who adored their mother. Oh—and Horance Forte, the barkeep at The Copper Pot Inn. So far, there hadn't been many instances to like the supposed stronger sex. Most of them had only ever used it to bully, bluster, and burden women, and worse yet, all their behavior was protected by the law of the Kaloma government.

"Good day, Miss Fareview."

Tarley's spine snapped straight at the voice, knowing the moment she turned who'd be standing at the bar. When she did finally turn, holding the last of the tankards she was filling, she wasn't surprised to see Dr. Allean Rufus smiling at her. That smile made her grit her teeth.

The thing was, he wasn't a terrible looking man, and his appearance wasn't off putting as much as her nerves informed her he was. Had she put all stock in how a person looks, then Allean Rufus had everything in his favor. His blond hair was slicked into a side part, neat and tidy. He had a lush mustache that was full and stylish along with one of those clefts in his angular chin. He wasn't egregiously tall, a middling height, she supposed, but tall enough to be slightly taller than her. He was wider, built lean, and strong if the way his clothing fit could hint at his strength. He always wore smart trousers, tailored shirts under dark vests and jackets with expensive shoes or boots. A gold timepiece hung from his pocket. Everything about him hinted at his wealth.

A newcomer to Sevens—an herbalist and healer like her mother—he'd once told Tarley that he "had brought his healing arts to the heathens to save them from the witches." The nerve, considering who her mother was. And so pretentious. Gods, she hated the man. She wished she'd punched him upon that first meeting. She would have saved herself the headache of his repeated attempts at courting her favor, and her repeated rebuffs of those attempts. It was a ridiculous cycle from which she hadn't been able to extract herself. She also couldn't fathom his persistence.

"Doctor." She grabbed the handles of the four steins.

"Did you give any additional thought to my invitation?"

"After my initial opposition upon receiving it?" she asked. "No. My answer hasn't changed." Tarley turned her head to Horance. "Which table?"

"That table of four." The barkeep nodded from the other end of the counter to the table near the hearth.

A man at the table where she was headed yelled, "Where's our drinks?"

Tarley rolled her eyes and said to Horance, "Taking them now." She scooped up the tankards.

"But Miss Fareview, I think a riverside picnic will be just the thing to demonstrate my regard." Rufus's head tracked her as she moved around the bar.

"No thank you, Mr. Rufus."

"Doctor."

She refrained from rolling her eyes. "Dr. Rufus. Not inclined, and I'm working, sir."

"But, Miss Fareview—"

Tarley left the doctor's declarations behind without looking back and worked her way across the room. Time with Rufus? Absolutely not. Time on her own for a solitary trip into the woods? Absolutely. A few days alone in the woods. Heaven. While her forays into the Whitling Woods weren't the safest of endeavors in Kaloma, especially for a woman—not with the threat of collectors and their roundups—she and her family had worked out a disguise to make the stints safer. Adding to it the lessons from her father in self-defense and using the forest to camouflage herself, she felt relatively safe disappearing into the wilds. She couldn't think about that now; she needed to focus on surviving work.

A strange energy filled with tension worked its way through The Copper Pot, which made Tarley tense as she moved between tables. Perhaps because of the impending visit of the Queen of Kaloma, who was set to arrive in the village of Sevens any day now, the village was on tenterhooks with anticipation. It was the most exciting thing to ever happen to Sevens in its whole existence, and the very reason Credence had given Tarley a position at the Copper Pot Inn.

Tarley had lived within the confines of Sevens for twenty-six years. While usually a sleepy, inconsequential settlement in the Whitling Woods at the northern edge of the Kaloma Kingdom, the news of the Queen's visit had caused the village to burgeon with new life. And, because it wouldn't just be Kaloma Royals visiting, but a royal contingent from the bordering kingdom of Jast journeying to meet the Queen for whatever it was the royals did, many new faces had arrived in the village, like Dr. Rufus—all hopefuls seeking to capitalize on the coin the royal visit would incur.

"There ya are," a gigantic stranger slurred as she arrived at the table.

"Four ales," she told the man and his companions as she set the tankards down on the table and offered a fake smile to each of them.

At one time, when Tarley and her sisters were younger, they lamented that there was no one their age in the village. But now there were so many strange faces, she wished they'd all go away again. This man and his party were among the newcomers. Most of the new life in Sevens were single men in search of fortune or gainful employment. And most of them were the very men who annoyed, belittled, harassed, harangued, and mistreated women already in short supply.

Sevens was a place that required a certain level of fortitude. It was why it was short of women and families and had been primarily a trading outpost for most of Tarley's life. Winter lingered for nine months of the year, then spring would arrive, and summer would play for a few weeks before it turned cold again. Her own family had eked out a living—barely—until Auri had found a key laden with gems in the woods after the *Great Nap Escapade*. With the wealth they gained from the key, they could have moved to the capital of New Taras—or anywhere in Kaloma—if they wanted, but her parents had insisted on staying in Sevens, in their tiny cottage within the confines of the hedge. They loved the life they'd built there. Besides, where could a woman go in Kaloma to escape the Law of Means? Sevens was as good a place to hide as any.

Tarley didn't love Sevens, but she loved the woods. Or rather, she loved the way she could disappear into the wilds and claim her independence. She loved being in a place so remote, no one questioned her. Except that had begun to change. Now that the Queen had put their small village on the map, and everyone had decided to make a run for their share of coin, it meant putting up with assholes like Mr. Four-Tankards and friends, who were presently making crude jokes, taunting her.

Ignoring them, she turned her back to the men to collect empty dishes on a nearby table. A meaty hand grabbed a handful of her skirt, including the right cheek of her backside, laughed as he did, and squeezed. With a screech, Tarley swung the used tankard in her hand, the cup connecting with the face of the offender, who yelped in pain.

The noise in the room fell into a chasm of silence.

"How dare you!" Tarley snapped. "Keep your filthy hands to yourself."

The man—Four-Tankards himself—a beefy tradesman who reeked of sweat and looked stained with dirt, moved from the wooden planks of the floor where he'd fallen to a knee and stood, a hand pressed to the side of his head. "How dare a woman swing on a man." He straightened, bringing him several hands taller than Tarley, his complexion rapidly reddening.

"But you'd swing on a woman?" she retorted.

"You bitch," he spat, spittle lingering on his lips.

Tarley took a step back. "Among other things," she said, narrowing her eyes and wishing she had more than a tankard as a weapon.

This was bad.

She took another step back and met resistance, colliding with the unforgiving wall of someone else. Afraid Four-Tankards would retaliate if she glanced away, Tarley kept her gaze forward, and realized Four-Tankards was frowning at whoever stood behind her.

"Excuse me?" a deep voice rumbled.

Tarley chanced a quick glance over her shoulder to discover the person behind her was Auri's suitor. He wasn't looking at Tarley, however, his dark, unnerving gaze leveled on the giant arsehole.

Mr. Uraiahs gently moved past Tarley, placing himself between her and the seething bull of a man who'd dared touch her.

"You should mind your business, stranger," Four-Tankards said, his skin mottled red. "This is between me and the wench."

Mr. Uraiahs turned his head to look at Tarley, his eyebrow arching over one eye. "Wench?" Then he turned to Four-Tankards again. "Is that how you speak with women, sir? It's no wonder you would have to manhandle one. If that's your tableside manner, one doesn't want to imagine what your bedside manner might entail." He glanced at Tarley and tipped his head. "Please excuse my coarse language."

Four-Tankards' face soured even further.

Mr. Uraiahs climbed a few notches in Tarley's esteem.

"It's a wonder he would know his way around a woman at all," Tarley added for good measure, stepping up next to Mr. Uraiahs, willing to fight for herself even if she was greatly at a disadvantage.

Mr. Uraiahs tipped his head back and laughed. It was a loud guffaw of mirth, and though perhaps a bit overdone, seemed to be committed with an intention to hit its mark, an arrow in the bullseye.

"I'm going to show you the way around my fists," Four-Tankards said to Mr. Uraiahs, his voice a low rumble of words ground through his teeth and a clenched jaw.

"Now that," Mr. Uraiahs said, his tone as cold as

granite with the added bite of winter, "I would love to accommodate." His mirth was gone, and a menacing look moved over his features that gave even Tarley pause.

"Not in my establishment you don't," Credence Crendell, the proprietress of The Copper Pot, yelled from across the room. She moved through the doorway past her brother Horance, who'd made his way around the bar. Credence's white hair was an explosion of tight coils that framed her brown face, shaped now by the frown. She pointed at the door. "Get out, the lot of you. And anyone getting handsy with my workers isn't welcome here."

Mr. Uraiahs took a step back and with the wave of his hand, gestured that Four-Tankards could lead the way outside.

Four-Tankards stalked past Mr. Uraiahs toward the door.

"Nix," Auri said, blocking Mr. Uraiahs. "Are you sure?"

Nix? Tarley was surprised at the familiarity and wondered if her sister was worried because Mr. Uraiahs was smaller than the dimwit who'd stomped outside. Not significantly shorter, but Four-Tankards had arms the size of small tree trunks. He didn't seem the sort to shy from a fight or a confrontation, which could put Mr. Uraiahs in physical peril.

But Mr. Uraiahs tipped his head to the side, gave Auri an arrogant grin, and arched that dark eyebrow again. "Now, Auri, are you worried for me?"

Auri? Tarley noted something secret passing between her sister and this man. She knew she would have to interrogate Auri sooner rather than later. If their mother found out about clandestine meetings with a suitor she hadn't vetted—Tarley shuddered at the thought of Scarlett's wrath. Her mother was going to know something was up if a suitor suddenly appeared.

Auri smiled sweetly at Nix, stepped out of his way, and watched him go, calling, "Maybe don't end him."

"You're not worried he's going to get hurt?" Tarley asked.

Auri glanced at Tarley, her cheeks pinking with a blush, then shook her head. "Not at all."

Tarley narrowed her eyes at her sister. "How well *do* you know him?"

Auri just smiled sublimely without a word, then started after the all-too-handsome suitor.

Tarley followed, stopping with Auri in the open doorway.

But by the time she reached the door along with the rest of the patrons, Four-Tankards was on the ground looking like he'd been through a raging storm, battered, bruised, his clothing rumpled and torn as blood gushed from his nose and mouth.

Shocked, Tarley looked at Mr. Uraiahs. His hands appeared perfectly fine. Not a bruise or cut marred his skin. Not a shred of his dark clothing was in disarray. He rubbed his hands together as if wiping offensive material from his palms and said, "Perhaps, sir, as you recover from these wounds, you'll take some time to reflect on your treatment of women."

"Who are you?" Four-Tankards sputtered.

"Your worst nightmare."

"I'm going to get you." Four-Tankards spat, the dark soil turning black as it mixed with his blood.

Mr. Uraiahs smiled an unholy smile. "You can certainly try."

Named after the evil god indeed, Tarley thought.

And with that, Mr. Uraiahs turned and walked away, completely unconcerned as he made his way back into The Copper Pot through the crowd that parted to make way for him. At the door, he turned to Tarley. "Are you alright, Miss Fareview?"

She nodded, speechless. He didn't have a mark on him, not a speck of dust, no hair out of place. His skin was as flawless as before. No indication of the violence that had taken place.

Auri threaded her arm through Mr. Uraiahs's with a bright smile on her face, her adoration shining in her expression.

Light flared in Tarley's vision, weaving golden threads between Auri and her suitor.

Tarley blinked.

That certainly couldn't be right. She shook her head, hoping she wasn't coming down with one of her headaches. After she watched them return to their luncheon, she glanced back at Four-Tankards in the street, now shrugging off his friends' assistance.

It was clear, she decided: not all men were created

equal.

"Tarley!" Credence grabbed hold of her and drew her back into the emptied-out dining room to the kitchen.

"I'm sorry—" Tarley stumbled.

"Don't apologize," Credence said, stabilizing her.

Mrs. Barnwell turned from slicing the fresh bread loaves to watch them.

"You weren't in the wrong, dear, but you need to get out of the village. That vile man will report you straight away."

"What happened?" Mrs. Barnwell asked.

"Gretta, would you prepare Tarley with another few days of food?" Credence's dark eyes returned to Tarley. "He'll bring a priest, or worse, a collector." She swallowed. "We won't have time to find your father. Let Horance and I smooth this over, yes? You go on your trip early."

"I'm so sorry, Credence. I didn't mean to—"

"Stop. What's a few hours difference? And I'm not worried about The Copper Pot, girl! I'm worried about you. Get to the woods." She pushed Tarley toward the back door and out into the yard. "I'll tell Auri, and don't come back until Mattias comes to get you. Now go."

Tarley didn't need any additional encouragement. She hustled up to her attic room, donned her disguise, collected her packs, and disappeared into the woods, taking several deep, grateful breaths of unfettered freedom.

Into the Woods

Lachlan

Lachlan Nikolas, first prince of Jast, heir to the throne, who at present carried a rather adept seat on his horse, Goldie, wasn't pleased about having to pretend to be someone else. Yet, that was exactly what he was having to do, because his father required it. And one didn't deny the king. Except Lachlan had, and now he was paying the price. Refusing to marry his father's selection for wife came with a price, which for the moment, meant traipsing through the Whitling Woods on the Kaloma side of the Whitling Mountain Pass.

The parade of horses carrying not only a stand-in

prince but also the disguised one, a bevy of royal guards, and a retinue of army soldiers and supplies moved along the narrow switchback path barely wide enough for two side-by-side, through the towering trees of the forest toward the tapered flats of the valley. To Lachlan's left was a steep incline that continued toward the mountain peaks frozen with perpetual snow, and to his right, a wilderness that obscured a stretch of land toward a deep ravine cut by a raging river below. It was cold despite being early summer, so they were dressed in thick clothing and over clothes. Their horses puffed steam as they traversed, jerking the riders at times with the steep steps.

"You did humiliate her," Ollie said from Lachlan's right. His friend's gray-speckled gelding plodded along next to Goldie. Ollie was dressed as the prince, his finery a spectacle in the woods, and wouldn't have ever been something Lachlan would have worn. It was too showy for his taste, the purple and gold of Jast on full display. They were on their way to the village of Sevens where they were to meet the Queen of Kaloma. Ollie had donned the ostentatious outfit Lachlan would never have worn, even to an event of state. But Kaloma didn't know that.

Ollie looked like a preening bird. A handsome one, however, with his dark, auburn hair tied back and his light brown eyes twinkling with mirth. Dressed like that, Lachlan wasn't so sure what Ollie had to be happy about. He was the bullseye of the target should anyone dare to attack the prince's retinue. And yet, the prime adviser to the king was all smiles about their circumstances, even if it was Lachlan's fault they'd been forced on this endeavor into the enemy territory of Kaloma wearing one another's identity.

"Humiliating her hadn't been my intention," Lachlan explained, reaching out to pat Goldie's neck. She nickered at his touch to tell him she was pleased.

"And yet it isn't intentions that dictate another's feelings," Ollie said. "It's the reality our intentions create."

Lachlan groaned. "No wonder my father likes you. You sound just like him." They rode in silence for a few more beats but for the sound of birds singing in the trees and the horses' hooves plodding against the earth, until Lachlan added, "How was I supposed to know that the worst gossip at court would hear me?"

"I don't know how you didn't know, Lach. You've lived at court your whole life." Ollie pulled the reins a touch so his dapple-gray bumped against Goldie, and they both veered a touch to the left. "Right, Captain?"

Johesha, the captain of Lachlan's guard, riding several paces ahead, glanced over his shoulder and smirked. "I'll keep my thoughts to myself."

Ollie laughed. "Wise, Captain. We might have a politician in the making."

Lachlan frowned, staring at the evergreen trees cutting the landscape with sharp points. "You're referencing the bit about when I said the shape of her nose looked like a thrush's beak?"

"You should have known—the court has giant ears

and trumpets for mouths."

He was right, as Ollie always was.

Ollie was five years older than Lachlan, which made them peers, but Ollie had been in service to the crown since he'd been twenty-two, when his own father had unexpectedly died. Ollie had been appointed a junior adviser in his father's stead, rising quickly in Lachlan's father's estimation and gaining the appointment of Prime Adviser by the time he was twenty-six. Ollie was a fine adviser and had trained his whole life to be one just as Lachlan had trained to be king one day. Lachlan didn't always like what Ollie had to say, but for the most part, Ollie hadn't steered him wrong. He just knew that Ollie was for Jast, so his advice never veered from what was best for the kingdom. It was why the man could be a sitting peacock pretending to be a prince for any would-be assassins and still smile.

"He didn't even ask me, Ollie," Lachlan said, a morose tone he usually tempered finding its way through. "Didn't even trust me enough to have a conversation about the betrothal." Lachlan was sure his past behavior might have solidified his father's mistrust in him, and he was pretty sure he didn't deserve to be crowned king.

"I wonder, Lach, if the truth is that you did want those in court to hear. That you did want the gossip to reach the princess's ears. That you did, in fact, want to sabotage a possible wedding rather than face the wrath of your father just by having a face-to-face with him."

Lachlan pressed his teeth together, hating Ollie's adept perception, even if he thought it was bollocks. The idea that he couldn't face his father wasn't something he wanted to consider. He preferred to be the victim in the situation. So, he didn't respond. A prince didn't have to.

"Your marriage to her would have secured a strong alliance," Ollie added.

"Freida Beaknose?"

"Yes, Princess Freida Truisante." Ollie rolled his eyes at him. "The alliance would have opened Jast's western borders and given us a straight route to the Mourning Sea. And if these negotiations with Kaloma prove favorable, Jast will have access to the southern border and the Dauntiss Ocean." Ollie sighed. "Now, we'll have to do damage control and hope Truisante isn't vindictive."

"Forgive me. I couldn't condemn my life to be married to someone I don't choose. Even for trade routes."

"Spoken like a young, headstrong, impetuous prince." Ollie tsked and shook his head. "Those in positions of power rarely have the choice."

"Do you think that's what my father is trying to teach me by forcing us on this trip and making us trade places?"

"No. I think it's an opportunity. And I think what your father wants is to protect you. The switch is only a safety precaution until we rendezvous with the queen."

Lachlan made a noise in his nose of incredulity. At twenty-five, he and his father rarely saw eye-to-eye. Nose-to-nose was a much better description of their relationship. If his father said "left," Lachlan went right. If Lachlan said "here," his father went there. Lachlan's mother had remarked that they were too alike, but Lachlan didn't see it. While he admired his father and thought he was a good king, there was a lot between them as a father and son that didn't work. It was fortunate they had so many people between them to build bridges. Lachlan's mother and Ollie, to name two very important ones.

"I think my father would prefer it if you were the prince, Ollie."

"Bullshit, your highness."

Lachlan glanced at Ollie, who was grinning, and smiled as a new noise was added to the clopping of the horses on the narrow path. It sounded like a quick tug on a horse's leathers while adjusting the saddle. Lachlan felt it move the air to the right side of his face, and out of the corner of his eye noticed the tell-tale shaft and fletching of an arrow as it skimmed the top of Ollie's shoulder. As if in slow motion, he swung to look, going for his sword as Captain Johesha yelled, "Attack!"

Lachlan turned, pulling up on Goldie's reins as Ollie yanked on the reins of his own horse, moving backward, away from Goldie, drawing the arrows away from Lachlan. The royal guard, including Johesha, swarmed, but one soldier near him—Jennings—

dropped. An arrow protruded from his neck and another from his side. Jenning's riderless horse darted forward, spooking Goldie. Another volley of arrows looking for purchase pierced her flesh and she reared.

Goldie bolted, leaving behind the chaos of the ensuing battle. With a glance over his shoulder, Lachlan caught Johesha's eye before facing forward to gain control of his mount. Lachlan was an excellent horseman, but his skills had been tested on the royal grounds of Jast. He hadn't had many opportunities to try and stay seated on his horse in mountainous terrain as his horse careened through the old growth forest of a land with which Lachlan wasn't familiar. He ducked low as they crashed through the forest, holding the reins and her mane, hoping to get her under control.

It was the wrong worry.

He and Goldie were moving fast.

Using his legs, his voice, and the reins, Lachlan tried to calm her, but his horse was frantic with fear and pain. When the edge of a cliff loomed ahead, Goldie seemed to sense the danger ahead and tried to stop, pulling up, but lost her footing, unable to gain it on the course rock. She slid, her momentum driving them forward, and before Lachlan could jump, his boot caught up in the stirrup, he and Goldie slid over the lip of the ravine and plummeted.

Lachlan, clinging to his horse, hit the raging water of the river. As they slammed against the surface, she took most of the impact of the fall, but she also became his anchor, her weight pulling him under. His breath was sucked from his lungs, and his body snapped against Goldie's in the current. He'd definitely broken bones, ribs. The water pummeled him as he fought against his horse's broken body, twisting and turning in the raging tumult. Every bone and muscle inside him screamed that he needed to be still, but his lungs needed air. Being tethered to Goldie, who was unsuccessfully fighting the current, drew them both deeper, the water holding on with cold and unforgiving hands.

Somehow, Lachlan found the dagger on his hip and used it to cut his way out of the stirrup. Though his lungs were on fire, he discovered he was caught in the reins too. He wasn't going to make it, he realized, but sawed through the leather anyway, unwilling to give up. There was an underwater tug and snap of the tether, and suddenly Goldie was drifting further away, rising toward the surface, completely still, without him.

His wet clothing dragged him down, his vision dappling dark like Ollie's gray gelding as his body slipped toward unconsciousness. Still, he managed to shed the weight of his outer layers, then found the will to kick. He needed air, needing to live more than he was ready to give up.

He broke the surface. Gasped a harsh breath, everything burning, his body refusing to cooperate.

Since he weighed significantly less, the current propelled him forward, and as he struggled to keep his head above the water, he caught up with Goldie, now drifting dead in the water. He grabbed hold of her and held on, pulling himself up onto her body as far as he could. The grief at the loss of his horse hit him in increments, but Lachlan couldn't stay in it, aware that death was coming for him as well. So Lachlan Nikolas, first prince of Jast, heir to the throne, floated down the Grimz River on his dead horse, broken but clinging to her for his life.

Tarley

At the birds' morning song, Tarley grinned and stretched contentedly under her blanket. She opened her eyes, reorienting to her surroundings under the linen-canvas roof of her small tent. Despite the circumstances that had pushed her into the woods, she was happy to be there. She could hear the music of the river moving in the distance, one of her favorite sounds. A light breeze drifted through the summer trees, moving leaves, shrubs, and tall grass. The bugs were buzzing, the birds flitting, and creatures scurrying. If Tarley could hide in the woods from Kaloma law forever, she would have, but the registry existed, which meant so did she. There was no disappearing.

Crawling from her bedroll, Tarley righted her bedding before donning the wrap around her breasts, then the boy's pants, tunic, and sweater given to her by her brother. She braided her hair, wrapped it in a coil, and pinned it before stuffing it into a cap. Finally, she flopped onto her backside and scooted forward to the entrance of the tent to stuff her feet into her boots before venturing out to start a fire and make herself some coffee and cakes.

The air, still carrying a morning chill, wouldn't warm much further, but that didn't bother her as she bent close to the smoking tinder and gently blew on it as it caught. It was summer in the Whitling Woods, which meant nothing more than no snow for a few weeks and summer plants to harvest for the winter ahead. Tarley added some more substantive pieces of wood to the burgeoning fire, knowing she only had a few weeks of the year when she could escape into the woods to hide from laws that kept her—and all Kaloma women—repressed. The thought grabbed hold of her heart and squeezed it mercilessly. She snapped a branch to add to the fire with a bit more fervor than necessary, then took a deep breath, unwilling to shed the happiness of being where she was for the oppression she would inevitably return to. The cool air cleared her lungs, and she reset as the heat of the fire settled her. She was glad when the coffee was done, sipping with her hands wrapped around the warmth of her cup as her cakes cooked.

Way back when, she'd argued with her father about her trips for this summer, especially after a woman had been found dead in the woods. Tarley had overheard the rumors spread by patrons of The Copper Pot that the woman's body had been defiled. Though she dismissed the rumors, she understood the reality. A woman was dead. Though it was likely that she'd been a runaway avoiding collection and was killed by her inexperience in the Whitling Woods by a wild woodland creature, Tarley couldn't help but be shaken by those circumstances as much as by something more sinister.

She shuddered.

That news brought out the desire in her parents to keep her from the woods. That was the way of her mother, after all. Protect at all costs. But the family needed the food Tarley hunted and caught to prepare for winter. She had promised to remain closer to Sevens. The other agreement, which she did anyway, was to remain disguised. The risk had always been being caught and claimed as an unprotected female. Based on Kaloma Law, any man could turn in a found woman and claim a reward. That was why collectors roaming the land were such a threat. She wasn't sure donning a cap and tucking up her hair made her look less female, but Brinna insisted Tarley could pull off young and boyish if she wanted.

"Just frown," her sister had said with a smirk.

The reality was, Tarley needed her trips to the woods like she needed air to breathe, having decided long ago it was because of the peace they offered. As one of five siblings, the Fareview cottage had been loud and constant. She adored her family. They were her life. But lately, even having the boon of working at the Copper Pot, she still felt as if she were missing something, something that was hers and hers alone. Their mother had made accepting the position at the Copper Pot difficult. Especially after Auri's *Great Nap Escapade*. Scarlett had been impossible before, now she was tyrannical. Just being allowed to work for Credence had been an exercise in stubborn persistence.

"I want my family here where I know you are safe," her mother had explained the day Tarley had finally won the battle of wills.

"Why wouldn't I be safe with Credence? It's Sevens!" Tarley had exclaimed. "Besides, it will free up some space here, since she's offered to let me stay above the stables. Plus, I'll be making coin, which will be helpful."

Tarley had watched her mother and her father exchange glances, wondered about it, but hadn't pursued her question because her father had asked, "How will she pay you?"

"Room and board, plus 25 luri a week."

He'd hummed his acknowledgement before taking a bite.

"I'm not a child anymore," Tarley had said. "I will take it."

Scarlett wiped the tabletop with the edge of her apron. "It isn't about being a child."

"Then what is it about? Because I'm not following your logic, Mother. I'm a grown woman."

"Yes. What is it?" Auri had echoed the question. "I'm tired of being a prisoner as well."

"That isn't... it's not..." But Scarlett, her eyes dancing between them, her ivory skin pinkening, hadn't finished her thought. Instead, she'd stood and left the room.

"How is that fair?" Auri had demanded. "It's a simple question!"

Their father had set down his utensils, dabbed his mouth with his napkin, and cleared his throat. "Your mother didn't have the safest life... before." Tomas's gaze jumped between Tarley and her siblings. "Forgive her protectiveness."

"What do you mean?" Tarley had asked, suddenly unsure, as if a haze had lifted, revealing how little Tarley knew about her mother before that moment. Her breath had tripped on the clarity, making her feel confused, before sliding away upon her father's reply.

"It isn't my story to share." Tomas had stood. "There's nothing wrong with you working in Sevens, Tarley, if that's what you want. You already go out on your forest trips. You're still in Sevens, which I don't think your mother can object to." He'd sighed and glanced at the red ribbon tied to her wrist. "I'll talk to her."

Because that was what their father always did, talked their mother off her ledge.

Tarley had nodded.

Now, she finished her coffee and stored her cakes for later, wrapping one into her pack for lunch. She covered the coals of her fire, collected her gear, and left camp behind. Fish for dinner, she decided, because there was a fabulous spot where she wanted to decompress.

Tarley walked through the woods, humming quietly, observing the sights and sounds as she went. The raucous cry of ravens, the warble of the songbirds, the buzz of insects, and the breeze rustling the foliage. The spindle branches of the deciduous trees clothed in rich, verdant leaves, reaching toward her like hands. She sidestepped them, drew some away, ducked under them, finding her way through the brush on a path she knew well, while the sky shone blue through the treetops overhead. A clear, perfect day.

She broke through the trees into the clearing, her steps crunching along the pebbled beach, anticipating the beauty at the river's edge. When she looked up, it wasn't the river she saw, but the carcass of a golden horse washed ashore. Next to it, a body.

"Oh my gods!" Tarley dropped her equipment and covered her mouth, the sound of her rapid breathing and her racing heart overtaking all other sound. Her thoughts jumped to the impulse to flee, to stay hidden and safe, but then went to war with her training to help, to heal.

Three beats of her heart.

One.

Two.

Three.

Many might shy away from death, but Tarley was her mother's daughter. She'd spent her entire life learning poultices, ointments, tinctures, balms, and a plethora of methods to help the sick and infirm. She'd helped deliver babies both human and animal alike. She'd set bones and wrapped them. She'd sat bedside for vigils and witnessed the death of a few, only to prepare bodies for those who couldn't. Tarley wasn't squeamish. After her count of three, she started across the clearing, knowing the bodies had to be burned to keep feral creatures and scavengers away.

The horse—which had been beautiful in its life— was still fresh, flies and other insects buzzing around it. It wasn't yet bloated, which meant the animal hadn't been dead long—or the body near it. One or two days perhaps. No smell of decay.

She knelt near the body.

A man.

One she didn't know. She hesitated. Even knowing he was dead didn't keep her heart from lurching, considering who he might have been in his life and the potential danger he might have once presented. She took a deep breath and moved to check his pulse to verify he was gone. Her fingers slid across his wet skin—cool but still pliant—and he shivered with a faint groan.

"Oh shit." Tarley scrambled back, her boots kicking up pebbles in the scree as she did. "You're alive," she whispered. She glanced around to see if this was a trap, but nothing indicated that was so. There wasn't anyone else waiting to nab her, no sounds in the forest beyond, no movement to make her think she was in danger.

She looked back at the man, the normalcy of the woods around them calming her slightly. After another deep breath, she assessed the scene with her eyes like she'd been taught. The man wasn't conscious, his body still partially submerged in the water greedily lapping at his legs. The tableau seemed more accident than set up. Besides, the stranger was barely alive, his body a painful testament to what appeared an ordeal. It seemed an extensive farce if it were a trap.

He might not be dead, but he wasn't far from it. She stood, wiping her hands on her trousers, and noted his shallow breaths. His dark hair was matted against his pale face. Thick, even brows framed his closed eyes, with dark lashes resting on his pale cheeks. It was a handsome face—or had been—when considered objectively, but Tarley knew handsome didn't mean safe. His soaked clothing was slightly strange, less homespun, and more tailored, which indicated the man was probably wealthy.

Tarley took a step away from him.

Wealthy men in Sevens, in the Whitling Woods, were uncommon.

But kingdom-appointed collectors were.

Tarley took another step away from him and swallowed, then another step. She couldn't help him and didn't know if her help would make a difference anyway, though her conscience argued she knew that wasn't true, all too aware that she was turning away from helping someone because she was afraid.

"Yes, I'm afraid," she whispered out loud to herself. *Why would she save a collector?* She spun on her toe, turning away from the stranger and the dead horse, certain she should walk away.

But after a few more steps—*What if that were Mattias?* the internal voice argued.

She stopped with a frustrated groan and turned back, her heart in her throat. Adrenaline made her shake as she hesitated, imagining him as her brother. "My brother wouldn't be a collector!" she whisper-shouted at the prone man who couldn't hear her.

But what if he isn't, that annoying voice pointed out.

"It's a risk," she retorted and grasped her hands in front of her with nervous indecision. "If he is…" She knew that it would put her in danger. "But maybe he'll die anyway," she reasoned, "and then my conscience will be clear, because at least I tried."

She sighed loudly; she couldn't walk away.

Returning to the man, she crouched down to touch him once more. "Hello? Can you hear me?"

He made a faint sound and mumbled something, though Tarley couldn't hear it, only seeing his lips move slightly.

"What is your name?" she asked, running her hand over his face and neck to check for a fever. His skin still felt cold to her touch, and he shivered—a bad sign.

He muttered again, and Tarley bent down, her ear

near his mouth. "I'm here," she said. "You're not alone," she added, in case he was on the verge of dying.

He muttered again, the faint brush of air from his exhalation and his cold lips a whisper against her skin. She shivered in response to the sensation, and leaned away from him, trying to ascertain what he'd said.

"Did you say? 'Ollie'?" she asked, but he didn't reply. "Is that your name?"

He was silent and shivered again.

"I need to get you dry, Ollie," she said, deciding that was as good a name to call him as any. With practiced hands, she ran her fingers lightly along his pale face nicked with scrapes, cuts, and red tells of forming bruises, relieved she didn't find any fractures. Next, she checked his head, moving her fingers through his hair to feel for lacerations and bumps. Though the silk of his wet hair was soft in contrast to the day-old growth on his cheeks, her hands came away clean. No blood. With an adept but light touch, she moved her hands down along his neck, over the sinew of his shoulders and arms, across his ribs—several broken, if his pained expression was any indication— down his flat stomach, over his pelvis, across his muscular legs and knees to the top of his very expensive boots that she wouldn't remove, yet. She couldn't be sure about a back injury, and aside from the ribs, all his bones seemed under the skin. She couldn't feel any obvious breaks aside from the ribs. She had to wonder if his ribs had punctured any of his organs. Without removing his clothing, she wouldn't be able to tell if there was internal bleeding, though he didn't have any blood on his lips, which gave her hope it wasn't so.

"Okay, Ollie? I'm going to help you."

Suddenly, his eyes flickered open, revealing a shade not quite gray, or green, or blue, or brown, but some combination of all of them. Like standing in the woods on a summer day, surrounded by a kaleidoscope of color. Tarley started, then froze as if caught like prey in a predator's gaze, only she didn't feel unsafe. Rather, she felt something altogether unrecognizable, as if she were floating for a moment in the vast expanse of a warm, summer-night sky, bathed in the effervescence of stardust. Which was ridiculous.

Then his dark eyebrows shifted, and though clear he was in pain, but he looked… panicked. "No!" With a jerk, he tried to scramble backward, to get away from her, only to yell out, grasping his ribs before he collapsed. "Get away." He grunted out the words between breaths and tried to yank at his wet shirt.

He was delirious, she decided. That meant grave danger. "You are hyperthermic, Ollie. I need to warm you up."

He closed his eyes again, breathing heavily, and began to shiver uncontrollably, lost to the haze of unconsciousness as his head lolled to the side.

Tarley stood, knowing what needed to be done. Fishing would have to wait.

Tarley collapsed next to the sledge where Ollie was lying unconscious outside of her tent. Dragging him back to camp had taken everything out of her. After burning the horse's body to keep the scavengers away, the fire had served a second and third purpose. First, by warming Ollie after she'd stripped him of his wet clothes and piled dry materials on top of him to insulate his body heat, and second, allowing her time to build the sledge to get him to safety. Now, having muscled both the large man and her gear back into camp, she was exhausted.

She rolled from her belly to her back in the dirt and looked up at the streaked sky beginning to turn dark. Her stomach growled, but she couldn't bring herself to grab the cake in her pack to eat. Not yet. There was still work to do to make sure Ollie would live.

Tarley sat up and looked at the unconscious man. "How am I going to get you into the tent?" she asked him, hoping he'd answer, but he didn't. He was still unconscious. At one point he'd stopped shivering but had started once more. The temperature of his skin had her worried.

She sighed and stood. "I guess I got you this far."

Moving around the crude sledge, she tried to figure out how to move him without causing additional injury. Getting him into the sledge had been difficult enough. He was tall—taller than she was—as well as muscular, which made him heavier than she'd anticipated. His clothing had hinted he was tall and thin, but as she'd removed the garments, she'd been surprised to find the compact and rigid plateaus and valleys of his musculature. His form was beautiful. She hadn't pictured a rich collector—if that's what he was—built so. She'd always pictured collectors as fat, living on the coin they made turning in women.

She glanced at the tent. Dragging Ollie was a terrible idea. Especially with his broken ribs.

But he needed warmth.

She considered leaving him there, and building a fire to keep him warm, but the darkening sky was peppered with collecting clouds. His lungs were already at risk. He needed to be out of the elements.

She looked at her tent again. "You can do this, Tarley. Just into the tent."

Instead of muscling him, however, she pulled the sledge as close to the outer wall of the tent as she could, unfastened it, then rolled up the canvas. Next, she prepared a space for him, realizing how cramped her quarters were going to be, considering his size. But there just wasn't anything to be done to change it, so Tarley focused on her task instead.

She removed his now dried clothes she'd laid over the leaves, then all the leaves and detritus she'd used to insulate him, until he was once again a naked, shivering man. Rather than think about his nudity—because she reminded herself nakedness was natural—she attempted to focus on what she needed to do. Unfortunately, she hadn't been able to unsee the beauty and bounty of his shape while undressing him the first time and forced herself to refrain from ogling him now by reminding herself he was a man and probably a horrible one at that. He didn't deserve her ogling.

"Okay, Ollie." Supporting his neck and back, she pulled him from the sledge. "Please. Don't. Make. Me. Regret. This." She grunted out each word as she dragged him from the contraption. Though she attempted to be gentle, she wasn't particularly graceful. He grunted in response to the movement but remained incoherent and incapable of assisting her. Finally, under the roof of the tent, Tarley pulled, but her foot slipped out from under her, and she collapsed with him landing on top of her. His head fell against her chest, his back to her belly until he slipped between her spread thighs, stretched out toward the sledge just outside the opening. She was pinned under his weight. Exhausted, she didn't fight it.

"Stars," she breathed and rested under him, gathering energy to finish the move. She closed her eyes, not hating his weight, even though she knew she couldn't take it for long. "Hold on. Hold on," she chanted, tapping into her reserves. "We'll get there eventually."

After a few more minutes, she wiggled out from under him, until he was on his back, and she was free.

She huffed and puffed a moment to catch her breath, then with as much care as she could muster considering the differences in their size, maneuvered him into a place where she could get him comfortable under blankets and still have room for herself.

With another sigh, Tarley rose onto her knees, and refastened the tent wall, then shuffled on her knees through the tiny space to check Ollie once more.

She reached out and pressed the back of her hand to his forehead. Burning up. "Shit," she mumbled.

Suddenly, her wrist was wrapped in his tight grip. "What are you…" he mumbled, his forest-colored eyes bright.

Tarley couldn't pull out of his grasp. "Ollie?"

"Are you trying to kill me?" he asked. "The arrows!" He tried to move but hissed in pain, collapsing back into the bedding. His eyes slipped shut once more, and his grip relaxed.

Her heartbeat thundering in her chest, she tentatively reached out to touch him. He didn't move, lost to unconsciousness. She couldn't make sense of his delirious visions, but she hushed him anyway, and continued to check him, making sure she hadn't missed any wounds. It was an intimate thing, but her mind didn't linger. Rather, she talked to him as her thoughts considered the things she would need to keep him alive. "I know it might seem rather forward of me to touch you this way, Ollie, but it needs to be done." She glanced at his face again, tight with his pain and whatever visions played within his mind. "I'm going to have to go look for some swennig root, to make you a tincture. That should help with any infection."

Her eyes skimmed his form, looking for anything she might have missed, all the while talking. "I'll have to look for some weeping wallosh to make you tea for your fever and pain. It's a good thing I found you Ollie. How long were you in the water?"

He didn't answer, instead moaning and mumbling in the haze that held his mind.

She pulled the blanket back up to his chin. "How does a rich man end up in the river?"

He didn't answer.

"Are you a collector?" she whispered, afraid he might answer that he was.

He didn't.

She tucked the blankets tighter around him.

Night was already oppressive by the time she was finished. Barely able to move herself, Tarley laid next to Ollie. Though she thought about all the things she still needed to do, her muscles and bones didn't seem to want to cooperate. So she listened. His breath was clear—no rattle—which was good for now.

She shut her eyes. "Just for a moment," she said and yawned.

Shoulder to shoulder with Ollie, she blinked her eyes back open and thought about getting food to cut the ache in her belly, but she didn't move. She considered going outside to build a fire, to sleep there, then remembered it might rain, though she knew she couldn't bring herself to move even if it wasn't a threat.

Besides, she couldn't leave her charge.

"Just another minute," she whispered to the roof of the tent. "I'll just rest for another quick minute," she murmured, closed her eyes, and drifted into the blackness of sleep.

Lachlan

Lachlan floated in oppressive darkness, his body undulating between gigantic and miniature, which added to his distress and discomfort. He needed to get outside of his form. He pressed at the bonds weighing him down, needing help and looking around, though seeing was impossible.

"Goldie?" he called out, blinking to clear his vision, and she appeared as if he'd willed it, floating just beyond his reach in the violent tumult of black water. "Why is the water boiling?"

His horse looked at him. "Ollie?" she asked.

But he knew that wasn't Goldie's voice—Goldie was a horse—and he wasn't Ollie, so he shook his head. "Goldie's dead," he muttered, and his eyes fluttered open as he pushed at the skin binding him to the black sea. No. It was a cauldron. "I'm boiling in soup."

"No. Keep the covers on." A shadowed face hovered over his, forcing the chains back into place, but he didn't fight, his attention fixed on the golden light illuminating the shadow from behind like a halo.

"You shot me," he accused and closed his eyes to find peace in the dark. But he moaned, his body undulating once more. "Out! I need out."

The shadow voice spoke in calm tones, but he wasn't sure what it said, exactly, only that the sound made him calmer.

He shivered violently, but he was on fire, burning in the boiling water. "Hot. Can't breathe."

The shadow swore, and fingertips carved a warm path over his icy-fire skin like piercing needles.

Goldie was with him again, but she was floating away. "Skin to skin," his horse told him.

Lachlan nodded to Goldie. "You saved me."

"Not yet—"

Goldie sank under the water and disappeared.

"Goldie!" he cried, reaching for her and grabbing hold of something else, a lifeline in the darkness, pulling the warmth closer. He held on and floated down the dark river, willing his body back to normal size before collapsing into the darkness. Taking a deep breath, he groaned, fighting against the water's hold. "Let me go."

"Hush," the shadow voice said and continued speaking, though the words sounded far away, indiscernible, and Lachlan sank away, back into the darkness.

Then suddenly, he was thrashing, fighting the current of the cold water, trying to get out of the icy fire consuming his skin. "The arrows are in my skin. The arrows," he cried, brushing them away.

His eyes flew open. It was dark, but not the dark of his mind, just the dark of night.

"I'm here, Ollie." The shadow voice was soothing. "I'm with you," the voice repeated, and the warm slide of the creature, an angel's velvet skin, was pressed against his, as soothing as the voice. "Just sleep," the voice said. "I'm not going anywhere. You aren't alone."

Lachlan listened, and dropped back into the chasm of blackness, grateful his body wasn't vacillating anymore.

Lachlan was familiar with having had too much to drink. As he became conscious, the fact his head felt as if it had been bludgeoned from the inside, that his mouth was three circles from the center of hell, and that his body was stuck under the rocks of a collapsed cavern made him decide he must have imbibed far too much the night before.

If only he could remember it. His memory wasn't quite connecting with the way he felt. In fact, his memory was just… blank.

Gods, he felt terrible.

He expected to be in his own bed in the palace, the glow of the fireplace revealing the dark blue canopy overhead, but as he blinked his eyes open, linen canvas fluttering above him, the essence of bright sun overhead making him squint, he knew he wasn't at home.

Where the fuck was he?

He turned his head, the innards of it feeling waterlogged. The rest of his body ached, as if he'd been pushing himself through physical training with Captain Johesha, who never held back when putting Lachlan through the paces.

Lachlan shivered, uncomfortably cold and yet had the urge to kick off the covers simultaneously.

Stars, he felt like he might lose his stomach. His gut rolled as he moved his head to determine his surroundings. A tent. A tiny one, barely large enough to accommodate him. The canvas wall to his right wasn't a foot from his head. He needed to move but felt pinned down.

"I think I'm going to be sick," he groaned, his voice hoarse and unfamiliar.

The weight pinning him down shifted, then was gone.

When Lachlan looked up, a naked woman was

crouched over him. "Ollie?" she asked.

Surprised, he wanted to say something clever, but was afraid if he opened his mouth, it wouldn't be words coming out. He waved a hand at her instead, wishing he felt better to appreciate her nakedness, that he could remember their night together. When he tried to sit up, his body protested, forcibly keeping him on his back. He gasped, huffing with the exertion, the wave of nausea ebbing as the discomfort of everything else took precedence.

What the hell was wrong with him? Had he been in a fight?

"Take it easy. Nausea is normal. Do you need help outside?" The voice drew his attention, and he turned his head to the woman shrugging into a brown sweater.

"You're naked. Sorry, I don't remember fucking. We did, right?" he asked, though why was he in so much pain? Nothing was making sense. He pressed his fingers between his eyes as the nausea rolled back toward him.

She scoffed. "Absolutely not."

He opened his eyes to look at her again. Her tone of voice communicated her abhorrence of the idea, which confused him. Women always wanted to have sex with him. It was a perk of being the prince, even if he knew it was because he was a prince, not because he was Lachlan. "Then why are you naked?"

Her face—though streaked with dirt—turned red. She had large eyes, a unique shade of gray with thick lashes and dark brows gathered between them. He shivered again and noted she had a nice straight nose, pert and proportional. Her supple lips were pressed together into a thin line. His mind wanted to identify her emotion, but he couldn't make the connection; his mind felt like the wrong size and shape.

"I was warming you up."

"I'm still cold." He shivered and drew the blanket back up. His teeth chattered. "I feel like death."

Her hand pressed against his neck. "You still have a fever," she said, "but maybe you're past the worst–"

"The worst?"

She paused, her hand on his cheek. She pulled it away. "You almost died, and you're still not out of the woods."

"Died?" Lachlan tried to piece together his memories, but they were scattered and hidden away. "I don't understand."

"Hypothermia," she said.

The woman disappeared from his line of sight. He could hear the slide of fabric, which made him think she was dressing, but he couldn't lift his head to check. Her elbow bumped against him. "I'm going to get the herbs I need for your fever and the pain. Get a fire going."

Tea sounded awful He felt trapped inside his own skin. He wanted out of this tent. "Who are you?" he asked and tried to get up again.

She stopped him, pressing his shoulders back into the blankets. "Stay." She measured him with her gaze, her fingertips pushing the hair on his forehead out of his eyes, leaving his question unanswered. "I'll be back. Rest." Then she scooted from the tent and disappeared through the flap.

Lachlan stared up at the ceiling of the tent, listening to her move outside, shivering. The sound of birds and the breeze in the leaves. The sound of steps. The crack of wood and the eventual crackle of a fire. He was in the woods.

He tried to stay awake, fighting sleep, only his eyelids grew so heavy he couldn't keep them open. It brought physical relief to shut them. The incessant shaking of his body and chatter of his teeth was painful. He had the fleeting memory of being forced to drink something terrible, and when he opened his eyes again, his body was weighted with more covers, but he finally felt warm. He imagined the naked woman—who must have been a figment of his fevered imagination—had helped him, but he didn't have the energy to ponder that strange reality and drifted back into the relief of sleep.

"Ollie?"

His eyes opened to the woman's face hovering over him.

Her face drew closer to his, and she gazed into his

eyes, frowning.

"Are you real?" he asked. "I dreamed you."

She ignored him, her eyes taking in something on his face in a detached sort of way. "Your pupils look good. Know what day it is?"

He shook his head and winced with the movement.

She noticed his reaction. "What's your name?"

"Lachlan."

Her eyes narrowed, and she reached to touch his head. "You said your name was Ollie."

Lachlan tried not to notice the interesting color of her eyes—gray ringed with threads of violet—or the fullness of her mouth as she studied him. He also ignored the way her fingers probed his head, sliding across his face and neck drawing out chills that raced down his spine. "What?"

"Memory loss and confusion can happen when one experiences trauma," she explained. "Maybe you hit your head," she muttered, more to herself. "I just didn't find any evidence of it."

Her hand slid from his head, and he ignored the sensation that it felt like loss, until she drew the blankets away from his torso, which made him jerk forward with a hiss of pain. He grabbed the blanket. He wasn't shy. Never had been, but he clutched the fabric, suddenly uncertain. "Memory loss and trauma? What's going on?"

Her pretty eyes jumped to his. "I'm just going to check your binding," she clarified, pointing at the blanket. "Around your ribs."

His skin heated, suddenly feeling foolish as he realized that the gaps in his memory were more concerning than he'd initially considered.

"Who are you?" he demanded again, as the insecurity of that realization upended his sense of his predicament.

He worked over what he knew to try and make connections to what he didn't. He was injured somehow. As hard as he tried to recall the missing bits of information, the memories remained on the other side of that canyon he couldn't seem to cross. He tried to sit up, and pain shot through him as he winced, first sucking in a breath, then following it up with a groan.

"They're broken." She pressed him back onto the bedding. "Now stop being squeamish and let me check."

Lachlan released the blanket, too tired to put up a fight. "Who are you?" he repeated, but she continued to ignore the question.

Instead, she drew the blanket down to his waist, the cool air hitting his exposed skin. He shivered again and went to cross his arms, but his torso lit up like it was on fire. He sucked in another breath, hating that he was incapacitated, hating how weak he felt. The last time he remembered being injured was when he was twelve, breaking an arm after tumbling from Goldie. Since then, no one (other than Captain Johesha) was willing to face the crown prince at full force—afraid to hurt him. Not that he'd retaliate; people just treated him as if he were made of glass.

"Stay still if you can," she ordered him. Her fingers slid over the fabric he could see wrapped around his chest. When he winced, she moved along, unconcerned.

"Bindings look good." She spoke to herself again. "You're still feverish, which worries me." Then her hands proceeded to stroke him: his shoulders, his arms. "But it isn't as high." She stopped at his wrist, pressing her fingers there, and was silent several minutes, her mouth moving as she counted his heartbeats. "Sounds good," she murmured, then laid a hand on his chest. "This is going to hurt, but I need you to take a deep breath to check for a rattle."

He complied, pain flaring in his ribs as he did. He squeezed his eyes shut, adjusting to it, then opened them once more to allow himself to look at her while she listened.

"Now just comfortable breaths," she said and leaned down, pressing her ear against his chest, facing him.

He wasn't blind. The woman had a lovely face. Her jaw was soft, her cheekbones high. Her braided hair was a rich brown threaded with red tones. He followed the line of her neck down to where it disappeared in the collar of her tunic. The muted light of the tent gave her an otherworldly glow.

"Why are you wearing men's clothing?" he asked.

Her eyes snapped open to look at him, wide with— fright seemed wrong. She didn't seem like the sort that frightened easily, not with her hands all over him. She moved away just as quickly. "Why?" she asked, a bite in her tone. "What else would I wear in the woods? They're my brother's."

Not a noble woman, then. There wasn't a woman of his acquaintance who would ever do such a thing, at least not one who admitted it. The idea was intriguing. A woman with her guard down and unaffected by the fact he was the crown prince of Jast. He'd always been the object of stares, of flirtation, among other things to lure him to beds, to trysts, to proposals. This woman didn't seem to care who he was, but then she'd called him "Ollie", and he wondered if maybe she didn't know who he was.

Where the hell was he?

"A brother, then. Not a husband?"

She lifted the blanket back up to his neck to cover him, then snatched her hand back as if the blanket had thorns. "Does that matter to you?"

He suppressed a smile as the contrast, her sudden timidity juxtaposed against her earlier utility. "Why should it?" he asked, though he could admit to himself he was somewhat curious if she was taken. Then he wondered what kind of man she would be attracted to, who would garner her attention, but didn't understand why he was curious about that. She was a stranger.

He just needed more sleep.

"Do you have a name?" he asked again and wondered if she would ignore him once more.

She hesitated, searching his face, a battle playing out on her features, which interested him as well. He didn't understand it. Then, seeming to capitulate to whatever thought was winning, she sighed and said, "I supposed it's only right to share it since we've slept together."

"Slept together?"

"Not in the way you might be thinking," she clarified and frowned. "It's Tarley. My name." Her hands reached for the end of the blanket, tugging it up from his feet.

"Where are my clothes?" His hands shot down to his groin to protect his covering.

Her eyes jumped from his hands up to his face, and she snorted. "Nothing I haven't seen before." She snickered again. "So prim, Ollie. You see a manservant anywhere? Someone had to undress you." Her attention returned to his legs.

"Why are you calling me Ollie? Where am I?"

She stopped and stared at him, unease flickering over her features. "That's what you told me your name is." She covered him back up and tucked the blanket around him. "You're in the Whitling Woods near the village of Sevens. I found you on the riverbank of the Grimz, washed ashore with broken ribs, barely breathing."

The river!

Fuck.

The attack!

All the gaps in his memory rushed through him as if a dam had opened.

He tried to move, like an idiot, pain shooting

through him once more.

Tarley pressed him back into the bedroll with her hands on his shoulders. "You need to stay right where you are. You weren't far from the stars. Let your body heal." She frowned.

"My horse?"

"Ollie—"

"Is everyone gone?" He closed his eyes and shook his head. He wasn't Ollie, even if he'd been playing at it, but in his mind, he saw Ollie rear away from him. He remembered the arrows, the chaos, the attack, Captain Johesha shouting at him as Goldie rushed through the woods.

Lachlan opened his own eyes, now, and they clashed with hers. He felt a little wild, while her gray eyes were calm and serene.

"Take a deep breath. There wasn't anyone else. Just you."

"Did you say Sevens?" he asked.

She hummed an answer that told him yes. "It was just you and your horse. I'm sorry about her. She was beautiful."

It all came rushing back. Sliding over the cliff. The cold and pain when they hit the water. The pressure of needing to take a breath under water. The fear that he was going to die. Goldie. The rush of the current dragging them downstream. Holding onto his dead horse as they drifted. The loss of feeling in his limbs. He'd finally succumbed to the numbness of sleep, one hand wrapped tightly in Goldie's mane, the other gripping her saddle. The fates had intervened to get him closer to Sevens, exactly where he was supposed to be.

"This is Sevens?"

She tilted her head. "No. We're quite a hike from the village. I found you almost three days ago and brought you here. There wasn't any way I could have made the hike back to Sevens with you."

"How did you get me here?"

"A sledge. Dragged you here from the river."

"You? By yourself?" The shock hit him squarely in the chest. This woman had found him. She could have left him for dead and hadn't. "You saved me?"

"Not yet, I haven't." She straightened, looking at his hands folded over the blanket before her gray eyes jumped to his. "You still have a fever. We need to get that under control, and we'll have to watch for infection in your lungs over the next day or so." She tucked the blanket in at his sides, then added another.

Lachlan noted she drifted around him with efficiency.

"We're still immersed in the woods in more ways than one."

Lachlan blinked, exhaustion grabbing ahold of him again. "You're a healer then?"

She paused, then said, "At the moment, I'm what you've got."

Lachlan shut his eyes and nodded. "Thank you."

"Rest," she whispered.

With his eyes closed, he wondered if Ollie and the

rest of the party were alive? Had they made it down the mountain to Sevens, or had they turned around to return to Jast? If he was alive, Captain Johesha would come to look for him. Jast would need confirmation he'd perished to ascend his brother Lome as Crown Prince.

But what if Johesha was dead. And Ollie.

Then it hit him like an arrow. Someone had tried to assassinate him.

"Why did you help me?" he asked, his eyes still closed, a horrible uncertainty weaving its way between him and the woman who'd saved him, wondering if perhaps she could be part of the assassination attempt.

Why nurse him back to health, however?

Silence hovered in the small tent, and he wondered if she'd left, but when he opened his eyes, she was staring at him. She looked down and messed with the blanket even though there wasn't anything wrong with it. Then she frowned. "I couldn't leave a man to die."

The earnest way she said it messed with his equilibrium. He didn't know what to think, but his head was aching, and he was alive. He had every intention of staying that way. "Thank you," he told her again and closed his eyes.

"Thanks aren't necessary for doing the right thing." Her voice drifted away as she left the tent. "Rest now," she repeated.

Then she was gone, and Lachlan was left alone with his thoughts. What he did know was that the crown prince of Jast was in danger in the land of

Kaloma. Someone had tried to kill him, even if it hadn't necessarily been this woman. Tarley. He tested her name in his thoughts. But he didn't know he could trust her, even if she'd saved him. He didn't know her people. Didn't know her connections. Only, he knew he needed her, so for what was probably the first time in his life, he committed to what his father had asked him to do. He wasn't Lachlan Nikolas any longer because Lachlan had died in that river. He'd been baptized as Ollie, and that was exactly who he was going to be.

Tarley

arley hadn't slept well, her dreams filled with a man chasing her through the woods. He'd had sharp teeth while at other times he'd changed into a handsome man sent to trick her. There'd been harsh gray stone, chains with cuffs and locks, prison bars, and the cold, horrific cold, making her fretful, agitated, and unable to settle. It hadn't helped that since finding Ollie near death days ago, she'd spent most of the time trying to heat him up, then trying to control his fever by force-feeding him spiked tea, pain tonic to manage the pain of his broken ribs, and rousing him to keep him from succumbing to the deep sleep. Add to it the size of the tent, which Ollie took up most of anyway. Whether curled in the fetal position for warmth or sprawled out as the fever fluctuated, his large body took most of the space, meaning she'd had to maneuver around him.

Except the night she'd had to strip naked and climb under the blanket with him, which she'd spent the better part of the last two days forcing herself to ignore. She knew using her body heat had been the only way to warm his dangerously cold body. She forced herself to ignore the beauty of his form as she'd lain against it, and justified she'd been trying to save his life. In the moment, that had been absolutely true. Though, she'd wondered why she was still thinking about it. She wasn't beholden to him, and if—stars forbid—he was a collector, he deserved to die. Only it wasn't her place to decide, so she'd chosen to act, refusing to believe she was swayed to save him because he was a beautiful man.

She could keep to those lines and had to. She couldn't afford to let her guard down. The plan was to get him well enough that he could go back to do what he needed to be doing. She'd send him on his way and continue hiding in the woods until Mattias fetched her.

But Ollie had blurred the line, when at some point the night before he'd kicked out of the blankets yelling about assassins.

Tarley had bolted upright, her heart racing with fear as he panicked next to her inside an awful nightmare. Afraid he might hurt her, she'd backed up against the canvas wall and called out. "Ollie?"

He'd stilled and turned his head, his body falling still. "Tarley?"

She hadn't been able to see his face in the dark, but she'd moved toward him. "I'm here. You're safe." When she reached out to touch his skin—her fingers grazing his sweaty face, the fever broken—he'd grabbed hold of her, drawn her into his arms, and curled around her.

"Safe," he'd whispered and promptly fell back to sleep.

Now, weary and bleary-eyed with exhaustion, she reached out to check his fever once more. His skin was still cool to the touch. She scrambled up onto her knees and double-checked, feeling his head with both sides of her hand, his cheek, the side of his neck, his chest.

Cool.

Tarley couldn't contain her smile, sighed, and laid back down, relieved. Perhaps he'd turned around at death's door and was now making the journey back to the land of the living.

She'd done it!

Then she took a slightly easier breath, but her smile faded.

Now she had to worry about him being a collector.

She turned her head to look at him. He was on his back, sprawled wide in the tent so it was impossible not to feel some part of his body. His face was turned slightly toward her, relaxed in sleep, which made him look more boyish than man despite the beard growing in. He was very beautiful.

Tarley looked away and stared up at the tent's ceiling, unsure why she cared if he lived or died. She didn't know him, and the likelihood he was up to no good in the Whitling Woods was far more likely than not. It was a question she couldn't answer. She didn't know why she cared, but for some reason she couldn't shake it, and she hated that she did. Her heart compressed into a tight, protective ball at the thought of him dying.

She wasn't sure he was a collector, which was why she'd finally shared her name. It was in the things he'd said and the dreams he'd had since. Perhaps he was a rich man, but she had a feeling he was running from someone. Maybe hiding like her. *Why* was the appropriate question, and she was certain she didn't want to get caught up in it.

Heal him. Get him healthy. Get him moving. That was the plan.

It was nearing sunrise on the fifth day, the twilight teasing the flap of the tent. The birds were only beginning to sing, and though the music of the birds waking and the river beyond were usually her salve to get her moving, her eyes were so heavy, her body weighted with exhaustion. The sound of Ollie's clear breathing and the birdsong lulled her mind and senses toward sleep, so she shut her eyes.

Just for a moment, she told herself. *Ollie's safe. I'll rest. Just for a moment*, she thought and slipped into the rest of the darkness.

"Tarley?"

She stretched her body, uncurling, basking in the gloriousness of warmth and rest. Her hand dropped against something unforgiving, her head pressed against a wall. She moaned, disoriented, and grabbed hold of the mound under her quilt, trying to figure out what had crawled into bed with her.

"I've always enjoyed a good fondling, but I prefer it being reciprocal."

Tarley's eyes snapped open at the foreign sound— a man's voice with just the hint of an accent with which she wasn't familiar. Skin. That's what her eyes focused on. Lots of it. An arm. A shoulder. A jaw in need of a shave as she raised her gaze. Full lips arched with a smile, the bottom slightly fuller through the pronounced arches of the upper. He was grinning, and his eyes—a myriad of colors—were darkened with a ring of deep green at the edges.

Realizing she was flush against him, holding him, Tarley jerked back, scrambling to the opposite side of the tent, only there wasn't enough room to maneuver. She regretted the quick movement, her body protesting with aches and pains of not enough sleep.

"Ollie. I–" She couldn't meet his gaze.

"You were asleep."

Her cheeks heated, realizing she'd been holding him in her sleep. Holding onto him the night she'd been trying to save him flashed in her mind, reminding her she'd held him before. *To save him*, she snapped at her inner self.

Her eyes danced across the quilt until she found the bravery to meet his gaze. She didn't like being disoriented. It made her feel out of control and weak. She took a deep breath to slow her racing heart and closed her eyes to reset.

One.

Two.

Three.

Sleeping. She'd been sleeping. That was it.

She took another deep breath. When she opened her eyes, Ollie watched her, his head tilted slightly.

Calmly, she reached over to feel his forehead and decided to ignore the precarious position she'd awoken to find herself in. "You look rested," she told him, noting he was still cool, and his color was good.

"So do you." He grinned, showcasing lovely teeth.

Which made her want to growl in frustration as her eyes traced his smile lines before meeting his gaze once more. "Do you need some tonic for the pain? For your ribs?"

He shook his head, stretched some to test it and winced. "It hurts, yes, but at least I'm alive and awake." He stopped, his eyes jumping around her face as she reached up to tuck her hair back into her braid. "Thanks to you—"

She was self-conscious suddenly, knowing she looked awful. Dirty and smelly for certain.

"You slept most of the morning. I'm sorry I couldn't give you more room. Tried to move, but it was too difficult with the pain."

Tarley shot up to her feet but crouched over in the tent. "You must be ready to try and eat, and I've slept the morning away."

"A deserved rest–"

She backed toward the tent's entrance.

"Wait," he said, calling her back and looking away as if embarrassed. He sighed.

She stopped near his feet. "What is it?"

He scrubbed a hand over his face, the scratch of his beard loud against his palm. "I'm sorry to ask, but I really need to relieve myself."

Her cheeks heated again. "Oh. Right." She chastised herself for her response, severely annoyed by it, unsure why she was struggling around this man like a silly, blushing schoolgirl. He was just a man. She had done this before, for others. This was no different. She steeled herself and moved back toward him.

"It's just difficult to get myself up and around," he explained.

"Of course. Can you stand?" She knelt so he could use her shoulders for support.

Ollie, with her help, adjusted his body to a series of groans and grunts.

When the quilt dipped low enough in his lap to barely cover his nudity, Tarley averted her eyes, then grew angry with herself again for noticing. "Use my shoulder," she said, with more irritation than she intended.

Taking her suggestion, Ollie reached out, sucking in a breath with what she figured was the pain that accompanied the exertion, and got to his feet, bent at the waist over her head. To her mortification, his pelvis was eye level. She was offered an eyeful of flat stomach arched with muscle, skin bunched around his belly button, and a trail of dark hair leading under the blanket loosely held in his closed fist, threatening to slide from his slim hips.

She averted her eyes, and in her rush to move, stood up, ramming the top of her head into Ollie's.

He yelped.

"Oh!" Tarley bumped against the top of the tent.

Ollie had hold of his nose, his eyes shining with unshed tears.

"Oh stars," she said and grabbed his face with her hands. "Let me see."

"Did you save me only to make sure I was in pain when you killed me?" Ollie dropped his hand, smiling.

Relieved, Tarley took a breath, inspecting his nose. Such a nice nose. "It isn't bleeding." There was a small scar on the bridge, but otherwise, a straight, proportional nose. "I'm sorry. I'm not used to being in here with someone else."

Ollie chuckled, as if he knew why she'd moved so quickly, which made Tarley press her teeth together with annoyance.

"Let's get you outside," she said, wrapping an arm around him. Ollie leaned on her as they moved tentatively through the tent, hunched together. "It's good for you to be moving around," she said. "You just have to be careful." She didn't like the sharpness of her nerves, which made her feel like chattering to soothe them. She wasn't a chatterer—that was her sister Brinna and sometimes her brother Mattias. Not her. Ever. She pressed her teeth together harder.

Once they were outside, she straightened as best as she could under his weight. To be fair, he also stood taller, as much as the pain in his ribs allowed, and she couldn't help but notice how she fit under his arm slung across her shoulders. The thought was discomfiting. To take her mind off her trail of thoughts, she asked, "Can you walk on your own?" and tried to put space between them.

Ollie reached out and grasped onto her, refusing to let her go. "I think I might need a bit more of your help."

"Let's get you to that tree. You can use it to hold you up."

"You sure you don't want to keep an eye on how well I eliminate my water?"

Her eyes jumped to his.

He grinned down at her.

She looked away, unable to concentrate with his dimpled smile under that beard and his gleaming hazel eyes. "You're teasing me."

"I am." He leaned a bit more into her, which made her want to push him off. She didn't, holding true to her morals and ethics rather than her emotions. "Apologies," he said. "I couldn't resist. I must confess, I get a bit irreverent when I'm embarrassed."

"Why would you be embarrassed?" she asked as

they shuffled over the grassy loam, grateful for the soft grass to protect Ollie's bare feet and wishing she'd thought of something to protect them. He had nice feet. She snapped her head up to stare at the tree line ahead. "There's nothing to be embarrassed about."

"I haven't had to rely on someone else to help me with my basic needs."

She didn't try to invalidate his very real struggle. In his position, she would probably make a terrible patient.

They'd reached the tree line.

Ollie reached out, pressing his palm to a tree. "So, I think I can do this."

"Of course you can. I'll just leave you to it." She turned to go, hating that her cheeks warmed.

"Wait!"

She turned back.

"Take the blanket," Ollie said, and pulled it from his hips.

She shielded her eyes against his nudity.

"I thought it wasn't anything you haven't seen before."

Though she wasn't looking at him, there was a smile in his voice.

She closed her eyes. "Right." She dropped her hand, then opened her eyes once more, keeping her gaze on his face.

He smirked, seemingly at ease in his bare skin. "We wouldn't want the blanket to get dirty."

She took it from him, her eyes fixed on his, then

tilted her head and smirked back at him. "True." When his hand brushed hers, sparks shot from the origin, racing with heat along her skin until it exploded between her shoulder blades, but she concealed any reaction, maintaining eye contact and her smirk. Two could play at this game, she decided, unwilling to give him the upper hand.

"Might as well stay, until you're done," she said. "No sense walking back, then having to turn around to come right back to help you to the tent." She wadded the blanket up in her arms and crossed them around the bulk of fabric to wait.

"Perfect," he said and turned away, facing the tree.

Tarley let herself to look at his backside. Her eyes skimmed over his wide shoulders, the rounded planes of his shoulder blades, the dips and rolls of the muscle under his skin, the taper of his waist, divots on each side of his spine just before the muscle curved into a tight, beautifully rounded ass. She looked up at the sky through the trees surrounding them, slightly guilty for ogling him, but more annoyed that she liked what she saw, chastising herself for playing this game at all. But now felt as if she couldn't capitulate.

So she waited.

Ollie cleared his throat. "I can't seem to go–" He looked over his shoulder at her.

Tarley tilted her head.

"Not with you standing there."

She narrowed her eyes, and her smirk deepened. "I'll just walk back to get to the fire," she told him, backing away, glancing at his hand pressed against the tree. A nice wide hand, veined and strong, with proportionally long fingers. "Just call me when you're ready." She twirled away, grinning because she knew she'd won that round.

With a minute shake of her head to put her brain back into its proper place, she walked back into the camp, her stomach growling as it reminded her there were things that needed to be done for survival. Hers and Ollie's. It started with a fire. After some indecision on her part about what to do with the blanket, she tossed it back into the tent to keep it clean and returned to the fire pit. She raked the ash for hot coals, grateful there were a few, added some kindling and got it going once more.

"Tarley?" Ollie called.

With a deep breath to fortify herself, Tarley walked back and found him in the same place she'd left him. Only he was looking over his shoulder at her, his body turned to present his profile.

Her mouth dried out and she swallowed. Despite the cloth wrap around his ribs, along with the cuts and bruises blooming on his skin, he really was magnificent. Lean and long muscles stretched over his form, rounded in some places like his chest, and sharp in others, like the point of his hips.

She bolstered her defenses.

He covered his groin with one hand, pressing the other against the tree for support. His eyes drifted over her, eyebrows rising a few degrees with a question.

"Where's the blanket?"

"I left it in the tent."

He grinned. "Why is that?"

She rolled her eyes. "I didn't want it to get dirty."

"Is that why?" he asked, though his tone sounded like an amused accusation.

She didn't know him well enough to comment on his teasing smile and ignored that her skin had felt like it was on fire the moment he'd touched her. She ignored that her cheeks were burning. She was just doing a job. She'd done her due diligence by this man. In a few days—hopefully—he'd be strong enough to go his own way.

In tense silence, they retraced their steps, Tarley next to a naked man she decided was no different from the tree, even if she knew it was a lie she was telling herself.

If her family could see her—

The thought nearly made her trip. Her mother and father would be so angry. Not at the naked man part— she didn't think—but definitely that she had chosen to put herself in danger by helping him. One of them— hopefully Mattias—would be coming out to see her in a day or so to give her the all-clear. That could be problematic, though Mattias could be strong-armed into secrecy.

She glanced up at Ollie and wondered since he was stronger now and had the ability to move, maybe she should go for help to cart him back to Sevens, instead of waiting. That could avoid discovery and maybe was a safer option. But it would take her a day or more to do that if the weather held, and he wasn't that strong yet. Besides, she wasn't sure if it was safe for her to return to Sevens.

"Are you from the village then?" Ollie asked, breaking their silence. "Or are you a woodland fairy?"

That made her smile—on the inside. "Yes, I'm from Sevens."

"For all twenty-two years of your life?"

When she tilted her head up to look at him, he was grinning.

"Are you attempting to ascertain my age, Ollie?"

"I think the river may have not only washed away my charm but also my wits."

She wanted to smile back at him but didn't. "Twenty-six."

"And since I have no ability to ask in a roundabout manner as I traipse naked through the forest next to you—relying on your goodwill—I won't be mauled by an angry husband, will I?"

"Stars, no!"

"Such vehemence."

"I have no intention of ever marrying." She bit down on the words, angry with herself for saying it. Even if he wasn't a collector, he was a man, and men in Kaloma believed women were obligated to marry. Which she expected him to reiterate.

"Because?"

The question surprised her. "I like my woodland trips," she answered. "Besides, there aren't many prospects in Sevens."

"Why such slim pickings?"

"Location and opportunity. Who wants to live in a remote village tucked in the haunted Whitling Woods where Jast could cross the border and pillage anyone brave enough to live there." She paused when he did, his breath taxed. No, she definitely couldn't leave him.

"And has Jast done that in recent history?"

"No, but you know as well as I do, that's what every stars-fearing Kaloma citizen believes about the kingdom to the north. The king is a despot and his prince a vampire." The thought made her grin.

"A vampire?"

She laughed. "So they say."

"And you believe that?"

"It's an inauspicious beginning if you think I do believe that." They walked a few more steps.

"How do they say the prince became a vampire?" he asked.

She chuckled. "Really? Does it matter if it isn't true?"

He grinned. "No, but I'm curious."

She shrugged. "Not sure if the lore was created, but how's this? During the last blood eclipse, when everyone knows vampires wandered the Whitling Woods, the prince—on a dare—decided to challenge the legend of The Great Blood Walker. And lost."

Ollie barked a laugh—the sound startling a group of birds into flight from a nearby tree—then winced at the pain.

His laugh unsettled Tarley, though she wasn't sure why, and her impulse to cover up the feeling made her chatter again. "Sevens has grown recently," she offered. "Because of the Queen's visit."

"The queen is in Sevens?"

She tilted her head to look at him. "Not yet, but everyone knows she's on her way. Where have you been? Under a rock?" She adjusted her body against his.

"Just in a river."

"I'm—" She paused. "Teasing. Good one."

"Where are you from?"

He looked at her, then back to his feet. "North. Don't get a lot of news up there, but I did hear the queen was meeting a group from Jast. Have they arrived?"

"A Northman?" If Ollie was a Northman, she *was* a woodland fairy. "You have really nice clothes for a Northman."

Ollie stumbled, and she held him tighter to keep him upright. Then his eyes skimmed her features, measuring her, assessing. When he finally spoke, he asked, "Are you excited for the royal visit, then?"

Tarley noted he'd changed the subject. "For it to be over, yes."

His eyebrows rose over his eyes. "Really? Why is that?"

Tarley helped him skirt the fire. "My sister Brinna is looking forward to it. Not me. I'd rather not be reminded how far beneath them I am."

When they got to the flap of the tent, Tarley lifted it and backed in, offering her shoulders as a means for his support. "Duck," she said and looked up, making sure to keep her eyes on his face rather than the hand he used to cover himself.

He looked down at her.

"I promise, I'm not looking," she said with an eye roll.

"What if I was hoping you would?" He smiled and chuckled. "See. Sorry. Irreverent and inappropriate."

"You're a rascal," she said and hid her smile instead of growing indignant, then she sobered. What was she doing, encouraging him?

He laughed, then grimaced. "This really is strange."

"You can say that again." She shuffled a touch closer to him in the confines, trying to find a way to get him back in, only she'd forgotten about the blanket she'd thrown inside. Her foot got caught, and like a horrible dream, she lost her balance, toppling onto her back and dragging Ollie down.

She gasped as his weight landed on her.

He grunted as they hit the bedding, but somehow, he managed to keep from crushing her, stopping himself with his hands. "Oh fuck," he groaned, his head falling forward as he breathed through the pain she could only imagine was a fire moving though him.

His brown hair teased her nose.

"Are you hurt?" She pushed his hair back off his forehead and searched his face, her hands framing his cheeks. "Oh stars, are you hurt? Worse?"

"I'm fine. Are you?" His eyes opened and connected with hers.

The sensation of being dragged in tugged at Tarley. A pulse of warmth, light, and knowing started in her belly like a tiny seed and sat there, but she didn't understand it. Her heart expanded in her chest along with her breath, and in her mind she pictured Ollie standing near the tree on the green in Sevens, smiling at her, waiting for her.

With a blink, she returned to her body and tried to squirm out from under him, recalling, rather suddenly, his very naked body. Pressed. Against. Hers.

"Ollie. I. Can't. Move."

"Just having a bit of a… time." He cleared his throat. "You know. With a pretty woman squirming under me." He gave her a pained smile but didn't open his eyes, releasing a slow breath through his nose.

Pretty? She certainly wasn't pretty at the moment. She was dirty and would probably chase away a predator with how terrible she smelled. She made an incredulous snort. "Right," she muttered.

"Stop. Moving. Tarley," he said through his clenched jaw.

She recognized it then, his rigidity against her thigh, and she stilled, eyes widening.

His eyes opened once more, meeting hers, and he smirked with those infuriating dimples, completely at ease with the fact that … that … that …

Her breath rushed out. "It's the tonic, probably–" She looked away. "Makes it hard to–"

His eyes widened. "Makes it hard?" He chuckled.

Flustered, she shook her head. "No, I mean, the tonic makes it difficult to control things."

"I don't think it has anything to do with the tonic." His grin widened, his eyes skimming her face.

Tarley made a frustrated noise. Did he ever stop smiling? "Just roll a bit, and I'll get out from under you."

"Stop wiggling," he said. "You're making it worse. Unless that, too, is by design. Was our fall by design as well?"

Rattled, she stilled, her gaze meeting his. His eyes were darker now, greener, like the forest on a summer day. He was smiling, but it wasn't exactly amusement on his face. He shifted to one side as much as he could in the cramped space, and she found herself free to slide out from under him.

But instead of moving, she stilled. She knew she should scramble out from under him straight away, except when her gaze dipped to his mouth, she wondered–

Move, she chastised herself.

She extricated herself as gently as she could to keep from hurting him, then tried to help him with his covers.

He stopped her. "I've got it."

Unable to string a coherent phrase together, she nodded and turned to leave, then turned back. "Do you need anything else?"

"A bath? Something to clean my teeth?"

She couldn't speak, annoyed at how flustered she felt.

Ollie smirked again. She wanted to hit him.

Instead, she left the tent, lamenting that he'd won that round. Rather than get him something to eat—like she should—she went straight for the river. She needed to cool off.

Lachlan

Lachlan flopped back into the blankets—as much as he could flop considering the circumstances—and draped an arm over his eyes with a groan. Since when had he become an adolescent boy with no control over his body? Was he going on thirteen again, panting after Lord Anderon's sixteen-year-old daughter rather than a nearly twenty-six-year-old man? Ridiculous.

Only he couldn't get the images out of his head of Tarley asleep, draped over him, of her hand reaching out and squeezing his hip, then patting around trying to figure things out, of her one hard-earned laugh—because stars forbid she smile—when he brought up a hypothetical husband. His chest constricted recalling her body pressed against his only moments ago. He decided the accidental collapse and his accidental hard-on had just been the coalescence of all the right conditions.

He grunted at himself at his ridiculousness. Sure, Tarley was attractive—even under all the grime. She did have lovely gray eyes that reminded him of clouds on a rainy day in Opalant City before lightning struck. Her lovely lips were kissable. She probably wasn't spectacular, however, considering he'd cavorted with courtesans. She may have saved his life—and he was very appreciative because he knew she didn't have to—and for that he was grateful, but it didn't mean he needed to go getting an erection, for star's sake. He could control his urges.

He was losing his mind.

He wasn't attracted to Tarley. Couldn't be. His erection was probably what she said—the tonic— even if he'd played it off as something else. Right? Because she was a peasant, and princes didn't cavort with peasants on principle except for carnal whims—and he'd never crossed that line. It wasn't right.

Her rather decided opinions about royals were clear. She'd called him a vampire.

Tongue in cheek, he reminded himself, and smiled recalling her absurd explanation for his vampirism. Then he chuckled and shook his head. But her words about the royal visit hit him like one of those arrows, and his amusement waned.

I'd rather not be reminded how far beneath them I am.

She'd said it laced with that sarcasm, but it made him pause now. Made him think about Beaknose and Ollie's reprimand. Lachlan rolled his eyes at the thought, recalling the arranged marriage he'd writhed out of with his court machinations.

Did he think he was better?

No. No. He shook his head. That was outrageous. He'd done what he did to Beak... Princess Truisante because he didn't want his father controlling his life. He wanted a say in things. Maybe Tarley didn't understand how royals were bartered for status, treaties, and trades in the name of the kingdom. Despite what Ollie had told him, Lachlan did want the best for Jast, but not at the cost of being a puppet. He wanted his father to have faith in him, trust him, believe in him to make the right decision for the kingdom.

Lachlan rubbed his forehead with his thumb and index finger, working out the pain that had started behind his eyes and spread, realizing Ollie had been right. Lachlan had been underhanded about how he'd refused the betrothal. A boy's move as opposed to a man's. He was regretting it, but regret was a wasted emotion. What was done was done.

Lachlan rolled onto his side, and his gaze fell on the place where Tarley had spent the last several days taking care of him. Sleepy once more, he closed his eyes and imagined introducing Tarley to his mother and father, then snickered, imagining the shock on his father's face. Tarley traipsed on her own about the woods dressed in homespun boy's clothing covered in muck. He shouldn't judge her—she had saved his life. And he was sure that any lady of status—not that he believed Sevens had any—wouldn't be cavalierly wandering the woods by herself.

Knowing what he knew about Kaloma Law, her female independence would be abhorrent even if he found it enjoyable. Surely, she had a male relative—not a husband, since she found the idea repugnant— otherwise she would have been cloistered for her willful disregard of the law. A barbaric practice in a barbaric land. Kaloma existed as if it were still in the dark ages. His current circumstances—attacked and nearly drowned—were his first experience in Kaloma. Jast had its issues, but at least barbarity wasn't one of them.

This was one of the reasons he thought his father's desire for a truce was questionable. What exactly did Jast have to gain by aligning with Kaloma, other than access through the country to the sea? The technology was shoddy, the laws archaic, and their coffers—if one believed the intel—were stripped by the theocratic influence. It was the whole of The Law of Means stripping women in the name of "protection." Kaloma was as much in need of Jast's funds as Jast was of trade access to the sea.

Though Lachlan knew trade was an important and cost-effective reason for a treaty, he was pretty sure this trip had more to do with reconciliation for his father more than anything else. Queen Keyanna was Lachlan's first cousin—not that they'd ever met—and a direct descendent of the Nikolas line through Lachlan's estranged aunt, the very reason the countries had gone to war in the first place.

He wondered what his father was doing. His mother. Did they know he'd fallen to his death? Were they grieving even now? Had anyone made it back to Jast to tell the tale? The fact was, he didn't know, and he needed a plan, because if the wrong person discovered who he was...

He sighed.

He might be feeling stronger, but he certainly wasn't strong enough to get home. He'd barely been able to walk between the tent and a tree to take a piss. Embarrassing, but neither here nor there. And while he had some survival skills from his time serving in the royal army, he didn't think he knew enough to make it back to Jast. The Fates, however, had intervened to get him exactly where he needed to be: saved by Tarley— who did know how to survive—and within a day of Sevens where, Tarley confirmed, the Queen was expected.

Lachlan couldn't afford to make a boy's decisions anymore. He needed to channel Ollie's advice and do what needed to be done for Jast. And he needed to prove to his father that he was worthy of his trust, worthy to one day be the king. While Lachlan couldn't change the fact he'd ruined the proposed marriage to Beak—Princess Truisante—he could move forward with meeting with the Kaloma queen to secure the treaty. For the time being, that meant pretending to be Ollie. And he needed Tarley to survive. He could squash his ridiculous physical response to her.

Easily.

And once he made it to Sevens and the treaty was secured, he'd figure out a way to return home. Until then, figuring out that portion of the plan would have to wait.

It left him wondering though, who was behind the assassination attempt. Had it been the queen of Kaloma? He worked out the moves of that possibility and others in his mind, some with her as the mastermind, but he couldn't get it to make sense. No matter which way he flipped the scenario, he knew Kaloma couldn't afford a war. As he pondered the possibilities, the growing warmth of the tent lulled Lachlan to sleep.

He dreamed of Goldie. Of the river. Of playing human-sized chess. Of Tarley leaning over him whispering indecipherable words with a coy smile. When he opened his eyes, it was to the sound of someone else in the space with him.

He tensed, alarmed for a moment because he forgot where he was, then blinked to reorient.

The tent.

The Whitling Woods.

Tarley and her hard-won smile.

"You're awake?" she whispered from somewhere near him.

Lachlan cleared his throat. "Yes." He lifted his head to look at her. The sight that met him grabbed hold of his throat and squeezed. He'd suspected she was lovely underneath the grime, but he wasn't prepared. Had he thought she wasn't remarkable? What a stupid fucking thought.

She held out a tin of steaming liquid. "I brought you some broth with wild rice. It's important to start back slowly."

She'd bathed.

Stars, she smelled good. Something herby and spicy.

The soot that had coated her face and clothing was gone. The mess of her braided hair, gone. Fuck. Before him was a beautiful woman. Her face was tinted with healthy color from being outdoors in the woods. She was a wood sprite, her brown hair damp, loose, and wavy as it dried. She still wore boys' clothing—clean now—but even that couldn't disguise the way her beauty stole his fucking breath. "For star's sake," he muttered.

She scowled at him.

Yes. Her irritation was good.

"Ollie. Are you okay?" she asked.

He coughed and tried to choke out words, but nothing came out, so he nodded. "Fine. I'm fine," he was eventually able to say as he watched her set down the steaming soup and move around toward his head.

"I'll help you sit up."

He closed his eyes and gritted his teeth as she

helped him.

Then he forced himself to ignore how close she was, her hand still pressed against his back, as she used bedding and cushions to make him a seat, so he was propped up.

He tried to ignore what she'd said about royalty reminding her of her place.

He tracked her movement when she walked back around to face him, when she picked up the soup, and when she held it out once more to him. No smile, because she didn't offer them freely.

He thanked her and took the offered cup from her, keeping his eyes on the cup. When his fingertips brushed hers, sparks flew up his arm, lighting all the nerve endings until they exploded between his shoulder blades, making everything worse. He kept his eyes on the liquid sloshing in the cup. Trying to untangle all the strange ways his thoughts were scrambled was disconcerting. He found himself frowning at the soup.

"Eat, first, then I'll help you bathe. I have water heating for you, now."

He nodded and chanced a glance at her again, unsure where his normal ability to tease and cajole went—this wasn't like him—and watched her leave the tent. She didn't look back.

He glanced at the cup of steaming soup, and sipped the watery broth, which was tasty. Tarley's entrance a few moments ago was repeating like a loop in his mind. Round and round, and his shocked response irritated him, of how wrong he'd been about her appeal. She wasn't just appealing as a person who made him curious—something a courtesan had never done.

He couldn't get his thoughts under control because he was anticipating her return. His breathing strangely erratic, his pulse racing. Maybe she'd drugged him. He looked at the soup, then set it aside. Irritation gave way to frustration, which led to anger at his circumstances, at the inconvenience of it all, the isolation, the pain of his ribs making him unruly, so by the time she returned, he wasn't fit for company.

She held a stack of folded clothing, her refreshing scent preceding her. "These are your clothes. I washed them for you. They're dry."

"That doesn't look like a bath," he replied and hated the sourness of his attitude—not just his scent— making the air bitter around him.

"It's too difficult to cart you to the river, and I obviously can't bring the river to you."

He growled. What the fuck? Who growled?

She narrowed her pretty eyes at him. "Would you prefer to remain dirty?" she asked, annoyance lacing each word. "If that's what you want, you're strong enough to sleep outside."

He knew she was right, but his frustration with the whole situation was leaking out beyond his borders, infiltrating the space between them. "Fine."

"Did you wake up from your nap on the wrong side of the bed?"

"Bed!" He scoffed because that wasn't a bed, then

grunted at her, not wanting to put her and beds in the same thought. He needed to channel Ollie, not himself. "I'm fine," he said and hated himself for it. For being an ass. She'd saved his damned life! *What is wrong with me?*

"What is wrong with you?" she asked, echoing his thoughts as she helped him to his feet.

"Nothing," he bit out.

She ignored him, but so far, she'd been adept at doing that. "Let's take up the bedding first, then I'll help you with the sponge bath after. I want to lay the linens out to air them out." She handed him one of the blankets she pulled from the bed. "Hold this for me?"

He took it and held the wadded-up fabric in front of his groin, the perfect covering to hide behind, which turned out to be a boon because Tarley bent down and gathered up the bedding, her ass—in those trousers—pointed at him, all while making little noises as she did. He suppressed a groan as he grew hard again, an answer to the sight and the sounds she was making. Sex sounds. He couldn't explain this hard-on away as a one-off. He was fucking attracted to her.

Fuck.

Fuck.

Fuck.

Rather than look away, like he should have, he tortured himself by watching her. He noticed the way her shirt stretched as she reached. Noticed the way her hair fell over her shoulder and how after she tossed it back over her shoulder, the end of it seemed to reach for her ass, until it would slip forward again. He watched her lift her arms, collect her hair, and as she did, the fullness of her breasts pushed against the fabric of the tunic. She tied her hair back, her lips parted as she did, before resuming her movement.

"Ollie?"

He blinked, unaware she'd stood and was staring at him. "Huh?"

"Are you okay?" She reached out to feel his forehead.

He jerked back. He didn't want her to touch him. "Fine."

She stared at him, her eyes narrowing a smidge, then nodded and disappeared. It wasn't a few moments later she reappeared carrying a pot of steaming water, a cloth, and a bar of soap. "Here. I can help you."

"I don't want you to help me," he snapped, then thought better of it. "Or maybe I do."

Tarley stalled at his rude innuendo. "Who do you think you are? The king of Sevens?" She set the steaming water, the bar of soap, and the cloth down on the bottom canvas sheet of the tent. "Do it yourself." She turned to go.

Lachlan heaved a sigh. "Tarley, wait."

She stopped at the entrance to the tent but didn't look at him, her spine rigid.

"Forgive me. I'm not used to…" But he stopped at the unfinished sentiment. What he'd been about to say was a godsdamned lie. He wasn't the king of Sevens but he was the prince of Jast, and he'd been reliant on others his whole life. He was acting like an entitled prick. He'd been surrounded by servants who addressed his every need often before he even knew he needed them. He'd never said please or thank you. It had just been owed to him.

His skin heated. Here was a woman who had helped him out of no obligation but her own desire to help because he needed it. And he was alive because of her. She'd saved his life, and what had he done? Thrown a sexual innuendo at her, teased her, acted like a jerk, and treated her with disdain because he'd presumed she was beneath him.

Exactly what she'd said.

Fuck.

"Forgive me?" he repeated, his heart beating wildly with anticipation that he hadn't made his one lifeline hate him.

She turned and looked at him, her gaze drifting over his features, and it was almost as concrete as a caress. Her thoughts moved across her face. First there was annoyance shaping her mouth, then brows sharp over her eyes, until eventually they softened into acceptance. "Fine. I'll help you with your back, and you can do the rest yourself." She offered him a cloth.

He turned, presenting her his back, dropping the blanket, relieved his erection had waned some.

She tugged on the bindings around his ribs. "I won't be putting these back on. It's time for you to start moving."

To keep his mind occupied with thoughts other

than being naked in front of her, he looked for something to talk about. "You mentioned your mom and a sister named Brinna. Is that all your family?"

"I have four siblings."

"Five of you?"

"Yes." Her arm came around him again, and he caught that spicy scent with a hint of citrus. "I have an older sister named Jessamine. She's my mother's apprentice. And two younger sisters, Brinna and Aurielle. And a younger brother, Mattias. There's also my dad."

"A big family."

She continued removing the binding, alleviating the pressure holding his torso together. "You don't have a large family?"

"Not quite as big as yours. I have two younger siblings. A sister and a brother." He didn't say their names. "And my parents."

"The oldest then."

The binding dropped away, and Lachlan tried to take a deep breath; it hurt, but it was also freeing in a way. He heard the water behind him slosh, and he imagined her wetting the cloth. Next, he felt the warmth of the water skimming over his skin from his neck across his shoulders and down his back, the water slipping between his bare ass.

"Soap now," she murmured. "Okay?"

He nodded, unable to find his voice for some reason.

The soap slid over his skin, and a refreshing

scent—rosemary, lavender, and a touch of citrus—hit him. She'd used this soap. She worked the bar over his skin, then with the cloth, continued her ministrations. His heart beat wildly in his chest, moving his breath quickly through his lungs. For some reason, this was one of the most erotic things he'd encountered. He couldn't help these physical responses, just like he couldn't help the fact he grew hard again and didn't want her to see.

As she rinsed his back, he worried she would notice that he'd become a walking erection around her.

"I can take the used cloth. If you want," she said, standing just behind him.

"Oh, stars no." There was a beat of silence at his swearing. "I mean, I've got it," he stammered when he realized what he'd said. "I'll bring it out when I'm done."

"Okay," she replied, draping the wet cloth over his shoulder. He didn't turn around to look at her, afraid of it, of her for some reason. "I'll be out at the fire," she added.

He nodded and listened to her leave, closing the flap behind her. He listened to her beyond the tent, the sound fading the further she moved away. Then he let out a relieved breath.

"Fuck," he muttered as he grabbed the cloth and looked at the hardest erection he could remember since he'd been an untried youth.

This—whatever it was—wouldn't do; he was a prince. He had responsibilities.

He looked up at the flap of the tent where Tarley had disappeared.

Except you aren't a prince right now, his brain reminded him. *You're just Ollie, a regular guy*. Which made him watch the tent opening as he slid soap over his skin, pondering the possibilities.

He shook his head to right his thoughts and looked away. Pursuing Tarley for pleasure wasn't right, especially when he needed her.

He glanced back at the closed tent flap.

What had Ollie said? *Intentions don't matter if your behavior doesn't match.*

A woman like Tarley—one who had saved his life—deserved more than a temporary tup in a tent by a lying, scheming royal, even if he was interested in fucking her. He might have done something like that last week, but this week… well, he'd nearly died. That alone was enough to make him take notice of who he'd been, and he hated to admit it, but he wasn't so sure his father had been wrong.

Tarley

O llie's demeanor sent up a red flag, so the moment she was clear of the tent, she wondered if she should run. How had he changed from cajoling her so charmingly to being so antagonistic in a matter of hours? She'd gotten too comfortable, believing he wasn't a collector. Her eyes darted around, looking for what she might grab in a hurry to bolt, but most of it was in the tent where he was now bathing.

She could make it back to Sevens by morning if she walked through the night, though it was dangerous with the nocturnal creatures she might encounter. The only complication was if the priest was still looking for her in Sevens. She expected Mattias any day now to give her the all-clear, but what if she couldn't wait for him?

Her eyes flitted back to the tent.

She could return home, skipping Sevens altogether. But she knew what came with that return. Isolation with Auri behind the hedge. Her mother wouldn't gamble on Tarley's safety if there was any question. While she appreciated that about her mother, Tarley didn't really want to be trapped behind the hedge either.

There was another option.

She glanced at the tent again. She could lead Ollie out into the woods and leave him. Since she knew for sure he wasn't a Northman like he'd claimed, it evened out her chances of escaping. A Northman's skills in the woods were legendary and ruthless. Ollie wasn't either of those things—he was rather soft of hand. Well, he might be ruthless, though she had yet to see evidence of it. But she didn't intend to wait for it. Especially if he was a collector.

Except she couldn't reconcile the persistent nudge in her gut that told her she was wrong. That she was reading everything incorrectly. What did she actually know? He'd been near death, next to his dead horse, with no weapons. Nothing to help him survive in the wilds. He hadn't even been dressed for survival in the wilds. What collector wasn't prepared? Add to that no women, no carts, no tools for collecting. It didn't mean they didn't exist, but it was a factor to consider. He hadn't been—even with his current broody behavior—disrespectful, just unruly. He hadn't been in a rush to get back to any cache he might have lost when he went into the water. These things didn't prove he was a collector one way or the other, though she did have to wonder how a man who hunted women for a living might exhibit ways of being that were less respectful. She pictured Four Tankards and his audacity. That was how she could imagine a collector. Ollie was no Four Tankards.

She dropped wood into the fire. Sparks jumped into the darkening sky and burned away into ash, drifting in the smoke toward the woods. Ultimately, she'd do what she needed to do for her survival. Disappear.

A sound made her look up at the tent as Ollie emerged, dressed in an ivory shirt, dark breeches, and boots. Since the dark was stretching around them, the fire didn't offer enough light to see his features clearly.

"May I join you?" he asked, his voice reticent.

"You're a free man."

He moved across the space, one hand wrapped around his torso, the other pressed to his ribs. It had probably hurt, putting his clothes on.

Tarley hated that she felt bad about it, warning herself to be cautious and wise.

Ollie bent to set up one of the chopped logs as a seat, grunting as he did, unable to muster enough strength and coordination with one of his arms to get it moving in the proper way.

Tarley sighed, stood, and walked over to the chopped log. "Here." She pushed and twisted until it was sturdy in the dirt.

"Thank you."

"You're welcome." She returned to her seat across the fire.

They sat in silence, and Tarley refused to break it, willing to sit in the awkwardness forever. She didn't know him, even if she knew he was lying. Trusting him wasn't part of the deal. It didn't matter how pretty he was. Besides, he appeared content to sit in the silence as well, his eyes on the fire.

Eventually, she stood to get the sticks she'd gathered to whittle into skewers for roasting the fish she'd caught. When she returned to her seat, the sticks gripped between her arm and her side, with her knife in hand, she felt Ollie's eyes on her. Continuing to ignore him, she concentrated on her job, setting a switch in her lap and using her knife to pare down an end into a sharp point.

After some time, annoyed by his silent attention, she finally snapped, "What?"

"What are you doing?"

"Carving skewers. For dinner."

"How did you learn all of this?"

She scoffed, lifting her eyes to look at him. "You care?"

He seemed surprised, leaning away just a touch, smoke from the fire drifting between them. "Just making conversation."

"Oh. Is that what this is?"

With his face glowing orange-gold in the light, his brow furrowed. "What else would it be?"

She shook her head and looked back at the stick. "You didn't seem open to conversation a bit ago. Something change?" Too irritated at best to maintain her concentration—which she knew better than to do!—she slid the knife, but lost her grip on the stick. The dagger sliced through the meat of one of her fingers, and she hissed a breath. "Shit."

"Tarley?"

She dropped everything with a thud in the dirt—stick and knife—and stood, drawing her bleeding hand toward her body, pressing her other hand around the wound to staunch the blood as she turned away from the fire. "Fuck."

"Tarley?" He was close now, at her shoulder.

"Leave me alone," she snapped, angry at herself for being so careless. A wound out here could be a matter of life and death.

"Let me see it."

"Don't! Just stay back. I don't need your help."

"I know that, but–"

She paused, confused, and looked over her shoulder. "What's with you? I don't know you. You're hot and cold. I don't trust you."

He hesitated and swallowed. "Who would I be?"

"You tell me? Because you aren't a fucking Northman."

He shook his head. "You're right."

She stilled, surprised that he'd offered her this. "Then who are you?"

"Not a Northman as you'd know one anyway."

"Men are dangerous," Tarley said, her antagonism now equal to his earlier. "I don't know why the fuck I saved you." She hated that the thought made her want to cry. She didn't know why that was so, and yet the thought of him not being alive made her want to cry. And her making the choice to save him made her want to cry. And her feeling trapped made her want to cry. And her cut finger made her want to cry. She was immersed in her monthly flux, and that made her want to cry.

"Let me see it," he said, taking another step toward her. He grasped her shoulders, turned her toward him, then reached for her hand.

Tarley resisted.

His hand on hers, he said, "I was traveling through Kaloma with… friends, and we got separated."

She relaxed a degree. "And?"

"I'm not sure if you could tell, but I'm sort of hopeless in the wilds."

Tarley hated that she wanted to smile at him, and resisted, but did release the hand coated in blood. "The fabric—"

"Where's the wrap?" he asked.

"Hanging there—" She nodded at the wrap she'd used for his ribs.

Ollie gently grabbed her arm and led her across the camp, speaking as they went. "My horse got spooked, and I couldn't get her under control. By the time I realized we were headed right toward a drop off, it was too late."

"You fell?"

"Right over a cliff. Landed on her—which is probably both what saved me but also broke me." When they reached the fabric airing out on a branch of a tree, Ollie tore a small strip.

"You should be dead," Tarley said, trying to imagine what had happened to him.

"Yes. That's true. I'm shocked I'm standing here right now at all. Was pretty sure I wasn't going to make it. Only you made sure I did–" He folded the fabric, pressing it to the bleeding cut. "Why?"

Tarley worked her bottom lip with her teeth and watched him tie the bandage. When she looked up, she felt the truth sitting inside her mouth, a big round thing that needed dislodging so she could take a proper breath. She wasn't going to say it. He was dangerous, only there was that feeling still tingling up her spine and traveling to her head that his danger wasn't something she understood. The image that had flashed in her mind earlier—him standing near a tree smiling—resurfaced.

When she looked up at him, he was concentrating on her wound. His lack of eye contact made her admit, "I wasn't going to," releasing the truth between them. "I was afraid."

"Why did you?"

"I started to walk away, but as I did" —she stopped

a moment, unsure why she was telling him this but continued anyway— "all I could think about was what if it were my brother lying there near death." She looked up at him.

He turned his head away, his profile reflective rather than angry. When he turned back, he asked, "Why were you afraid?"

"I thought you might be a collector."

Even in the dark she could see the questioning look that froze his features. He titled his head. "A collector? What's that?"

"You aren't from Kaloma are you?"

He swallowed. "I don't know you. Why–"

"You have an accent I don't know. And you don't seem to recognize the normal things someone from Kaloma would know. Are you from a different kingdom?"

"What's a collector?" He repeated, ignoring her questions.

"They round up unprotected women for coin."

His eyebrows rose over his eyes. "I didn't...that's not what I thought–" His tone carried the breath of surprise.

Tarley turned away and moved back across the space to where she'd been sitting, picking up her knife again. "Are you from Jast?"

His steps faltered behind her, which told her she was on to something, before he said, "I'd rather not say." He paused and reached for the knife. "Here. I can do it."

"You think I should give you my knife? Do you think I'm a fool?"

He smiled. "You, Tarley, are no fool." He looked at himself, then sat down on the ground, removing his boots. "There. The knife for my boots. If I try to come after you, I'd have to do it without them." He grunted as he got back to his feet, his arm wrapping around his ribs again.

"And how do you plan on carving skewers with a busted rib?"

"See. Another advantage to you. There's no harm in letting me try." He crouched and picked up the dropped twigs.

As he stood, she offered the handle of the knife.

He took it, the twigs under one arm, and shuffled back to his seat across the fire from her. "Tell me about the collectors."

"I don't know much," she admitted. "Only what I've heard, since it isn't in my best interests to get close to find out."

"What have you heard?"

"That there are men who hunt women—runaways trying to flee to other kingdoms. Rumor has it, they'll even abduct women with male covering, if they can get them alone."

"And then?"

"They take them to the church convents where the collector is given a reward."

"And the convents take them? Even if it's fraudulent?"

She nodded.

He sighed and shook his head. "Barbaric."

"So where are you from, Ollie?"

"The north."

"But you aren't a Northman?" Jast was looking more and more like the proper answer, but she couldn't figure why he wouldn't he admit that, not with a treaty imminent? Unless maybe he wasn't supposed to be in Kaloma.

He shook his head. "If it's all the same to you, I'm going to need to keep my secrets for now, Tarley."

"Because you don't trust me, even though I saved you?"

He smiled, sliding the knife through the wood. "No. Because I'm not sure how dangerous my secrets might be to not only myself."

She hummed a noise, willing to accept his request. She could relate to it. "Shall we use a couple of those skewers to cook dinner? Feel like solids, Ollie? Or do you need some more watery broth?"

He grinned. "I'm willing to take my chances."

After fish and normal conversation about why she loved the woods, and how she'd learned, she realized Ollie had gotten her to talk more about herself than anyone else she'd ever met. She'd shared about growing up in Sevens, and the lessons given all her siblings by their father.

Ollie was quiet and listened, patient and interested, peppering her with questions that kept her talking. The more he listened attentively, the more curious she became about him. She wasn't sure she could name a man of her acquaintance who had ever been interested in her life stories. It made her want to know more about him, but she knew he wasn't going to unlock more than he'd revealed. And for some reason, because the awareness was connected to that warm feeling traveling her spine, she was inexplicably willing to accept it.

"How about some more lore," he said after she stood to ready the camp for bed. "I especially enjoyed your vampire story."

Tarley suppressed her smile and washed her hands, wiping them on a cloth. "You did?"

"Well, truthfully, I would have liked more of it, but beggars can't be choosers, I suppose."

"Right." She carried the water toward him. "Hands?"

He held his out. She doused them with water, handed him the cloth to dry them.

"Would you retie my bandage?" she asked.

Ollie stood and stepped a touch closer, taking the fabric bandage she'd removed to wash her hands.

A new kind of tension lingered between them. She wondered at it, fully cognizant of each of his movements, his breathing, the shift in his body as he bent over her hand. When he was done, he stepped away.

"Thank you."

He cleared his throat. "So? A story?"

"I think it's your turn to talk," she said and moved

to the fire, breaking up the coals in the pit. "I've talked more tonight than in the whole of my life, I think."

"Okay. Let me think about it."

When the fire was doused, she walked into the tent, Ollie behind her. Though it was dark inside, and she was able to move based on memory. She tried not to think about lying next to him, reminding her they'd been in this tent together for nearly a week. Only this was different. He'd been fighting for his life then; now, he was decidedly better. She decided to ignore the tension, since that was the easiest, and untied her trousers, sliding them down over her hips.

"What are you doing?" he asked.

"Taking off my pants."

He made a strangled noise.

"Do you need help with yours?"

He paused for several beats, then said, "Yes."

"It's dark. I mean, I won't be able to see anything. And sleeping in your clothes isn't a good idea anyway," she said, babbling as she reached toward him. "Better to rely on your body heat so that if you need additional insulation, it works properly."

He hummed.

Her hand met resistance. She wasn't sure what she was touching and didn't want to think about it too much. "Can you guide me?"

"Yes." His fingers wrapped around her arm, then slid down covering her hand to pull her gently toward him.

She took another short step closer.

"Here," he said quietly, pressing her hand to the thick fabric, which she assumed was at his waist. There was also the softness of skin against her fingertips, and she took a deep breath.

Detach, Tarley warned herself. *You're just helping.*

"Can you shift your hips? Toward me," she asked and reached with her other hand to match the one he'd placed for her.

She felt his hips, her hands framing them, his slight intake of breath as the movement taxed his ribs. She slid the fabric down and shifted to her knees at his feet. "Put your hand on my shoulder."

Instead, his hand found its way into her hair, and rather than move it, Ollie shifted his fingers slightly, his fingertips drifting into the strands. Chills from that simple caress raced down her body like the current of the river.

"Lift your leg. The right one," she said and pulled the fabric from his body. "Now the left one."

He complied, his hand still in her hair, his touch light, as if concerned he might hurt her, or scare her away.

She had a fleeting thought that she wouldn't mind feeling his hand wrapped tightly in her hair, then banished the thought as strange and unhelpful. "What about your shirt?" she asked, deciding it would be helpful as well.

"It's—"

"Unbuttoned?"

His hand moved, then, sliding from the top of her

head to her shoulder as he knelt before her with a pained breath. Though it was dark, her eyes had adjusted some, and she could make out the outline of his shadow, the slope of his shoulders. She reached out for his shirt and met his hands when he reached for the buttons at the same time. Their fingers tangled, and Tarley's heart hitched in her chest, twisting, but she didn't move, didn't apologize. She waited, and when he didn't move away or push her away, she found a button. Ollie's hand tangled with hers and helped her release a button. Finally, he let her hand go, and started on a different button, until together they'd unbuttoned them all.

She pinched the front placket of his shirt and slid her fingers up to the collar, careful not to touch his skin, afraid for some reason that if she did, something would happen she wasn't sure she wanted. Though the quickness of her breath told her that was exactly what she wanted.

She didn't trust him, she reminded herself. She didn't know him.

She pushed the fabric open, sliding it to his shoulders, the warmth of his skin finally grazing her palm—a relief considering where he'd been only a day ago—and she leaned forward, pushing the shirt down his arms.

"Thank you," Ollie said.

"Need help lying down?"

"No," he grunted.

She listened to his sounds, as he gingerly worked

his way into the now fresh bedding, the shift of the blankets. Once he was settled, she laid next to him, her shoulder pressed against him, her bare thigh to his. She knew she could roll away, but she didn't.

Relative silence, besides the normal night sounds in the forest, drifted around them. She listened to him breathing and felt the slight shift of his body as he sighed, wondering what he would do if she rolled toward him and touched him. She didn't dare, annoyed with her trail of thoughts. It wasn't hours ago she was afraid he was a collector, and now she imagined touching him. Her skin heated with shame, at her weakness.

She rolled away from him, closed her eyes, and tried to go to sleep.

Lachlan

Why had he gone outside? Now he'd screwed himself. She wasn't just some person who'd saved him. She had a story. She had a family who loved her. She had fears and hopes. As he laid next to her in the dark tent, knowing he knew he wasn't ever going to find sleep, not after the feel of her hands undressing him. Not after imagining it was leading somewhere else and chastising himself for wanting it to. They were strangers.

So to distract himself, he said, "I think I finally have a story."

The night cracked around them at the intrusive quality of his voice, but that was what he needed.

Tarley shivered next to him.

That he didn't need. It reminded him she was lying next to him. He could feel the knobby fabric of her tunic against his arm, and since she'd rolled away, recalled the silky feel of her leg against his.

He swallowed. "Cold?"

She reached down and pulled another blanket over them. "I'll be fine. The story?"

Maybe she needed the distraction as much as he did.

"So, the prince–"

"Of Jast."

"Yes? Who else?"

"Just clarifying."

"The prince of Jast, on the day he was to enter the woods to meet The Great, um–"

"The Great Blood Walker?" she asked.

"Yes. The Great Blood Walker," he said and smiled in the dark. "He decided that if he was going to defeat the vampire king, he would need a secret weapon."

"A secret weapon?" Though he couldn't see her, he felt her turn back toward him. "What kind of secret weapon could be used against a vampire?"

Lachlan rolled his head to face her. "The great royal advisers had done some research in the royal archives for years, studying the compiled tales of the horrible menace that stalked their land. And for centuries, they hadn't been able to stop the horrible Vampire King. According to the advisers, the creature had no weaknesses. The prince, however, knew this couldn't be true. Everything has a weakness, and after much meditation—"

"The prince meditates?"

"Why not?"

He felt her shrug next to him. "Can I continue?"

"As you were."

Lachlan smiled again at her royal decree. "After his serious meditation—"

"Serious? Is meditation humorous?"

"Do you want the story or not?"

"Sorry."

He took an exaggerated deep breath, though he didn't feel frustrated in the slightest. "The prince—"

"Lachlan," she said.

His heart froze in his chest at the sound of his name from her lips. He hesitated. "What?"

She rolled toward him. "The crown prince's name. Lachlan Nikolas."

"Oh." His heart resumed its scheduled beat, only now a touch faster and off kilter. She hadn't been talking to him, but she knew his name, knew of him, which felt strange, suddenly. He wanted to know more about what she knew, what she thought, how it might connect them. "Right. Prince Lachlan decided that the Great Blood Walker's one weakness must be his excessively long life."

"Why would that be a weakness?"

"Consider all the people you would have to watch die if you were immortal."

"But as a vampire, he could make them immortal."

"But what if he didn't want to? What if he hated the fact he was a vampire, and felt as if it were a curse, and didn't want to curse those he loved with it."

She hummed, considering. "Okay. Continue."

For some reason, Lachlan felt as if she'd bestowed upon him a favor, which made him want to chuckle. He didn't but did continue the story. "The prince–"

"Lachlan."

"Right. Lachlan… determined that the vampire was weary of his curse, heartbroken because he'd had to watch the love of his life die, leaving him behind angry and miserable. That was why he was bent on collecting citizens who wandered into the woods."

He paused for a moment and waited for her to interject, but she didn't. "What? Nothing to add?"

"Nope," she said. "I'm intrigued."

"Lachlan decided he needed to take a secret weapon."

"I still–"

"Hush, Tarley," he said, rolling toward her, then groaning because his ribs protested.

She reached out and her fingers drifted lightly over his arm. "Are you alright?"

"Just shouldn't have moved," he admitted, and reoriented himself anyway to find a comfortable position. He knew they were facing one another even though he couldn't exactly see her. His eyes had adjusted enough to make out her shadow, but he couldn't see her face.

"The secret weapon?"

"Himself."

Tarley offered a restrained laugh, a quiet sound of amusement that Lachlan realized he wanted to hear more of. "Oh my stars. The prince believed he was the secret weapon. Figures."

He imagined she'd rolled her eyes. "Why 'figures?'"

"The royal arrogance to presume they can fix any problem."

Lachlan bristled at her criticism, but reined it in. It was a story, and she lived in Kaloma, where the government had failed her.

"How, pray tell, was he the secret weapon?"

"He was the sacrifice," Lachlan said. "He decided the Great Blood Walker was exhausted and wanted his freedom from his endless walk. So the prince entered the forest and offered himself as a sacrifice to the Walker, provided the Walker would end his torment of the people of Jast."

"And did he agree to the prince's plan?"

"Obviously. All that royal hubris can't be for nothing. But the prince had gotten it all wrong."

"Why's that?"

"Because the Great Blood Walked wasn't a *he*, but a gorgeous she. So he didn't have to make a sacrifice at all, becoming her continuous meal." Lachlan laughed, and Tarley reached out, tapping his shoulder playfully. "And that is how Prince Lachlan Nikolas became a vampire."

Tarley rolled away from him. "That was a good one," she said, and he could hear the smile in her voice.

He felt as if his chest expanded under that knowledge.

She shuddered.

"You okay?"

"Yes. I think I'm going to have to put my pants back on." Tarley sat up to find them.

Lachlan hesitated, then said, "Or we could share body heat. For survival purposes."

He expected her to reject the idea, and perhaps she had planned to. Silence stretched on for several extra beats in the dark.

"It's a good idea," she admitted.

He still expected her to say, "but," only then she moved, and slid in next to him, her body fitting against his perfectly. He tried not to think about how her tunic was only a bit of fabric between his body and hers. Or about how easy it would be to slide his hand underneath to feel her skin.

"For survival purposes," she echoed, and her fingers closed around his arm. She pulled it around her so her back was flush against his chest, and his arm was wrapped around her ribs.

Lachlan had the disjointed image of laying with her like this before but thought it must be his imagination. He took a deep breath, inhaling her satisfying scent, resigned that sleep was going to be nearly impossible. Before he knew it, however, he found that listening to her breathing, and hearing it slow as she found sleep, allowed him to relax. He was content to be there in that moment, content to accept this, whatever it was, because he understood that this was probably all Tarley would ever allow him that he could claim as his. And just as he fumbled with the exhaustion infiltrating his thoughts, claiming his waking consciousness, he wondered why he'd even thought that?

Tarley

Several days later, a routine with Ollie had found purchase in their little woodland space. He was getting around better, though his ribs were far from healed and would take several more weeks to return to normal. He didn't let that keep him from helping around camp. He collected firewood and water. He took care of the fire and helped her cook the food—he knew so little—she brought back with her. Every night, they sat around the campfire talking about her life and snippets of what he would share with her, then they'd tell stories. Most of the time, she was fighting laughter. He had a way of charming her into it, and when he succeeded, he always looked so pleased with himself.

But she wouldn't admit she was worried. Worried she'd let her guard down with him too easily. Worried that Mattias hadn't arrived to give her the all-clear or to replenish her supplies. Though to be fair, no one knew she had another mouth to feed with her. She could survive in the forest without supplies, if necessary, but it was clear the longer she was with Ollie, he couldn't. Not indefinitely. The more they were together, the more she realized she needed to get him back to civilization, if not for him then to return to some semblance of what was normal. Ollie was chaos incarnate to her sense of self.

With the bedding spread out over bushes again to air out in the sunshine, she stopped and took a deep breath filling her lungs and reminding herself this was what was real. The woods. The freedom. The truth was Ollie was getting to her, breaking her down, which she found annoying and disconcerting. The ease with which he disarmed her, the cuddling at night to conserve body heat, the laughter. She needed him gone and fast, but even as much as she wanted him out of her hair, she wasn't sure she could risk returning to Sevens yet. For her own safety. That—to protect her—had to be the reason Mattias hadn't arrived with the all-clear.

The sounds of the steps made her turn.

Ollie was walking across the camp. His brown hair was unruly and damp. Her breath caught. He was so very appealing, and she hated that she noticed. Hated that for the last three days, she'd anticipated when he'd return from the river looking this way.

"Good bath?" she asked, turning back to the bushes, tugging on the corner of one of the blankets to keep from looking at him. Only, as much as she willed it, she couldn't unsee him, his image burned into her brain. She ignored the way her body wanted to respond, to lean toward him, to accept any offering of attention he'd give.

Annoying.

She needed some space.

"Did you need some help?" he asked.

She gritted her teeth. Even the timbre of his voice was alluring. She cleared her throat as if that might clear her brain and recalibrate her body. "No." The word came out rougher than she intended, but she didn't correct it.

Suddenly, he caught her hand. She let her eyes flit up form, his hand holding hers to his face before sliding away.

"How's your cut?"

"Healing."

"Are you angry?"

She shook her head, feeling like he'd caught her in the act, and pulled her hand from his grasp.

"Then what is it?"

She wiped her hands on her shirt as if it would clear away the chaos inside her chest at the way his unmarred skin felt against her calloused hands. "Nothing?"

A line appeared between his disconcerting eyes.

They looked a bright green today, like the woods filled with spring growth after winter. "It's been a while since you seemed like you wanted to pummel the chore you were doing."

She shot him a glare and stepped around him, moving toward the fire.

"Are you infuriated at everyone? Or just me?"

She ignored him.

"Just me then."

"No." She chanced a look at him over her shoulder.

He grinned. "Everyone."

She rolled her eyes. "I'm going to the river to fish."

"I'm coming."

She glanced at him, looked at him holding his chest. "You were just there."

"Is there a law that says I can't go more than once? The law of Tarley I take it?"

She huffed a frustrated sound. "Fine, but I'm not waiting for you." She picked up her pole and tackle.

When she reached the river, the sight suddenly melted away in front of her like hot wax, revealing a hazy view.

Tarley saw herself, dressed in Mattias's old clothes. There was a fire. The campsite. The sound of footsteps. Vision Tarley turned and looked at the forest. A shadow appeared. Then everything was gone, and Tarley stood at the edge of the river as dizziness threatened to topple her.

She took a step, bent slightly at the waist, shook

her head as she blinked, unsure what had just happened, then took several breaths, waiting, worried that perhaps she was getting one of her headaches. Squeezing her eyes shut, she waited a breath, and reopened them. Her vision remained steady, and there wasn't any pain or nausea. Several more breaths later and no plausible explanations, she decided she was just overly tired.

By the time Ollie stepped out from the woods onto the riverbank, she had already baited her hook and was casting it into the current, the strange incident sliding down the river with the water.

"You weren't kidding about not waiting."

"Why would I joke?"

"Most people–" But he stopped.

"Most people what? Coddle you?" she asked and waded deeper into the moving water.

"Why would you say that?"

She looked over her shoulder at him.

His gaze moved from her to his shirt, as if to check he'd redonned his clothing properly. He smoothed his hands down the fabric. "What? Why?"

"Rich man's clothes," she said and turned back to the river. With a flick, she cast the line into the moving water, then glanced at him once more. "Soft hands," she muttered.

"You seem excessively preoccupied with my clothes." He glanced at his hands, opening them wide.

He'd obviously heard her, and his fading smile at her snipe made her feel guilty. Unable to look at him, she turned back to her line.

"Why is that?" he asked.

She shushed him and forced herself not to turn, irritated and put out by his presence, even if he was easy to look at. She pulled the line back in and recast it, her thoughts trying to put together the details Ollie had shared that weren't adding up. A rich man from the north but not a Northman? It was like a riddle. Jast made the most sense. She glanced at him over her shoulder and wondered if he could be part of the royal party—one of the nobles—then looked back at the swiftly moving river and flicked the line, reeling it back in. But why would he be separated from them?

After a few minutes, a rock plopped into the water near her.

She turned and looked at Ollie standing on the shore and watched him throw another rock into the water near her. He grinned.

Irritated—mostly at herself for wanting to smile— she narrowed her eyes. "You don't want to eat?"

"I do. I'm just bored. I need some entertainment."

She bristled and turned back to the water. Of all the stupid things… this was her time. Hers! And here she was, having saved his life, and he was chasing away dinner. And she wanted to flirt with the man. A man who'd probably never been hungry in his life, wearing boots like that.

Another rock—a much larger one—plunked into the water near her. The splash doused her.

Angry, she turned.

Ollie was standing a few feet away, holding his side and laughing.

She waded toward him and slapped the pole against his chest. "You catch dinner then."

He winked at her.

The audacity.

She stomped to a rock nearby and sat to wait.

And he started humming.

The nerve!

Tarley wanted to scream but pressed her teeth together instead to keep from letting him know how annoyed she was.

When he grew silent, the warmth of the sun coupled with the music of the water moving through the forest lulled her. She glanced at the river. At him. His back was to her, and she let herself to admire the way his shirt stretched across his shoulders and back as he moved. The way the fabric bunched and flowed over his muscles.

He pulled the line and cast. Pulled and cast. Checked the bait. Cast and pulled. It was a beautiful rhythm, and Tarley admired the view.

She was pleasantly surprised to learn he could fish. But she couldn't watch him any longer and looked away as her thoughts slid toward the physical impulses in her body. Toward the memories of laying in his arms the last several nights, her body protected in the heat of his. Of the warmth of his breath caressing her skin. He'd been a complete gentleman, hadn't crossed any lines, though his body moved through its normal courses as hers did, and she'd certainly noticed his morning erections. Her breath tightened considering it, her pulse quickening, a heaviness between her legs.

All unwelcome.

She leaned back onto her hands and tilted her face toward the sun. The river reflected the green of trees and the blue of the sky. The sun headed toward the horizon cast a warm glow over everything, and its warmth made her eyelids heavy. She laid back onto the rock and gazed up at the sky, the clouds drifting overhead.

A sound forced her eyes open.

The sky was a swirl of orange and violet, the sun hovering near the horizon. With a gasp she sat up, but she wasn't in the fishing spot anymore. Instead, she was at her favorite swimming hole. It was where her father had taught her and her siblings to swim with stories of giant fish looking for wishes and fresh-water mermaids seeking to capture children.

The light from a fire caught her attention. Near it, stood a shadow of someone. Ollie. He was bent over, dropping wood into the growing fire. The yellow-orange light drifted over his features, undulating as if dancing. He was the most beautiful man she'd ever seen, Auri's suitor Nix notwithstanding. For a moment, his physical inducement made him dangerous, but she dismissed the initial thought for one more pleasant.

"How did we get here," she asked.

He grinned at her.

"Stop smiling. I don't like it," she told him.

He didn't reply, continued smiling, and walked toward her, his steps so light she couldn't hear the crackle of pebbles she knew were supposed to be there under his boots.

She blinked, disoriented, and Ollie was suddenly standing before her, and she was standing with him. She wasn't sure when she'd stood. When had his shirt gone missing? She thought she should step away and comment on his missing shirt, but instead her body propelled her forward. "Where are your bruises?" she asked.

He lifted his hands and slid them over his chest as if looking.

Her mouth dried out and her tongue thickened, and on impulse, she reached out and touched his chest, tracing the trail he'd made with his own hands. Moving around him, she slid her hands over the width of his back. His skin was smooth, supple, and the need to feel more of it kept her hands in place.

Ollie faced her, grabbed her hands, and slid his hands up her arms to her shoulders, wrapping his fingers around the back of her neck. "Kiss me," he ordered. His words were a growl near her mouth before his lips met hers, his hands tangling in her hair.

Her heart slammed against her rib cage, his mouth igniting new sensations inside her like that dancing fire. While she should have put an end to it, her curiosity won out, and she grasped his shoulders, rose onto her toes, and kissed him back. She slid her hands into his hair and his arms, having moved to hold her against him, tightened in response. He exerted pressure on her, a gentle coaxing. She arched her back against him, and his mouth dropped to her neck. When his tongue swept against her skin, she moaned, the sound reverberating through her, around her, loosening the plaster that held her together. Her insides liquified.

"Tarley," he said against her neck. "I need you."

She liked the sound of her name in his voice.

He pulled back, searched her eyes, then smiled, showcasing his fangs.

Fangs?

She tensed. "Wait. What?"

With a feral sound, he descended, sinking his teeth into her neck.

She gasped, and her eyes flew open.

"Tarley?"

She was still on the rock near the river. The sun was lower in the sky, golden light filtering through tree leaves, casting longer shadows.

Ollie, leaning over her, straightened. "You fell asleep, and I got dinner." He held up four fish, beaming.

"I slept?" She sat up with start. How could she have fallen asleep? The dangers!

"Yes. So soundly that when I looked over, you were drooling." He grinned, then laughed when she wiped her mouth.

Tarley scrambled from the rock. "It will be dark soon." She grabbed the pole from him and collected the tack before staring through the woods, unnerved that she'd let her guard down so easily. "Are your ribs feeling alright?"

"Are you always like this?"

"Like what?"

He was quiet for a beat, then said, "Responsible. Efficient."

"Anything less means starvation and death." She glanced over her shoulder. "But then maybe a rich man wouldn't understand that."

"You bring that up a lot."

"You being rich?"

"Yes."

"When you grow up with nothing…" Tarley let the unsaid finish her thought.

Their footsteps against the ground and the movement of the trees and bushes as they walked offered the only sound for some time, until Ollie's voice changed the cadence. "Would you tell me about that?"

"What? Being poor?"

"Yes."

She stopped abruptly and turned. Ollie stopped just before bumping into her. "Because my experience is a story for your amusement?"

He shook his head and sighed. "No."

She turned and started again to the camp, confused by the emotions she couldn't reconcile. When they got back to camp, she stoked the embers of the fire, needing the distraction to burn up the dream kiss still scorching her neck, confused about why when the dream should have made her feel afraid, when what she really felt was unquenched desire.

Lachlan

Lachlan was one of the fish hanging from the line he held as he watched Tarley hustling around the camp. She bent to restart the fire, and he realized he spent a lot of time watching her. His eyes were always straying to find her no matter what he was doing. Just earlier, he'd watched her sleeping longer than he should have, those same fish hanging from his hand.

He'd turned to show her, wanting to cajole her into being irritated with him some more. Her ire offered him amusement, though he couldn't exactly identify why that was so. Had he ever in his life tried so hard to get and maintain someone's attention? Had he ever needed to? He couldn't recall an instance. But there was something about getting a reaction from Tarley that brought him such enjoyment.

The moment he'd turned, however, ready with a jibe about his obvious fishing abilities, she'd been curled up on the rock, her hands under her cheek, asleep. She hadn't been drooling like he'd told her. The vision she'd made had caught his breath in his lungs. Though they'd been sharing sleeping quarters—cuddling, which he'd always been averse to, until now—he'd never seen her asleep. It was the first time he'd seen her vulnerable, the rigidity in her countenance, which he hadn't realized was there, gone.

Tarley was beautiful. He'd recognized it, of course, but this way—unguarded—whoa.

Her brown hair was threaded with strands that looked like the late summer wheat fields of Jast's outer provinces at sunset. Her features had been soft, her eyes closed and her lashes fanned out over the ridge of her cheek speckled with a smattering of freckles. Her lips had been relaxed, soft, and a shade of pink that reminded him of a confection the chef made for special dinners at the palace, sugared and plump. Lachlan had resisted a fleeting impulse to lean over and touch his tongue to them, curious if they would taste as luscious as they looked.

He'd shaken his head, needing to dismiss thoughts he couldn't afford if he intended to sleep curled around her, and had taken a deep breath to release them. He was in Sevens for a purpose, and it wasn't to spend time rhapsodizing about a peasant girl.

"Tarley?" he'd asked.

She'd moaned in her sleep.

His body had responded, his groin tightening. He'd closed his eyes, cleared his throat, made an adjustment in his pants, and reminded himself he was a grown-ass man.

"Tarley," he'd repeated and reached to gently shake her awake—only her eyes had flown open, and she'd sat up with a start. The haze of sleep still lingered in her gray gaze, but she'd blinked, righting herself.

Now, they were back at the campsite, and Lachlan was watching her hurry around. It was a wonder she wasn't always sleeping as often as she was moving. The efficiency with which she did things tired him out. No wasted movements. Everything with a purpose. He wasn't sure she ever just stopped to exist. Well, perhaps him doing the fishing and her falling asleep on the rock was the first time. He found the things he'd initially found strange about her mattered less and less, and in fact, he liked it. He liked her.

"Are you just going to stand there?" Tarley asked. She hadn't looked at him and added more wood to the fire as if she were trying to make a giant bonfire. It glowed bright as the sun set, casting the place in long, blue shadows.

He started toward her, irritated by her tone. "Do you need all that wood?"

Her gaze found him, and her eyebrows arched. "You're welcome to do it."

"I don't need to anymore. You've done it, excessively, just as you do everything."

"You're welcome to do more, your highness."

Lachlan tripped and righted himself. "What's that supposed to mean?"

She stared at him, then looked away. "Nothing." Stomping toward him, she snagged the fish from his hand, then stormed across to the wooden plank.

"What are you doing?" Lachlan advanced on her.

"Everything. Excessively," she said with a caustic bite, slapped the fish on the board, and unhooked the first one. "Why didn't you clean them?"

Lachlan rounded the board and nudged her out of the way with his body. "I can do it."

"Obviously you can't," she snapped. "It's supposed to be done away from camp." She glared at him. "So bears don't come looking."

"I didn't—" Lachlan felt stupid. He knew that. He'd learned it in one of his many survival sessions when he'd served in the royal army. And yet he'd forgotten, more interested in pushing Tarley's patience.

"Know?" She looked down at the fish. "I'll take them—" she bit out, reattached the first fish, and grabbed the line.

"I'll do it." Lachlan grabbed the line at the same time.

Tarley tugged.

Lachlan tugged back. "Let it go."

"You let it go."

"I said I'd do it." He leaned toward her.

"But you didn't. And now I have to fix it." Tarley leaned closer.

"I can clean my own messes," he said, and his eyes jumped to her lips as his heart thrashed in his chest.

Her eyes flitted to his mouth before she leaned back as if pushed, releasing her hold. "Fine," she said and stormed away.

"What is wrong?" he called after, even more confused. Sure, he'd messed up with the fish, but her anger felt like the bonfire she'd made, way bigger than it needed to be. He hadn't imagined that she'd thought about kissing him, as he had her. Right?

She disappeared into the brush—probably to look for skewers to cook the fish—ignoring his question.

Lachlan didn't appreciate being ignored. In fact, he couldn't remember a time in his life where that had ever been the case. Even his father acknowledged him. Frustrated, he left the fish and stalked after her, following a narrow path from the campsite until he found her hacking at some twigs, still in range of the bonfire's light.

"What's wrong?"

She whirled and let out a frustrated groan, rolling her eyes before turning back to the twig.

"What have I done?" Lachlan realized her answer mattered more than it should. He tried to tell himself that she was no one to him, and yet he knew it to be a lie. That might have been true a week ago, but now it wasn't. She'd saved his life. She'd kept him alive since. She'd provided for him when he wouldn't have been able to provide for himself. They'd laughed together, cuddled. There was so much more between them, even if it was undefined. "Is it because of the rocks? The fish?"

"No."

Hack.

"But it's something?"

"No!"

Whack. The twig came loose, and she started on another.

"How am I supposed to apologize if I don't know what I've done?"

"Is that what you plan to do? Apologize?" She hit another branch, and it detached on the first swing of her giant knife.

Lachlan took a step back to stay clear of her knife wielding. Apologize? He wouldn't have normally. He'd never felt the need to apologize for anything. He hadn't even apologized to Princess Truisante. But being with Tarley as Ollie had done something to him, even if he wasn't exactly sure what it was. He just felt… different. "If I've done something wrong, yes."

She harrumphed a sound through her nose and hit another branch, knocking it loose. Then she turned and marched past him.

Lachlan wanted to grab her and order her to talk to him, but he knew that wouldn't go over well, so he turned and followed. "I'm sorry for throwing rocks. But I caught the fish. That should be a good concession."

She whirled on him. "Would you just stop! Stop. You're driving me to distraction. It's infuriating!" She poked her temple. "I try to get away from you and I can't."

Lachlan's heart slowed and stumbled in his chest. He took a step away from her.

She blinked and stepped toward him. "I didn't–"

"That was pretty clear," he said. She didn't want him around. She wanted him away. Like his father.

"No. I mean. I just need some space. I can't–" But she stopped.

He might have pressed her to finish the thought, but all he heard was that he wasn't wanted, and he godsdamned knew he wasn't needed.

"Right," he said, taking a step back and crushing his fledgling feelings. "I'll just–"

"Ollie–" Her step followed him.

"I'll just, um, go–" He walked past her, grabbed the fish and the knife, and moved to take them back to the river to clean them.

"Where are you going? That's not what I meant, at all."

"What part of 'I'm trying to get away from you,' doesn't sound like you want me to go?" He kept walking.

"I don't want that," she called after him.

"That's okay, Tarley. I get it." He turned and started back into the forest, holding up the fish. "The fish have to get cleaned." And he walked away, though the light had faded quickly. He needed to recenter his thoughts. The normalcy of just being a regular man in the woods with a regular woman had gotten away from him. He was Prince Lachlan, the useless prince, sent away by his father and now by a peasant woman.

"Wait! Ollie. It's getting dark!" she called.

"Giving you some space," he yelled back and pushed through the brush, leaving her and the camp behind.

Tarley

Tarley watched Ollie disappear, angry with herself for pushing him. He hadn't done anything wrong, and she'd been purposefully antagonistic. Forgetting to clean the fish at the river was a minor thing, and she could have overlooked it. And now he was angry with her, but worse, she'd hurt him, had seen her words had hit their mark in the dejected way his usually amicable countenance had sort of wilted. She found she hated knowing she'd caused it, especially because his hurt was justifiable. She'd been mean.

Now, she sharpened the skewers, angry with herself for being so hostile. She'd pushed him away because that was what she was good at. And now it was dark. Her heart slammed up against her throat with a tremulous beat.

After finishing the skewers, she busied herself so she didn't have to ponder Ollie in danger beyond their fire. She pulled the blankets from the bushes, hoping he was safe, then carried them to the tent, realizing how quiet the campsite was without him. As she laid the bedding inside the tent, her worry grew, wishing Ollie were with her so she knew he wasn't hurt. The thought unsettled her even as she kept looking at where he'd disappeared.

She'd been sure keeping him at a distance was safest for them both. Once he'd recovered, he would leave. She would remain in Sevens, and the world would go back to being what it was supposed to be. Only she'd lost the dividing line somewhere, letting him in, and that was why she was angry.

At the sound of footsteps, Tarley hurried from the tent, figuring Ollie had returned. She was going to say she was sorry.

Only it wasn't Ollie. It was a stranger.

She straightened, swallowed, and took a step back, but she couldn't move farther without backing into the fire. She suddenly wished she'd taken more care. She'd spent so much time concerned with Ollie that she'd forgotten to remember the real danger. Yet with her very next thought, she wondered if he was okay.

The stranger stepped from the shadows into the ring of firelight, one hand holding the straps of his pack, the other on a dagger at his hip. He was of medium height and a stocky build, though it was hiding under dirty garments. His leather jacket was lined with fur, hinting he was familiar with being in the forest. Blond hair hung a bit long and unclean, obscuring his bearded face. He'd clearly been in the woods a while and had the appearance of a hungry, wild animal.

"I smelled your fire," he said, revealing teeth that hadn't been cleaned for some time, if ever. "And you're a woman." He smiled, his gaze raking over her.

Tarley shuddered. "I don't have anything of value," she said, looking at his sharp, lean face. "I was just getting ready to make some fish."

"Oh. I wouldn't say that." He tilted his head, and his grin widened. "Looks like I hit the jackpot." She knew he wasn't talking about the fish. "You alone?" He glanced around looking for evidence that she wasn't.

"No," she said and lifted her chin.

"I don't see no one," he said, stepping toward her. "You're unprotected. Makes me within my rights to take you in. Collect the coin. But if you're her—"

"Who the fuck are you?" Ollie's voice snapped the tension as he stalked into camp, his brow heavily weighted over his eyes with anger. His gaze jumped to Tarley, assessing her.

Relief flooded her, and she rushed to his side, taking the clean fish.

As the stranger watched Ollie, his feral gaze shifted to something less predatory. "I was just trying to keep her safe."

"That's my job," Ollie said and pressed his hand to her back, his eyes asking if she was okay. "Not a stranger."

Tarley tilted her head to look at Ollie, knowing she couldn't take charge, that it was up to him to save her. But trusting him to do it warred with her sense of self. While it felt wrong on every level of her being, she was so used to relying only on herself, the relief when Ollie had arrived was a visceral charge moving through her body. The very real threat of what might have happened had he not appeared was taking root. And somehow, letting go and letting him take charge felt right.

"What's yer relation if I may? Brother?"

Ollie glanced at Tarley as if looking for guidance, but her tongue was tied, unable to guide him. To fool this man, they would have to showcase her place, or he'd sniff out the lie. And if the stranger was what she thought he might be, he might be desperate enough to hurt Ollie. She wouldn't let that happen.

Ollie's gaze danced across her face, then back at the waiting stranger. Taking a step forward, Ollie placed himself between her and the man. "She's my wife. Now bugger off."

Tarley took Ollie's hand, surprised by his choice, but grateful because it was perfect. "I promised him some fish."

Ollie glanced at their joined hands and pulled her closer, then leaned to say into her ear, "I don't like his look."

She pressed her mouth to his cheek and said, "He's desperate." Then she leaned back and offered him a smile, hoping he could read what else she was trying to say. If they didn't feed him, he might do something worse.

He nodded and turned to the man. "My wife has such a kind heart. Dinner?" His tone wasn't friendly, but he'd adequately read the situation.

The stranger nodded and took a seat at the fire, dropping his pack with a thud onto the ground.

"Sit," she told Ollie. "Let me serve you."

Ollie's eyebrows shot up and he grinned at her, but she noted the tension underneath his smile. "Allow me to get another seat first," he said, "for you. But come with me." Holding out his hand, he murmured, "I don't want you out of my sight."

Tarley took his hand and walked the few paces with him to the edge of their small woodpile at the edge of the light. They could still see the stranger looking over their camp, his dark eyes jumping between them and their supplies, them and the tent.

"Can you lift it?" she asked Ollie quietly.

"I'm lifting it regardless," he whispered. "He can't know–"

She understood what he meant. This stranger seemed daring enough to find any way possible to get coin. "You could reinjure yourself. I don't–"

"Tarley," he whispered. "I'll be okay. Are you okay?"

She nodded. "You're sure?"

"Let me—"

And she knew what he didn't say, running back to their angry exchange. He wanted to help, to take care of her for once. Acquiescing, she nodded and watched Ollie bend down, pick up a log large enough to sit on, and cart it into the camp, where he set it next to his. "There." He twisted it to make sure it was secure, then sat without so much as a flinch, a grimace, or a groan, as if nothing were wrong in the bones of his chest. "I'm Ollie," he told the man. "You are?"

"Gan," the man said.

"You from around here?"

"No," Gan said.

Tarley offered him some water, which he accepted, his gaze drifting over her face and down to her shirt.

"Why she dressed like that?" he asked Ollie.

Ollie looked at her, his eyes communicating his frustration. "Practicality."

Gan smiled and took another sip of water looking over the edge of it at her. "You one of those then?"

Tarley handed a skewered fish to Gan, whose fingers brushed hers as he took it. She suppressed a shudder and fisted her hands, wishing she could hit him for what he insinuated as if it were nothing at all.

"I don't know what you mean."

"You like the boys."

Ollie stood, and Tarley moved to his side. "This is how you repay kindness?" Ollie asked.

Gan chuckled. "I meant nothing by it, lordling."

Tarley touched Ollie's arm. "Mr. Gan will enjoy his fish and be on his way, love."

Ollie's eyes met hers, and a look she didn't understand passed between them. He worked his jaw in frustration before sitting once more, though she could see his anger coiled and ready to strike. Rather than strike out at Gan, he grabbed her waist and sat her down on his lap.

"But dinner for you—" she protested.

Ollie pressed his mouth to her cheek. "You're all the dinner I need," he said loud enough for Gan to hear.

Her cheeks heated as she noted the smile spreading across Gan's face. He chuckled, his eyes on the fish instead of her. She turned her head to look at Ollie, eyes wide. "What are you doing?" she whispered.

"Exactly what he thinks I should be." He lifted a hand and pressed it to the side of her face. Tarley had the impression he was thinking about kissing her, his eyes drifting to her mouth—like earlier—and her heartrate pounced once more, expectant, but when he leaned forward, he pressed a kiss to her cheek instead. "I don't like the way he's looking at you," he said against her skin.

"He's looking at me like most men in Kaloma look at women. Like chattel."

Ollie ran his hand from her head, down over her shoulder and dropped to the juncture between her hip and thigh, his thumb riding the seam of her leg.

Her body responded to his touch inopportunely, a

deep thrum of need spreading warm and low.

He gave her a squeeze. "I don't want to let you up, but I need protein for later." He gave her hip another squeeze and let go so she could stand.

Gan laughed loudly. "Keep 'em in their place—on their backs."

She skewered two fish and handed the stick to Ollie, who looked utterly disgusted at Gan's comment. Then she skewered a fish for herself and sat next to Ollie.

"What are you doing out in the woods?" Ollie asked, staring at his cooking fish.

Tarley watched Gan, who took his time answering. "Hunting."

"What kind of game?"

"Woman."

Tarley heard Ollie's breath stop, then restart with a rush before he asked, "Excuse me?"

"Seems there was a ruckus in a village nearby. A serving wench got it in her head to strike a man, then ran. Priest called in a hunting party."

Tarley straightened. He was talking about her.

"There's more of you?" Ollie asked, horrified.

"Was," Gan said, oblivious, and checked his steaming fish. He tested it with his filthy teeth, and Tarley worked to keep her expression neutral. "Few of the men kept tabs on her family. Thought they were hiding her but turns out wasn't the case."

Which was why Mattias hadn't surfaced.

"Few of us decided to hunt the woods," Gan

continued, picking at his fish. "But you know, not many of the weaker sex is willing to charge the haunted woods, so that was a longshot. If she did, she's probably dead, some Northman's new toy, or a collector got to her first. Huntin' party disbanded and went home, 'cept me. You're the first I've come across." His eyes drifted back to Tarley and lingered. "Pretty woman, I hear. Was hoping to have a go at her before I turned her in for the reward."

Ollie stood, pointing his skewered fish at Gan. "Take your fucking things—take the fucking fish—and get the fuck out of this camp."

Gan remained seated and just stared at Ollie as if surprised by his outburst. "What climbed up yer ass, lordling?"

Seeing Ollie wanted to beat the man to a pulp, Tarley's her heart further softened toward him. She could also see he recognized the man wouldn't get his anger in that way. "You keep looking at my wife." He stalked around the fire still holding the skewer.

Gan jumped up and grabbed his stuff. "I'm not getting ideas about your property."

But Ollie didn't stop, and Tarley wanted to cry out for him to be careful, to mind his ribs, but held her tongue. He grabbed Gan by his thick jacket with one hand and dragged him across the expanse toward the woods. "She's mine. All mine. And I won't have some other man getting filthy ideas."

She knew he was acting, but the words did something to her, working their way inside of her so that her heartbeat raced. *His. All his.*

"I don't got no ideas," Gan yelled, trying to get his feet under him, only Ollie was moving too quickly.

And he didn't stop until Tarley lost sight of them beyond the firelight and the shadows of a dark forest beyond. She heard a scuffle, a succession of thuds and grunts, crashing in the underbrush, and the crack of wood. Then it was silent.

Her heart thudded, echoing in her ears. "Ollie?" she called out and took a step toward the shadows.

Gan hadn't been overly large, and under normal circumstances, she was sure Ollie would have the upper hand, but he was injured. Gan had a knife. Her imagination raced. What if Gan had hit Ollie? Stabbed him? What if Gan was coming back to claim her. She glanced at the forest and considered hiding, but what if Ollie was lying in the shadow dying again, his ribs crushed, his lungs bleeding.

She took a step toward where they'd disappeared. "Ollie?" she repeated, only she whispered it this time, terrified that Ollie was gone, and knowing suddenly, she didn't want him gone. She hadn't really wanted it, and that realization made tears burn her eyes.

She didn't want to be alone.

A shadow moved through the forest toward her and into the clearing. The light didn't need to touch his face for her to know it was Ollie.

"Ollie!" She ran across the clearing and launched herself at him.

He grunted in pain.

She stepped back. "You're hurt?" Her hands were all over him, feeling, pushing at his shirt, but he grabbed her wrists.

"I'm okay."

Tarley stilled, looking up at him. "I was afraid something happened to you."

"Fuck, Tarley." He grasped her face between his hands. "You happened to me," he said and pressed his lips to hers.

Lachlan

The hurt and anger from their fight had burned away the moment he'd entered camp to a stranger saying he would turn Tarley in for coin, as if she were nothing more than a farm animal who'd wandered into the woods. His heart twisted with dark anger at the threat.

Lachlan had heard the discourse about Kaloma, of course. Sitting in on his father's royal council meetings made it impossible not to. Though he'd honestly wondered why it mattered, since it didn't affect Jast. Now he wondered if the "Kaloma Problem," as Lord Arting had referenced, was so much bigger. Arting's lands extended to the border between Jast and Kaloma, and the noble had lamented the intermittent refugees crossing over. Lachlan's father had extended full asylum, but Arting had been less than happy about it, citing the financial burden placed at his feet.

"And what if it were your daughter, Arting?" his father had snapped. "Your wife? Mother? Sister?"

Arting had bristled.

Lachlan's father had added, "The problem is that it shouldn't matter if it were your family. The problem in Kaloma is sanctioned abuse, and that is on each of us to care. Jast can't stand idly by on this any longer, not now that we have an opportunity to act."

Suddenly, having heard the stranger's threat against Tarley, clarity had moved through Lachlan like a sand wash against his insides as he connected the dots. Was this why his father had pushed so hard for this treaty?

When Gan had admitted he would hurt a woman—force her—he'd lost it. Disarming Gan and then speaking to that idiot with his fist had been satisfying. But he knew it didn't solve the overall problem.

As he'd walked back into camp, having tossed Gan in the water, Tarley's relief at seeing him, which had begun the moment he'd returned from cleaning the fish, grabbed hold of his angry heart and twisted it back into place. Then it filled with heat, swelling inside his chest with longing.

And he'd kissed her.

Gods, he'd kissed her.

She'd kissed him back.

Her lips soft and addicting. Her breathy moan when he'd wrapped his arms around her and pulled her close. The sensation of her hands gripping his arms, holding onto him for support.

Then she stepped away, ending the kiss and blushing. And in typical Tarley fashion, got efficiently busy.

Now, they sat side by side sharing the only fish remaining.

She'd kissed him back. Lachlan glanced at her again, his thoughts hanging up on that fact.

"Here," Tarley said, holding the fish toward him.

He glanced at her mouth. *Tarley had kissed him back.*

Lachlan pinched some meat between his fingers. As he ate, his gaze drifted up to Tarley's face once more, enamored with it.

She'd kissed him back.

She hadn't slapped him, hadn't been angry. Her hands had grasped hold of his shoulders. She'd relaxed against him, let his tongue mingle with hers, had equally participated. Her body had hit his. Her touch had taken his measure. Worried. Concerned.

Now, his heart hopped up before diving toward his stomach with his distracted thoughts about the night. Their fight. Wanting to kiss her then, fighting over fish. Touching her, claiming her, having her in his lap, of his hands on her ribs, her hips, her lips against his.

His racing heart wouldn't stop, offering a familiar rhythm he understood in an old way but felt entirely new.

She'd kissed him back.

When she'd ended the kiss, she'd stopped with a wide-eyed look, shocked, as she'd pressed her fingertips to her lips and looked at him.

He hadn't apologized for kissing her. He'd wanted to do it for days.

He glanced at her once more. He wanted to do it again.

Though they were sitting at the fire sharing the fish, they weren't talking about the one thing that he knew he was thinking about that wasn't Gan. The kiss. His ribs might be smarting inside his chest with each breath, but it wasn't because of a broken rib. There was something between them, but if he'd learned anything about Tarley, he knew if he was too forward, she'd run.

He tried to wrangle his mind to focus on something else, and said, "He said he came from a village. Which one?"

"Sevens. It's the only one close enough."

"Do you know the woman he was talking about?"

She held out the fish but wouldn't look at him, and he knew.

"You're the woman?"

Her gaze slid up to meet his. "Does that make you think less of me?"

"For what?"

"Striking a man?"

"If he was treating you half as disrespectful as Gan, he deserved it."

"He put his hands on me."

Lachlan's jaw tensed, and he had the urge to put another beating on Gan to pay for the stranger who'd touched Tarley. "Then he should be in the ground," he bit out.

"I had to run," she admitted and swiped a hand down her thigh. "I expected my brother days ago, but now I know why–" She paused. "I hate to cause my family undue worry. It was hard enough–" But she stopped.

"Hard enough to?"

Her eye flashed from the fire to his face, then back. "It was a bit of a battle to get to come out here on my own."

He could imagine. If Tarley were his–

Lachlan's brow furrowed at the thought. He shook his head again. She wasn't his. "Because it's dangerous?" he asked.

She shrugged. "Everything is dangerous. Everywhere I go."

"Because you're a woman?"

She looked at him again. "Because I'm a woman." She looked down at herself, then back up. "Disguised as a boy."

"To be fair, though, Tarley, you've never looked like a boy." He offered her a grin.

She didn't respond and picked at the fish, putting the small bite in her mouth.

He noticed the shape her lips took around her fingers and looked away, concentrating on the fire. "Are you wanting to return? Is it safe?"

"If that man's claim is to be believed, the search has been called off."

"And will they just forget what happened so you can return?"

"Most likely, the man who made the claim will be gone like most of the passers-through. I'll be vouched for, and the claim will be dismissed. I have my father."

Lachlan stared at the fire pondering that, then suggested, "Another few days, then?"

"Except Gan knows where we are."

"He won't be back," Lachlan said, still raging at the man and his comments about what he would have done to Tarley. "I made sure of it. Besides, he thinks you're a taken woman."

Tarley fidgeted next to him, then cleared her throat. "Are you strong enough to make the hike?"

"I can make it, but I can't guarantee I can walk quickly." He wondered if Ollie was alive and in Sevens. The curiosity burned through him and ignited his willingness to make that hike but didn't fan his desire to leave the comfort of what this camp had become to him.

He glanced at Tarley. *She'd kissed him back.*

She hummed, thinking, and held out the fish. "Eat the rest."

Lachlan took the skewer.

"We'll wait one more day," she said. "Then start back."

Lachlan ate some of the fish, then picked out a bone and flicked it into the fire. "I'm surprised your protective family approves of your trips."

"It was like going to war—a battle of wills between my mother and me." Her hand went to her wrist, and she rubbed it, an unconscious action that Lachlan realized he'd seen her do several times. "I guess it's always like that between us." She gave him a wan smile.

He looked closer at her wrist, at the red ribbon tied there. "What else?"

"What do you mean?"

"Why are you so preoccupied with my boots?" He smiled. "I'm preoccupied by the fact you're a pretty woman attempting to disguise herself as a boy, who knows the healing arts, how to take care of herself, and is distressed at causing her family worry."

She looked at him and bristled. "I'm not preoccupied with your boots."

"You are. You bring them up every three or four sentences."

She huffed a noise, but her tension deflated. "I don't want my mother using this against me, is all."

"Would she?"

"I imagine so."

"And your father?"

"He was the one who insisted on the disguise."

Lachlan pointed at her. "That disguise is terrible."

"Not from a distance."

"Except Gan got close." Lachlan wondered if his worry was written on his face.

Her head tilted the other direction, and she hummed as she considered. Then she said, "Is that the first time you've encountered a hunter?"

Lachlan tossed the used skewer into the fire. "Are you trying to wheedle information out of me, Tarley?" He smiled at her, then sobered. "Yes. It was." He paused, then asked, "Why doesn't the queen do anything to stop it? Surely, she has the power to change things."

Tarley snorted. "When her father died, she was the default heir. If the rumors and gossip brought to Sevens is true, then the royal council wants to oust her because she's a woman."

"What?" Lachlan's heart stalled and hung there, realizing that Keyanna reaching out after all this time might be more about survival than just repairing familial ties.

Tarley's eyes narrowed. "What? No news in the north?"

"So this treaty with Jast?"

"What about it?"

"Is the royal council in favor?"

"I would venture to guess that she's facing opposition. Gan's in the majority here. The laws are set up to make sure it stays that way, and those who make them—the traditionalists—have opposed every change the queen has attempted to make."

"I see."

"The Archpriest—if the rumors are true—is running things. I've heard whispered theories that her reaching out to Jast is a last-ditch effort to maintain her tenuous hold on her power."

"And if she doesn't?"

She shrugged. "I don't want to think about how it could get worse in Kaloma if she's deposed—"

Lachlan swallowed, grappling with this new information, considering what he'd just experienced with Tarley. "A mass exodus to the borders," he predicted. It wouldn't be one or two crossing, but a flood of people over the Jast border. And while he thought the kingdom could accommodate a surge of people, he could imagine the political ramifications with the nobles, how it might impact the economy, their resources. If they didn't open new trade routes, it could massively impact Jast's financial well-being, the food supply. "How do you know so much about it?"

"Why? Because I shouldn't?"

Lachlan shook his head. "No. Please don't mistake me–"

"–but because I'm a woman wearing peasant's clothes in the middle of the woods, why would I know?"

Shame hit Lachlan, because he had jumped to those conclusions in a myriad of ways since meeting her. Perhaps not about this issue, but about many others. "I have judged you, yes. As you have me." He lifted a boot.

One side of her face quirked up, and she huffed her amusement. "If you're a Northman, I'm the queen of Kaloma."

Lachlan chuckled.

When the amusement faded, Lachlan sat side by

side with Tarley, silent for some time, watching and listening to the fire. Usually this was when one of them made up a story about the creatures in the Whitling Woods. The night before, Tarley had told the story of the Witch of the Woods, but the fun of those last few nights seemed so distant. His thoughts felt heavy with what had happened with Gan and with the kiss they weren't talking about.

Tarley broke the silence. "I'm sorry about earlier," she said and began breaking apart the coals inside the firepit in preparation for bed. "I didn't mean to insinuate I didn't want you here. I... I didn't mean that."

"Tarley—"

"No." She turned and looked at him. "Please forgive me."

That apology meant something, especially from her. He could see the earnestness with which she offered it, her need for absolution, and he would give it, of course. He nodded. "Forgiven. I'm sorry for being so useless."

The last words dropped from his mouth like boulders. He hadn't intended them, and there they were, so ugly and vicious. And he understood, then, that was how what had happened with his father and how it had made him feel. Useless. And Tarley maybe hadn't intended it, but that insecurity had risen anyway.

"Stop—" she said, tossing the stick into the fire and grabbing hold of him. "That's not true."

"Isn't it?" he asked.

After standing on the shore of the river stabbing fish, ripping out their guts, and throwing the entrails into the water, his insecurities tied with anger at his father, but the hurt festered in how Tarley saw him. He could understand now. It was that kiss. He'd developed a layer of feelings for Tarley rooted in something other than attraction. Attraction to be sure. But friendship, too. Challenge. Fun. Respect.

"Ollie. Please don't think that's what I think—"

Her earlier words had thrown fuel on the insecurities his father had already stoked when he'd tried to broker a marriage deal without consulting Lachlan. He'd felt useless, worthless, little more than something to be traded away. And now, with Tarley, he wanted to be something more, only he didn't know how. He'd never had to be more than a title before.

He looked at Tarley, awareness hitting him in the chest. "My father thinks that—" he said and offered her a grin that he knew he didn't feel. Pulling away, he moved to right the camp, maybe understanding her default of being busy.

"What do you mean?"

The fire had died to coals. They stood facing one another in the dark, and Lachlan knew he couldn't tell her everything, but he trusted her enough to share the truth that mattered. "My father arranged my marriage without asking my permission."

"You ran away?"

"You could say that—" he hedged.

"But—"

"He didn't trust me enough to ask me."

"That doesn't mean anything about whether you're useful or not."

"What if I deserved it? His mistrust because of who I was."

She paused, considering, if that was what her silence meant. "Are you that same man?"

"It would be hard to nearly die and remain the same, I think."

He wondered if she'd smiled, because her shadow shifted, her head tilting down, which she often did when she was fighting one. She grabbed hold of his hand and wrapped her arm around his as they walked toward the tent. "I suppose the only thing to do, then, is live your second chance different."

She released her hold on him and ducked into the tent. Lachlan followed, and they moved through their routine—undressing and slipping between the blankets, pressing against one another for warmth—and she chattered, which he'd learned she did sometimes when she was uncomfortable or nervous.

The stillness of the night infiltrated the tent as Lachlan laid there, pondering the night's events, how raw and exposed he felt.

Tarley was right. He had a second chance, and perhaps he hadn't deserved one, but she had made sure he had one. That meant rising to the challenge to be the man his father needed him to be. A man worthy to be the king of Jast.

"Are you going to tell me where you're really

from?" Tarley asked, cutting into the silence.

"Someday," he said, tightening his arms around her. "In the meantime, I prefer a bit of mystery."

"Even if I'm putting myself in danger by helping you?"

He sobered, recalling the moment he'd seen Gan in the camp, the moment Gan had stared at her like she was something to take, and the subsequent thought that still startled Lachlan. *Mine.* "Trust this, Tarley, I will protect you with my life."

Tarley

Thoughts swirled in Tarley's brain as she drew the blanket tighter around her. The kiss. The awful events with Gan. The kiss. Lachlan's vow to protect her. The kiss. It was why she was now laying outside in the loam staring up at the starry sky instead of curled up with him. She shivered but didn't get up to return to the tent. Not yet.

It had been a day since they'd kissed, a day since he'd shared about feeling useless. Things were slightly strained between them. Ollie's teasing had tapered off to barely a trickle, as if he were in his thoughts.

Her body felt coiled and ready to spring when he was near. Every time she looked at him, she couldn't keep her gaze from his mouth, the kiss on her mind. Oh stars, that kiss. The heat of it. The fear of the moment and extended longing, a powerful elixir. She wanted to kiss him again, except she reminded herself Ollie wasn't being completely honest with her, and she didn't know how to reconcile that with her sensibilities.

All his incongruencies, added one upon another, screamed she needed to pay attention. Like his boots. Like not knowing about collectors and hunters. Like his accent. Like his manners, that were impeccable. Granted her father and brother weren't disgusting like some of the men she'd served at the inn. Her mother wouldn't have tolerated it, having taught all her children to have manners befitting "a prince and princesses." Like he used words to assuage, charm, and cajole. She just couldn't put all the pieces of the riddle together to solve it.

That kiss, though. She'd felt it in the marrow of her bones as if a magical spell had been cast between them, melting her insides so all she could feel was him and the sensations he created within her.

Yes, she would kiss him again regardless of not knowing everything about him, replaying that moment when he'd kissed her over and over in her mind.

But it was also why she'd retreated from their tented cocoon to find perspective in the stars. She shivered, looking up at the sky through the treetops, their dark outline framing the sky. She wasn't being wise, out in the cold of the night with the remnant of Gan's appearance a loud echo, but after two more nights laying with Ollie thinking about that kiss and listening until his breathing evened out with sleep, her own evaded her. Rather than disturb him, she got up. She knew Ollie would have insisted on remaining together, especially after what happened with Gan, and she wouldn't have blamed him, but he needed his sleep to continue healing for energy to return to Sevens.

Tarley would be lying to herself if she said she was looking forward to going back. Days ago, she'd thought that would be the answer to her lack of focus, but somewhere between then and now, there'd been a shift in her wants when it came to Ollie.

She'd known he was handsome when she'd found him, and in the adrenalin of trying to save him, hadn't spent time thinking about it. Now, though, after allowing herself the luxury of getting to know him despite her best efforts to keep him at arm's length, she was tired of trying. Her own thoughts made her blush, imagining his hands on her, his mouth. And though she didn't have identifiable feelings for him—unless one counted frustration—she was certainly attracted to him. He made her smile—or want to. They talked and worked together. He was kind and respectful.

Allowing her mind or her body to take her toward experiencing the physical aspects people shared terrified her. That loss of control frightened her. But that kiss. Ollie had taken it, only it hadn't been as if he'd stolen from her. She'd felt as if maybe she hadn't been the only one at a loss. That he'd given as much as he'd taken. She'd enjoyed it.

Most of her experiences with men were in the disgusting and abhorrent way they treated the women in the village. Though she realized there were alternative examples of men offering their respect and regard. Mr. Uraiahs with Auri, for one. Horance. Trevis. Mr. Cobble. Her father and brother. There were good men, she supposed. Even Ollie, whose unwillingness to tell her the whole truth appeared to be less about dishonesty to her than it was about something circumstantial regarding his own life.

She watched the constellations above, the shadows of clouds drifting past, and thought of Auri. Watching her with Nix in the booth at The Copper Pot weeks ago had stabbed Tarley with a sense of longing. And suddenly she understood the ache in her chest for what it was: loneliness.

She was always alone even when she was surrounded.

She couldn't look at it.

So she mentally turned away and ignored it.

She would return to Sevens and resume what had been in her life before this adventure. Before Ollie. And he would move toward whatever it was he was seeking. She refused to let the sadness to enter, adding another lock to the door.

She yawned and watched the stars twinkling in the velvet sky above, her denying the emptiness that careened around inside of her, and eventually succumbed to sleep.

"Tarley?"

She blinked her eyes open, dizzy with sleep, and shivered.

"What are you doing out here? It's freezing."

She shivered again. "I didn't want to kiss Ollie."

"Help me," the voice said. She recognized the tone, found comfort in it, but couldn't get her cold mind to reconnect to its identity. "I can't carry you," the voice said. Strong arms wrapped around her. "Did you want to? Kiss Ollie?"

She got to her feet and hummed an affirmation, her arms wrapped around the shadow's shoulders. "Yes."

He chuckled. "He won't kiss you if you don't want him to."

"Because he doesn't want to?" she asked, ducking into the dark tent.

"Oh, he does," the shadow said, and helped her lie down, sliding into the bed behind her and pulling her tightly against him. "Let's warm you up."

She shivered again and the shadow's arms tightened around her.

"You're safe," he whispered. "I promise."

With that, she slid easily back into a deep, comfortable, and warm sleep.

When her eyes opened again, the blue twilight of the morning hinted the sun was coming soon. A sharp wind yanked at the fabric overhead as the drumbeat of rain tapped against the taut linen, dripping down the outside of the tent in streaks.

A hard, warm form was pressed against her backside, and when she moved, the arms banded around her tightened.

"Not yet," Ollie said, his voice deep with sleep. Alluring. She felt it in the heat of her lower belly. "It's raining, and you're dry and warm. Here. With me."

She wanted to fight him on it. She wanted to jump to her feet and direct them toward a hike back to Sevens. To put distance between what would protect her and what she was realizing she wanted. Badly. And she rationalized the weather would make it muddy and slow, and with Ollie recovering, he needed another day.

She relaxed. Leaving the warmth of his arms, of this bed, wasn't what she wanted. She wanted to lie here and imagine that the man holding her was her lover. And she wanted to understand the feelings pulsing through her like those twinkling stars she'd consulted the night before.

A little while longer.

"Did I fall asleep outside?" she asked.

He hummed an affirmation.

She felt that sound between her legs and pressed her thighs together.

"How did I get back in?"

"I came and got you. I woke up and you were gone."

"Is that why you're squeezing me to death?"

His arms relaxed a touch. "I freaked out a little bit." His even breaths filled the silence, until he asked, "Would you like me to let you go?"

Her brain was at war with her body, especially at his words. Her body was winning the war. "No."

She knew he smiled even though she couldn't see him. "We probably shouldn't hike back in this."

"Agreed."

"If it clears–"

"Tomorrow will do."

"But–"

"Why are you always moving? What are you running from?" he asked. He released his hold to caress her, his hand skimming over her ribs, her waist to her hip and back again. Back and forth.

Her breath hitched, rediscovering a rhythm, her concentration on his hand and the possibilities. "I'm not–"

He squeezed her waist gently. "In the time I've known you, you've collapsed with exhaustion every time you stop moving. Otherwise, you're in constant motion." She felt him shift behind her, leaning closer somehow, though she wasn't sure there was much space between them as it was. "Don't lie, Tarley."

He was right. From moving between the cottage and The Copper Pot. From making the means to be out in the forest where movement was a requirement to living, a requirement to not allowing emotions like loneliness a grip on her. "I don't think I've ever thought about it before."

He hummed, and she felt his breath move through her hair like a caress. Chills coalesced at the nape of neck and raced down her spine. Then she felt his morning erection pressed against her backside. Her own breath caught as that familiar heaviness returned between her legs.

She arched into the feeling. When she did, Ollie responded, his breath stalling, restarting, and his body shifting. His hand fisted against the linen of the tunic covering her belly, and the length of him pressed even tighter against her bare bottom.

Then the pressure was gone, and he moved. "Maybe–"

She moaned, a refusal, tightening her hold on his hand on her belly. "Stay–" Her body needed the feel of him more than the need to flee.

"Tarley." Ollie realigned his body behind her and leaned forward, pressing his lips against the skin between her neck and shoulder.

Her heartbeat pitched, slamming up against her ribcage, and a deep breath escaped her. She clasped onto the back of Ollie's head, holding him there, and tilted her head, offering him more space. "I want to feel you–"

"I promised–" His mouth moved across her skin, the silk of his tongue creating a hot trail.

"Promised what?" she asked on a breath, driving her bottom back against his erection.

"To keep you safe." His hand opened and pressed more firmly against her belly as he tilted his hips against her, moaning softly, "Tarley–"

She took a deep breath, alive with all the sensation moving through her. "I don't feel unsafe." She rocked her hips back, against him again, her core melting with need.

He groaned. "Stars. You feel—"

She caught hold of his hand, and his breath caught.

"I feel… like… I need—" She panted the words, unable to catch her breath, and guided his hand lower until it was pressed between her legs. "I need… I need…"

"I know what you need," he said, his voice rough and demanding. His fingers skimmed through her sex, until he found the cluster of nerves that made her suck in a breath the moment he connected. "So wet—" he murmured and bit down on her shoulder.

"Oh," she gasped.

"Fuck, Tarley. Is this okay?"

"Yes." His finger circled her clit. "Yes," she repeated and tilted her hips toward him.

"Spread your legs wider for me," he ordered.

She did, draping one of her legs over his and reveling in the sensations he created. He slid a finger inside her, and she sucked in a breath, then moaned and rocked her hips as he pleasured her.

His lips and tongue fluttered over the skin of her neck, and suddenly his hand was gone from between her legs.

"No," she whimpered. "Ollie—"

He grasped her hand, gripping his arm. "Show me how you like it," he said and placed her hand between her legs, his hand resting over hers. "You've made yourself come before?"

She nodded.

"So hot, Tarley. Show me."

She'd had the privacy to explore her own body—now that she lived alone—but she'd never thought someone would watch her. The idea of Ollie watching her excited her, her heart beating with the bewitching idea of it.

He pressed his hand against hers. "I need to see."

She slid a finger into the silk of her hot warmth, then up to the apex where her clit was swollen. Moaning at the pleasure of her own ministrations, she rubbed her backside against Ollie behind her as she rolled her hips, seeking release.

He grabbed hold of her hip and drew in quick breaths as he watched, squeezing harder. Then, as if he couldn't stand just watching, he slid his other hand under her tunic up over her ribs to a breast, curving around and kneading, then grasping a nipple.

She gasped at the pressure, feeling it like a jolt between her legs.

"You like that, Princess?" he asked, doing it again.

She bucked against his erection, and he groaned. "Fuck." The word was rumbled, like thunder deep inside his chest. "Fuck," he repeated. "I like how you love yourself."

With slow, deliberate circles, she continued. She felt powerful, arching her back, pressing her head against Ollie's shoulder as she pulled her own pleasure from inside out. She panted, then moaned, louder now, each sound stacking upon the next, less restrained with each passing second.

Ollie pressed his hips against her backside, his hard

length finding resistance against her ass as she rocked, her rhythm quicker, his breath quickening as she did.

"Fuck, Tarley," he murmured near her ear. Then with one arm banded around her, he reached down and covered her hand with his, inserting a finger inside her once more.

She cried out. "Yes. Please," she panted.

"I want to feel you come." The added weight of his hand against hers, the warmth of his palm hot against hers as she moved against her own fingers and now his only increased the sensations. He ground his hips against her backside. Warmth spread from where she was touching herself, to the feel of his finger sliding in and out of her.

He inserted another finger, murmuring, "So hot."

All of it, the sensations, his body, his words, her touch became overwhelming. The pleasure whipped up like a storm in the forest, overtaking everything with its intensity. Her breaths came quicker, sharper, building inside her chest as she panted. "Please," she cried and rocked against both of their hands. "Please," she repeated over and over.

"Yes, Princess," Ollie said into her ear. "Let go."

And she did. All the worry, the struggle, the loneliness broke apart inside of her, as her body tightened around his fingers, around her heart, and cracked everything under the pressure. "I'm coming," she whimpered. Heat raced through her, burning her up, disintegrating everything else until all that was left was her. And Ollie.

"So tight," Ollie said gruffly. "Fuck. I want to feel you grip my cock." Then he groaned, pressing his lips against her bare shoulder.

The storm eased, breaking up, until she relaxed, loose and languid in the glow of her release, and sighed. Relief flooded her, and she couldn't keep the smile from her face.

Ollie withdrew his fingers from inside her and ran his hand over her body from her hip back up to her breast, squeezing it as he pressed kisses against her exposed skin.

She moved, withdrawing her leg draped over his hip, but Ollie reached down and grasped her thigh. "Not so fast," he said. "Where do you think you're going?"

She stilled and twisted, tilting her head to look up at him. His eyes were dark, like that stormy forest—gray, brown, dark green, black—and her heart lurched in her chest, then found that quick rhythm once more.

"Breakfast?" she asked, though her voice sounded breathy and insubstantial in her own ears.

"Not yet." He shook his head and lifted his eyebrows. "It's my turn to make you come."

Lachlan

Lachlan moved gingerly, drawing himself out from behind Tarley.

"Oh, but–" She followed him with wide eyes.

"Nope. Can't talk me out of it," he replied with a grin, rocking back onto his heels, his hands gripping his rather impressive erection, if he did say so himself.

"–you're injured." She pushed up onto her elbows.

He chuckled and looked at her lips, trailing his gaze over her reclining form, the stretch of the ivory tunic pulled off her shoulders, but tight over her breasts. Her nipples were pebbled under the fabric. He licked his lips. "As if that could keep me from what I want to do to you."

He wanted to see more of her, suddenly wishing he'd insisted on watching her face as she came, though the feel of her body clenching around his fingers had been like discovering a buried treasure.

"This breakfast is going to be amazing," he said, reaching out and touching her knee, urging her to part her legs.

"What?" She pressed her knees together and sat forward. "What does that mean?"

Slightly confused by her response, since she'd been so open with him just moments earlier, Ollie stopped and looked up to her face, surprised by what now looked like panic. "Have you never?"

She shook head. "No."

He sat back slightly. The thought that he could be her first experience tightened the muscles in his chest around his already haphazardly beating heart. "Wait. Never?"

She tried to get up.

He grasped her thighs, stopping her. "Don't mistake my question, Tarley. It isn't a judgement. I'm surprised, that's all."

"Why?" She settled back and tilted her head to study him. He could see she was wary, building a wall back up that he'd somehow been able to walk through his morning.

"Because… fuck—look at you, Tarley. You're so beautiful. And smart. And accomplished. Who wouldn't want this… with you?" He blew out a breath and ran one of his hands through his hair, the other still on her knee. Kneading the flesh of her thigh with the other hand, his slid it higher to her hip. "Your trust earlier meant so much." He looked unto her eyes, closing as she relaxed.

Leaning forward, he ran the tip of his nose along her jaw, his lips skimming her skin as she sighed. "I promised," he said.

"Promised what?"

"To protect you."

Tarley turned her head toward him. It was slight, as there was little room to maneuver between them, but it was enough that her lips were aligned with his. She reached up, skimmed her hand over his jaw, and closed the minute distance, pressing her lips to his, communicating what she wanted.

There was sweetness in the kiss, a confection of lips and sighs. Lachlan, his hands framing her face, went slow, afraid to scare her now that he knew, but she surprised him, opening her mouth under his, and touching his lips with her tongue.

His internal organs twisted up with desire, and he pulled her tighter against him. His ribs protested, but he ignored them. This. This moment with Tarley felt like everything. When she grabbed hold of his hair and moaned, opening her mouth wider under his, he lost the battle with taking it slow, pressing her back into the blankets, and draping her body with his, his knee pressed up between her legs.

She moaned, shifting her hips against his leg,

seeking friction, her hands now trying to find purchase on his back. That knowledge, the feel of her slick heat against the skin of his leg, her movement, pushed him toward a frenzy.

"I want to look at you. May I?" He breathed the words against her lips.

While he thought she might balk, she didn't, relaxing with a shiver, surprising him. "Yes."

He reveled at the look on her face, trusting and hungry, as if the more guarded Tarley receded to allow the real one to emerge.

Sitting back, he pushed one of her legs wider, then the other, until she was spread open before him. He stared, licked his lips, and swallowed. Her sex glistened, swollen with her earlier orgasm, enticing him. If it was even possible, he was even harder. His eyes jumped up to meet her gaze, as he gripped his cock. "See what you do to me?"

Her eyes tracked his movement, and she offered a sound that grabbed hold of his spine and tugged him forward. When she reached between her legs to touch herself again, Lachlan stopped her hand with is and trapped it gently on her belly. "My turn, remember?" He grinned at her.

Leaning down, he pressed his lips against the inside of her knee. "I'm in control." He gave the other side equal treatment. "Do you hate that?" He glanced at her and could see she wanted to reply but didn't.

He kissed her again, sliding his tongue along her inner thigh. "Is this alright?" he asked.

Her eyes darted over his features. Her mouth opened as if she wanted to protest, only she didn't. When his tongue teased a sensitive spot at the seam between her leg and pussy, she gasped, "Yes. Ollie, yes. I want this. I want to watch. To feel you–"

His breath caught at her admission, and he swallowed again, as if the movement could keep him contained. He found himself hesitating. He was lying to her—by omission. He'd promised to keep her safe, but gods, his moral compass was fucked this close to her promised land. So he justified that he wasn't going to fuck her—not with his cock anyway. His tongue was another matter.

He slid it through her velvet heat, encouraged by the moan that escaped her when his mouth found her clit. That sound added kindling to the fire already raging inside him.

When she pulled her hand from under his on her belly, then fisted both in his hair, arching her back and gasping, "Oh, gods," rather loudly, he lost control, wanting to take her apart bit by bit and then put her back together.

"Tarley," he groaned against her sex. "I love your taste." He inserted a finger inside her again, then another, her walls snug around him. "You're so godsdamned tight."

The revelation she'd never been with anyone else and was choosing him ignited something inside of him he'd never experienced before, possession, perhaps, and something feral and primitive. *Mine. Mine. Mine,* chanted in his head again, though he knew she wasn't.

An intensity consumed him. He parted her, licked and sucked, used his fingers and tongue to drive her as wild as he felt. Her hands in his hair held close as she moved against his face. When he pulled away, she cried out. "No! Please."

"Not yet. Patience." He growled the word, slowing things down, pushing her toward a sharper edge of want with him. Gods knew he wanted to drive his cock into her, but this was about learning her. Only the longer he played, the more his desire for his own release with her increased. To alleviate the pressure, he pressed his erection into the soft cushion of the bedding, groaning with his own impatience. "Fuck, Tarley. You're making me crazy."

He grasped her legs and draped them over his shoulders, then maneuvered, driving forward to hold her in place with his shoulders and mouth. Unable to keep his own pleasure in check, he feasted on Tarley with his tongue and took his cock in hand. The essence of her pleasure, her mewling and moaning, her hips trying so hard to move with him even as he pinned her, the primal way it all felt with a storm raging around them—Lachlan embraced the moment.

"Oh. Ollie," she cried out. "I haven't. With. Someone–" She gasped each word. "I can't–"

He eased up, finding a rhythm she liked. "You can. You will," he commanded. He let go of his own pleasure, for hers, looking for the right way to please her. A soft lick, a suck, a stroke of his tongue. He reached up and fondled her breasts.

And suddenly she struggled against him. "I can't-"

He stopped and looked up at her. "Tarley?"

With her eyes squeezed shut, she said, "I don't think I can–"

Lachlan stopped. "Tarley. Princess, look at me."

She opened her eyes. He kissed her hip bone. "Look at me," he said, and slid his tongue over the skin of her lower belly. "Do you want me to stop?"

She lifted her head and looked at him. "No."

"Does it feel good?" he asked, kissing her pelvic bone.

She followed his tongue with her eyes. "Yes."

He continued, climbing her body with his mouth. "Where did you go?" he asked, then kissed her ribs.

She sighed and moved her hips against his belly. "In my head…" She closed her eyes.

"Open your eyes," he ordered, now at one of her breasts.

She focused on him at the same time he licked her nipple, savoring it with his tongue.

She drew in a deep breath.

"You like this?" he asked and closed his mouth around her, sucking and drawing the peak into his mouth, then scraping it softly with his teeth.

"Yes," she moaned and closed her eyes.

"Keep your eyes open," he said, continuing his attention. He gave the other breast equal attention while she watched, then reached down between her legs, caressing her folds with his fingers, sliding them gently back and forth, fondling, sliding a finger around her clit while his mouth explored her breasts. "Does that feel good?" he asked.

"Oh. Yes," she said, her focus going hazy.

"What do you want me to do, Tarley?" he asked, inserting a finger, then withdrawing it to swirl the tip around her sex. "You feel so good."

His words somehow broke her barrier.

"I want your tongue," she said. "I want to come on your tongue."

He grinned, then dipped his head. "Eyes open, Princess," he ordered, "and hold on." He flattened his tongue against her sex, pressing and pulsing, licking, swirling.

Her chant began. "Oh, gods. Please-"

The refrain loosened his ability to concentrate.

"Yes," she cried. "Please, Ollie."

As much as he wanted to, Lachlan couldn't maintain control at the feel of her coming apart under him. So when she cried out, "I'm coming," her cunt clenching and her clit swelling against his tongue with her orgasm, he took hold of his cock and stroked it, following her orgasm with his own.

She breathed heavily, boneless as he released her legs, his breath coming in gasps as he too came down from the high.

"Oh gods, Tarley," he said, his cheek on her belly, enjoying the feel of her skin.

The orgasm surprised him. He'd succumbed to his fair share of coming both at his hand and the hand—

and mouth—of another, but this was different, somehow. Only he wasn't sure how, exactly.

He lifted his head so he could see her, her hair loose and spread out around her, watching him with her ancient gray eyes, their smoke dark with the aftermath of being undone and remade.

His chest tightened, and he felt the need to press his fingers against his heart, but he dismissed it, smiling at her as she studied him.

He moved up her body until he held himself above her. "I'm afraid I made a mess on the blanket."

She lifted her head as if to look but didn't get very far with his body pressing her back against the blankets, his hips flush against hers, a latent hope that perhaps he might still get to fuck her even knowing he shouldn't.

"Is that bothering you? The idea that there's a mess?" he asked.

Her eyes flashed back to his, then narrowed. "You think you know me so well."

"I don't. You've shocked me."

Her cheeks reddened and she tried to push him away, but he stayed where he was.

"Wait. You don't regret it, do you?" he asked and skimmed her face with his fingertips. "I don't. I think I could spend a lifetime feasting on the way you taste."

The scarlet of her cheeks deepened. When her gaze met his again, it ran over his features until it settled on his lips again, then jumped back up to his eyes. "I don't regret it."

"But?"

She moved then, drifting out from under him as if she were made of smoke.

Lachlan missed the feel of her, which was disconcerting in and of itself since he wasn't one to linger after sex. Only her lack of answer unsettled him even more. He didn't like that she wasn't smiling, not that she often did. But she'd had two orgasms, for godssake.

"But?" he repeated, watching her get to her feet. "You think we made a mistake?" His words shocked him. In the whole of his life, he'd never had a woman say being with him was a mistake. Women wanted him, did what they could to lure him and tried their best to keep him. He was a prince, after all. "You didn't enjoy it?" he asked, getting to his knees.

Standing an arm's reach away, Tarley adjusted her shirt, pulling it so it was righted against her thighs, as she looked down at him. "I did." The blush that bloomed on her cheeks told Lachlan she was telling the truth. "It's just we barely know one another, Ollie. It probably shouldn't happen again."

Ollie.

Fuck.

She was right.

He was lying to her. She thought he was someone named Ollie. And yet, the thought of never being with her in this way again tightened his chest uncomfortably. Even as he nodded understanding because she was right, they hadn't known one another very long, the thought hit him: he did know her.

He knew that she worked hard. That she was thoughtful and kind. She cared about her family, and stories made her smile. She liked to be clean, and always braided her hair to keep it out of her face but not until it was dry. And he was sure, if pressed, she knew him too.

So his body rebelled, wanting her even more. He wanted to grab her by the waist and pull her back onto the blankets. He wanted to kiss her into submission, and prove to her that she knew him, probably more than he'd ever allowed anyone to know him. He wanted to push his cock inside of her and claim her as his–

Wait.

She doesn't know your name, his brain argued, stopping his thoughts.

She disappeared through the tent's entrance in only her tunic.

"Where are you going?" He got up, grabbing his trousers and shoving his legs inside. "It's raining!" He scrambled after her, pulling the pants over his hips as he hopped from the tent.

Tarley turned to look at him, her loose hair getting wet along with the gauzy linen of her tunic, which then stuck to her skin, making it even more see through. She wasn't wearing anything underneath, so he could see her the dusky outline of her nipples and the shadow of hair between her legs.

Lachlan's breath caught. She was one of their

stories about these woods come to life. A wood nymph there to bewitch him. Mission accomplished. When his breath seeped out of his chest, everything he'd ever decided about what it meant to feel for someone else escaped. It was the vision of this woman standing in the rain refilling him with what was honest. She was the destination, the treaty, the very thing he wanted to claim for himself.

Only she didn't want him.

Her arms came out to her sides, and she tilted her face up toward the sky. The rain fell with a gentle rhythm that wasn't oppressive but rather fulfilled a need of sorts.

"What are you doing?" he asked, needing to clear his throat to say it.

"I'm going to the river."

"In this? It's raining."

She turned her head and regarded him with a rare upturn of her lips. "I'm already wet."

"But it won't be warm. There isn't a fire."

Instead of answering him, she gave him one last look and disappeared into the brambles toward the river.

Lachlan wasn't sure what had just happened. He spun to the tent, then spun back to where Tarley had disappeared. Rationalizing he was worried about her safety, he rushed after her.

"Tarley?" he called, following the trail from the camp, calling after her, his clothes soaked through. When he came to the clearing between the forest and the river, he stopped short. She stood in the river, submerged to the waist, naked, her tunic discarded on the shore.

It was at that moment Lachlan knew that no matter what she said, what they'd shared that morning hadn't been a mistake, and there was no way in the underworld that it wasn't going to happen again.

Tarley

"Tarley," Ollie's voice called from behind her, collapsing her resolve to get away from him. The experience with him in the tent had been an earthquake, fracturing the very foundation of all the things she thought about herself, about men, about partnership, about sex.

Her perception was fixed in the beliefs reinforced by her usual experiences that men were selfish creatures who used and abused women. Only that wasn't what had happened at all. She didn't feel used or abused. She'd felt worshipped. It upended everything she thought she knew. And somehow amid all the sensation, she'd fixated on it. On how wrong she'd been as Ollie's mouth and hands made her feel… so much. As she'd slid toward being undone, she'd dug in her proverbial heels, afraid—and hated admitting that even to herself. Afraid of giving that power to Ollie, even if she trusted him to keep her safe. But instead of doing what might have been easy, he'd centered her pleasure.

She hadn't felt used or weak doing what she had with him. In fact, she'd felt powerful somehow despite giving away a piece of herself. Wanted. Necessary. Her preconceptions crumbled, leaving her a shell of awareness and insecurity about what to do with the newness of it. Did it make her weak to continue wanting Ollie?

The easiest thing to do was to run.

She hadn't expected him to follow.

Now, Ollie stalked from the tree line toward her, his face dark with whatever emotion she was witnessing, though she didn't know him well enough to discern it. The vision he provided was a punch to her core, pushing sensation out toward the furthest reaches of her fingers and toes. He was shirtless. His brown hair, darker when wet, hung in his eyes, his scruff adding to the wild look. She wanted to run her hands from the slope of his neck to the rounded definition of his shoulders. When he got close enough to the water's edge, he waded into the river, his trousers open and a trail of dark hair from his navel disappearing underneath.

She thought about him holding his erection earlier. Thought about how much she'd wanted all of him. As he moved toward her, power evident in his stride, tension in his body, she swallowed and backed up, the current tugging at her legs, even more aware of him, of the way his look seemed to stake a claim.

Ollie didn't slow. "It wasn't a mistake," he said, and grabbed her face and pressed his mouth to hers with an animalistic growl. His tongue didn't meander, it claimed just as his hands grabbed her ass and tugged her roughly against him, her bare skin slick against his.

And she loved it, grabbing onto him so she wouldn't float away.

He lifted her, and she wrapped her legs around him. "This doesn't–"

"Hush."

She listened, unable to resist. There was something altogether commanding about his order, as if the forest would bow to it, would listen, and obey.

He waded back to the shore, carrying her with him. "This isn't over," he said against her mouth, his hands gripping her thighs. The rain continued to fall. The roar of the river drowned out any noise she might have had in her head. She listened for it, but it was empty. All of her was filled with the sensations Ollie had awoken. But her mind grasped onto her doubts, and she went to war with it. Allowing herself to be driven by this desire wasn't safe.

Wanting someone else was dangerous.

She undid her legs from around his waist and

pulled back from his kiss. "You don't get to decide." She stumbled.

Ollie caught her and pulled her back. "I do."

"No. You don't," she said and pushed against his chest.

"You want me, Tarley, as much as I want you. Your kiss tells me so. Your tongue." He reached down and cupped her sex. She moaned, pressing closer despite her resolve. When his fingers attended to her most sensitive place, her body ignored the resolve as well, and she leaned into it, grasping onto his shoulders for support. "That tells me." His lips found her mouth, kissing her deeply, his hands doing things inspiring a moan from her that he swallowed. "Your sounds tell me."

She pushed him away, angry at herself for being so pliable with him. "You don't get to decide."

"I'm—" But he stopped, shutting his mouth.

"You're what?" she asked.

He shook his head, refusing to give voice to what he'd been about to say.

"I'm a grown woman, Ollie. I've been taking care of myself without anyone, and I will continue to take care of myself without anyone. That is what I want."

His eyes narrowed, and she noticed the captivating shade of green and gray threaded with something darker.

"Is it really Tarley? Or are you just pushing me away because I'm upsetting whatever it is you have in your head as the way it should be?" He stepped closer, and she held her ground, refusing to give him the satisfaction of knowing how much his proximity was messing with her resolve. "No one *wants* to hide in the woods alone."

An angry flint sparked in her chest. "When the world is filled with liars, they do." She knew she'd hit her mark because he took a step back. She poked at him. "You can't even tell me the truth."

He shook his head. "I did. You just didn't believe me, and you've spent the rest of the time reminding me how I couldn't know things because of my fucking boots." He leaned toward her, his chest heaving with annoyance, but his eyes flitted to her mouth, then back to her eyes. He straightened. "You tell me, Tarley. Why would I trust you with the truth?" He turned, walked away, and disappeared through the woods back toward the camp.

Unsure what he meant, she whirled with a frustrated huff back to the river running swiftly past. The rain was waning, now just intermittent droplets. She tried to recall him telling her and couldn't recall it. He was lying, but she couldn't fault him for it. If only her words hadn't made her feel slightly ill-at-ease with her choice.

But this was safest.

It wasn't as if they had a future.

When she got back to camp shivering inside her wet shirt, Ollie had a fire started, and he'd strung up the blanket to dry. The sight of him made her cheeks heat, thinking about what had occurred between them earlier, but she knew this—distance—was easier in the long run. She didn't need the complication of coming to want something with him.

He didn't love her.

She didn't love him.

They would go their separate ways.

He glanced at her when she walked into camp, then looked away quickly as he poked at the fire.

"Are you pouting?" she asked.

"No." He stabbed at a coal.

She stepped up next to the fire and held out her hands toward the heat. "You seem like you're pouting."

He looked at her, his eyes skittering like a rock skipping over water, then looked away. "I'm not pouting."

She bumped him with her shoulder, trying to cajole him into a better mood like he was always doing to her. "I'm sorry for insinuating you were a liar."

He shrugged at the fire, not looking at her. "It's fine."

But she could tell it wasn't. He was different. His teasing was gone. The banter had slid down the river with the rain, and she found she missed it even when she'd thought it irritated her.

She suddenly swayed and grasped onto his arm to keep herself upright. Ollie, the fire, the campsite, the woods beyond jerked back and forth in her line of vision, then flared bright so she had to close her eyes. She stumbled again and there was Ollie's voice in the distance, but she couldn't discern what he said.

A black dot in her vision rushed toward her, the sensation making her feel sick. She lost her balance—or perhaps she already had, because there was Ollie somewhere beyond, calling out to her. The black dot widened, until she could see it wasn't a dot at all, but a keyhole. She peered inside at her mother and Jessamine bent over a bed. Someone was in it, but she couldn't see who. When she blinked, they were gone, and in their place was the hollow sound and stabbing pain of one of her headaches.

"No. No," she mumbled, her stomach rolling with nausea.

"Tarley? Please. Talk to me."

She realized she was in Ollie's arms near the fire.

"I'm here," he said. "What's happening?"

"A headache," she whispered with her eyes tightly shut. "I need the tea. The herb I gave you—"

"Which one?"

"Wallosh." She swallowed, and knew she was going to be sick. "With the purple...I need—" But the nausea took over. She rolled her head away from Ollie, gagging and spitting up bile, but there was nothing in her belly to eliminate.

"Fuck, Tarley. What can I do?"

It sounded like yelling.

"Sleep. Quiet," she whispered.

Suddenly, her body was floating. "Your ribs—"

"Hush. Don't worry about my ribs."

But his grunt told her she should worry, only she

struggled to piece together why she was supposed to worry. "I've got you."

Ollie laid her in the tent.

"The tea—"

She curled into a ball and prayed the balm of sleep would come for her. Sometime between the strike of the powerful headache and Ollie forcing the bitter tea into her, she slept. By the time night fell, the tea had begun to work, and she opened her eyes. The remnant of the headache lingered, making her mind sluggish.

Her wet tunic was gone, and she was covered with a dry blanket, with her head in Ollie's lap. His hands were in her hair, his fingers brushing the strands with soft, gentle strokes. She turned her head and looked up at him, wincing at the residual pain as her mind caught up with her senses.

His gaze met hers, worried. "What can I do?" he asked.

"You've done it," she answered and allowed herself to accept his nurturing. For this moment, at least. She shut her eyes and just existed, imagining this could be more, even as she knew it couldn't. Awareness gradually dawned that she'd been completely helpless, and Ollie had stepped up once again.

"You kept your promise," she said.

"What do you mean?" His voice was light, like his touch in her hair.

She wasn't sure how to explain it. Had she been with Gan when a headache hit, she knew a man like that wouldn't have been taking care of her this way. She'd have been in danger.

She turned her head and studied Ollie. His head tilted down as he watched her, his usually smiling mouth serious, and usually smiling eyes tight with worry.

"I'm sorry—"

"Tarley. Don't—"

"You didn't have to—"

"Of course I did. You nearly fell in the fire." He stopped, his fingertips pressed against her scalp, and took a deep breath. "When you went down—" He cleared his throat.

She frowned against his chest as the vision she'd had returned. Jessamine and her mother in a room attending to someone. She'd had many headaches, but they weren't usually accompanied by images. Lights, sounds, smells—yes. This had been one of her worst. "Thank you. For helping me."

"Thank you isn't necessary. You fucking saved my life," he said, his voice deep and resonant with her ear pressed against his chest. "It's the least I can do."

Right. Payback. After rejecting him so thoroughly earlier, she shouldn't have hoped there was another reason. Though what would that reasoning be? What did she hope? Nothing. There was nothing to hope for.

She sat up, gingerly pushing away from him to right herself. She held a blanket to her bare chest, realizing he'd stripped her of her wet clothes. Smart.

"Maybe just stay—" Ollie said.

But Tarley straightened, knowing she needed to be the one to hold herself up. That was the way of things, the way to be safe.

"About earlier–" he stated.

"Forgotten," she said and attempted a weak smile.

He frowned.

Her throat suddenly felt too tight with emotion that wanted out, though she couldn't understand its origin. This was what she wanted. She cleared her throat of it, deciding the best way to move forward was to avoid it.

"We can start for Seven's tomorrow morning."

"Are you sure? You seem, weak–"

Tarley bristled at his statement even if it was accurate just then. She was—but didn't want to be thought of that way. Unable to meet his gaze, she said, "I just need a good night's sleep and some breakfast. All will be well. Did you eat dinner?"

"Tarley. Now's not the time to be efficient and responsible. Rest," he said and moved toward the tent's entrance. "I'll get you–"

"I don't want you to go to any trouble."

He scowled at her, shook his head, then ducked out of the tent.

Tarley took a deep breath, clearing away all the confusion clogging up her thoughts. She hated the way her heart snagged in her chest, as if there were a sharp stake inside of it, scraping at the soft tissue to make it bleed on the inside.

She was sure that returning to Sevens was the right

course of action. He could get a horse and return to where he came from. She could return to the safety and predictability of her routine. Only those thoughts made her innards feel weighted with an anchor. There was a sensation that in moving toward Sevens, she'd be moving away from something very important and toward the unknown of a something dark and lonely, which, she knew, was a foolish thought indeed.

Out of the Woods

Lachlan

The hike to Sevens was slow and arduous. It left little room for talking, not that Lachlan was inclined to talk even if he'd been able. His body—usually healthy—had other intentions, it seemed, since he spent so much time trying to catch his breath. Tarley hadn't driven them, stopping frequently to check on him, giving him the opportunity to rest, and ascertaining if they were moving too quickly.

She forced him to stop when he tried to push, giving him rations and water. At the halfway point, she offered to make camp, worried he might be overexerting himself, but he'd insisted he was fine.

Really, what he needed was distance. Her proximity made it impossible to think clearly.

"I need civilization."

She'd chuckled quietly. "Sevens as civilization," she muttered, still amused as they continued.

The night before had punched a hole in his self-awareness. Witnessing Tarley collapse, watching her descend into unconsciousness, seeing the pain she'd faced. His helplessness had been aggravating. He'd only wanted to take it from her, willing to face death again if only to keep her from what she'd been going through.

As he'd sat in the tent, her head in his lap as he caressed her hair, he realized for the first time with utter clarity, and then shame, how right his father had been. Lachlan was selfish and immature. He had been underhanded and a coward. His father's criticism had been right.

Perhaps Lachlan's incredulity at not being included in decisions about his own marriage were fair, but he couldn't forget his father's harsh words following his ridiculous behavior. *"How could I trust an immature boy with the welfare of a nation?"* his father had asked, is face red with anger at learning what he'd done to Princess Truisante. *"You have never thought about anyone beyond the tip of your nose. You will go to Sevens, Lachlan. I hope while you are there, you will find the means to grow a backbone and the sense worthy of being a king of Jast one day."*

Lachlan had sat in that tent, tending to Tarley, eyes shut remembering his father's frustration, ashamed with such a harsh truth about who he'd been, and what it had taken to make him recognize it.

Rather than consider his shame and Tarley's astute observations of his character based on his stupid boots, he focused on the Whitling Woods. As they approached the village, they left behind the mountains of their former camp giving him a change to appreciate their surroundings. It was beautiful when considered it objectively, something he hadn't done before the attack. He'd been so preoccupied by his predicament, he hadn't stopped to consider what was beyond the tip of his nose.

Sevens, according to Tarley, was situated at the edge of the woods at the last curve of the River Grimz before it opened up into the rich fertile farmland of the Fulstrom Valley. Giant evergreens rose like guards on duty, their jutting limbs creating shadows that seemed to hide the forest's secrets. Peppered in between like flocks of animals were grove after grove of deciduous trees clothed in various shades of green, some flowering, some with the new fruit too young to eat. There were bushes and brambles, animals scurrying to hide in them as they walked.

Though it was daytime, Lachlan couldn't shake the feeling that they were being watched from the shadows, even as he told himself he was being foolish. His mind was playing tricks on him because of the stories about the witch in the woods, the vampires, the master of ravens, the fairies.

Tarley tried to engage him in inconsequential

camaraderie. She was chattering again. While he shrouded his feelings in silence, she did it with noise and movement. She was trying to smooth things over on a superficial level with him. He was still stinging at her rejection and worried by her unexpected collapse the night before, but he was more concerned about the potential danger they were walking into that might get her caught.

Tarley's amusement about Sevens representing civilization became clear as they walked through the village. She hadn't undersold the size of it, and he couldn't imagine how any of its inhabitants were able to make a living. As they walked, Tarley explained that the Queen's visit and the retinue set to arrive from the Court of Jast had provided an influx of coin and people.

He noted a few wooded homes with shingled roofs, a main thoroughfare, a giant meeting house which she pointed out as the marketplace, a few two-storied buildings where commerce occurred, a mercantile, an apothecary and healer—though Tarley pointed out it wasn't her mother's shop—a blacksmith, a leather worker. There was a Sun Church—a nondescript building rather than an actual cathedral where most of the ostentatious sects of Sun worshipers met—near a giant tree at the center of things which Tarley called "the green," and beyond that was the inn. The Copper Pot was the only pub and accommodations in Sevens it seemed, though Tarley mentioned a skin house a bit further out of town.

By the time they entered the courtyard of The Copper Pot Inn, Lachlan was too tired to be irritated with even himself. He was too tired to feel much of anything aside from the ache in his ribs and the blisters on his feet.

The inn rose two stories with jutting dormers at equidistant intervals. Mullion windows glowed with yellow light as the sun sank below the horizon. The building wrapped around a cobblestone courtyard where a nicely kept stable was situated. It matched the stone and wooden facade of the inn, with mullioned windows and an attic room with an outdoor staircase that led to a wooden door. The River Grimz cut behind the inn, flowing through the village. Tarley pointed out the shingled roof of a mill further down river.

As he followed Tarley into the courtyard, a young man—no more than seventeen—rushed out from the stables.

"Tarley? That you?"

"Evening, Trevis," she said. "All clear?"

Lachlan knew she was asking him about the hunters.

"As a summer night." The young man's eyes caught on Lachlan and narrowed. "Who's this?"

"This is Ollie. He was injured. Has my mother been about?"

"Injured, you say? Your mum was here last night with Jessamine. She's here." His gaze lingered on Lachlan. "Dr. Rufus is dining in tonight. Want me to get him?"

"Oh gods, no," Tarley said. "Absolutely not." Lachlan watched her shudder and wondered about it. "Credence?"

"Running the meal."

Lachlan listened to their dialogue, hearing the inside knowledge, the shared history between them, and hated being outside of it. He'd had Tarley's full attention for nearly two weeks and suddenly resented having to share it, which was ridiculous and immature. It also wasn't befitting a prince.

"Ollie?"

"Apologies," he said, trying to adjust the pack on his back and wincing, his ribs reminding him he wasn't completely whole yet.

Tarley came to him immediately, removing the pack. "We need a place for Ollie, Trevis."

"He can bunk with me in the stable."

"Can you check in with Credence, and if she's unavailable, with Horance? Let them know I'm back but not to send for my father."

"Mattias is here. He brought Jessamine."

"He is?" Tarley smiled, and it was the first time Lachlan could remember seeing that kind of smile grace her face. There was no hesitation, no trepidation, no tempering of emotions. It was beautiful. "Did he say why?"

"Who's Mattias?" Lachlan asked.

"He was worried they couldn't get to you sooner," Trevis said, ignoring Lachlan as he crossed the courtyard. "Was getting ready to head out at first light."

"My brother. Remember?" she asked Lachlan, and he felt foolish at the twinge of jealousy he'd felt.

She called out to Trevis, "Tell Mattias, will you?"

"Sure thing, Tarley."

"Oh, and Trevis?"

The boy stopped again and turned.

"Would you ask Mrs. Barnwell to heat some extra water for a bath?"

The boy nodded and continued to a doorway where he disappeared.

"Come," Tarley said and helped Lachlan to the stables. "Think you can climb a ladder?"

Lachlan might have been aching, but he wasn't about to show it. "I can manage."

The stables were impeccable. Horses were shut away, their stalls clean and smelling of fresh hay. A few nickered and snuffed as they passed, which gave him a pang of grief and longing through him for Goldie. He looked for Ollie's dappled gray with the white forelock or Johesha's mahogany quarter but didn't see either. Disappointment and fear weighed heavily on his shoulders. Had they not survived the ambush?

Stars, he was tired, and the thought of trying to solve his problem—being stranded—seemed too big just then. With the closed border, how was he going to get word to his family that he was alive? How was he going to get home?

When they reached the ladder, he stopped, put his hands on the rungs, and looked up.

"You're sure?" Tarley asked and laid a hand on his

back.

He looked over his shoulder at her, took in the concern riding her brow. "I've carried you. I can climb a fucking ladder, Tarley," he groused. Her comforting hand disappeared from his back, and he climbed the ladder and stepped onto the platform.

"Trevis sleeps up here," she said from behind him.

Lachlan moved aside and leaned to help her up, grabbing hold of his ribs as he did.

"You did too much today," she chastised, swatting his hand away as she stepped up next to him, and reached to check his ribs.

He fell back both grateful and resentful of her hovering, though he wasn't sure how those went together.

She pulled her hand away, looking suddenly timorous, which Lachlan hated because Tarley wasn't timid. Swallowing, she moved beyond him. "I'll have Trevis set up a palette for you. He'll also help with water for a bath. And it will be warm."

"Warm water. An indulgence," he replied on the off chance he could reconnect to the rhythm from before, missing it.

"I'll be sure there's soap." She pressed a finger to her lips, tapping as she considered things that needed to be done, and it dawned on Lachlan he'd kissed her only a day and a half ago, but it might as well have been a month with how much had changed. He wanted to do it again, but she clearly didn't.

"And clothes," she added.

She'd rejected him. He didn't want what she didn't. So, he quelled the thoughts about kissing her, and looked away. "Thank you."

"I'll gather some bedding," she said and moved to the ladder, disappearing over the side of the platform.

He walked the length of the narrow loft, stopping to study Trevis's space, which had a palette situated between the raw wood of a dormer. A small crate next to the bed held extra clothing folded neatly inside. Next to the oil lantern on top of the crate was a small book, the cover wrapped in etched leather. Lachlan wanted to pick it up but didn't, knowing it wasn't his place. It made him curious about the boy.

Besides Trevis's accommodations, there were bales of straw, barrels, and crates of materials, the area above the horse stables serving as a storage space in addition to the boy's sleeping quarters. In contrast, Lachlan's suite of rooms back home weren't ever anything he had to worry about. They were cleaned and cared for, the sheets changed each day. He had running water and a bathing room, a closet filled with clothes that he never had to clean. He looked down at his boots now, four inches caked in mud. While he'd had muddy boots before, of course, he'd never had to clean them.

He glanced at Trevis's meager accommodations.

Suddenly Tarley's criticisms felt appropriate, and Lachlan felt ashamed of his own entitlement.

The sound of voices and footsteps echoed across the stone corridor of the stable, snapping him back to the present.

"What do you mean you've been alone with a man?" a male voice asked.

"What was I supposed to do, Tai? Leave him to die?" Tarley answered, her tone frustrated.

They'd stopped walking and Lachlan peered over the loft's railing. Tarley stood below, her back to him, facing a giant of a man—a young man, no more than eighteen or nineteen. Though Lachlan's view was skewed, he could see that the young man was taller than Tarley by at least a foot. Their coloring was similar, brown hair, light skin, though the young man was trying to grow a beard. It was patchy. Her brother, Lachlan decided.

"What if you'd been caught?" His long arms came out to his sides.

Tarley crossed her arms across her chest. "A hunter showed up–"

"Tarley! What?!"

Unable to see the brother's face, Lachlan could still hear the panic in his elevated tone and choppy words.

"I'm standing here, aren't I?"

"How?"

"The man I saved helped me—Ollie. I'll introduce you."

"He's here? What if he's in on it?"

"You don't think I considered it?" Tarley snapped at him. "Don't you trust me?"

In on it? Lachlan's face bunched, then relaxed. He hated that she'd thought it but understood. He'd been a stranger then, no one to her other than a representation of the kind of person able to hurt her.

"This isn't about trust. Mother—"

"She can't know, Tai. She'll never let me back out."

"I don't want any of my sisters to die," Mattias said in a low voice; Lachlan had to strain to hear his words. "Or be carted off because of some stupid law. And now—"

"And now what?"

Mattias looked behind him, grabbed hold of Tarley's arm, and walked her deeper into the stable so they were unseen beneath the loft. "Something's off between Mother and Auri," Mattias whispered. "They went out late a few nights ago."

"On a call?"

"I don't think so. When does Mother take Auri on calls?"

"Never."

"Exactly. Jessamine and Brinna said Auri was acting strangely the day before. Then—"

"What?"

"They left. That's when they found the Royal caravan."

"The Queen's here?"

"Attacked, Tar. Burned out. No survivors. Auri said the bodies were unidentifiable, except for a single soldier wearing Jast armor."

"Jast armor? Only one?"

Lachlan straightened, frowning. That couldn't be right.

"And the queen?" Tarley asked.

"Thought she'd been among the dead, but she's here."

"What?" Tarley nearly shouted it.

Mattias hushed her. "Showed up the night before last. The guard died getting her here, and she hasn't woken up yet. Mother and Jessamine have been with her nonstop."

"Stars, Tai. This is bad."

"You see?"

Silence stretched between them as Lachlan reeled at the information. It didn't make any sense. Jast wouldn't have attacked the queen. He was sure it hadn't been the queen's order to attack him. Who was behind the assassination attempts?

When he heard them move, Lachlan stepped away from the railing and waited for Tarley and her brother to climb into the loft. His assessment of Mattias was correct, clearly young and untested, but by the look Lachlan was getting, very protective of his sister.

"This is Ollie," Tarley said, then turned and faced Lachlan. She didn't meet his gaze. "This is my brother Mattias."

Lachlan uncrossed his arms. "Hello."

Mattias grunted.

Tarley backhanded his arm.

"Hello."

"Ollie has broken ribs, so help me move his pallet, Tai." She walked to Lachlan. "Hold these." She shoved linens into his arms.

Then she and Mattias went about setting up a

wooden pallet in a corner of the loft, similar to the position of the other boy's palette. Trevis arrived carrying a lantern and pitched in while Lachlan stood watching, feeling useless. When he tried to help, Tarley scolded him, and the boys snickered, though not at his expense. They both looked at him in commiseration as if they too had been at the other end of her razor-sharp tongue.

Then Tarley was standing before him, her skin tinged pink with exertion, her eyes bright, her hair askew. She was still dressed as a boy, and yet he couldn't remember ever seeing anyone more beautiful, his mind conjuring her standing in the rain.

"Ollie? The linens." Her hands were out, waiting.

"Oh. Right." He handed them to her. "I'll help."

When they were done assembling his bed, Tarley stood.

Mattias started for the ladder. "Let's go. Mother and Father will be relieved to see you."

"You're leaving?" Lachlan took a step toward Tarley, feeling as if the rope tethering him to shore was being cut, leaving him adrift. To drown.

Tarley nodded. "I'll be back tomorrow."

He took a slight breath of relief, but it didn't alleviate the root of his panic, though he couldn't exactly identify what that root was.

"I need to check in with my family. After what happened." She picked up a pile of fabric Trevis had dropped when he'd arrived. "Here's some clean clothing." She handed him the stack. "I'll see you tomorrow."

Lachlan watched her descend after her brother. She glanced at him once more before disappearing, and her look communicated something he couldn't decipher but he wished he could.

"Would you like that bath?" Trevis asked, his blue eyes assessing what Lachlan figured was his horrific appearance.

He nodded.

"It'll be this way."

Lachlan followed, because what else could he do? He was alone in the very kingdom where Jast was going to be framed for the attack on Kaloma's queen, and the one person he considered an ally had just left him alone.

He had no plan, no way to contact his family, no way to get home. Taking a deep breath, he resolved that a bath might help his perspective. Only he found himself wishing for their tiny tent in the middle of the Whitling Woods once more.

Tarley

"A man?" Scarlett snapped, smacking a wadded-up towel on the counter next to the stove. "Have I not impressed upon you all the danger strangers possess!"

Tarley stood just inside the front door. She'd barely made it over the threshold as Mattias had shared the news: *Tarley was alone with a strange man in the woods.*

"Tail!"

"Sorry, Tarley," her brother replied, though the look on his face—the arched brow and grim set of his mouth—told her he was anything but. He wasn't keeping secrets about her safety.

The rest of her family were in various places in the

small space of their cottage. Her father stood near her mother in the kitchen. Brinna was sitting in the living area near the fireplace mending something, and Auri was setting the table for a late dinner. Jessamine, at the inn, was the only one absent.

"A man?" Brinna grinned with a dreamy smile on her face, her mending forgotten in her lap. "Was he handsome?"

"A man?" Auri snorted and set another dish on the table with a touch more force than necessary.

"A man?" Her father, harrumphed the phrase as if he were chopping wood, cutting the words down into bits. He crossed his burly arms over his wide chest. "We agreed on the disguise, Tarley. There shouldn't have been any strangers. None at all."

"It was a matter of life and death."

"Just like having you flee in the first place," Scarlett scolded. "If you'd been in the cottage like I said in the first place, this wouldn't–"

"Mother–" Tarley started, annoyed, knowing all along this was how the conversation would go.

"I saw him," Mattias said, removing his outer garment and hanging it on the wooden tree their father had made. "Good looking fellow," he said and added, "Stared at Tarley a bit too much."

"He didn't," she said but felt her skin heat recalling what had occurred between them—a secret she had no plans on divulging.

"He did."

"He was safe," she insisted even as the thought

caught in her brain and spun on itself contemplating Ollie walking through the river and grasping hold of her, kissing her, claiming what had happened between them hadn't been a mistake.

"You're blushing?" Scarlett asked, smacked her wooden spoon into the pot, and started across the room toward her.

"Just a man—Ollie—and as I've already told Tai, he was near death. I couldn't leave him."

"You could have." Scarlett closed the distance and grabbed Tarley's hand to push up her cuffs, exposing her red ribbon.

"What are you doing?" Tarley jerked her hand away. "You wouldn't have."

Scarlett smiled, then kissed Tarley's knuckles. "You're safe."

"Are you going to lock her up in here too?" Auri asked, her words laced with bitterness.

"I don't have to," their mother said.

"Because she didn't lose her ribbon." Auri slammed something against the table.

"What does that have to do with anything?" Tarley looked at each of her family members before removing her jacket. "What has gotten into you? You're acting strange."

"There were hunters after you, Tarley—"

She looked at Mattias, hopeful he'd keep that part secret. Sure, it was a part of the safety, but the threat was past whereas Ollie wasn't. There wouldn't be any point in sharing it, and she hoped Mattias would see it that way too. There wasn't any sense in adding to their mother's panic. She begged Mattias with her expression, and Mattias's eyes widened with his obvious conflict about it. But then he stayed silent and Tarley took a deep breath.

Scarlett returned to the kitchen. "Go clean up. You're filthy. Then join us when you're done."

Tarley mouthed a "thank you" to her brother and left the room. Baffled by her family and the added lunacy, she leaned against the closed door of the backroom. Usually when she returned from a trip, there were greetings, along with shared business as usual as her family filled her in on anything she'd missed. Then there were things like any new babies born or house calls Mother had made. Sometimes it was a spooky story shared by her father while he and Mattias were in the woods. Other times it was something as mundane as who had the chores that week. She supposed her flight to the woods, the queen's appearance, and her arrival with Ollie were only the most interesting thing to happen since the *Great Nap Escapade*. Mattias was right, though— something did seem off.

Tarley stripped out of her dirty clothes and stepped into the steaming bath, sighing as she slipped down into the warm water. The lovely rosemary and citrus infusion her mother put in the water reminded her she was home. She leaned back and closed her eyes, memories of Ollie flashed in her mind. His arrogant grin, his needling her to react as he threw rocks, his head between her thighs. Her eyes flew open, and she busied herself with washing. She didn't need to be thinking about Ollie and his magical tongue. But then she recalled the way he'd watched her from the platform of the stable as she'd left, and her heart pinched in her chest at how alone he'd looked.

As she slid the soap across her skin, a knock came at the door.

"May I come in?"

Auri.

"Yes."

Her youngest sister's face appeared followed by the rest of her body as she squeezed through the crack in the door. Auri looked out once more as if to check if she'd been followed, then shut it. When she whirled around, her face looked pale. "So much has happened."

"She found out you were sneaking out, didn't she?"

Auri pushed away from the door and came to sit outside the tub. "Here. I'll help with your hair." She massaged the soap into Tarley's scalp. "She already knew."

"How?"

"I don't know." Auri was silent, her fingers working through the strands of Tarley's hair. "I swear to you that woman has spies everywhere."

"Unlikely," Tarley said, enjoying the feel of her sister's ministrations.

"You'd be surprised."

"What happened?"

"Nix and I got into a fight."

"What? Why?"

"A petty disagreement," Auri hedged. "As you can imagine, it put me in a terrible mood. We were in the garden, and I sort of snapped at Mother. Accused her of lying."

Tarley tried to turn, but Auri held her head. "You what?"

"Stop and close your eyes."

Tarley complied as water sluiced over her head and down her face back into the tub.

"It's the only thing that makes sense."

"Why? How does that make sense?"

"Hear me out–"

Another knock sounded at the door. "May I come in?"

Brinna.

"Yes!" Tarley called, her eyes still shut as Auri continued washing her hair.

The door creaked open, then clicked shut as Brinna slipped inside.

"I wanted to talk to Tarley," Auri said.

"Me too!" Brinna exclaimed. "You aren't the only one who wants to hear about this man."

Auri sighed.

Tarley opened her eyes and swiped the water from her lashes. Brinna was sitting at the foot of the tub, smiling hopefully. She looked so pretty, her wheat-colored hair shining in the lantern light.

"Yes. You're right," Auri conceded, letting go of

whatever she'd been about to tell Tarley.

"There's nothing to tell." Tarley moved the water around with her hands.

"Lies," Brinna said with a gleam shining in her gray eyes. "You blush every time he's mentioned."

"That doesn't mean anything–"

"I had a dream about you," Brinna added, cutting Tarley off.

Tarley sat forward, interested, the water sloshing as she did. "A dream? Do tell."

While that didn't always mean anything, sometimes it did. Brinna's dreams told stories, and sometimes parts of them added up to something important, like the time she'd dreamt their father got a new white coat, and two days later he'd been trapped in a freak blizzard. But then sometimes she might dream she kissed a man with golden eyes, and no such man arrived to do the kissing.

"You were in the woods," Brinna said, "and the sun was super bright—like this golden color that shone down on you. And there was this entity with it, and everywhere it went, the golden light followed it."

"Entity?" Auri asked. "Is that a replacement for the word 'monster'? A monster with the golden light?"

"No! It wasn't a monster. There weren't any bad feelings with it. But I couldn't exactly see its face. I had the impression it was an important part of Tarley's story. You were smiling."

Tarley scoffed. "I smile."

"Not like that–" Brinna said.

"You're a grump," Auri said, washing Tarley's back.

"Hey." Tarley turned to glance at Auri over her shoulder. "Who covered for you?"

"One, that doesn't make you less of a grump. And two, it didn't help."

"So tell us," Brinna demanded.

"Tell you what?"

"About the man!"

Tarley sighed. She didn't want to offer her sister hope where there wasn't any. Ollie was leaving. They weren't in love, and she knew that was exactly what her dreamy sister was hoping to hear. "I promise. There isn't much to share. His name is Ollie. He fell in the river, and I saved him. He got separated from his party, so he came back to Sevens until he's well enough to go after them."

"Maybe he'll stay," Brinna said.

"I don't think so."

"Is he handsome?"

"You can decide that for yourself. He's staying at the inn."

"Oh!" A smile cracked Brinna's pretty face—the fairest of them all—as she clapped her hands together. "Maybe I'll invite him for a picnic."

Tarley bristled at the thought, hating the idea of Ollie offering any other woman attention, but in the next thought it felt ridiculous of her to ponder it. "Do what you want."

When she looked up at Brinna, her sister had a sly

smile on her face.

Brinna laughed. "Right. That's okay, Tarley. You have feelings—"

"I don't have feelings!"

Brinna giggled and looked at Auri. "I think she protests a bit too much."

"What did you want to tell me, Auri?" Tarley asked, needing to divert Brinna from her speculation.

"Mother's lying."

"Tell me what you really think." Tarley laughed. "About what?"

"I suspect a buried treasure trove worth."

"How do you know?"

The door opened, revealing the very subject of their discussion. "Auri? Brinna? What are you doing?"

"Just getting caught up," Brinna said.

"Helping Tarley with her hair." Auri poured more fresh water over Tarley's head, and Tarley sputtered, not ready for it.

"Spinning tales?" Scarlett asked Auri, but it sounded more like an accusation.

"I did learn from the best," Auri said, dumping more water over Tarley.

"Stop," Tarley said through the hair over her face and the water.

"Auri!" Brinna admonished, glancing at their mother.

Tarley shoved her hair off her face, waiting on doomsday to break out between Auri and their mother.

Scarlett turned to look at Tarley, ignoring Auri and

Brinna for the time being. "I came to tell you dinner is ready." Then she left.

Tarley stood, grabbing a cloth to dry off.

"Divert us, sister. What does Ollie look like? Is he handsome?"

"Why did you get in an argument with Mr. Uraiahs?" Tarley avoided Brinna's hopeful look, maintaining focus on drying off.

"You've met him?" Brinna asked, her eyes wide with surprise. When she looked at Auri, she looked hurt. "I haven't."

"Don't blame me. You were out in the woods, and Mother and Jessamine on a call. I made a run for it."

"The one time," Tarley told Brinna and shrugged into a clean chemise.

"Why we argued doesn't matter," Auri said. She sounded miserable. "He's gone."

"He'll be back though?" Tarley asked.

Auri shrugged, and for the first time Tarley noted the paleness of Auri's skin, the pinched look as if she might be in pain. She'd seen this look before, just after the *Great Nap Escapade,* when Auri looked about as brittle as a fire-ravaged tree.

"Aurielle?" Tarley grabbed hold of her sister's arm. "He'll be back?"

She nodded. "There's little choice of it."

Confused, Tarley jerked back and tilted her head. "What does that mean? You don't want him to return?"

"Of course I do," she bit out, then shook her head,

but not before Tarley caught the tears shining in Auri's eyes. She seemed to collect her emotions and stash them somewhere for safekeeping before saying, "I'll tell you later, after we eat. I'm sure you're hungry." Auri offered her a wan smile.

Tarley's gut twitched with concern, but she nodded.

Brinna and Auri disappeared through the door, and Tarley hurriedly dressed in one of her everyday dresses, a dark burgundy cotton splashed with tiny ivory blossoms. She left her hair unbound to dry and joined her family at the dinner table.

Once they were seated and Tomas offered thanks, they dug in to eat.

"How is the queen?" Mattias asked, scooping a helping of mashed root vegetables onto his plate. He passed the dish to Tomas and turned to Tarley for the next dish of fowl covered with fragrant herbs.

Tarley blinked, and the room shifted, swirling away revealing a dark room beyond, a woman—a stranger— sitting up in the bed looking at her. Her face was marred with bruises and cuts, her eyes ringed with dark circles.

"Tarley?" Mattias snapped.

She blinked, the image gone, and looked at Mattias holding the dish now.

"Are you okay?" he asked.

She glanced around the table, each member of her family staring at her. "Jessamine is with the queen?"

"What is it?" Scarlett asked, her brow drawn

together with worry.

"Just got a bit dizzy," Tarley said, unsure what to say to keep her mother at arm's length, and hesitant to admit that it had happened before, unable to explain the sensation away again, even if they were slightly different. She knew the moment she did, her mother would jump into action with healing remedies—but Tarley wasn't sure what she'd be trying to heal. She blinked, wondering if the headache would follow, but while her stomach expressed a touch of discontent, her head remained clear.

"Yes," Scarlett answered, though she was still watching Tarley with her shrewd eyes. "She's watching the queen at the inn."

"Is she going to make it?" Tarley asked and blinked again at the vegetables on her plate wondering if it would happen again, but her plate remained the same.

"She was in and out of consciousness when I left," Scarlett said, adding leafy greens to her plate. "I'll check on her again in the morning."

"Do you really think it was Jast?" Brinna asked. "Such a shame if it was. We could have visited another kingdom."

"Visited? I'd have moved," Tarley added with a sarcastic chuckle.

"It seems far-fetched." Auri added a hot bun to her plate. "A single piece of armor and a single arrow in Jast's colors hardly seems like evidence. And those were the only bits to have made it through the inferno that ravaged everything else. It was as if—"

"—someone placed them there after the fact," Scarlett said.

"Why would someone want to make it look like Jast?" Mattias asked, then took a bite of his dinner, smacking around the bite. "It's good, Ma."

"Mouth closed," she corrected, then thanked him.

"Maybe to keep the treaty from happening. Perhaps to start another war," Tomas said.

Brinna dropped her fork with a clank. "A war! Why?"

"How late is the royal party from Jast?" Tarley asked.

"Both are late," Tomas said. "Over a week. Though traversing the mountains can be treacherous any time of year." He took a bite.

"What if they were attacked too?" Mattias asked.

Tarley's heart leapt, then began to pound. She set down her fork and pictured the horse, how beautiful she'd been. The beauty of the embellished silver tack. The man washed ashore next to her—Ollie in his finery. The boots. *I'm from the north*, he'd said, over and over. She'd considered Jast, but suddenly a memory she'd dismissed surfaced in her mind. He'd been delirious with fever. He'd called himself, "Lachlan." And just a few days ago, he'd snapped, *I told you who I was. You dismissed it.*

"Who's the king of Jast again?" Tarley asked, pushing the greens around on her plate.

"The king? Mallor Nikolas. But rumor is he's not coming. That he's sending the crown prince."

Lachlan. Lachlan Nikolas.

He had told her the truth.

She'd saved the fucking crown prince of Jast.

Tarley stood, her plate barely touched. "I need to go back to the inn."

"What?" Scarlett asked. "You just got home. And I have some things I need to—"

But a sound outside the door interrupted.

Scarlett froze and each of them looked at the doorway waiting for a knock.

But the knock never came. The door burst open. It was Jessamine, Trevis just behind her.

Scarlett stood. "What is it? Is something wrong? Why aren't you with the queen?"

Jessamine looked frazzled, her black hair slicked in a tight bun but for a few strands that had escaped, and her brown eyes alight with panic. She had obviously raced there from the inn with Trevis, who stood behind her, hat in his hand.

"Mother. You must come quickly."

"What is it?" Scarlett moved out toward the door, already going for healing kit.

"It's the queen," Jessamine said. "She's awake."

Lachlan

Lachlan sat at a wooden table near a large fireplace in the dining room of The Copper Pot Inn. It was late enough that any remaining patrons were bellied up to the bar, and the remaining tables were empty aside from a table in the corner with a lone man. He followed Trevis in when a woman approached, holding a crock of steaming food.

"This him?"

"Yes'm," Trevis answered.

Her dark eyes flitted over him. "You don't look like much, though Horance's clothes would make anyone look like they were swimming," she said. "Let's put some meat on those bones. Ollie?"

He nodded.

"I'm Credence. I own the place. Well, my brother does—in accordance with the law."

"Thank you for your kindness," Lachlan said and watched her set the bowl in front of him. It smelled divine. Game roasted on sticks in an open fire had its place, but this. "Your hospitality is appreciated."

She harrumphed a sound. "Don't go thinking I'm offering charity. I'll put you to work to earn your keep unless you've got the coin to cover it?" Her smile was bright and welcoming, reaching her dark eyes, making them warm.

He grinned. "Fair enough. I'm very obliged."

"Now, tonight notwithstanding, most of your meals you'll take in the kitchen with Mrs. Barnwell. Bunking with Trevis will do. Got anything you're good at?"

Lachlan had to think about it. What had he been trained to do besides lead a country? He swallowed. He could do many things, but most of them showcased skills that weren't particularly useful.

"Never mind," Credence said. "There's plenty of work to be done, regardless."

"Miss Credence?" a voice interrupted.

Lachlan looked up at a pretty woman with sleek dark hair and dark brown eyes. She leaned close to Credence and spoke quietly. Lachlan's mind compelled him to look away, his gaze sliding back to his stew. His mouth watered, and he picked up his spoon.

"Trevis," Credence said. "You accompany

Jessamine and bring Scarlett—"

Trevis jumped up, and Lachlan watched him move as the woman he had to remind himself had just been speaking with Credence followed Trevis through the dim room toward the main doorway. Lachlan had the urge to look away and did, focusing on his food once more and wondered what he'd just been doing.

Credence's hand was on his shoulder. "Eat up, Ollie. The Fareviews will be here soon, and I have a feeling it might be a long night." She moved across the room to help a blond man sitting in the corner booth.

As Lachlan was finishing his second helping, the door opened. A woman walked in, a dark blue cloak around her shoulders, a satchel in her hand. She pushed the hood back and her eyes scanned the room. Her gaze stalled on the blond man, who dipped his chin in her direction. Then her head turned, taking in the rest of the room, stopping at him before moving on. When Trevis appeared at her side, Lachlan knew this was Scarlett, Tarley's mother.

With efficient steps—so much like Tarley— Scarlett crossed the room to the bar. "Credence?" she asked Horance, who nodded toward the back with his large head. Horance, Lachlan had learned in the hour he'd been sitting at the table, was a man of few words.

It wasn't but a few minutes later that Tarley appeared, followed by what Lachlan knew must be her family. She wasn't in her boy's disguise, and instead of the braids she'd hid under a hat, her hair was pulled back at her nape, loosely tied with a ribbon. She was wearing a dress, a dark color with white splotches. Lachlan didn't care much about the details except seeing her made his chest warm.

He stood.

Tarley froze when her eyes met his.

His chest compressed, making it difficult to draw a breath, which was ridiculous. She'd rejected him. And though they'd just been together hours earlier, he wasn't sure why he felt as if he hadn't seen her in eons. That the world hadn't moved in the proper direction since.

He offered her a smile and hoped for one in return, though he wasn't sure why. She rarely bestowed them. Instead of a smile, however, there was something strange about the way she was looking at him. It was soft, somehow, and reflective, as if she'd unlocked a treasure she was planning to share with him and him alone.

"Miss Fareview!" A voice cut the moment. Everyone in the dining room whirled at the sound toward its owner—the blond man, who'd been sitting in the corner.

Lachlan watched Tarley's body go rigid. It wasn't subtle. Where her gaze had been… easy, now she frowned. She ignored the man and walked toward Lachlan. There was something altogether satisfying about watching her move toward him rather than another man who obviously knew her. Lachlan had the impression that he and Tarley were involved in a game of wills, and this move—whatever it was—was setting up the rest of the game in his favor. He smiled at the thought.

"This way," Credence said from a doorway behind Lachlan.

"I need to speak with you," Tarley told him quietly and reached down to grab his empty dish.

He took it back from her. "Should I be worried?"

Her eyes skipped around his features before she looked away. "Of course not."

"Fareviews! Mr. Fareview? Might I have a word?" the blonde man called after them, scooting out from the bench seat where he'd been seated.

Tarley whirled and looked at a tall man, who had a very strong resemblance to Mattias. "No, Papa," she whispered, then turned to the other man. "Evening, Mr. Rufus." She dipped into a quick curtsy. "We have something to attend." Then she herded Lachlan in front of her Credence, who stepped aside to allow their group into the kitchen.

"Doctor. It's Doctor." But his voice faded as they disappeared through a hallway, leaving him behind.

"A bit pretentious," someone said.

"I swear to you, he's a menace," another voice added—Mattias.

"He sure doesn't look the type, though," the first voice replied. "I mean, he's handsome enough."

"Appearances are deceiving," Tarley said.

"I'm not so sure about that," the first voice giggled.

"Brinna," Tarley warned.

The voice belonging to Brinna laughed harder.

Once in the kitchen, Tarley took Lachlan's dish once more and dropped it into a bucket of water before joining him at the work island where everyone else had crowded around. He looked at the faces, wondering why he was there.

There was Credence, a woman he'd learned was named Mrs. Barnwell, Mattias, the large man Tarley had called Papa, and two women. One of them was smiling, her gray eyes bright, her hair like colored wheat threaded with sunlight and copper rather than the brown of Tarley's. The other, he'd seen earlier, dark haired, dark eyed, but her face seemed to slip through his mind and into obscurity as if she'd never been there at all. Each time looking at her felt like he both knew her and had never seen her before.

Of them all, he was the odd one out. The stranger. Tarley was the reason he was standing there at all, which made him look over at her.

"She's up there now," Credence said.

Tarley kept her gaze fixed on Credence. "Have we heard anything?"

"Not since she went up."

"I'll get everyone some tea," Mrs. Barnwell said, though the rest of them refused, not 'wanting to put her to any trouble.'

Lachlan leaned toward Tarley as side conversations broke out. "You wanted to speak with me?"

"Not here," she said, still avoiding his gaze, which made Lachlan wonder what she wasn't willing to say in front of her family. The thoughts he came up with made his insides heat, but he doubted her intentions had anything to do with that, even if he was hopeful. She'd rejected him, and Lachlan realized he was absolute rubbish at trying to decipher her.

"Scarlett?" Credence asked.

The party turned collectively toward the stairs where Tarley's mother stood, her cloak draped over an arm along with a bag she carried. "She has her memory."

There seemed to be a shared sigh of relief.

Scarlett's gaze scanned the party and stopped on him, jumped to Tarley and then back. Her disconcerting gray eyes narrowed. "You're the man Tarley found?"

He nodded. "Saved."

Her frown deepened as she studied him, as if looking into the depths of his soul and measuring his quality. When she seemed satisfied with her study, she turned to Tarley. "She wants to see you."

"Me?"

"I told her about you," Scarlett admitted, her eyes back on Lachlan, "and the mysterious stranger near death in the woods."

"You think I had something to do with this?" Lachlan stepped forward, shocked at the accusation he heard in her voice.

He heard Tomas and Mattias shift behind him. Lachlan knew it was defensive because he was defensive.

"It is strangely convenient, isn't it?" she asked.

"Mother–" Tarley stepped slightly between Scarlett and Lachlan. "He didn't have anything to do with it. The timeline doesn't work."

Scarlett waved a hand. "Details."

"I wouldn't hurt the queen," Lachlan said.

"And how would we know that?"

He knew he could tell them who he was, but he had nothing to prove it was true. It would just be his word, and they didn't know him from any other stranger who moved through these woods, many of them with sinister intentions. Rather than make any claim, he just said, "My actions will have to prove the truth."

Tarley looked over her shoulder at him, as if he'd surprised her. For once.

"Go up," Scarlett told Tarley, "but don't overtax her. She's recovering."

Tarley turned to Lachlan and held out her hand. "Come with me."

Lachlan took her hand.

"Wait," Scarlett blocked the doorway. "You don't know he's safe–"

"I do." Tarley refused to back down, and Lachlan had the impression he was witness to an epic battle of wills. "Mother. I need you to trust me."

Scarlett narrowed her eyes and glanced at someone behind Lachlan, though he didn't turn to see who it was. When she looked back at Tarley, she shifted to let them pass. Halfway up the stairs, Scarlett called, "We're staying."

Lachlan wanted to ask what was happening but was equally concerned that if he spoke, it would break the spell. Tarley's hand was in his, she'd spoken up for him, she'd looked at him as if he mattered in her world. He didn't want that to change.

"Tarley?"

She squeezed his hand. "It's alright."

Trusting that he was behind her, Tarley led him into the room of Queen Keyanna Rose Hollis. She was sitting up in bed, her sienna skin glowing with recovery but her dark eyes hollowed out with weakness. Her shrewd scrutiny tracked them across the room.

Tarley froze in place. "It's you–" she breathed.

"The last I checked," the queen said, her voice raw. Her eyes jumped to Lachlan, and he knew the moment she recognized him.

"Forgive me, your majesty." Tarley curtsied.

"Up. Just Rose for now. I'm in disguise, you know."

Tarley straightened and glanced at Lachlan, then back at the queen. "Yes. Rose."

Keyanna's brown gaze met his. "You don't look like a Northman," she said. "A horrible disguise with boots like those."

Tarley's hand flew up to cover her smile, and he caught the amusement in her eyes as she looked from his boots to his face.

Lachlan released Tarley's hand and walked to the window, turned, and leaned. "I'm from the north. That's all I said."

"So it's Ollie, I've been told?"

He didn't look at Tarley, knowing she was about to find out just how much he'd duped her. But curiosity drove him, and when his gaze met hers, she wasn't frowning. She had that gentle look once more, her features and eyes yielding.

"I know," was all she said.

And Lachlan straightened and unfolded his arms, pushing away from the wall. "You know?"

She nodded.

"How?"

"I figured it out." She sighed. "Plus, you *did* tell me."

The queen cleared her throat.

Lachlan tore his gaze from Tarley to look at Keyanna, whose gaze was jumping between them. "Forgive me. How are you feeling?" he asked.

"I have been better, cousin, as I'm told has been the same for you recently." His nod seemed to be all the confirmation she needed. She turned to Tarley. "As I understand it, you saved this man."

"I helped him," Tarley replied, her eyes wide with the surprise of confirmation. She turned to the queen.

"She saved me," Lachlan corrected. "I wouldn't be here had she not taken the risk."

Keyanna looked from Tarley back to Lachlan. "It would seem we both owe our lives to a Fareview."

"I'll leave you to talk," Tarley bowed.

"Stay," Lachlan asked. "I mean, one of us could collapse, and we'd need a Fareview to bring us back."

He grinned at her. "Besides, you're owed the truth—'"

She dipped her head. "Very well…"

"Lachlan," he said.

"Lachlan Excelsior Orion Nikolas," the queen finished. "So many names. Tell us what happened."

So he did.

"Ambushed as well?" the queen asked. "Probably best you keep Ollie as your name for now."

At Ollie's name, Tarley's eyes shifted to meet his.

Lachlan looked back at the flames in the hearth. "Yes."

Keyanna groaned. "Miss Fareview? Help me adjust my pillows?"

Tarley jumped into motion, helping the queen, stuffing pillows behind her back. Her eyes remained fixed on her job, and Lachlan wished she would look at him again. She didn't.

"My whole party was murdered. The captain of my guard made it out with me, but—" The queen cleared her throat of emotion, but it didn't leave her eyes. Lachlan recognized her sadness, understood the way the people closest to you, who put their lives at risk, were like family.

"Are you in pain… Rose?" Tarley asked.

"Yes, but I need all my faculties," she said. "There are decisions that need to be made and time is critical, it would seem." She took a deep breath and turned her head slightly so she could see Lachlan at the end of the bed. "I'm afraid your attack, Lachlan, along with mine, was committed by the hand of a group called Fiedel."

"How do you know?"

"When my father died, I inherited his cabinet. And as I'm sure you've gathered, Kaloma isn't as forward thinking as other countries on the continent." She winced.

"Are you sure you wouldn't like something for the pain?" Tarley leaned over the queen. "You need to rest and heal."

Keyanna looked at Tarley. "What I need is to get a message to my sister immediately. I fear her life is in danger. Is there anyone you trust to deliver it?"

"I trust my brother," Tarley said.

She nodded. "I'll need a pen and paper."

Lachlan watched Tarley leave the room.

When the door closed, he turned to Keyanna. "How did you know it was me?" he asked.

She offered a smile, macabre with the wounds on her face. "Did you not think I would have spies in Jast? You have them here."

He'd seen her likeness, so he nodded. "My father wanted this to work. For many reasons."

"We have a lot going against us now."

He nodded. "Tarley suggested your cabinet isn't supportive of your leadership."

"Smart girl."

"Very."

"I suspect they might be behind this attack. That some of my nobles are colluding to fund the Fiedel. And what of your party?"

"I don't know what happened. If they are even

alive. I haven't found a way or an opportunity to get word to Jast. Short of hiring a smuggler—not a lot of opportunity here."

Keyanna sighed and watched the fire for a time. "While our assassinations were unsuccessful, it doesn't preclude that our negotiations can't be." She looked at Lachlan. "To be frank—perhaps a bit course and undiplomatic as well but it appears we don't have the time we need for diplomacy—I need this treaty, cousin. If I don't bring change to Kaloma, I fear not only for my people–" She paused, then said, "There's a growing darkness, and I'm not convinced it will stay within Kaloma's borders."

Lachlan turned and looked out the window. It was dark and the hint of his reflection in the leaded windows bounced back at him. "What do you need?"

"First, open trade routes. My people need an infusion of funds."

"Which will add to your coffers."

"Yes. Rather than what's happening now."

"And with the people behind you, you become the people's monarch."

She nodded. "The support of the people will be most important. It's hard to argue against the injustice of religion. People get so stuck in their thinking, but financial stability has the potential to equalize things."

Lachlan nodded and turned back to her, leaning against the windowsill. "Jast wants an open trade route as well as direct access to the Dauntiss," Lachlan told her, knowing it was what his father wanted, what he knew was in the best interests of Jast. "Is that all you need?"

She shook her head. "I need access to Jast resources."

"What kind?"

"The military kind."

"Why?"

"Opening the border between our countries would offer an infusion of new ideas. Stars know Kaloma needs new ideas, but my throne is threatened by a theocracy. Remove me and my sister, it paves the way for that, and I fear if that should that happen–" She stopped, and Lachlan understood her fear. He and Tarley had already discussed the state of things. Ushering in a theocracy with the kind of laws that had already been made would create the atrocity his father warned his own cabinet about. "It could mean a civil war. I don't have the resources to raise an army, but the church does."

"So framing Jast for your assassination isn't about staring a war," he said.

"What do you mean?"

"The armor and weapons found at the site of your attack. Whoever is behind it wants to undermine any possible treaty."

"And what better way to divide a country than under the guise of a holy war," Keyanna added.

Lachlan paced near the fireplace. "I need to get a message home."

Keyanna sighed. "I want the border open, Lachlan,

but I need assurances."

He stopped pacing and looked at her. "Military assurances aren't enough?"

"A trade agreement opens the border and provides unencumbered access to the Dauntiss, but things can't remain the same in Kaloma. I want a Jast contingent here to help me eliminate the threat to the Hollis throne."

"You want assassins?"

"I need a new cabinet."

"Jast can't be behind that, Keyanna. You know that. If it were to ever come out–" He put his hands up. "War would be justified. I can't agree to that." He took up his pacing again.

She nodded. "What about a marriage?"

Lachlan froze. "Excuse me?"

She laughed, then winced. "You look as if I've stabbed you. Not us, Lachlan. I'm not interested in being married." She wrinkled her nose.

"So unite nobles?"

"No, I want *you* to marry someone from Kaloma." She stopped and searched his face. "I can see the idea is as pleasing as eating sour grapes. Is that why you spurned Freida Truisante?"

"You know–" he started but then recalled the spies. "Is that why you have a harem? Just to piss off your theocratic cabinet?"

Keyanna laughed. "No. I have a harem because I enjoy having a harem. And your deflection was rather elementary, Lachlan."

He crossed his arms. "Why?"

"Why do I like my harem?"

He couldn't remain irritated at that and chuckled. "No. Why a marriage?"

"Think of it this way: marriage ties our kingdoms today–"

"Our kingdoms are already joined in marriage," Lachlan reminded her. It hadn't been a happy alliance, but it was still true. "We are family."

She made a short noise through her throat and relaxed back against the pillows. "You know that isn't the same. It also ignited a war resulting in the current closed borders." She shook her head. "We need something new, a new union to showcase our alliance. Something for the people of Kaloma to celebrate. My people need to see Jast not as the enemy bent on our destruction, but to change the narrative that we are family. What better way for that to happen than through marriage? Then Jast's influence in my cabinet wouldn't be secret or a cause for war."

She wasn't wrong.

He turned and looked out the window, the milky pane revealing nothing more than darkness as he pondered her proposition. What would his father think? It seemed a stronger position for Jast overall. But to marry for it?

Ollie's words stabbed at him: *People in your position rarely get a choice.*

It wasn't the idea of marrying for Jast that Lachlan hadn't wanted. It was that his father hadn't given him a say in the matter. This, however, was his decision, and he recognized it was all he needed to prove to his father he did have what it took to be a leader, to make a selfless choice for his kingdom.

"Is it the thought of marrying that has you unsettled?" Keyanna asked. "You will need an heir."

"As will you."

"Yes. Someday. Or my sister will accommodate that in my stead."

"It isn't marriage."

A knock interrupted.

"Rose?" Tarley reappeared through the doorway, holding Keyanna's requested paper and ink.

"What is it, then?" Keyanna asked him.

Lachlan glanced at Tarley, then forced his gaze away from her, because he couldn't seem to keep from seeking her out when she was near and found Keyanna watching him. He hated the idea of marrying a noble woman Keyanna chose, but he could feel the walls closing in on him, knowing he had to decide this for Jast. He sought Tarley again, following her movement with his gaze, wishing he could have just remained Ollie a bit longer. Then he looked away and shook his head. "It's nothing."

Keyanna turned to Tarley. "I think I would like the medicine for my pain now."

"I'll get my mother." Tarley disappeared again through the doorway.

Keyanna waited until the door was shut. "A Kaloma commoner."

"What?"

"Marriage."

"I don't think–"

"Don't think like a royal, Lachlan. Think like the people. What better way than to secure the love and support of the people than to choose a new queen from among them? A romantic story they can write poems and songs about."

"As the queen of Jast," he said. "How do you think that would go over in Jast?"

"I don't know, Lachlan," Keyanna said, her eyes narrowed. "Your kingdom went to war with mine over a marriage."

Lachlan felt like he'd lost any high ground and was slipping down a very steep incline. It was true. While it was initially justified for the kidnapping of a Jast Princess, the ruination of Kaloma had been for spite. "You're suggesting I marry a commoner from Kaloma?"

Keyanna slipped deeper into the covers, looking smug. "Think of it. People will celebrate that kind of marriage because a commoner is someone who represents them." She paused and tapped her chin. "Yes. A commoner singled out by the crown prince of Jast. Her circumstances improved by Jast. A reparation after the war… it's perfect."

"I'm not sure all of them would agree." He took a deep breath and turned away, resigned. Everything she said made sense for Kaloma, and while a commoner queen wasn't exactly in line with expectations, the rest of the agreement aligned with Jast's goals. His own father had been willing to marry him to a neighboring kingdom for the sake of trade. "Kaloma might be amenable to the terms. The question is how Jast would perceive the alliance, as well as how Truisante would view it in light of the slight against them."

"Which, Lachlan, isn't my problem."

He knew that was true. He'd made that mess on his own.

"When Jast merchants and nobles are filling their coffers because of an easier trade route, they won't care who you marry," she pointed out. "Besides, you're the playboy prince. They probably expect you to do something impetuous and rash."

"Your spies are so thorough," he muttered, wanting to snap at her assessment but thinking of his father's criticism. She wasn't wrong. As much as the idea of marrying for an alliance wasn't his first choice, he had to think of the kingdom. Opening the route to the Dauntiss along with influence in Kaloma's government at the highest level would be a win-win for Jast.

"Do you have someone in mind? Or do we have to go through some process to find the right candidate? A ball or some such nonsense?"

"No ball. That would take too much time. But I do have someone in mind." She stifled a yawn, pressing the back of her hand to her mouth.

"Who?" he asked, ready to wrap his head around his future, and hating that he wished he could return to the woods and hide from it.

"Tarley Fareview," the queen said, her eyes closed and a smile on her face. "The commoner who saved your life."

Tarley

Scarlett pushed away from the counter as Tarley entered the kitchen. "Is everything okay?"

Tarley looked around, slightly dazed. How had she seen the queen, before she'd ever met the queen?

She focused on her mother, ignoring what she couldn't fathom just then for something she could. "I can't believe you accused him," she said, shaking her head.

Ollie wasn't Ollie. He was Prince Lachlan. She'd been right. Her eyes tracked everyone moving to get the kitchen cleared and closed for the night. The action was so normal, only everything felt strange and surreal.

"I need some pain medication. For the guest."

Scarlett nodded and hurried around to the stove. "I didn't accuse him."

"Close enough."

"He's a stranger. We don't know him."

"A stranger he may be, but I think I'd know if he was an assassin."

"You can think you know someone," Scarlett said, smacking the kettle onto the stove with a bit too much force.

"A cute stranger, your Ollie," Brinna said, defusing the tension as she stacked clean bowls on the shelf.

"He's not mine, Brinna."

"But you do think he's cute!" She giggled.

"He is handsome," Jessamine smiled, lifting a tray covered with clean mugs. "Auri will be so disappointed to have missed meeting him." She disappeared into the dining room with the tray.

Tarley ignored her sisters' jibes. "Rose needs to get a message to her sister. I said she could trust Mattias."

Mattias, carting heavy pots from outside, glanced at Tarley. "Trust me for what?"

Scarlett bristled. "Send him from Sevens? No. Absolutely not."

"He's old enough. Smart. Strong."

"I'm nineteen," Mattias confirmed, setting down his load and flexing his arms. "What am I going to do?"

"Nothing." Scarlett jerked the satchel of tea from her bag.

"Delivering a secret message to Princess Meera."

Tarley dropped her voice to whisper the name.

"What?" Mattias stopped moving. "Why?"

Scarlett straightened, her back stiff. "Absolutely not. Everything I have done has been to keep you all safe from danger. Why would I agree to send my son into the heart of it?"

"Mother, she's in danger. Failure to act–"

Mattias stepped forward, looking as if the world suddenly made sense. "I can do it."

"What's it to us—to our family?"

"It could be everything, Mother!" Tarley exclaimed. "Do nothing and the Law of Means possibly becomes something worse?"

Scarlett sighed.

"Tarley's right," Tomas said, stacking wood next to the stove. "The queen and her sister are Kaloma's greatest chance for change. Without them–" He shook his head.

"I can do it," Mattias leaned over the counter. "It will be easy."

"That would be an overstatement," Tomas warned.

Mrs. Barnwell walked in through the door. "Well, look at this! I need you Fareviews here every night!"

Scarlett sighed and filled a steaming cup. "I'll take this."

Tarley put a hand on Scarlett's arm. "I'll do it."

Scarlett looked like she wanted to argue, but then didn't and slid the cup toward Tarley. "This will make her drowsy."

Tarley squeezed her mother's forearm before retracing her steps back to the queen's room. At the door she stopped and took a deep breath.

Ollie is Prince Lachlan.

Her cheeks heated, recalling his head between her thighs.

She shook her thoughts away and took another deep breath, knowing she couldn't afford to allow her past to invade her present. He was a prince. She was a commoner. The two didn't mix. When they'd still been in the woods, she'd accepted he would leave, and she would remain. Wanted it even. She would pack the experience away in her mind to take out and treasure every so often.

After a quick knock, she entered. "Your tea, Rose." She shut the door and crossed the room to the queen's bedside.

"Just the woman we were discussing," the queen said.

"Keyanna—" Lachlan warned.

Smoothing her skirt, Tarley's gaze jumped back and forth between Lachlan, whose presence reminded her what she wanted to forget, and the queen, whose smile unnerved her.

"I need you to—" the queen started.

"Keyanna, wait," Lachlan interrupted. "Please—"

"Please what? Tarley's a Kaloma subject. She'll do what her queen needs her to do."

"I know how that works," Lachlan said, sounding annoyed.

Tarley's heart tightened in her chest. "Excuse me?"

Lachlan pushed away from the wall. "Cousin. Let me–"

"You will marry the prince." The queen smiled. "For the sake of Kaloma."

Tarley swallowed, and though she wanted to look at Lachlan, she couldn't. She didn't want to see his face, afraid of what she would find in his expression. So she kept her focus on the queen and opened her mouth to speak, but nothing came out. "What?" finally escaped.

"As a condition of a treaty between Kaloma and Jast, I would like you to marry Prince Lachlan. He has agreed to marry–"

"I haven't agreed," Lachlan said.

Now Tarley's eyes shifted to his face, her heart dropping into her gut.

He wasn't looking at her.

"But you agree it is a worthwhile idea," Keyanna said. "And Miss Fareveiw is the perfect candidate."

"Miss Fareview is an exceptional one," Lachlan replied, his eyes finally rising to meet Tarley's, only instead of the warmth she'd once seen, his look was distant.

"Your Majesty. You can't mean it." Panic filled Tarley. "Are you jesting?" She struggled to meet the queen's eyes as she sat covered with blankets, the firelight casting moving shadows across her battered face. The same moment from the vision she'd had earlier. Tarley fidgeted with her hands and forced herself to stop.

The queen, despite her injuries, her face swollen so she was almost unrecognizable leveled Tarley with her stare. Tarley had leveled a stare like that once or twice in her life. Perhaps daily, but never had anyone frozen her with a stare like that.

"Why would I tease you?" the queen asked. "Do you think me cruel, Miss Fareview?"

Tarley dropped her eyes. "No, your ma…Rose. I just… I'm not… I'm not a noble, I mean. Surely, there must be someone at court better suited to marrying royalty?"

"Perhaps so," the queen conceded, "but it wasn't a noble that saved the crown prince of Jast, now was it."

Tears threatened to fall. "But I'm–" She stopped about to say she was *no one*. "We don't…" she started to say *suit*, but they shared chemistry in abundance. Only, she'd rejected him and hated that she had. "I hate–" She stopped herself from saying Lachlan. The truth was, she didn't hate him. She certainly didn't hate his mouth on her. So she amended, "I'm common. I would make a terrible emissary for Kaloma, your majesty."

The queen chuckled, but Tarley could hear the pain in it.

"What are your objections, Miss Fareview? Only that you hate Jast?"

Tarley glanced at Lachlan leaning against the wall, his arms crossed over his chest, and his face uncharacteristically aloof. "I don't hate Jast." She looked back at the queen. "Do I have to say?"

"You think he shouldn't hear?" The queen nodded at Lachlan without looking at him. "He's already heard your objection to marrying him. Don't you think he should know why?"

Tarley wanted to wilt under the pressure, but she wasn't made that way. Tarley Fareview didn't wilt. So she straightened her back and straightened her skirt. "Fine. As you wish," she said and lifted her chin. "I barely know him."

"Better to not know the defects of one's marriage partner, I think," the queen countered.

"He's from Jast—"

"Which might actually be in his favor, considering what Kaloma has to offer."

"He lied."

"With reason. Someone did try to kill him. I'm doing the same."

"He's arrogant."

"As are most of the weaker sex, Miss Fareview." When Tarley didn't raise any further objections, the queen raised her eyebrows and said, "Is that all?"

Tarley tried to reason her way out of it but couldn't. "I'm sure I'm just as objectionable to him, your majesty. We don't get along at all." Though that wasn't exactly true.

Lachlan's eyebrows rose, as if in challenge.

The queen glanced at him. "Royal marriages aren't designed because the partnership has tender feelings for one another. Isn't that right, Prince Lachlan?"

Tarley's eyes flew to the man she'd thought of as

Ollie until a few hours ago. The man she'd allowed between her thighs. Her cheeks heated.

Lachlan cleared his throat. "True."

"Are you opposed to marrying Miss Fareview on the objections she'd voiced in conjunction with your own?"

"I'm willing to forgo any of my objections on the basis that doing so will align our two kingdoms. This is what my father sent me to do, and it must be done. If that means I marry–" He paused, his gaze sweeping Tarley from head to toe and making her feel both hot and cold simultaneously. "If it means I must marry, so be it."

The queen looked at Tarley. "The prince will have you."

"I don't want him to have me–" Tarley snapped then pressed her lips together. Raising her chin, she said, "I have no intention of marrying."

The queen chuckled. "You have fire, Miss Fareview. A good quality in a queen, I think. A good quality in many areas." She glanced at Lachlan. "I want this union, so it will be done. It is a story the people will love—a commoner saves the prince of Jast, and they fall in love—it's the stuff of fairy tales, and Kaloma needs a fairy tale. Kaloma needs hope, Miss Fareview, and I believe you can be that hope. We'll see it done tomorrow," she said. "Now, I'm tired. Leave me."

"Tomorrow?" both Tarley and Lachlan said.

"No. Absolutely not," Lachlan added. "I need to

get word to my king. There could be ramifications–"

The queen's brows rose. "Fine." She closed her eyes. "Let's throw a party—a country dance. A fortnight. We'll make the announcement then."

"And how do you suggest I get a message to my kingdom?"

"Use a falcon. Sevens should have a falconer, but code the message," she said and yawned, waving them away. "I'm excessively tired."

Tarley dipped into a curtsey, refusing to look at Lachlan, and walked from the room. As soon as the door closed, she hurried through the corridor, past her mother and family readying for home. Her mother tried to stop her with a question.

"I can't talk–" Tarley said and hurried away, toward her space above the stables. She needed to be alone. She needed to think.

The woods.

She could run away, hide, and she wouldn't have to marry him. He wouldn't have to marry her. She'd be saving them both.

She raced up the steps at the back of the stables, moving through the doorway of her small room, lit the lantern. Then her eyesight wavered, and dizziness forced her to grab hold of the mattress. Her surroundings receded, giving way to the woods, in the brambles, the blackberry bushes near the river. She turned to find Dr. Rufus too close, backing her into the brambles.

Tarley blinked, and found herself in her room once

more, her stomach unsettled. She took several deep breaths, taking in the hint of pain lingering like the aftermath of a headache. Standing upright, she took several more breaths, unsure what the vision meant. Was it a prediction, or more like Brinna's, a waking dream matching her reality with unconscious thoughts?

Grabbing her pack and adding in a few extra things for cold weather, she blew out the lantern, dropping the room into dark, and moved to the door. She couldn't survive the winter in the woods, but Lachlan would be gone in a few weeks.

When she opened the door, Lachlan stood blocking the way. He leaned forward, his hands on either side of the doorframe, his eyes dropping to her bag. "Going somewhere?"

"Away."

He straightened, pushed away from the doorframe, and walked in as Tarley retreated. "With what appears to be your belongings? That looks more like you're thinking about committing treason."

"You don't want to marry me," she said, deflecting.

He laughed, but it wasn't joyful. "You still think someone in my position is ever able to consider what they want?"

"I'm not in your position."

"You are now."

Unsure how to respond, she stepped back as he stepped forward, closing the door quietly behind him, his large frame blocking any lingering light.

She couldn't see his face, but she heard him sigh.

She lifted her chin. "Let me go."

"Let me guess…" he said, his voice deeper, rough, with a note of… disappointment? That didn't seem right. "You're running. To the woods."

Her ire rose. "What do you care?"

His shadow shifted. "I care about Jast, and you represent what Jast needs at the moment."

She narrowed her eyes. "I'm just a pawn in your game, then?"

"We are all pawns."

"Then change it."

"Sometimes sacrifice is the change needed to do it."

"Well don't sacrifice yourself on the altar of matrimony for me. I don't want it. I don't want you," she snapped, and even as she said it, she didn't believe it anymore. She did want him, but the cost was too great. She would forever be the commoner elevated by marriage to a prince.

He moved toward her, the wood floor creaking. "Am I that objectionable?"

"Why didn't you tell me?"

"What? Who I was?"

She nodded, then remembered he couldn't see her. "Yes."

"I did."

"You didn't trust me when push came to shove."

He took another step. "And how would that have sounded? I'm the crown prince of Jast, Tarley." He stepped again, the thump of his boots somehow louder. "Someone tried to kill me. And you were a stranger."

He was right. She'd known that was why even before he'd admitted it, but her petty heart couldn't get over the weak way she wanted him. "And after you had your mouth between my legs?" she snapped, grateful he couldn't see the way her face flushed.

He drew in a breath, and his shadow drew closer. "You didn't want me, remember?"

Tarley took another step away, the back of her knees bumping against the bed. She couldn't catch her breath, for some reason. She knew if she just reached out, she'd touch him. "Why do you care if I'm running away? Committing treason? Going to the woods? Any of the above saves you from marriage. From the sacrifice."

"You think if you run, I won't have to marry?" he scoffed. "You aren't that naïve. If it isn't you, Tarley, the queen will find another suitable candidate." He took another step, and she could sense his heat. "Want to know why I'm in Kaloma at all?" he asked.

"I don't need to know." Though, the thought of Lachlan marrying someone else annoyed her, her irrational jealousy thinking about his mouth on someone else annoyed her further.

"My father promised me to a Princess Truisante—"

"That was a true story?"

"I've never lied to you other than failing to tell you my true name, Tarley." He paused then said, "I was a prick to the princess. Made fun of how she looked so she'd call off the marriage rather than just tell my father I didn't want to marry her."

"She called it off?"

"Yes." Lachlan stepped closer. "And I got sent away from Jast because my father couldn't bear to look at me. He called me immature and weak. Not fit to be a king."

"Why are you telling me this?"

"You told me a couple of days ago that I should use my second chance to make the change I want."

"Yes."

"This is me doing that."

She dropped her pack with a thud. "But you don't want to marry. I don't want to marry. We can look for another way. There must be—"

"I've never said anything about not wanting to marry," he said, his fingertips skimmed her cheek. "I must marry. If I don't make the choice, my father—or the queen—will." He traced her face.

She swallowed, feeling as if she was losing ground somehow.

He leaned forward, his warm breath caressing her ear. "I don't mind the idea of marrying someone I can't stop thinking about fucking," he said quietly.

Her breath stopped up in her chest. She should push him away. But she didn't. She couldn't. She knew what a hypocrite that would make her. She hadn't stopped thinking about what had happened between them. She still wanted him.

"It's not enough to base a marriage on," she said instead.

"I'm aware. I heard all the reasons I'm not good enough. We wouldn't suit. I'm arrogant, among other things on your list. I'm not enough."

"I didn't say that."

"You didn't have to. It's been clear since the woods—" He pressed a finger against her racing pulse. "But, I believe you want me as much as I want you." He moved so their bodies were pressed together, his thighs rustling her layered skirts. "I want to hear you tell me you don't want me," he whispered and pressed his lips to the pulse in her neck. "Deny it."

"I don't want you." But the words were weak, said on a breath. Then she negated them by tilting her head so he could have better access.

He chuckled and wrapped his arms around her.

Angry at her own traitorous body and at him for being right, she pushed at his chest. He stepped back as she fell onto the mattress. "You are an arrogant, presumptuous ass."

"Now who's lying?" he asked from above her.

She lifted her chin and willed the words out, but instead of 'I don't want you,' the words "I hate you" came out instead.

"Another lie."

She watched as his shadow crouched in front of her. Then, with his hands on her hips, he yanked her toward him, settling in between her thighs as best as he could, given her skirts.

"Hate me then," he whispered, squeezing her ribs with his large hands, running them up to frame her breasts.

Her lungs filled with longing, slowing her breath, and she arched against his touch.

"Show me how much you hate me."

Without a thought, Tarley shoved her hands into his hair and crashed her lips into his. She moaned into his mouth, kissing him with all her pent-up frustration.

A rumble left him, from somewhere deep in his chest, reverberating through hers.

"Yes," he groaned and dragged his mouth from hers to her jaw, to her neck.

"I hate that you can do this to me."

"Fuck, Tarley." He grabbed her breast and kneaded. "I need to feel you."

She grabbed his head and held him as his tongue found one of her nipples, licking, sucking, biting it through the fabric, then moving to the opposite side.

 Reaching between them, she rubbed a hand down the front of his trousers, seeking the heat of his cock. "Do you feel me?"

He grunted. "Not enough," he panted.

She fumbled with his belt until she could wrap her hand around his silken heat. "Oh," she said into his mouth. This was the first time she'd touched a man. The first time she'd felt such a soft and yet unyielding thing. "I don't know how—"

He groaned but moved away from her touch.

Her chest heaved with unspent need. "What's

wrong?"

"This heat, Tarley," he started, then paused. "Why am I so objectionable?" he asked quietly.

"It isn't you–"

"You had a list of reasons."

"I'm not–" But she didn't finish her thought and shook her head, unable to voice how she was the one who was objectionable. Backed into a corner, she'd blustered about ways they didn't suit, but really it was just her and her fear that he might look closer and see her for what she was: a weak woman. She couldn't be a queen.

"Fuck, Tarley," Lachlan said, still kneeling before of her.

She wished she could see his face.

"I never said I didn't want to marry."

Tarley shivered. "There is physical connection between us, but in the long run, you would be miserable, and I would be angry and bitter."

Lachlan stood and adjusted himself. She heard him refasten his belt. He started for the door but stopped and turned. "Would marrying me be so bad?"

She didn't answer. To say 'no' felt like a betrayal of herself, except she couldn't honestly say that the idea of marrying him was any more abhorrent than marrying any man would be. "You don't love me. I don't love you," she said instead, as if that alone dictated things.

His shadow stood near the door for several more breaths, before he said, "Give me a chance to change your mind." Then without waiting for her to reply, he disappeared, shutting the door behind him.

Lachlan

After leaving Tarley, Lachlan climbed into the loft, hopeful not to wake Trevis. Turned out the boy was a light sleeper.

"Everything okay?" Trevis asked from the dark.

"Yes," Lachlan lied and laid on his own palette.

Trevis returned to sleep, but it eluded Lachlan despite his exhaustion and the early morning hour.

So much had changed in the last few hours, and yet nothing had. He'd agreed to maintain the pretense of being Ollie for the time being, he was still stuck in Kaloma, and he was still reliant on the goodwill of others. But Tarley knew who he was, and he'd hurriedly negotiated a treaty on behalf of Jast which included he marry Tarley for the kingdom.

Now he had to find a way to get her to agree, but as much as he considered it—framing it as his duty— he couldn't banish memories of the heat between them. He wasn't opposed to marrying Tarley. And as much as she said she abhorred the idea, her body made a liar of her.

The problem was her stubbornness. He needed her to come to heel and getting that done was just going to make her dig her heels in deeper.

Proving his worthiness to his father meant making sure this treaty worked. That meant figuring out a way to get Tarley to agree. For the good of Jast. He had two weeks to change her mind, and he excelled when there was a strong inducement. A willing Tarley in his bed was a strong motivator.

Lachlan finally fell asleep smiling, considering the challenge.

Several days later, Tarley was making it impossible. He'd taken to hoping for glimpses of her as he moved through the various chores around the inn. She was avoiding him, and then he'd find himself pouting about it as he repaired cobblestones in the courtyard, or angry as he helped cart wood for the fireplaces, begrudging the fact that Prince Lachlan had never had to work so hard for a woman.

Then, he'd picture Tarley outside the tent, her hair free as the rain fell, and his breath would catch. He'd remember her standing in the river and recall his own thought that he hadn't wanted their encounter to end. Then he'd think about their last kiss and the riotous passion between them, and his mother's wisdom would flit through his thoughts: *anything worth your time should require your effort. It makes the acquisition so much sweeter.*

Lachlan knew he wasn't the most patient of men. He was impetuous, mostly, and probably a bit spoiled now that he thought about it. But he was smart. And he was loyal. And he was willing to do what needed to be done for something he wanted. Which was to see this treaty to fruition. For Jast.

If he had to marry for Jast, he wanted a partnership, and though he hadn't known Tarley long, he was sure that could be achieved. Only, he was going about wooing her all wrong, somehow, but for the life of him couldn't figure how to go about it right. When had he ever had to chase anyone?

For the last hour, he'd been with Mrs. Barnwell cleaning and chopping vegetables, then cleaning and chopping more vegetables as his mind wandered beyond Mrs. Barnwell's boring but pleasant chatter.

Besides the attack, he wondered about Ollie and the guards. He thought about his mother and father, his brother and sister. He wondered if the falcon message had arrived in Jast and how they would react knowing he was alive in Sevens. He wondered if his father would be proud he'd negotiated a treaty for Jast. And when those thoughts ran dry, every noise beyond the kitchen drew his attention. When it was Credence or Horance, disappointment weighed him. But every so often, Tarley would flit in and out without a glance his way. He tried to catch her eye and felt foolish for doing it, and yet he tried anyway. And occasionally, Tarley would give him a tentative glance, then look away and disappear once more.

"Ollie? Have you never helped your mum in the kitchen?" Mrs. Barnwell asked, her face scrunched at his latest attempt at chopping carrots.

He could confidently say even Ollie hadn't done that. "No, ma'am. I've wielded a knife while hunting."

She nodded. "So you know how to dress out the animal."

His eyes widened because no, he'd never done that either. Servants did that.

She sighed. "What are you? A lordling?"

He coughed uncomfortably and was saved from answering when Tarley hustled into the kitchen with a tray of dirty dishes.

"Godsdamned oafs," she snapped.

"Handsy patrons?" Mrs. Barnwell asked.

"I need another three bowls of the fowl. Is there bread?" She dropped the empty bowls into the soaking barrel, then leaned against the workstation where

Lachlan sat. "Stars. My feet hurt. Handsy is an understatement. If only everything was as it should be, then these awful strangers could go back into the bowels of hell from whence they came."

Glad for Tarley's interruption because she was talking instead of running from him, he realized seeing her was becoming both a boon and a curse. She looked as she ever did in her white blouse and skirt the shade of a fall plum, a muslin apron tied around her trim waist. Her shirt was rolled to her elbows, and he could see that her wrists—one tied with a decorative red ribbon—were delicate but sturdy. An interesting contrast. Wisps of her brown hair escaped her braid, and her cheeks were bright with exertion.

It was hot in the kitchen, Lachlan decided, feeling the stuffiness and needing air. "Do I need to go and kick them out?" he asked and stepped back from the countertop.

Tarley leaned past him to collect something he wasn't paying attention to, and he caught her lemony scent. "These are your cut vegetables?" she asked, studying his pile. The carrots were a haphazard mess of various sizes, as were the other roots and stalks. "Have you never chopped vegetables before?"

Lachlan tried to ignore her scent, somehow stronger now, suppressing the urge to lean closer and inhale. His mind drifted back to their last kiss, her hand around his cock, and his groin surged. What the fuck was wrong with him?

"Don't worry about my work," he said, his tone

acerbic as he worked to get himself under control. This woman was making him brutish.

Mrs. Barnwell chuckled as she set three bowls and slices of bread rolled in cloth on the tray.

Tarley studied him as if she had a question she needed answered, but he couldn't guess at it. He had a question himself, involving kissing, touching, and sex. Her blatant regard was the first she'd taken the time to look at him, but then she shrugged, looked away, and fixed her tray to balance it.

Tarley one. Lachlan zero.

"Be careful out there," Mrs. Barnwell warned. "Get Horance to boot any offenders."

"That handsy?" Lachlan asked but already knew and hated the idea of someone putting their hands on Tarley. Hated the idea of her having to put up with that. Hated the idea that someone was defiling his future queen.

"Yes ma'am," Tarley said.

"Those customers can't seem to keep their hands to themselves," Mrs. Barnwell said, pointing her spoon at him. "Should have been here the other day. One of the patrons grabbed a handful of Miss Tarley here."

"Mrs. Barnwell—" Tarley said, hoisting her tray. "Ollie doesn't care about that."

"Sure I do," he said, but Tarley had already disappeared into the noisy dining room. He turned to Mrs. Barnwell. "Does that happen a lot?"

"Sad to report that Mrs. Credence, Miss Tarley, and Miss Genevieve share at least one story each day. They are lovely women—not old like these old bones—and there are more than enough miscreants who seem to believe that a pretty girl deserves that kind of treatment. It's a shame. Law doesn't help."

"You aren't old, Mrs. Barnwell."

She laughed. "You're trying to get out of chopping, young man. Mr. Barnwell says I'm too set in my ways, but that's neither here nor there to the story. What sent Miss Tarley into the woods was a big oaf who manhandled her, and she hit him with a stein–"

"She hit him?" He'd heard Tarley's short version of events but enjoyed Mrs. Barnwell's recollection. He could picture Tarley defending herself and found himself smiling.

"Got him so good, he fell off his chair, I heard. Had it not been for another patron's intervention—I can't remember the details—she might have been roughed up pretty good. Good thing Credence sent Tarley into the woods. She saved you."

Lachlan wasn't relieved to hear Tarley could have been hurt by a customer, and glanced at the entrance to the dining room, repressing the urge to go out and watch over her. And Miss Credence too, of course. "What happened after?"

"Oaf went to the priest. Now mind you, our priest, Acolyte Primrose, isn't as fanatical as some, but he had to respond. Hired a pack of hunters. Gross misuse of church funds, if you ask me."

Lachlan could work out the rest. "Perhaps another man working in the dining room would help? You know?"

"I'll mention it to Credence. It's clear that kitchen work isn't your thing." She snickered and turned away from him.

When the lunch run finished, and Lachlan had washed most of the dirty dishes, Tarley joined to help scour the pots and pans. Lachlan helped her carry what he could out to the water pump. They each rubbed the pots with a rag and scoops of grit, then rinsed them until they were clear. They didn't talk, which felt strange to Lachlan since their ease in the woods. He missed that. Their stories. The laughter. Sleeping curled around her every night. He wished he could find a way to broach this divide that had appeared between them.

"Are you angry with me?" he finally asked. "Because I think you're avoiding me."

"Avoiding you." She hummed a sound but didn't comment.

"We need to talk about this."

"About what?"

"Our marriage."

"I don't remember agreeing." Her scrubbing became a touch more aggressive. "I don't even know you."

"What do you want to know?"

"When's your birthday?"

"Summer solstice. Yours?"

"Fall equinox. See, opposites."

He puffed a laugh. "Actually, opposite would be

the winter solstice."

She rolled her eyes.

"What's your favorite color?"

"The color of the woods on a summer day. Yours?" She looked at him.

Lachlan took the opportunity to dive into her eyes. "In Jast, just before a thunderstorm, the sky turns this beautiful color of violet. That color." Her eyes held that color in bursts.

She looked away, but not before Lachlan noticed her blush.

"Maybe we should talk about what happened in your room," he said.

"No."

"What are you afraid of?"

Tarley's eyes jumped to his. "I'm not afraid."

"I think you are. I think that's why you're avoiding me."

She scoffed. "And what, pray tell, is it that I'm afraid of."

"That you might actually like me. That I might actually change your stubborn mind." He grinned. "That you might actually think marrying me isn't such a bad idea."

Tarley straightened and schooled any expression that might have been on her face to look bored and indifferent. But Lachlan noticed her jaw protrude as she pressed her teeth together.

"What I actually think," she said, laying her rag over the lip of the barrel, "is you can finish these up."

And she walked away without a backward glance.

Had Lachlan been a less arrogant man, he might have felt downtrodden by her response. But he was a prince, for godssakes. So rather than feel upset by her response, he found himself grinning from ear to ear. She'd blushed, which told him she felt something. "I'm beginning to think it's an excellent idea," he told the pot he was cleaning.

One point Lachlan.

Tarley

Tarley stomped up the stairs and pushed into her room, slamming the door and leaning against it. She huffed, fanning her shirt to cool her fevered skin, and stomped a foot against the floor, then winced at her immaturity.

Lachlan was infuriating. That arrogant grin like he knew her. That cocksure way he did everything even though he was doing it wrong. That way he would look at her with a smirk on his face telling her he was thinking of the last time they'd been alone.

She did. All the time. Dreamed about it, in fact, and hated it was so. Her dreams had them consummating the act and delighting in the different variations.

And now she was dreaming about it with her eyes open. Seeing him only made it worse.

Watching him replace cobble stones, his sleeves rolled to display his tanned arms. Watching him cart loads of wood in the wheelbarrow, his shirt stretched across his muscular frame. Watching him lift pots for the wash, water sloshing on him so that everything stuck to him, watching the muscles of his perfect thighs in his perfectly fitted breeches.

Everywhere she looked, Lachlan manifested her fantasies, and all the ways she wanted to taste him, feel him, hear him ran through her head. She couldn't get away from him.

She should have run away, but she didn't want to give him the satisfaction. Better yet, she should have left him in the woods, but the thought pinched her heart, leaving an ache in her chest.

But his charm and arrogance didn't match with the words he'd shared in the dark. *I'm not good enough.* Her heart not only smarted from the idea of him not being there, but of him believing she didn't think he was. If he only understood why she was keeping him at a distance. He barely had to do a thing for her attention, and that was horrifically dangerous in his favor.

She snatched a basket from the table to go pick berries for Mrs. Barnwell and hurried from her bedroom, stomping from the inn's yard. By the time she reached the meadow by the river, she finally found her breath coming easier.

What she hated more than anything was how close

to the truth Lachlan had been—accusing her she was afraid. She hadn't truly reconciled it, however, not until he'd said it. She'd rationalized she was maintaining her independence and power. But Lachlan's words had been like a dart thrown into the bullseye.

Careful to avoid thorns, Tarley plucked some berries and dropped them in her basket.

She did like him and liking him meant keeping her distance was the only way to protect herself. Only she wasn't sure what she was protecting herself from anymore. Lachlan hadn't once tried to take her agency. He'd misled her, but with good reason. He was honest and forthright in all the ways it mattered. She could feel herself softening toward him more and more each day, and that was what she was afraid of—falling for him.

It wasn't just the physical. It was the way he tried even when he knew he'd fail. The way he could have admitted he was the prince to her mother and hadn't. The way he spoke to her in the dark, the vulnerability he expressed, even if he was telling himself lies. The stories. The laughter.

There was the errant possibility she would fall in love with the man she'd been asked to marry, but he might never feel the same. He'd never claimed to love her—or that he could. *Royals marry to beget heirs.* They were an arrangement. Where would falling in love with him leave her? That imbalance of her heart would leave her at a clear and painful disadvantage.

"How is he?" a voice interrupted.

Tarley jumped and spun, her hand at her throat.

"Dr. Rufus." She hadn't heard him and shuddered at her carelessness. "You frightened me."

Dr. Allean Rufus bowed slightly at the hips, his hat, and black bag in hand. His dark jacket and trousers were a stark contrast to the shades of the forest around them. "My apologies," he said. "The patient?"

She wasn't sure to who he was referencing. The queen? But she knew no one had been told. "I'm sorry?"

"The man you saved in the woods." He straightened.

"How—"

"It's all over the village, Miss Fareview." He walked slowly through the meadow to her, then reached around her to pluck a berry, dropping it into her basket. "He's working at the inn, now?"

"Ollie? Yes. He's doing much better." She didn't want to share anything with Rufus. "What are you doing here?" She glanced around the glen, finding it strange he was there at all.

"Returning from a call." He lifted his bag before setting it on the ground at his feet. "Why didn't you send for me? With this Ollie?"

Tarley turned back to the berries, hoping Rufus would take the hint and leave. "Besides being near death a half a day's journey from Sevens? He was mended by the time we returned. Didn't need your assistance."

"I find your… trips into the woods alone… problematic. Dangerous. There are evil things lurking in the woods."

"Well, it's a good thing your opinion isn't of my concern, and my actions are none of yours." She plucked another berry.

"I don't like that you were alone with him, Miss Fareview. It's all untoward. And with the village talking about it, too–" He picked another blackberry and dropped it into her basket, his hand brushing her arm.

Tarley gritted her teeth and yanked berries from the bush with a bit more fervor. "My whereabouts and with whom I choose to spend them has nothing to do with you."

"But they are, you see. It seems your current protector is doing a poor job of keeping you safe. Once you're my wife–"

Tarley sighed, shaking her head. "This really is tiresome, Mr. Rufus–" A thorn stabbed her finger. "Ouch." She removed the thorn put her finger into her mouth without thinking.

"Doctor." His voice sounded strange.

When she turned her head, he looked… odd, his eyes a shade darker as he studied her finger in her mouth, a peculiar grin on his lips that gave her pause. She shoved her hand into her pocket and gripped the fabric. "I will never be your wife, and I don't want to revisit that with you now or ever."

Dr. Rufus's grin faded to a frown, and he stepped closer, his body crowding her into the bushes. "Tar– Miss Fareview—" He grasped her arms. "I can–"

"Mr. Rufus. Unhand me."

Had he just sniffed her?

"Call me Allean." He pulled her toward him.

Tarley tried to disengage but ended up deeper in the bush, thorns grabbing her clothes and pressing into her back. "Dr. Rufus. Stop."

This suddenly felt familiar. As if she'd been there before.

"Our alliance would be a boon for you and your family. Just think how I can provide for you. For them."

Her vision. The brambles. Dr. Rufus.

"Stop!"

Her vision! Like the vision of the queen! How many others had she had? Her mind raced trying to remember them while also wondering if she was in trouble. Is that what the visions were communicating? But there'd been one, the one she continued to see, of Lachlan standing near the green, smiling at her.

And as if she'd conjured him— "Tarley?"

Lachlan.

"Here," she cried. She pushed harder against Dr. Rufus. "Speaking of Ollie. Here he is now."

"You call him by his given name?" Rufus took a step away, releasing her, just as Lachlan broke through the brush.

Lachlan was grinning. "I'm surprised I was able to…" But the words dropped off when he saw that Tarley wasn't alone. Now, knowing him better, she could feel him sorting through what he saw. His eyes narrowed. His smile broke, and Tarley was sure he noticed every detail. Like how close Dr. Rufus was standing. Where the doctor's bag had dropped at his feet. How he'd shoved her into the bush. Her anger. The blackberries. The doctor's unwelcoming frown.

"Who are you?" Lachlan demanded, surprising her. She expected his disarming charm, which she'd witnessed several times. Was he angry with her? He could have interpreted the scene incorrectly.

"Dr. Allean Rufus." He offered Lachlan a slight bow.

Ignoring him, Lachlan strode across the meadow and helped her from the bush, looking her over. "Are you alright, Tarley?"

Relief flooded her.

"Miss Fareview," Rufus corrected.

Lachlan's gaze flicked to the doctor and back to her. "Tarley," he said, and she knew it was to annoy Rufus. "Credence is looking for you."

"Picking blackberries," she said, raising the basket so he could see. "For Mrs. Barnwell."

"And you are?" Dr. Rufus asked.

Tarley watched Lachlan turn, noted the aristocratic way he examined the doctor, as if he'd stumbled across something bothersome. She didn't see Ollie, but a prince. "Ollie Berkman," he said. His tone wasn't pleasant.

Dr. Rufus hummed, then waited, as if he had more investment in what was happening near the blackberry bush than he did. His eyes returned to Tarley, and she imagined he looked… hurt. Maybe desperate, but the look slipped away.

"Well." Dr. Rufus picked up his bag and placed his hat on his head. "I should be off. Pleasure, Mr. Berkman." He tipped his rounded, bowler hat. "I'll see you soon, Miss Fareview." Then he disappeared down the trail through the woods.

Tarley turned and stared at the blackberries realizing that Dr. Rufus hadn't just happened to have been walking in this meadow. She turned and looked at where he'd disappeared. He would have had to come from the road.

"What was that?" Lachlan asked.

His tone captured her attention, a tone that seemed to match her trepidation at the realization Rufus must have followed her. Though she'd dismissed the doctor as an oddity, she wasn't sure she could anymore. He'd all but threatened her. What might have happened had Lachlan not arrived?

Lachlan was scowling.

Tarley turned to pick more berries. "You met him."

"Why was he here? With you?"

Tarley reached deeper into the brambles, hoping Lachlan wouldn't notice her trembling hands. "It would seem that I have more suitors than I want."

She could feel Lachlan's gaze on her but refused to look at him. When she didn't, he turned and helped, grumbling each time he encountered a thorn.

"The key is to avoid those sharp things."

"Right." Lachlan pulled a berry and sucked in a breath. A bead of blood welled at his fingertip.

Tarley set down her basket. "Here. Let me see it."

Lachlan held out his hand.

"You're being a baby."

"I think pampered prince is probably a more apt description."

Tarley couldn't help herself, she smiled and looked up at him. "Perfect description."

Lachlan grinned.

Her heart answered, dancing around inside her chest with too much fervor. Ignoring it, she withdrew the scrap of fabric she used for her braid from her skirt pocket, pressing it against Lachlan's finger.

"Stop," he said. "It's fine. You're always trying to save me," he added but he didn't pull away. "Who is that man to you?"

"Jealous?" she asked.

"Yes." His eyes were steady and serious.

Her smile faded, and heat streamed throughout her at his admission. "I think this time, you might have saved me." She looked up at him once more. "Though I'm not quite sure how—"

Lachlan looked chagrined, his gaze sliding from her face to his hand. "I might have watched you leave and followed."

Tarley dabbed until the blood stopped welling. Though it didn't take long, she didn't release him, instead holding his hand as her heart flipped in her chest. She recognized how easy it was to be with him, how safe he made her feel, and knew it was too dangerous to let down her guard.

Chastising herself for not releasing him, she said, "Well, thank you." Then she did something ridiculous and squeezed his hand.

Lachlan stepped closer. "Tarley–"

She looked up and glanced at his lips as she did, but just as she thought he might lean forward to kiss her, she cleared her throat and stepped away. "I think that's enough for pie." She picked up the basket. "We should get back."

Though she could tell he wanted to argue, he didn't. Instead, he nodded. "Lead the way," he said, "and I will follow."

Lachlan

After finding Tarley cornered in the brambles by that ridiculous doctor, it took Lachlan several days to work out his anger. He'd wanted to pummel that stupid man's face for cornering Tarley like that. Then he'd wanted to haul Tarley over his shoulder and lock her in her room to keep her safe. Neither, he knew, would ever change Tarley's mind about marrying him, even if his motives were to protect her.

As he worked off his frustration, he'd worked in the dining room, which had been a disaster the first time he'd seen someone put their hands on Tarley, then cleared rooms and done laundry with Genevieve, who was sweet but chatted his ear off about nothing. He found out he wasn't attuned to the finer details of cleaning, and it was when Credence had finally suggested he work with Trevis in the stables that he discovered a comfortable rhythm. The downside was how infrequently he got to see Tarley.

While the barn usually made him feel content, today he was feeling sorry for himself.

There'd been no message from his family, nor the arrival of guards, which only increased his worry that something worse had happened on that pass than even he knew. If his father had gotten his message and the men had perished, it would take longer to assemble a new team to make the journey to Sevens.

The queen was adding to his stress with pressure about the impending marriage to a reluctant bride.

And it was his birthday.

While he wasn't necessarily one for his birthday, he knew had he been home, there would have been a party. Here in Sevens, no one knew, which made him feel even more alone. Feeling sorry for himself was ridiculous, but he couldn't seem to help it.

"Ollie?" Trevis called from the tack room.

Lachlan lifted a shovel full of horse manure and dumped it into the wheelbarrow. "Yes?"

Trevis appeared in the doorway to the small room, an oil cloth and tack in hand. Given he was only sixteen, the young man's skill with leather astounded Lachlan, though he'd learned from their conversations that Trevis's father and his father before him had been tanners and leather smiths. Credence and Horance had taken Trevis in after an illness orphaned him.

"You think the only gift a girl might like receiving is flowers?" Trevis asked.

Lachlan paused and studied Trevis. He remembered being that age, though he hadn't had to work very hard for a girl's attention. "I'm probably the wrong person to ask—being as I'm not a girl." He grinned at the boy before scooping another shovel full. "I'd venture a guess that a woman would like any gift, flowers or not, depending on the motive behind the gift."

He thought about Tarley, wondering what he could give her.

"You got a specific girl in mind?" he asked Trevis. Over the last week, they'd come to know one another better and spent most nights on their respective pallets reading, then chatting about what they'd read. Lachlan loved that Trevis was a deep thinker, often delving into philosophical questions Lachlan felt well-equipped to handle, thanks to his extensive education.

Lachlan emptied his shovel into the wheelbarrow when an extra-large shadow blocked the light in the doorway.

"Greetings, Horance," Lachlan said and pushed the shovel through the pile of muck once more, grateful his newly developed callouses had stopped his hands from smarting.

The big man shoved his hands into his back pockets, an action Lachlan noticed Horance did when he was uncomfortable. He glanced at Trevis. "Ollie, you take a break," Horance ordered in that deep voice of his. There wasn't a preamble or explanation. Just *take a break.*

Lachlan straightened, one hand holding the shovel, the other draped over the top. "I still have one more stall."

Looking at the stalls he'd completed, he realized he liked the work, and the accompanying accomplishment. While his family would have been appalled that he was standing in horse poop and dirty straw, his boots no longer so pretty, there was something altogether satisfying about being Ollie and finishing the task he set out to do. About being the man who worked to do something that needed to be done. It made him feel... fulfilled.

It was a far cry from his life before. A prince who lived for what was easy and fun. It wasn't a surprise his father had believed what he had about him then. He wondered if his father saw him now—besides the shit-covered boots—would he recognize Lachlan? He felt so different.

He knew, however, that getting this treaty to work would be a strong way to prove he'd changed, that he could do what needed to be done for Jast. Now if he could just get Tarley to say 'yes.' He had less than a week to do it.

"Trevis," Horance called.

Trevis's curly blond head peeked out from the tack room once more. "Yes, sir?"

"Finish up that stall and meet us in the kitchen."

"Will do."

Horance's dark eyes returned to Lachlan. "Credence needs you."

Lachlan nodded and leaned the shovel against the wall, closing the gate behind him and shrugging into a shirt, pretty sure it meant he'd been summoned by the queen. "Is she kicking me out?" He replaced the suspenders.

Horance laughed. "Not yet."

Lachlan followed the other man across the courtyard, their heavy steps cutting through the loose rocks. When Horance disappeared into the kitchen, Lachlan followed, blinking against the relative darkness.

When his vision adjusted, all the people he'd come to know over the last few weeks at the inn stood in the kitchen. "Happy Birthday!" They chorused.

Lachlan stopped short. Set on the workstation was a tall sweetcake frosted in white with fresh berries, a narrow candle flickering in its center. His eyes bounced from Mrs. Barnwell, to Credence, to Horance, then to Genevieve and Trevis—who'd obviously raced through the other entrance of the inn to make it to the kitchen—and finally to Tarley.

"You remembered?" he asked Tarley.

His eyes moved from the cake to Tarley again. Some wild and unruly bird unfolded its wings in his chest. He knew he was attracted to her, but this sensation was different, like watching her in the rain. A moment that hit him squarely in the chest. The way her eyes were tilted up at the corners, softened as her mouth into the semblance of a smile. Then she looked away.

"Yes. Tarley's to blame," Mrs. Barnwell said.

"How young now?" Trevis said and leaned forward to look at the sweetcake.

"Twenty-six," Lachlan answered and tried to keep his eyes from Tarley.

All these weeks, he'd looked for her. His favorite time of day was as the sun began its descent. He knew it was the right time because the light in the stables turned a vibrant hue of gold. He knew he'd find her out in the courtyard, pulling the dry linens from the clothesline. He'd see her silhouette on the other side of the sheets. He'd watch her fold bedsheets, the sunshine touching the red-gold strands in her brown hair. Seeing her like that did the same things to his insides as they were doing now. It made it difficult to draw a breath.

"This is so unexpected," he said, remembering himself and his audience and offering a smile to each of them.

Lachlan had spent each of his birthdays at a party. Each year the nobles and ladies attended. Each year there was a decadent dinner, dessert, and dancing. All for him. Each year he was given elaborate gifts from people he barely knew and who barely knew him, sycophantic gifts meant to outdo the next. And he'd expected it.

But this.

He hadn't expected it, only wished for it, and somehow Tarley had made it come true.

He swallowed.

"I made you this," Trevis said and slid a band of leather toward him. "It's a cuff, you know, like those bracers soldiers wear, but smaller. I didn't have enough…" His words faded.

"Trevis. This is—" Lachlan picked up the dark leather. Trevis had worked it so it was supple and soft, with leather laces to wrap and tie it. It was less bracer and more bracelet, but Lachlan was touched by the thought. "This is incredible. Can you tie it on for me?"

Trevis's cheeks reddened, and he dipped his head as he helped Lachlan fasten it.

"I made the sweetcake," Mrs. Barnwell said.

"It looks delicious. Can we eat it?" Lachlan asked.

"No. Gifts first!" Credence exclaimed. "Then the sweetcake ceremony."

Lachlan had never heard of a sweetcake ceremony, but he nodded, delighted at the prospect.

Genevieve had embroidered a kerchief with the letter "O." Horance and Credence had bought him some ready-made clothes—a new pair of dark trousers and a linen shirt that looked his size.

Then it was Tarley's turn. She wouldn't meet his gaze as she slid him something wrapped in purple fabric that reminded him of her. When he pulled at the string the fabric fell away to reveal a bar of soap and a familiar fragrance—the rosemary and lemon.

"You said you liked it," she said, her voice

uncharacteristically quiet.

He nodded, though she probably didn't understand why he liked it so much. He picked it up and brought it to his nose, closing his eyes to inhale the scent as he imagined her underneath him, her lips swollen with a kiss, her chest heaving as excited breaths pulsed through her lungs, her vibrant gray eyes shining with desire. Lachlan snapped his eyes open to quell the thought and keep his cock from announcing to everyone else where his mind had gone. He nodded at Tarley. "Thank you."

"Ceremony!" Trevis said.

"Tarley," Mrs. Barnwell called. "You do the honors, since you planned it."

Lachlan couldn't keep his eyes from her. She had planned this. For him. Maybe she was warming to the idea of marrying him. It made his heart feel light, floating inside his chest with buoyant hope. But why would he hope for a marriage of convenience? The thought confused him. He would be marrying for Jast, but just then, feelings had pulsed through him that hadn't reflected duty.

Tarley moved around the workstation until she stood in front of him, a knife in hand.

"Please don't stab me," he joked.

She arched her eyebrows and said, "You don't have a birthday ceremony where you're from?" It was said like a challenge, though Lachlan was sure he wasn't hearing her properly with her standing this close.

He shook his head. "We celebrate birthdays, of

course, but I'm not sure what you mean by a sweetcake ceremony."

She lifted the knife. "This is for the sweetcake. Not for you. But don't tempt me."

Everyone laughed.

"She has been known to hit men with steins," Mrs. Barnwell joked as she met Tarley with a dish.

Tarley grinned and cut a slice of the cake. "Another year, another sweetcake layer," she said, as if reciting a passage. "Each layer on the cake represents a year of the life you've lived. This celebrates your past and who you were."

"Twenty-six?"

"Twenty-five."

Lachlan looked at the cake. Sure enough, there were layers upon thin layers of light brown cake, as if a tree had been sliced open to reveal its rings, only these were parallel lines inside the cake. The labor that must have gone into making it—he met Mrs. Barnwell's eyes.

"It was a breeze."

Lachlan was sure it had been anything but.

"And a lit candle to celebrate today," Tarley explained. "The candle represents a celebration of this new year—your present—added to your old life."

He looked at the candle flickering.

"Give a blessing," she said and handed him the plate. "By giving it away, you are offering a blessing to someone else's year in hopes of bringing a blessing to your new year."

As Lachlan took the plate, his hand brushed Tarley's. The spark traveled up his arm and landed in the middle of his back. "What if I want to give it to each of you?" he asked.

Tarley smiled, "You will. We'll all share the cake."

He turned and handed the plate to Credence. "Do I have to say anything?"

Credence smiled. "Blessings upon blessings," she said, and Lachlan recited it. "Thank you, Ollie."

"Thank you," he said and turned back to Tarley, who opened her mouth, then closed it before turning and facing the cake.

"Do the rest!" Trevis said. "You can't skip the last part."

Tarley took a deep breath but kept her eyes on the cake. "Offer a kiss to seal the wish made on this birthday." Her eyes slid to his. "Now, you make a wish for your future, and offer someone a kiss."

Lachlan swallowed, wanting more than anything to kiss Tarley. "The past, the present, and the future?"

Tarley nodded.

He made a wish for his future—that he could be the king Jast needed him to be and that Tarley would want him—but instead of kissing Tarley like he wanted, he kissed Mrs. Barnwell's cheek. She *tsked* with pleasure, blushed, then smacked his arm, saying something about Mr. Barnwell being jealous.

When Lachlan returned to his place, he looked for Tarley, but she'd moved to the opposite side of the room, standing just slightly behind Genevieve. She glanced at him, then looked away.

After the cake was cut and distributed, they all wished him another united 'happy birthday', then stood around the worktable shoulder-to-shoulder, eating the dessert, laughing, and sharing stories of birthdays.

Lachlan had been to many birthdays, but in all his years, he'd never experienced one that gave him greater enjoyment, knowing these gifts were offered at great expense to people giving them. It gave him pause, to consider that in his privileged life, this here, with these people, with—his eyes slid to Tarley across the table, her head bent to listen to Trevis—Tarley, filled his chest with emotions he wasn't sure how to process.

As the celebration wound down, Tarley plated another slice. "I'm going to give Rose a piece."

His impulse was to grab Tarley, to drag her to the back stairwell where he'd show his thanks. He wanted to touch her, give her pleasure, in the same way that his heart was pulsing with it. But he suppressed the impulse. The feeling moving through him was too big. For her, especially. Hell, it was too big for him, and he didn't know what to do with it.

So he watched Tarley disappear up the stairs, letting her go and afraid it was all he was ever going to get to do.

Tarley

"Come in," Queen Keyanna called from inside the room.

Tarley found the queen standing at the windows. "I brought you some of Lachlan's sweetcake."

The queen, looking slight in hand-me-downs much too large for her, turned toward Tarley. "His birthday?"

Tarley nodded, setting the cake down on the table where the queen had been taking her meals. She could imagine the queen was feeling cooped up. She would.

"And the sweetcake ceremony?" the queen asked. "I'm not sure Jast has one."

Tarley smiled and pressed her hands to her skirt.

"Of course, your Maj–"

The queen held up a hand. "Rose." She lifted her skirts and drifted across the room to the table. "Who did he kiss?" Her dark eyes met Tarley's filled with a mischievous glint.

Tarley often had the impression that the queen was ageless while being an ancient soul simultaneously. But at that moment, Tarley realized Keyanna couldn't be much older than her sister Jessamine—twenty-nine—give or take a year or so. Under different circumstances, perhaps they might have even been friends. "Mrs. Barnwell."

"The cook?"

Tarley nodded.

The queen hummed. "Perhaps he isn't as adept at persuasion as I had hoped."

"My qu–" Tarley checked herself. "What do you mean?"

Keyanna sat at the table and took a bite. "Delicious."

"Mrs. Barnwell is a magician in the kitchen."

"Any word on my sister?" the queen asked. The same question each day.

"None," Tarley said, equally worried for her brother, who hadn't sent a single message, though she was sure he couldn't.

The queen sighed. "Give me better news. Have you agreed to the marriage?"

The rate at which the queen could disarm her, then hit her with the heaviness of her situation was fearsome. "I haven't."

"And why is that? It's clear that Lachlan is a handsome devil. Maybe too handsome for his own good. He probably hasn't had to work for much."

Tarley snickered.

"And it's clear you agree." The queen smiled.

"He is handsome, yes, but one doesn't marry for looks alone."

"Ah," Keyanna said. She took another bite, then set down the fork. "You want to marry for love?"

"Isn't that what we all want?"

Keyanna hummed. "Perhaps. Royals aren't always given the option, but it is a noble desire." She looked from the cake to Tarley. "Are you familiar with the story of my parents?"

Tarley shook her head.

"They weren't a love match. Rather my father, young and dumb, became obsessed with my mother, and rather than ask permission for her hand, he stole her away from Jast to Kaloma." She paused. "Sort of fits doesn't it. With Kaloma's history." She sighed.

"Started a war."

"Among other things. Word is that is why he was cursed with only daughters and dead sons."

"Why didn't she run away from him?"

"Maybe she initially tried, but ultimately, my father convinced her to be his bride. She must have found something redeeming about him. And maybe she was carrying his first child by then."

"The one that died?"

"One of many." Keyanna stood. "I tell you the story to say that marriages are strange things. If they could make a marriage…" Her words faded as she looked at the sweetcake. "I don't plan to marry, though if I'm able to remain queen, I realistically know I may not have that choice. It may become a necessity." She returned to the window. "But I only ever knew my parents in love. Their inauspicious beginning might have predicted a tumultuous partnership, and I supposed it was initially, but by the time I was a child, I was witness to their deep mutual respect. Her death ruined my father."

"Your point being that should I marry Lachlan, the lack of it being a love match doesn't necessitate that love won't eventually bloom."

"You're smart, Tarley. Lachlan will make you a queen. And queens have power, which I suspect is something you desire."

"I desire the power to decide my own life."

"Yes. I know." Keyanna sighed and crossed her arms around her middle.

"Being forced to marry someone doesn't feel like empowerment," Tarley said, unwilling to hold her tongue on the matter.

The queen remained fixed at the window. Her silence made Tarley think she'd been dismissed, until the queen said, "I need you to marry Lachlan, Tarley. Kaloma needs it. If I have any hope of changing those barbaric laws and avoiding war, I need the backing of the people." Keyanna turned and gave Tarley a pointed look. "And the backing of Jast. Do you understand? See the power in your hands to make a difference?"

Tarley nodded, but she needed to get away to think. "Can I get you anything else?"

Keyanna shook her head. "Thank you for the sweetcake."

Later that evening in her room, Tarley undressed and cleaned her body before slipping into her night shift, but she didn't get into bed. Rather, she paced, processing what the queen had said. Wishing she could talk to… Lachlan.

She stopped.

That was the truth. Somewhere her point of confidence had shifted from her family to the man who pushed her, needled her, made her both frown and in the next instant smile. And if that wasn't something to build a marriage on, well, there had been less. He seemed to like her. If she lost her heart to him, maybe he could learn to love her?

Needing to find him, she grabbed her shawl and opened the door.

Lachlan, stood outside, his arm raised as if he'd been about to knock. He looked unsettled, his hair unruly if he'd run his hands through it, his linen shirt open at his neck, the hem haphazardly tucked into his trousers. He swallowed and dropped his arm.

"Oh–" she said. "You're here?"

"I… I'm sorry to surprise you." Lachlan took a step closer and put a hand on each side of the doorway as if to keep himself on his side of it. "I just wanted to say thank you, for today."

Tarley looked at him and nodded, her heart thrumming in her chest. "Of course. No one should miss–"

"Tarley," Lachlan started, and she loved the way her name sounded on his lips. It made her think of his mouth filled with her. "Where were you going?"

"To–" She stopped, feeling flustered, and considered a lie. "I was coming to see you."

His eyes took her in, and she could see his assessment, like that day at the meadow when he'd happened upon her and Dr. Rufus. His gaze skimmed her unbound hair, her night shift, her bare feet. "Like that?"

"I guess I hadn't thought that part through," she said, looking down at herself before tilting her head back up toward him.

The queen was right. He was handsome. A girl could go a long time having had the attention of this man. But that wasn't all that was on her mind, even if it seemed to be taking up all the space.

Lachlan dropped his arms and stepped across the threshold. "I gave a kiss to Mrs. Barnwell–"

"I was there."

"I didn't want to kiss Mrs. Barnwell," he admitted and leaned toward her.

"You didn't?" Tarley heard herself ask, though it sounded more like she'd breathed it. Her heart was beating in her chest so loud she could hear it in her ears, the sensation of it sending ripples to zip across her skin.

He filled her doorway, his hands in his pockets now, but still leaning toward her. She could see the muscles of his arms below the rolled sleeves of his shirt. Heat rushed through her, and she grasped the neck of her nightshift, fluttering it to cool off her suddenly burning skin.

His eyes tracked her movement, and he shook his head. "No. I wanted to kiss you."

"Why didn't you?" She licked her lips.

His gaze followed her tongue before finding her eyes again. "I knew that the kind of kiss I wanted to give you—well, that wasn't the right place."

She swallowed and realized she was staring at his lips. Her eyes drifted back up to meet his. "What kind of kiss?"

"Tarley?"

"Yes?"

"May I seal my wish?"

"You did."

"It feels like it should have been with you." His voice was low, quiet, and somehow demanding.

There was a time when she wouldn't have even considered it. Except at that moment, standing nearly chest to chest with Lachlan, she didn't feel powerless. She felt powerful, because she could see he was also affected, his chest rising and falling, his muscles tense, his eyes speaking to her with an emotional intensity that matched what was moving through her body. She didn't feel weak just then.

She nodded. "Yes."

Lachlan smiled, a smile with teeth and bright eyes, and she liquified.

His heavy boots thudded as he stepped closer. One arm slid around the small of her back to pull her against him, his other hand in her hair at the back of her head. "I'd hoped you'd say yes, Miss Fareview."

Tarley clung to his shoulders.

He dropped his head but then stopped before their lips touched. His warmth mingled with hers, and his eyes searched her face as if to make sure. Her body vibrated with anticipation. Then his eyes slipped shut, and he pressed his mouth against hers.

His kiss was better than she'd reimagined, her fantasies paling in comparison to reality. A vision coalesced in her mind of Lachlan standing on the green in Sevens, smiling at her. A vision that felt vaguely familiar, even if she couldn't place it. She pushed it away to focus on the kiss, on the feel of his lips, his hands pressed to her jaw, his fingers wrapped around the back of her neck.

Before she was ready, he drew away. Her eyes fluttered open, blinking to reorient herself, and she met his gaze.

He was breathing heavily, the rise and fall of his chest a clear indication he was as moved as she was, but he didn't kiss her again. Instead, she saw the muscle in his jaw twitch, and his eyes flicked down to her mouth. "I shouldn't have done that," he said and before she could ask why, he released her from his grip. Stepping back, he added, "I know what it's like to kiss you. It's all I'm going to be thinking about."

Tarley's mind went blank. There was something she'd wanted to tell him. That's where she'd been going, only as she thought about the craving coursing through her, she just wanted more of his kiss, his touch. They'd awakened that before—in the woods— but here, things had been different.

He stepped back once more, though it was clear he was fighting himself, his hands fisted at his sides. He cleared his throat. "Will you save me a dance?"

She nodded.

He took another step back and offered her a smile, and she anticipated he was going to say something charming. Instead, he turned and started down the stairs.

She watched him go, wanting more than anything to call him back. But she didn't. Maybe she was willing to marry him, but she wasn't sure she was willing to give him complete access to her heart.

Tarley

arley—having gone home to prepare for the dance—now rode back to Sevens in the wagon with her family. She glanced at their mother, dressed in deep sapphire, to their father in his best clothes, to Auri, ecstatic that their mother had released her from the confines of the cottage for the event.

Dances in Sevens were a rarity. In fact, Tarley couldn't remember the last time they'd been to one. But as much as she tried to relax into the joy of it, she was too cognizant of what this dance represented.

"I love our dresses," Brinna exclaimed, preening in her aqua taffeta.

"Good thing we ordered them when we did,"

Jessamine said, referring to the catalog Mr. Martin kept handy to order ready-made dresses from New Taras. She wore a rose gown that shimmered like a pearl.

"We could never have made them in time," Brinna added.

She and Jessamine continued their conversation about the fabrics, which always bored Tarley to tears but for the moment let her lean toward Auri and ask, "Will Mr. Uraiahs join us?"

Auri turned her head, then shook it. Her emerald gown with its off-the-shoulder neckline and cap sleeves, was the perfect cut for her. The bodice wrapped around her to a drop waist, where it flared at her hips. But not even Auri's stunning gown could change the pall that had become more pronounced in the weeks since Tarley's return.

"Is it because of the argument?" Tarley asked, trying to hide her alarm.

"Not the argument," Auri whispered. "Because of what I asked him to do."

"Which was?"

Auri opened her mouth, then hesitated and said instead, "I love your dress."

Tarley thought it was pretty; she felt pretty in it, but the sweetheart neckline had her cleavage on display. Brinna had insisted the neckline was perfect to showcase Tarley's assets. The loose sleeves draped around her shoulders, and the dress pinched her waist, then exploded with sheer fabric Brinna called tulle. Whatever it was, it was pretty. She'd wondered why she couldn't just wear a normal dress, but Brinna had raged at her—and Brinna never raged.

"I wish Tai was here," Brinna said.

"Hush," Auri said, glancing at the front of the wagon where their parents sat. "You'll get Mother worked into a fit." It was a point of tension, Mattias still on his errand. The longer it stretched on, the worse Scarlett's mood grew.

Brinna blanched. "You're right."

"The point is to have fun and forget the stress of the last few weeks, yes?" Tarley pointed out, though this night was anything but fun for her. The event would end with her betrothed. The stress of it was making her feel faint, and she didn't faint.

By the time they arrived at the meeting house, it was bustling with people—a strange sight in Sevens. With all the new members of the village, it was an actual party, and Tarley couldn't help but smile.

She was sure they were a sight, climbing from the back of the wagon in fancy dresses, but it wasn't like they were royalty rolling up to a country dance in a carriage. Too bad they didn't have magic to change it for the night.

Golden light spilled from the windows of the wooden building to light the surrounding woods, music drifting from the open door. They entered the room packed with people, all dressed up in finery. The chandeliers shone, candelabras adding light along the floor near each window. A fire hazard, Tarley thought it a bit preposterous having gone to the lengths for a fancy ball when it could have been something less ostentatious. But the queen had insisted, saying, "The fairy tale must be believable."

Ivory ribbons held sprays of forest greenery, and Tarley had to admit it was like being transported to a fairy woodland. Credence, Mrs. Barnwell, and the queen had pulled it off.

It was a fairytale for her and Lachlan, all set to enhance the announcement that they were betrothed. It was a farce, even if she'd decided to relent. Their fairytale wasn't a real one. It was an arrangement, except she hadn't been able to tell Lachlan she'd agreed yet. While the queen had been right, being a queen someday would give her power, the secret in her heart was that she was falling for Lachlan which had nothing to do with power. And that is what ultimately terrified her.

She scanned the crowd, looking for Lachlan, Unable to find him, she stayed with her family as they moved through the space, stopping to say hello, making excuses for Mattias's absence. When she saw Dr. Rufus moving through the crowd toward her, she ducked behind a tall man, drawing Auri with her.

Brinna danced with someone. Jessamine wasn't, a wide swath of space around her, which she didn't seem to mind. Auri looked pale but smiled. Tarley just wanted to see Lachlan.

Suddenly the crowd quieted.

Credence and Horance entered the room with their visiting distant relation, Rose.

Tarley gaped. Credence looked like a queen in her deep scarlet dress, her white hair piled on her head in an explosion of ringlets. Horance escorted her on one arm, and on the other, Rose looked younger than her years in an understated pink gown.

Hoping for Lachlan, Tarley swallowed her disappointment.

"Miss Fareview?" someone said from behind her.

Tarley and Auri turned.

"Nix?" Auri breathed. "How can—"

Sure enough, Mr. Uraiahs bowed before her, looking as beautiful as he had the first time Tarley had ever seen him, though he had the same strange pall about him as Auri's. He was dressed in formal black, his usual color, it seemed. His dark hair was a touch long, and his face a bit scruffy, but it worked for him. "I'd hoped that perhaps you would save me a dance."

Auri threw her arms around him, and Nix crushed her against him. "I'm so sorry," Auri whispered. "I didn't mean it. Don't go again. Please. I don't care about it."

Tarley watched her sister's pallor rapidly fade, her cheeks pink, her eyes vibrant, her smile infectious once more.

Mr. Uraiahs, whose color had also returned, whispered something in Auri's ear. Then they abruptly pulled apart and glanced around, obviously looking for Scarlett, who was dancing with Tomas.

There was another man with Mr. Uraiahs, tall and imposing, the exact image of Auri's suitor, only his antithesis, blond and golden as opposed to the dark and mysterious. The stranger's face, however, was devoid of emotion, a living statue.

"Lucian," Auri said, her tone curt, cutting.

The golden man dipped his head, and a smile broke out on his face as if there were a joke occurring between them, "Aurielle." Then he looked away, as if resuming guard duty.

"Auri?" Tarley asked. "How?" She couldn't understand how her sister knew these two men.

Auri offered her a smile, pure and unadulterated Auri, which grasped hold of Tarley's heart and squeezed. It didn't matter, really, only that her sister was happy. And this man offered that to her. Wanting that, Tarley scanned the room for Lachlan.

But he was nowhere to be found.

Her heart squeezed again, only this time with worry. What if he'd changed his mind? Or worse, what if he was hurt somewhere?

"Tarley?" Auri captured her attention. "This is Lucian. Nix's brother."

The blond man offered a nod of acknowledgement.

Tarley curtsied. "How do you do?"

He grinned. "Better now."

Tarley blushed, her eyes skittering away to look for Lachlan once more, wanting it to be him flirting with her.

"Dance with me?" Nix asked Auri.

Auri's gaze skated to Tarley. "Do you mind?"

"Go." Tarley gave her sister a smile, happy that Auri looked herself once more and realizing she was going to have to speak to their mother on Auri's behalf. Leaving her stuck at the cottage wasn't healthy.

She watched Nix lead Auri away, then looked for Lachlan once again. The realization that she didn't want to be without him punched into the soft tissue of her heart, and she feared, as she scanned the crowd that he'd finally come to his senses.

"May I offer you my companionship as a dance partner?" Lucian asked.

He was being polite, but Tarley offered him a charming smile and inclined her head. "I'd love to."

Lachlan

He was late. He hadn't intended it, but Trevis had an accidental spill on his pants, then ranted that everyone would think he'd "pissed himself." Lachlan, rather clueless, had used his common sense, but that meant waiting for the fabric to dry to not showcase the offensive darkness in the region of Trevis's crotch. Lachlan had spent the last hour working hard not to laugh. Trevis wasn't in the mood.

The queen was going to be put out. And Tarley. He'd made gains with her since the blackberry picking and his birthday and the kiss, but he had a terrible feeling that Tarley was… well, he wasn't sure, and when it came to Tarley, he never had been. Being late might seal his fate. They still hadn't come to an understanding about Tarley as a willing bride, but the queen was rolling ahead. He supposed if worse came to worse, if Tarley refused, they could break the engagement down the line, though the thought antagonized him.

When he entered the meeting house—a far cry from a ballroom but appealing in a magical wood kind of way—he immediately scanned the room for Tarley. When he found her, several things happened. His lungs stopped working because she was the most radiant woman in the room, then his heart expanded, because he was going to get to marry her, then his mind stalled, because she was in the arms of a very tall and handsome stranger—blond, bright, smiling— someone he'd never seen before in Sevens.

And she was returning his smile. Laughing with him.

Trevis said something, which Lachlan didn't hear, then disappeared into the crowd, leaving Lachlan to his own devices. Which weren't good.

He knew that but didn't check himself, his impetuosity ruling as he stalked through the room. That man didn't get Tarley's smiles or her laughter. That man didn't get to dance with her. That man was dancing with his woman… Lachlan wanted to rage, throw his fists. But halfway there, he stalled and stopped.

He'd never felt like that before. Not about anyone.

He glanced at Tarley, and his heart eased,

tempering his fit of jealousy.

She deserved to look at a man like that, even if it wasn't him.

She deserved to smile and be adored by everyone.

She deserved to be happy, even if it was in the arms of another.

As much as it pained him: she deserved it all, even if it wasn't with him.

And he was on the way to steal it from her through their forced marriage. She was entitled to her fun tonight. So instead of being an ass, he veered course toward the punch, hoping it was spiked with something stronger, and found a wall to lean against.

When the queen found him sometime later, she was glaring at him.

"What are you doing?" she demanded. She was such a petite thing, and so fierce. "You look like you're pouting."

"I might be."

"Why?" She followed his gaze. Tarley wasn't with the blond giant any longer but standing among several men like a queen holding court. "Why aren't you over there?"

"I'm giving her space. You know, to enjoy the night."

"You are such an idiot. I don't know how you're ever going to rule a kingdom," she snapped in a subdued whisper.

Surprised and hurt by her virulence, he leaned away. "She's been pretty clear that–"

"Look at her face!"

Lachlan hadn't taken much time to notice, too wrapped up in his own misery watching Tarley shine. He wanted so much to be who she chose, and yet she was surrounded by a bevy of men. But when he let himself look at her face, she looked... angry, like the Tarley he knew when she was ready to throw something.

Lachlan smacked his cup down on the table. "Time to save my queen," he said and left Keyanna behind.

When he made it across the room, he could tell she was seething.

"But it's apparent," one of the men said, "that the fairer sex needs help in all matters."

Tarley's eyes widened, but her mouth remained shut, her usually plump lips pressed into a firm line.

"As I've always said, there isn't a woman who knows her own mind. She needs a guiding, but firm, hand."

Tarley tensed, her arms dropping to her sides and her mouth opening.

"Miss Fareview," Lachlan interrupted.

All six faces of the men surrounding her swung toward him, each expressing varied states of irritation at Lachlan's interruption.

Her face turned red. She closed her eyes, and when she opened them back up after taking a deep breath, she narrowed them on him.

Uh oh.

"May I have this dance?" he asked.

She bristled, and he thought she might decline, but then she seemed to consider the alternative and offered him a short nod, taking his outstretched hand.

Lachlan tucked her arm into his elbow and led her to the dance floor.

"Where have you been?" she snapped.

"Across the room." He nodded to where he'd been standing.

"The whole time?"

"You were dancing when I got here, with some golden god."

She turned her head to look at him, the shape of her eyes softening. "Were you jealous?" Her grip on his arm tightened.

"Exceedingly," he admitted. When she looked down at the floor, he continued, "I was afraid I might make a scene of epic proportions—you know how spoiled I can be when I don't get my way."

"I do." She looked up at him with a grin. A real one, and Lachlan's heart constricted in his chest.

"So I just stood over against the wall and felt sorry for myself, because the most beautiful woman in the room wasn't paying any attention to me." Lachlan swept her into his arms, one hand on the small of her back, the other holding her hand.

"Were you pouting?"

"I was."

"You poor thing," she said, her eyes twinkling.

"Really." He nodded and grinned. "Then I got scolded by Rose for failing to read the room properly.

She isn't sure I'll make a very good king."

Tarley's hand on his shoulder tightened, then moved deeper over his shoulder blade. "You saved me, so I believe you're on your way."

"I think if I hadn't, you might be under arrest for murder."

She laughed then, bright and musical, and Lachlan knew he had finally done something properly when it came to Tarley. "You know me so well," she said, but her smile faded, and she grew serious again. Quiet.

"You are an excellent dancer," she said after they'd taken a turn about the room.

"One thing I'm good at it would seem. I've had extensive training and practice," he teased.

But she remained pensive.

Unsure why her demeanor had shifted so suddenly, he wasn't as confident he'd made any of the right choices when it came to her. They shared several more dances, Lachlan as her escort, teasing and cajoling her. But her unguarded smile never returned. In fact, the longer the night wore on, the more tense she became, until he couldn't take it a moment more.

"Would you like to get out of here?" he asked.

"But the announcement?" she whispered.

The reason for her anxiety.

"Can't make the announcement if we aren't here," he said and offered her another grin.

"Let me tell my sisters," Tarley said.

When she returned, Lachlan offered his arm, but she took his hand, and they walked out into the night.

Tarley

Lachlan's hand in hers felt right. Leaving the meeting house for the inn felt right. Everything about the moment felt right, but Tarley still couldn't bring herself to tell him what she'd decided. She didn't want to adulterate the rightness of just being with him this way with the pressure of what those words would mean.

"This almost feels like the woods again," she said instead.

Sevens stretched out in front of them, the dark buildings appearing like shadows. The dirt roadway was a soundtrack to their steps as they walked. The dark windows watched them as they passed.

His hand tightened around hers. "Why do you say that?"

Rather than answer his question directly, she said, "I don't like dressing up."

"You look divine, however."

She smiled. "That's sweet of you."

"It isn't. I always have an ulterior motive."

She turned her head. "Oh?"

"Yes. I'm hoping it grants me a kiss later."

Tarley felt the smile in her heart even though she looked away. "When I'm in the woods," she said, returning to the original subject, "I feel like my most authentic self."

"And you don't like this?"

"I do, just a different—not as confident—version of her."

"I understand."

"You do?"

"I've never felt like a more authentic version of myself since knowing you."

Her throat closed with emotion, threatening to fill her eyes. She swallowed it but didn't trust herself to speak for fear of losing control. When she finally could, she asked, "What about before?"

Lachlan walked with her for some time before saying, "I think I was a very different version of Lachlan Nikolas. One you would have hated."

They passed the green, the shadow of the tree looming large, the church beyond it. Tarley imagined Lachlan standing on the green, wearing a purple coat with white and gold accents. She blinked and watched the shadows as they passed, knowing she'd seen that vision before. It filled her with peace. Rightness.

"Hate is a strong word," she said.

"I underhandedly sabotaged my father's choice of bride by assassinating her appearance in court. Hate might be too weak of a word." He cleared his throat.

"Why did you do it?"

They walked in silence for a bit, then Lachlan said, "I was too scared and too weak to just come out and tell my father I was angry with him. And rather than face him, I embarrassed her into calling off the betrothal."

"You didn't care what she thought?"

"Not in the slightest. She wasn't the only one I did it to."

"Really?"

"No. I'm ashamed to say. Princess Freida Truisante was one of many princesses and noble women I've insulted."

Tarley wished she could offer words to exonerate him but knew there were none. "This isn't the Lachlan I've come to know," she said instead.

"I don't think it would be fair to this better version of me to lie about what I once did. But I feel... different now from then."

Tarley squeezed his hand, loving that he was sharing this with her. His willingness to open up to her made her feel connected to him in a way she'd never experienced before. "How so?"

"My perspective before meeting you—before nearly dying—was always connected to how things affected me. Never someone else. This second chance has forced me to look more closely at myself and untie the self-centered way I was. What a horrific reflection when I looked closer."

"That's a bit of an overstatement."

"I'm a selfish man, Tarley. Let's not muddy those waters. I'm still selfish," he said, looking down at the path as they walked into the courtyard of the inn. "I think that was what my father was trying to teach me by sending me to Sevens. That as king, sometimes one must make choices that don't always align with what we want, but rather what our country, our people need."

Tarley started up the steps, pulling Lachlan along behind her. "I don't know about then, but I know about now. And I don't think you're selfish. You care about Trevis and Credence and Horance. You never complain about tasks. And when my mother accused you of trying to hurt the queen, you didn't boast about who you were, you decided to demonstrate your character."

"I care about you," he said quietly.

She stopped at the door, opened it, and turned to look at him. "You've put your kingdom above yourself."

He took a deep breath and stepped closer. "I can't say that's true anymore."

Tarley tilted her head to look up at him and knew

what she wanted more than anything. She wanted him. She wanted everything. He made her smile and laugh. He made her angry, but he also challenged her in ways no one else ever had. Perhaps she would be the only one to fall in love, but she knew he cared. So when she backed across the threshold into her room, she kept hold of his hand and pulled him in with her.

It just felt right.

"Tarley?"

"I think you've earned that kiss. If you still want it," she said and reached around him to shut the door.

"I do. But–"

"But what?"

"I don't think it's true I'm putting my kingdom first anymore."

"Why?"

"Because I want you. For me."

"Yes or no Lachlan?" she asked.

"Yes. Yes," he said in the dark of her room.

She grasped his face and brought his lips to hers, then stepped closer, needing to feel his strength pressed against her.

The fabric of her dress rustled with their movement. When she opened her mouth and touched the seam of his lips with her tongue, Lachlan made a deep rumbling noise, grasped her hips, and pulled her against him with a force to match hers. He angled his head for a deeper connection, his tongue sweeping against hers, an addictive tangle.

She grabbed hold of his bottom lip with her teeth

and pulled, sucking, and Lachlan stilled, his shadow looming around her.

He pulled back. "Did you just bite me?"

"I did," she admitted. "I feel like I'd like to bite you everywhere."

"This is it, Tarley." He reached down and grasped her ass to lift her, walking her backwards.

"What?" she asked, not really wanting him to talk.

"My birthday wish."

"You wished for this?"

"Sort of."

The admission did something to her heart, melting a layer of ice and rock she'd built around it for protection. "You wished for me?"

"Oh stars, Tarley. Yes." He helped her onto the bed, and she laid back, pulling him with her. It groaned under their combined weight.

"I've been dreaming about you," she admitted. "For weeks."

"Sex dreams?"

She nodded.

"Have you touched yourself thinking about it?"

"Yes."

He moaned and kissed her. Lips. Tongue. Teeth. Raw hunger claimed them both. Lachlan grabbed the hem of her dress and looked for her leg underneath. When his hand found her skin, he slid his palm up her bare leg, his new callouses rough and welcome.

His mouth left hers and made a trail to her neck, licked, sucked, tasted, savored, his hand near her knee.

"May I touch you," he asked.

"Please. Please," she said and turned toward him, drawing his mouth back to hers.

Lachlan reached up and caressed her breasts over her dress, molded them, conformed them to the palm of his hand. "Gods, you look so good in this dress."

Tarley arched her back into his touch, and his mouth left hers again.

"What did you dream?" He asked the question against her skin.

"This," she breathed, her hands in his hair as he moved lower, his warm mouth closing over her nipple, the soft silk creating a pleasing friction. She moaned and closed her eyes. "Your touch. Your kiss. You inside me."

"Tell me more."

"I can't think—" she said, wrapped up in all the sensations his hands, his mouth, his body was igniting in hers.

He pulled back, his eyes seeking hers, his hands smoothing her hair. "Marry me, Tarley."

She paused, knowing she could say *yes*, but the word lodged in her throat.

He didn't wait for her answer, as if he had his mind made up about what she intended to say, sighing as if resigned. "What's wrong with me that you won't even consider it?" He moved off her, the creak of the bed and the cool air that moved across her highlighting his absence. "Is the idea of being my wife—my queen— so terrible?" He sat on the edge of the bed, arms pressed against his thighs. "Help me understand."

She sat up, his words feeling like knives in her heart. "Is that how I've made you feel?"

He looked over his shoulder, but his eyes separated from her. "Your kiss tells me something different—"

"What does it tell you?" she asked, pressing a palm to his back.

"That you want me as much as I want you." He looked at her then.

"The day of your birthday," she said, "I was coming down to tell you I would marry you."

He turned to her, eyes were wide, his mouth slack. He tilted his head. "You were?"

"I was, only I wanted to—"

Lachlan moved, lightning quick, pressing her back into the bed once more. "You agree?"

She nodded, reaching up to move a strand of hair away from his eyes. "I want to tell my family."

He nodded and pressed a kiss to her cheek. "Yes. Anything." He pressed another to her jaw. "Tell me what you need." Another kiss to her opposite cheek. Then he pulled back, smiling, and Tarley's heart stretched thin, making the beats painful, because his look wasn't one of someone being made to marry her. He seemed genuinely happy, and that happiness seeped into her own body, filling her with light.

"Then perhaps I've overstayed," he said and leaned down, pressing his lips to hers. "Because," he said between kisses, "I want you so bad." He ground his hips into hers, and she gasped at the feel of his erection through the fabric of her gown. "And now that you've agreed, there's nothing to keep me from fucking you other than your word on the matter, Tarley." He reached down and grasped her hips, tilting them so he could press his body closer.

She moaned, unable to contain it, and knew she didn't want to anymore; she fixed her arms around him, keeping his weight where she needed it. This felt right.

"Don't go," she begged.

Lachlan

"Don't tease me, Tarley," he growled against her lips, pressing his erection between her legs, the layers of fabric between them denying him relief.

"Lachlan–"

"Say my name again. Please." He ground his hips again, drawing in a breath, shocked by how much he wanted her. His body was wound up with it. There wasn't a time he could recall feeling this wild with need.

She moaned again, the sweet sound filling his head. "Lachlan. Oh, Lachlan. I want you–" Her hands slid down his back and grasped his ass, holding him against her. He felt her tilt her hips toward him, seeking that friction.

Frenzied, Lachlan lifted his hips, missing her, but needing to be closer. He helped her stand. "This needs to be off." He tugged at her dress with impatience.

"I'll—"

"Sorry," he told her and kissed her lips, then pressed his forehead to hers, simply breathing there for a moment. "I've lost my wits. You make me come undone, Tarley Fareview." He turned her and started in on the buttons that ran down her back, until the dress fell to offer him bare skin, the dress pooling around her hips. Leaning forward, he pressed his lips to her shoulder.

"You smell so good," he said and pushed the dress from her hips, then reached around and palmed her breasts. "That soap. I've pleasured myself to that scent so many times thinking of you."

She gasped and leaned into his touch.

Lachlan ran his tongue along her shoulder to her neck, until she turned her head and met his mouth with hers. The kiss was charged and filled with promise, their tongues dancing the same rhythm their bodies vowed to discover.

When she turned in his arms, he drew back to look at her in the moonlight. He'd seen her before. In the tent, spread open to his kiss. Her body barely hidden by a wet linen shirt as she stood in the rain. Naked in the river, and now, this.

"You're so fucking beautiful," he said, trailing a hand from her shoulder down her arm to thread their fingers and pull her closer.

"Your turn." She reached for his shirt, pulling it from his trousers. Lachlan helped her, drawing it over his head and dropping it on the floor next to her discarded dress.

"Stars, Lachlan." Her eyes roamed his body. "You're beautiful yourself." She reached out and touched him, and Lachlan loved that she wasn't shy. Her finger skimmed down his chest, over his belly, to his erection tenting his pants.

He shivered.

"These too, yes?" She pulled at the fastener.

He nodded. "Yes. Nothing between us anymore." He removed them with haste, then helped her with her underclothes, needing to feel her skin against his.

When they were done, naked before one another, they touched, lingered with fingertips and kisses, until they were both lying on the bed, Lachlan's hips settled in between hers.

"My heart is racing," he admitted between kisses.

"Mine too."

He felt his impatience, wanting to bury himself inside her, but willed himself to slow down. This was her first time. This was their first time. He looked up at her. "Are you sure, Tarley?"

"I've never been surer about something I wanted," she said and grasped the back of his head, pulling him back to her, kissing him as if she'd been made to do so.

Lachlan kissed her harder, skimming her skin with his hands, kneading, touching, drawing out her sounds of pleasure, allowing his mouth to stray from hers. He licked and sucked and bit at her skin, excited as she mewled and writhed under him. He spent time kissing her breasts, enjoying the moans his attention elicited, including the way she held the back of his head to keep him there. While his tongue lavished attention on her nipples, his hands slid lower to the cleft between her legs, seeking the knot he knew would produce the most pleasure, excited by her wet heat, her readiness.

When he touched her, she tensed, sucking in a quick breath. "Oh. Yes." She moaned his name.

His name, connected to her blissful sounds, spurred him forward. He dragged his mouth from feasting on her gorgeous breasts, down her belly, until he was settled between her thighs to taste her again. "I told you," he said, looking at her sex, finding it as enticing as the woman, "I told you this wasn't over." When his tongue slid up her seam to her clit, she gasped, her fingers threading in his hair. She pulled his hair as she arched her back, her pelvis tipped, her hips seeking his mouth. "Lachlan," she repeated. "Yes. Yes," she chanted.

"I fucking love to hear my name in your mouth," he said, inserting a finger.

As he pampered her with his tongue, she tightened around him, releasing his hair and reaching for the sheets, gasping and panting, rolling her hips against his tongue. He draped one of his arms across her hips to keep her where he wanted her. Her sounds grew louder. He loved it, wanted it. Her hips sought friction as her pleasure intensified, bucking against his face, the bud under his tongue more pronounced until suddenly she cried, "Oh gods," her pussy tightening around his inserted fingers as she panted out, "I'm coming. Oh gods. Lachlan, help me. Please."

"Let go, Tarley. I'm here," he said against her skin. "I'm here," he repeated, gentling his attentions, kissing instead of sucking.

She whimpered, her body riding the pleasure of her orgasm.

"Good?" he asked after her body melted and grew pliant under him. Lachlan kissed up her belly, drawing his skin across hers, loving the feeling of that friction, her softness juxtaposed with his rigidity.

She sighed. "You know it was." She opened her eyes, met his gaze, and smiled, a true, unguarded smile.

It devastated him.

When he lined up with her body, settling into the cradle of her thighs, he held her face between his palms. "Tarley?"

"Yes?"

"Is this still what you want?" he asked, afraid she might change her mind.

She searched his face and nodded. "Yes. I want this... with you."

"I don't have any protection, to prevent pregnancy."

"I have herbs for after. And then for both of us until we decide–" She stopped, as if the reality of what they were doing sunk in, and Lachlan's heart expanded.

When they decided to have children, he finished in his head. This was real. This was happening.

He leaned down and kissed her with all of him, not just his body.

"That's a yes, then?"

"Yes." She kissed him. "Yes." Kiss. "Yes." She grasped his ass and pressed.

Her permission made him whole.

He pushed into her, going slowly, restrained, though everything in him wanted to claim, to dominate—but he wanted her to enjoy it. "I don't want to hurt you," he panted the words.

"It doesn't," she gasped out as he pushed a little deeper. "It feels"—she sucked in a breath— "like"— another panted breath— "finding my way home."

He slid a little deeper and moaned, both because she felt so good gripping his cock with her tight heat, but also because her words pulled his heart in deeper. "You feel so good," he said. "Fuck, Tarley." Still, he held back, sweat beading on his skin as he restrained himself.

"More," she said, still holding his ass and testing movement with her hips. "Lachlan," she whimpered. "Please."

"Spread your legs wider," he ordered. "Tilt your hips." He reached down and grabbed her thighs, drawing one up and settling it on his hip.

She complied, allowing Lachlan the range to move a little deeper, and she gasped, nails biting his skin.

He smiled. "I never thought you'd do what I asked

you to–"

She grinned, then gasped as he pushed all the way in, his hips flush against hers.

Lachlan froze, unwilling now to rush this, because stars. "You feel so fucking good, Tarley. Oh my–" Sweat dripped down his arms as he held himself still, seated inside her.

And suddenly she moved, tilting her hips further to test the friction. "Oh," she said and moved some more.

"Fuck. I'm not going to last, Tarley," he groaned, his heart beating frantically inside his chest. He grunted as she moved against him again, knowing she was feeling him inside of her as much as seeking pleasure against her clit. "Tarley, I can't–"

"Let go, Lachlan," she panted. "I'm here. Please."

Her words—his words given back to him—unmoored him. He ground his hips against hers and she cried out, "Yes! Lachlan. Please," her nails biting into his back.

Suddenly he couldn't hold back. He withdrew, and she grabbed to pull him back, as he thrust all the way into her.

She cried out. "Yes. Lach, yes," over and over, until Lachlan lost himself, the rhythm erratic because he all he had become was need.

Her volume increased with his movement. The bed squealing, the frame hitting the wall with rhythmic thumps.

"Please Lach. Please," she begged.

He couldn't think, but he wanted to feel her come around his cock. "Tarley. Tarley. Touch yourself." He pushed into her, as she reached between them, touching herself as he drove into her again and again. Her cunt tightened around him, and she gasped then, whimpering as she found release once more.

Lachlan let go. His body tensed, everything exploding into her tight, wet, warmth. He grunted, sucked in a breath, and held it until the spasm of his orgasm abated. Then he eased himself down against Tarley, who wrapped her arms around him tightly.

Lachlan caught his breath against her shoulder, waiting for his vision to clear, enjoying being in her arms. Her hands in his hair, her fingers threading his locks, offered him something he'd never known he wanted. He'd been with women before, but he didn't stay, didn't let them to stay. Tarley's hands in his hair, moving over his back, down to the curve of his ass, back up to his neck, over his arms, back to his hair, made him feel as if he'd never been more known. More seen. As himself.

He nestled deeper into the crook of her neck. "Are you okay?"

She hummed. "Are you?"

Lachlan looked up so he could see her face illuminated by the moonlight. "I've never felt more like myself."

She was smiling as she opened her eyes and looked at him. "I feel… perfect." She stretched under him, the silk of her skin tantalizing.

The realization that he was going to marry this woman hit him in the center of his chest. Weeks ago, his father had insisted he marry a stranger. He'd balked and done everything in his power to undermine any possible betrothal negotiations. In retrospect, if he hadn't been an ass, he wouldn't have met this woman.

When Keyanna had suggested Tarley, he'd known it wouldn't be a hardship. Tarley was smart, determined, and pleasing to his eyes and body. He had decided they could forge a partnership amenable to both for the sake of Jast.

Now, though, looking at this woman lying under him, stretched out, content, offering him the smile he'd longed for and providing a touch he hadn't known he wanted, Lachlan recognized what he had with Tarley wasn't about Jast anymore.

This wasn't a matter of whether he would fall in love with her—he already was. But if Tarley Fareview couldn't learn to love him back, he wasn't sure how he'd ever recover.

Tarley

arley raced up the back stairwell, taking the steps two at a time to the queen's room to tell her the news. She anticipated the queen would be put out because she and Lachlan had disappeared but would ultimately be relieved at the outcome.

Watching her steps, Tarley navigated the dark corridor a bit more treacherous than the main stairwell with the ease of familiarity, her steps light with happiness, then slowed, knowing her smile might give her away. This morning she felt buoyant but didn't want to consider it too long or look too closely, because she knew Lachlan would be at the center of it.

He'd snuck out just before dawn, to be in his pallet when Trevis woke. One more reason he warmed her heart. Adding it to everything else. They'd lain in one another's arms talking about their lives. Lachlan told her about growing up in Jast, the pressures that had been put on him by his father. She'd shared about her mother's over-protectiveness, of growing up in Sevens. And just as the sky hinted the sun was nearing the horizon, she'd kissed him at the door and watched him slip down the stairs and back into the stables. She hadn't realized she'd missed what they'd created in the woods, until then.

Her attraction to him was a raging fire in a dry and brittle forest. She knew it wasn't just because she was lonely in Sevens, that when along came a handsome stranger, and she was just easy and desperate enough to fall into the trap of wanting him. Tarley had accused Auri of the same and insisted how could Auri know. Then she'd gone and done the same thing. She knew without a doubt, she was falling for this man, and it was more than their physical connection—it was the emotional bond they'd been forging for some time.

"Good morning, Tarley."

Tarley's gaze snapped up from her feet, and she tripped up the last step into the dark corridor, nearly falling into Dr. Allean Rufus.

Her smile cracked, breaking apart the joy in her chest. "What are you doing here? In the servants' hall?"

"Miss Crendell asked me."

"To what?"

"Check on a guest, I'd suspect."

The corridor was too small. Tarley's chest tightened as she recalled the incident in the woods. Grasping the wall to steady herself, she wrestled with the seed of a feeling she couldn't identify —but she knew she felt the need to flee.

The doctor was at her side, then, bringing his malodorous scent with him, a tense war between the loam of the forest, the musk of minerals, and something astringent. "Are you unwell, Miss Fareview?"

She stepped away. "I'm fine."

He sniffed as if smelling her, then cleared his throat, running a hand down his jacket, and tilting his blond head to offer her a sugar smile that curled the tight edges of his bright blue eyes—though Tarley had the impression his eyes weren't smiling. He just worked to make it look as if it were so.

"You avoided me last night, Miss Fareview."

Tarley straightened her spine. "Were you there?"

His bright eyes jumped to her face. "I'm wondering about your avoidance of me. Do you anticipate a better offer for matrimony coming your way? These things," he said, "are business endeavors to some extent. Should something happen to your father, or brother, I would care for you and your sisters."

He'd invaded her space, and Tarley's back was against the wall.

"Is that a threat?"

"Why would I do that?"

Footsteps on the stairwell weren't cause for Rufus to give her more space. Then Credence's voice resounded through the hallway, calling her name, "Tarley?"

A dark look clouded Rufus's features, and though she couldn't be sure in the dim light, his teeth looked wrong as he said, "I smell him," his voice a dark hiss of seething rage.

Credence stepped into the hallway. "What's going on here?" she asked, her gaze shifting between them. "Dr. Rufus?"

Rufus took a begrudging step back.

"He said he was up here to meet you," Tarley said, trying to understand Rufus's last comment, her heart flopping about in her stomach, drowning.

"The patient?" Dr. Rufus asked her.

"Not up here," Credence said. "The man is in the dining room. He fell–"

Rufus straightened and bowed his head slightly. "My mistake."

Rufus's gaze returned to Tarley one last time, and she shrank back against the wall, knowing without a doubt that whatever Rufus was playing at was over. He was going to be a problem, but she was at a loss how to address it. His mustache twitched with annoyance, but he retreated, then disappeared down the stairwell.

Credence watched him go, then turned and looked at Tarley. "What was that?"

"I don't–" she started.

The door to the queen's room cracked open, and

Scarlett's face appeared. "Is he gone?"

"He is," Tarley said.

Scarlett squeezed out the door. "An odious man."

"I take it you don't want me to accept his offer of marriage?" Tarley deadpanned. "It's only his third or fourth by now. Maybe I can finagle a fifth."

Scarlett rolled her eyes.

"I'll go see that he finds the right place to be," Credence said, then turned back. "Found your daughter, Scarlett."

"Thank you."

"How is she?" Tarley asked.

"A picture of health," Scarlett replied. "A bit miffed about something not going the way it was supposed to last night. Know what that's about?"

Tarley shook her head.

"What are you doing up here?"

"I came up to see… Rose."

Scarlett hummed. "Want to know something interesting? I went to look for you last night, and you were nowhere to be found."

"I left early."

"And Ollie was mysteriously absent as well."

Tarley didn't respond, figuring her mother was astute enough to put that together on her own. There wasn't any reason to confirm or deny. Not yet, anyway.

"Tarley."

"Mother. Don't."

"Where were you last night?" Scarlett grabbed Tarley's arm and slid her thumb against the ribbon tied around her wrist. "There was quite a stir with Auri. I knew she'd been sneaking out—but we met–"

"Nix."

Scarlett took her measure, her eyes drifting over Tarley's entire form. "You knew?"

"I've met him."

"When?"

"Weeks ago. But is that any of your business?"

"She lost her ribbon."

Tarley's hand circled her own. "What does it matter?"

"Everything!" her mother snapped, then lowered her voice. "Everything!" She stopped and glanced at the stairs. "There are things… I only want to protect each of you. You understand?"

"From what?" Tarley didn't understand her mother's adamancy. "Keeping Auri corralled in the cottage isn't good for her. Nix—whatever your objections—makes her happy."

"You don't understand anything."

"Because you haven't told us anything. You have all these…" Whatever it had been slipped away along with the thought. She blinked and couldn't remember what she'd even been thinking about.

"Why him?" Scarlett asked.

"Who?" Tarley blinked again, reorienting her mind, only she felt like she'd skipped over something.

"The stable boy."

"Trevis? Or Ollie."

"Humor me, Tarley. You know I'm not referring

to Trevis."

"Ollie is…"

"Be cautious. He isn't what he seems."

"And you would know?"

Scarlett's eyebrows rose in high arches, a look she'd perfected over the years. Then her eyes narrowed, and she drew a deep breath. "Perhaps you should bring Ollie home for dinner, then? Since you insist on… whatever it is you insist on."

Tarley was sure her joy about Lachlan was written all over her face, and her mother had a way of finding out the truth no matter the circumstances. She seemed to know all things, which was why Tarley knew Auri couldn't get away with sneaking out to date her handsome suitor.

"I'm a grown woman, Mother, and am perfectly capable of choosing my own path," Tarley whisper-yelled so as not to disturb the queen.

Scarlett caressed her hand and took a deep breath. "Bring him with you to dinner then—through the hedge." Scarlett released her. "Let us get to know him."

Tarley watched her disappear down the stairwell feeling as if her mother had acquiesced too easily, that there was more to her invitation than she was revealing. Then she turned to the doorway ready to face the queen, which she hoped would be an easier conversation.

Later, when Tarley walked into her small room after a full day's work with an appeased queen and a family dinner to attend, it was hard not to think of Lachlan in there with her. She missed his presence. When she looked at her bed, she imagined his large body between her thighs, his bulk under her quilt. Blood rushed to her extremities when she thought about what they'd done together, wishing he were with her now so they could do it again.

She'd seen him passing throughout the day. In between sightings, she'd extended an invitation to dinner, to which he'd grinned, informing her Scarlett had also stopped by the stable to invite him. His swagger was maddening. They agreed to meet at the mercantile, so she could pick up whatever her mother had ordered that morning, then walk together to the cottage.

She changed into a nicer dress for dinner, then she locked the door behind her, passing the stables without looking in to see if Lachlan was there, and walked down Sevens only thoroughfare.

It was filled with people, so unlike the night before when she'd walked it with Lachlan. Most with faces she didn't recognize, but those she did were friendly.

"Hello, Miss Fareview!" "Good afternoon, Miss Fareview." "How is your family, Miss Fareview?" She stopped to converse, happy to do so. Not a single soul brought up Ollie and her discovery of him in the woods—or their disappearance the night before—though perhaps they wouldn't when she was the center of speculation. When those conversations concluded, she continued.

Until she saw Rufus emerge from the door to his practice. Her step faltered, and she glanced around for an escape. *Turn the other way. Please turn the other way,* she intoned in her head as if perhaps her words could control him. But Dr. Rufus, turned in her direction, caught sight of her, and walked toward her with purposeful strides.

Tarley considered walking the opposite direction, but her pride kept her from it. Rather, she didn't want Rufus to know that seeing him made her want to run like a scared rabbit. While his initial attentions had proved tedious, now there was an undercurrent that frightened her, and she wasn't sure how to manage it.

"Miss Fareview," he said when he reached her and doffed his hat politely, only she knew he wasn't polite. He'd threatened her. He'd been cryptic in the hallway, but the tone had been menacing. As if proving her feelings right, he stepped close, his leg shifting her skirt.

She moved away from him. "Dr. Rufus. We need to stop meeting this way."

He smiled, showing nice, even teeth, his lips hidden

under groomed facial hair. The smile didn't reach his eyes. "We can finish our conversation that was so rudely interrupted."

"No, thank you," she replied and stepped around him.

He stepped in front of her. "I saw you. With him." He rasped the words, producing a strange sound in his chest. "You don't understand–"

"Saw me?"

"Last night."

Chills raced across her skin. "I don't know what–"

He leaned closer. "Lies." His eyes dropped to her waist, and he licked his lips. "Given the fact you were alone together in the woods, it won't come as a surprise to Sevens folk. Add to it your disappearance together last night." He tsked.

Tarley shouldered past him and continued walking.

Rufus caught up and grabbed her arm. "I would never hold any possible impending children against you should you find yourself in a way and would gladly… relish any bastard of yours."

She pulled her arm free from his grasp, hissing when she felt something sharp but didn't look, afraid to take her eyes from Rufus. "Leave me alone." She continued, hurrying to get to the mercantile.

"I can't, you see. It's impossible now."

She reached for the mercantile door, but Dr. Rufus spun her to face him. "I won't let you go, Miss Fareview."

She yanked out of his grasp and looked at her arm

noting the puncture marks in her sleeve. "You have done nothing but insult my person, my intelligence, and my womanhood. I wouldn't want to be near you, much less marry you, if you were the last man in the kingdom."

He had the decency to look abashed, but it quickly turned to something dark as he grabbed her shoulders, squeezing her too tight. "I'll escort you home. It isn't safe for a woman to journey through the woods on her own. There are stories about these woods—"

Her vision receded, Dr. Rufus, the buildings, the forest collapsing into a dark hole and leaving a view of the darkness behind, the sound of rapid breathing, the awful sense of fear. Then she blinked, back once more in the grip of Dr. Rufus.

She struggled, and his grasp tightened. She knew she couldn't go anywhere alone with him. "Unhand me."

"Are you going to make me say it?" He'd leaned closer.

She recoiled. "Let me go."

He yanked her closer. An unpleasant bolt shot through her body at his nearness, a warning.

"It was supposed to be me," he hissed, "and you soiled yourself with a stable boy. Disgusting," he said through a clenched jaw, as if he were trying to maintain a smile and present the illusion all was well between them to passersby. "You spoke to me, first. Me. You're mine. Why are you denying me?"

"Because she's already engaged," a voice

interrupted.

Looking over Rufus's shoulder, Tarley found Lachlan's hard gaze, and relief filled her chest.

Momentarily startled, Rufus's grip relaxed, and Tarley yanked free and stumbled away.

"The stable boy," Rufus sneered. His gaze raked up and down Lachlan. "Why am I not surprised to see you? You have a way of inserting yourself between me and what's mine."

Lachlan took several slow, even steps toward Rufus. Tarley noted the glaring contrast between them. Lachlan was tall and fit, Rufus was several hands shorter. Whereas Rufus appeared light, Lachlan was dark. Except, Rufus was evil to the core, if the last few moments were any indication, while Lachlan had proven his nobility of his character time and again.

Rufus took a step to avoid Lachlan, and Lachlan bypassed him, coming to stand before Tarley. "Do our plans still stand?" Lachlan asked and grinned at her.

"Yes," she answered and she loved that his smile deepened. "You're right on time."

"Excellent." He turned his attention to Rufus. Tarley thought she saw his smile harden and his eyes turn cold. "If you know what's good for you, Rufus, you'll forget you ever knew Tarley Fareview. In fact, let's make it any of the Fareviews. Your sight sickens me, and I can't guarantee that this *stable boy*, as you put it, won't use his fists the next time he sees you. Is that understood?"

Dr. Rufus's face reddened, but he seemed to know

he wouldn't be able to contend with Lachlan. "You have no idea," he said, his eyes dark.

"I think I have some. You're not a nice man, Rufus. So one more thing," Lachlan said, straightening Rufus's lapel on his jacket, a little roughly. "If I hear one word disparaging Miss Fareview's character or any word of insinuation that she's beyond reproach for saving a man's life, just one word"—Lachlan tapped Rufus's chest with enough force to make a sound— "I know who I'll look for first. Are we clear?"

"Shall we, then, Ollie?"

Lachlan offered her his elbow. "We shall."

Sliding her arm through his, she caught his scent— a heady concoction of the same scent of the soap she used but smelling so different on him—that both invigorated her and made her feel safe. She loved how she had to tilt her chin to look up at his face, now offering her that smile—a gentle look just for her. His dark brown hair framed his face, giving him a mischievous, boyish quality.

"Following me again?" she asked, glancing over her shoulder as Rufus skulked away.

"I told you I would, remember?" His eyes danced as he looked at her, a jaunty shade of gray green with a ring of copper near his pupil that burst outward. "Wherever you go, I will follow."

Tarley reached out and touched him, smoothing the jacket that was a touch too big. "Thank you."

His smile faded. "I saw his hands on you, and I wanted to end him. Maybe I should have."

Tarley swallowed at the dark words, but they didn't make her feel fear, instead pushing the pace of her heart, making her want to kiss him.

"Let's forget Dr. Allean Rufus." She linked her arm with his. "Are you sure you want to face dinner with my family?"

His eyes curled at the corners with his grin. "How could I possibly say 'no' to my future mother-in-law?"

Tarley opened her mouth, then shut it. "There aren't many who can deny Scarlett Fareview," she finally said. "You'd think she was the queen of Sevens."

Lachlan laughed. "I thought that was you."

"Well," she said as they left Sevens behind, "don't tell me I didn't warn you."

Lachlan

Scarlett Fareview had stopped by the stables before she'd left the inn earlier that day and had invited Lachlan to dinner. "Come with Tarley," she'd said. "She's supposed to invite you, but knowing my daughter–"

"Yes, ma'am," he'd said, understanding immediately what she meant, but elated because Tarley had indeed invited him. "I'll look forward to it."

Trevis had then proceeded to badger him about Scarlett's invitation the rest of the day, teasing and cajoling, but even that hadn't kept Lachlan from smiling like a fool.

Of course he'd started the day rather proud of himself, after the night before. Each time he thought about Tarley crying his name as she'd come, knowing he'd given her pleasure, he wanted to go find her and do it again.

But he didn't. He dug in with his tasks instead, and suddenly Tarley was walking past the stables dressed in a dark dress and looking as pretty as a painting. He'd slapped soap and water where it needed to go, changed into his nicest clothes, and hurried toward the mercantile where they'd agreed to meet.

Working with Trevis had been an education about all things in Sevens, providing Lachlan could sift through the kid's extraneous information. One point included the importance of the Fareview family. Lachlan hadn't really understood until he caught up with Tarley and discreetly followed her down the street, admiring the view. She stopped and spoke to a host of people along the way. With each one, she smiled politely. In every interaction, the people she interacted with were enamored, which he understood completely.

Tarley Fareview was beautiful and smart and poised. And she was equally tough and stubborn and opinionated. His insides surged as he observed her, not only knowing her as he did now, but also knowing she was his. That possessive awareness twisted his gut with the memories of kissing her, of being between her thighs and hearing her come apart under him. This frustrating, beautiful, independent woman was dragging him into a different version of himself, and he couldn't say he hated it. But it just made him uncomfortable. And worried. What if she changed her mind?

But then, tonight was about telling her family, and she hadn't sent him back to the inn after the showdown with Dr. Rufus. At present, they were walking down a shadowy lane toward her family's home. Though, Lachlan was still seething after seeing Rufus's hands on her, hearing his vile words, and he frowned and glanced at Tarley, sure that despite her calm demeanor, she must have been affected by the interaction. He had been.

"How are you?" he asked, breaking the silence. "After Rufus."

She looked at him, then back ahead. "I'm fine."

"Are you?" he asked and looked at her sideways. "I'm not sure I am."

She glanced at him. He adjusted the packages he carried for her.

Tarley stopped him and took some. "I was worried. But now I'm not." She offered a slight smile. "He seemed to get your message."

Lachlan leaned forward and pressed a kiss to her cheek, lingering for a moment. He wasn't sure Rufus had gotten it. There was something odd about the man.

"I'm glad you were there," she said quietly.

Lachlan pulled back to look at her face, then grinned. "That sounded like it was hard to say."

She smiled then, her face tilted down to hide it.

Lachlan hooked a finger under her chin and coaxed her gaze up to his. "Don't hide your smile, Princess. It's too beautiful and does things to my insides."

She blushed and turned away, resuming their walk down the lane.

"So what should I expect?" he asked, changing the subject. He needed to, based on the direction of his thoughts.

"Chaos."

"That sounds pleasant."

She snickered. "My family is… something. The truth is, I don't know how it will be. None of us have ever brought anyone home."

"Ever?"

"Lach, you've been in Sevens for weeks now. Can you imagine me bringing someone home?"

He hung up on the way she'd said his name. A nickname, and it made his insides sputter and his brain stall, replacing it with the sound of her coming. He cleared his throat. "Right. I guess not. That makes me excessively happy."

She glanced at him, then stared straight ahead once more.

Lachlan had grown up in a palace among royals and nobles. He'd been to court and watched the interplay and politicking. He might have hated it, but he could engage with the best of them. And Tarley, common woman from this tiny village of Sevens at the northernmost settlement of Kaloma, would have fit into the palace with her affect as much as anyone he'd ever met. She was going to make a perfect queen, and the realization filled him with pride.

"Excessively?"

"You have no idea." He grinned. "How often do you take this journey from the inn?"

"Usually once a week."

He frowned at the thought of her walking this alone. "By yourself?"

"Sometimes."

He swallowed. The Whitling Woods were beautiful, but they were also terrifying. The gnarled tree trunks grew in tight profusion, their covered branches, stretching out to cast dark shadows over everything.

"You don't find walking through these woods frightening?"

"Why? Do you?"

"Yes." Lachlan was confident enough to admit fear. He figured it was foolish to pretend otherwise. "Do you think less of me for it?"

She glanced down at her feet, a smile touching her lips. "Not at all."

"Surprised?" he asked, happy she did.

Her arm brushed his. "I haven't met many men willing to admit being afraid of something."

"Maybe they're hesitant to appear weak."

"Do you see it as a weakness?" she asked.

He turned to her, following the line of her jaw with his eyes, then the slope of her neck, wanting more than anything to press a kiss there, but also knowing that doing so would mean foregoing their conversation.

That felt far more important in the scheme of their future. "I don't, but there are many who might. What's more important to me is if you do."

She turned her head to look at him again. "I don't."

"And why is that?"

"I think even the bravest of us feels afraid. It isn't being afraid that's weakness, it's how we behave in the face of fear."

Lachlan couldn't respond at first, her words resonating deep within him. "Spoken like a sage," he finally said.

They continued walking, silence weaving between them. Lachlan could almost hear her thinking, his own thoughts so loud between his ears.

"Are you afraid of tonight?" she asked.

"Terrified." He grinned.

"Be serious."

"I am. Goodness, your father and brother could squish me and then use me for fertilizer in these woods." He shuddered theatrically.

She stifled a grin. "Mattias isn't home."

"I doubt your father is less effective on his own. He's a giant."

She smiled openly at him, her face brightening.

Lachlan stopped, drawing her to a stop. "I love it when you smile."

Her smile faltered, but he could see it wasn't because she had lost her joy. Her eyes flicked to his mouth. "Would you like to hear what I am truly afraid of, Tarley?"

She nodded.

"I find myself afraid of how I feel," he said, hoping this risk would be worth it.

She swallowed. "Feel? What are you feeling?"

"So much all at once."

She nodded, and that made him hopeful.

"And I can't seem to grab hold of any one to assign it a name."

"Why does that make you afraid?" she eventually asked after they'd resumed their walk.

He glanced at her, understanding how hard she made him work for her attention. Each time she bestowed it felt like a gift. "Things have been given to me, handed to me, fixed for me. Gifts have been bestowed and I accepted them as if these things were my due. I have taken and withheld without consideration to consequences."

"And–"

"And," Lachlan said, then drew a deep breath, understanding now where he was going with his thoughts. "I have never been afraid that my feelings might not be reciprocated."

"Why?"

"Because I didn't care. I didn't reciprocate anyone's feelings—not that common feelings were shared. I think perhaps in most of my interactions except for my family and Ollie, and you, others used me as much as I used them."

"And now?"

He stopped walking and turned to her.

Thinking back to all his interactions with Tarley since meeting her, she had only met him with resolve, stubborn pride, and annoyance. He wanted to prove himself to her that he could be more than just Crown-Prince Lachlan. He wanted to earn her favor because she clearly didn't bestow it easily. This woman didn't care who he was in his past, only who he was in the present.

"I guess that's the right question," he said. "Because I do care, now. Very much."

"Hmm," she said and continued their walk.

Lachlan wondered if maybe he should have said more but didn't know what to say, slightly insecure in her silence. Was it believable to think he loved her? Was he even capable of love?

"We're here," she said when they reached an opening in a hedge. He'd have missed the doorway had he not been with Tarley. The tall natural wall appeared as if the forest had grown up and around whatever was inside, shielding it, dense with dark green foliage and bright, white blooms with a pistil a shade darker.

He followed her inside to a corridor even darker than the lane. Lachlan looked over his shoulder, but the doorway had disappeared, leaving him to wonder if the path was curved, even though he'd been sure they'd been walking a straight line.

It wasn't much longer they emerged from the corridor into a forested glen, where he followed Tarley through the meadow, past a barn to a quaint cottage. Wisps of smoke rose into the blue sky streaked with orange, the sun now hovering above the horizon. Golden light reached through the mullioned windowpanes, the flower boxes beneath were bright with sprays of blooms of varying colors clearly cared for with adept hands.

The door opened before they were even to the steps and Brinna darted out, squealing with joy as launched herself into Tarley's arms. "I had a dream—" Brinna stopped abruptly when she noticed Lachlan, and pulled away from Tarley, smoothing the front of her blue dress. "I was afraid you'd finally succumbed to Mr. Rufus's persuasion."

Lachlan suppressed a smile. He could see Brinna was teasing Tarley.

"Why would you think that?" Tarley frowned. "You remember Ollie?"

"Good evening, Miss Fareview."

"Call me Brinna," she said, "otherwise you'll be 'Miss Fareviewing' the lot of us, and it will get overly confusing." She grinned, and Lachlan was entertained by this sister's energy. Tarley was so different from her.

"Watch out, Brinna," Tarley said in that dry, acerbic way of hers. "I'll bet you're next on Dr. Rufus's list. You or Jessamine, that is," Tarley snickered.

Brinna linked her arm with Lachlan's. "Certainly not." She wiggled her eyebrows. "What about Auri?"

"Her too."

"Have you met Auri's suitor yet? I don't think he'd approve and might turn Dr. Rufus to ash with one of his looks."

Tarley laughed, which Lachlan loved. "That's so true," Tarley exclaimed. "He's a sight, isn't he."

Jealousy pulsed through him like lightning at the sound of her assessment of this other man.

"He is a dream," Brinna breathed.

Tarley looked at Brinna, her eyebrows high. It was clear that Brinna seemed oblivious. "He's here?"

"Yes!" she whispered, leaning around Lachlan toward Tarley, who was realizing he was inconsequential in this conversation.

"You both have given me hope." Brinna's gentle gray eyes threaded with shades of blue flicked to Lachlan as she laughed. "There's hope for Jessamine and me yet."

"There's always Dr. Rufus," Tarley said from behind him as Brinna, guiding him toward the cottage, laughed good-naturedly. Tarley leaned forward and said for him alone, "Enter at your own risk."

Lachlan smiled as his gut clenched with desire for her; he adored Tarley this way, playful and unguarded.

Brinna pulled him through the arched doorway, and Lachlan looked over his shoulder at Tarley, who offered him a smirk, then mouthed, "I warned you."

Once inside, the rest of the family moved about in a flurry around a small main room of the cottage. Within the main room, there was a living area where Tomas stood with another man—dark haired and handsome in a broody way—an area where Auri and their oldest sister were setting a large table, and a kitchen where Scarlett was hefting a pot toward a countertop. It smelled divine—rosemary and garlic with a tinge of something spicy.

"Ollie's here," Brinna announced, releasing his arm to drift to the table, leaving him just inside the entrance. Tarley stopped at his side as Auri and Jessamine turned their way. Their faces and bodies leaned to catch Tarley's eyes. It wasn't subtle.

"Mother said to set a place for him." Auri grinned and winked.

Lachlan glanced at Tarley. "She did." It was his turn to smirk.

Tarley blushed.

"I did," Scarlett said from across the room. "Auri, be sure to introduce him to Mr. Uraiahs."

Auri beamed, plates in hand, and moved across the room to the handsome man next to their father. "A quick interruption. Nixus, Ollie." She waved between them. "Ollie, Nixus."

Lachlan shuffled the packages more securely in one arm. "How do you do?"

"Never better, considering this is my first invitation. There's time to change my mind," he said, offering Auri a hint of a smile along with an arched eyebrow.

"Ignore him," Auri whispered to Lachlan. "He's in a funk because Mother invited you right away, and it took him months to secure an invitation."

Nixus huffed. "I'm not in a funk."

Tomas chuckled.

Lachlan wanted to explore his invitation a bit

further, as if it was a sign of sorts, but Tarley interrupted, her eyes meeting his.

"Let me take those." She leaned forward, and as she reached for the packages; her hands brushed his. Sparks burned through him with memories of touching her, kissing her. He wanted to do it again, suddenly.

"This is going to be fun," she whispered, her lips near his jaw. Then she walked away, still smiling.

He'd never seen her like this, as if every barrier she'd put in place was gone. There'd been glimpses of it when they'd sat around the campfire telling stories. There'd been her letting go last night. This, however, was another facet of Tarley that made her shine even brighter in his eyes. His heart compressed, and he wished they were alone. He wanted to tell her… What did he want to tell her?

Tomas stuffed his hands into his back pockets and rocked back onto his heels. "Nice to see you again, Ollie. I don't remember catching your family name last time we met."

Lachlan nodded, reminding himself not to use his real name. "Berkman, sir. Has Mattias returned?"

Tomas frowned, his eyes flickering toward the kitchen, then back to Lachlan. "Not yet, and best we avoid that topic. Fareview women aren't ones to withhold their opinions–"

"I'll say," Nix muttered.

"–and I've heard mightily from Mrs. Fareview about allowing her only son to ride toward danger," Tomas finished.

"He seems a capable young man," Lachlan said.

"I sent my brothers when Auri mentioned it." Nixus took a sip of whatever was in the glass he was holding.

"You did?" Tomas tilted his head.

"Auri expressed her worry."

That was all he said, and Lachlan understood completely.

When the silence stretched a bit too long, Nixus added, "He probably won't know they are there, but you know—just in case."

"Hmm," Tomas said, his tone so much like Tarley's. "I'm obliged. Though measures of safety rarely matter to mothers, as I'm sure you can attest to." He glanced between Nixus and Lachlan.

The mention of his mother hit Lachlan in the chest. Stars, he missed her. He nodded.

"Now." Tomas clapped Lachlan on the back. "Call me, Tom." He paused, then muttered, "Berkman. Berkman. That name sounds familiar. I can't remember where I would have heard it." His warm eyes looked over at Lachlan.

The whispers drew Lachlan's attention to the four women—Jessamine, Brinna, Auri and Tarley— standing shoulder-to-shoulder, staring at him and Nix.

Tom laid one large hand on Lachlan's shoulder, the other on Nix's. "Don't worry about them. They are gatekeepers for one another, but they are a good sort." Then he walked past, instructing his daughters to be nice.

Tarley rolled her eyes and turned away, saying loudly, "It was him or Mr. Rufus."

"No contest then," Lachlan said, joining them at the table.

The sisters howled with laughter.

Tarley glanced at him, smiling, happy.

At that moment, clarity hit him in the breastbone like a punch thrown by Captain Johesha. He loved her. It wasn't just a cascade into love he'd thought he was sliding through. That had started in the woods the moment he saw her standing like a woodland fairy wet with rain and golden with pleasure. No. The kaleidoscope of feelings he'd been trying to untangle couldn't be unraveled because they represented a part of the whole design. That complete picture was that Lachlan was completely in love with his future bride.

His forced future bride.

His heart pinched in his aching chest.

He swallowed.

Scarlett set a final dish on the table. "Welcome, Ollie and Nixus."

He took his cues from the rest, moving around the table to their places. Tarley grabbed his hand and pulled him to her side, making room for him to sit next to her on a bench.

The wooden table had clearly been made by an artisan, the wood smooth and polished but simple with two benches, one on each side, and two chairs, one at each end. It was set with the flourishes of a home: simple dishes, simple flatware, simple glasses, and sprigs of flowers and herbs.

Lachlan was used to beauty and an opulent table. Gilded dressings of candles, of flatware, and dishes threaded with gold and silver. Crystal wine glasses that sparkled in the light. Rich, decadent food, overflowing and served to him. Yet, standing there, looking at that family surrounding that table, the love that went into setting it, made it the most beautiful table he'd ever seen in his life.

Tom gave thanks the forest for its bounty, and when he'd concluded, the family erupted with movement and sound.

Tarley offered him a bowl of mashed potatoes toward him. "I'll hold it while you put some on your plate," she said, not meeting his gaze.

"Thank you," he said and scooped a spoonful onto his plate. When he took the dish, their fingers brushed, and those pulses of lightning sizzled Lachlan's thoughts. He handed the dish to Tom and turned back to the next, wild greens in herbs and butter, and the next, slices of roast pork followed by herb gravy, then wild fruit that Tarley suggested he put on the meat. With everything was dished out, he found he missed the ability to touch her and wondered how he might find a way to do it again, content for now to feel her leg pressed against his.

"Have you been to Jast, then, Ollie?" Scarlett asked. "Living so far north?"

"I thought the border was closed," Jessamine said.

"It is." Lachlan pressed a napkin to his mouth.

"But people cross all the time."

"Berkman," Tom said again, and Lachlan knew he was putting puzzle pieces into place, and once he had them, he looked at Lachlan again. "The Prime-Advisor-to-the-King-of-Jast Berkman?"

Lachlan wasn't surprised Tomas would place the name if he was half as astute as Tarley. Nerves coiled in his back with concern. It wasn't so much that the Fareviews might ascertain who he was but rather that he'd been lying, and Tarley along with him.

All this suddenly felt wrong somehow.

Lachlan's breath caught, and he glanced at Tarley frowning next to him.

He had to call off the betrothal. He wanted Tarley, but not because she'd been forced to marry him. He couldn't take her from all she loved. Perhaps that wasn't what was best for Jast. And maybe his father was right—he'd make a terrible king because he couldn't put Jast ahead of his feelings for her.

Lachlan replaced his napkin in his lap, his arm brushing Tarley's. "Yes, sir."

Tom's eyes flew to Tarley. "Did you know that?"

Tarley turned her head to look at Lachlan, and the strands of lavender in her eyes flaring with awareness, but also something else. "Actually–."

Tarley was going to tell. He reached under the table, grasped her hand, and squeezed. Her eyes swung to his, confused. "It's a long story," he told Tomas.

"One you obviously haven't shared," Brinna said.

Tom made a harumphing noise. "Well, there's not

a lot of pomp and circumstance in this house, but we might have tried a bit harder."

Nixus made a noise.

"Are you pouting?" Auri asked.

"I don't pout," he answered. "I brood."

Jessamine giggled. "I'm sorry, Father, but as much as you'd like to think we would try, what you see is what you get, Ollie."

Tarley pulled her hand from his, and he could tell she was angry with him, confused. He noticed the way her head turned as she spoke with her mother about the queen.

Suddenly, Lachlan needed to finish this meal, even as much as he was enjoying it. He needed to get Tarley alone, to explain. He would lay his heart out on the altar for her to either take or sacrifice, but it was time to face his fears.

So he sat, polite as he'd been groomed to be, and waited, anxious to face feelings and lay himself bare to the woman he loved, terrified to face repercussions that had the power to eviscerate him. But he knew it was time to stop pretending.

Tarley

Tarley sat at dinner wide awake, wondering how she'd been wandering through Sevens asleep all this time. She couldn't get her conversation with Lachlan on the way to the cottage out of her mind. He was right. She was afraid of all she was feeling. Afraid it was weakness rather than strength.

Except his honesty illuminated her own struggle. Her weakness wasn't the fear, but her failure to face it. She was always running away. Worse yet, lying to herself that doing so was her being strong and capable, but instead it was just hiding and making herself smaller and invisible.

Maybe the queen had given her an opportunity to

be strong, to sacrifice herself for the greater good. And Tarley was ready to sacrifice herself on the altar of Kaloma for all women, only last night, being with Lachlan hadn't been a sacrifice at all. She hadn't given herself away but rather staked claim to who she was, complete.

With Lachlan.

It was ludicrous. She was sitting with her family as images of being with Lachlan, the sensations, the pleasure accosted her, all because Lachlan was sitting next to her, his thigh pressed against hers. All because there was this energy arcing between them every time she looked at him and found his eyes following her. All because he'd shared what growing up in Jast was like, because of what he'd said to Mr. Rufus, because he'd admitted he was afraid of the woods, because he spoke to her like an equal. All because he was kind and gracious interacting with her family. All because she'd agreed to a marriage and the lines of what that truly meant were blurring.

"Did you know?" her father was asking because he'd just placed the name Berkman with Jast. She knew he'd figure it out. And now was as good a time as any to share the news.

She glanced at Lachlan; she wasn't going to run anymore. "Actually," she started.

But then Lachlan squeezed her hand under the table.

"It's a long story," he said, maintaining the ruse.

Her heart cramped with unease and confusion as

her eyes swung to meet his. She pulled her hand from his, and his eyes begged her to understand, to trust him, which melted away just as quickly. "Our group was attacked like the queen," he said, turning back to her father. "And I got separated from the royal party."

Afraid that what was happening was beyond her control and her newly acknowledged feelings were about to be crushed, she sat, heart pounding, realizing Lachlan maybe hadn't ever given her a reason not to trust him, but he had the capability to hurt her.

"Are they–" Brinna started, her face pale.

"I don't know," Lachlan admitted and shook his head. "I've sent word with the help of Rose to find out."

"Have you heard any word?" Scarlett asked.

Lachlan looked down at his plate. "I haven't."

The conversation moved forward, eventually offering Tarley an opportunity to lean toward Lachlan. "What are you doing?"

He turned his head and whispered, "It's just–" But he stopped.

Tarley leaned back to look closer at him.

He shook his head slightly and glanced at the table.

"How did you meet?" Tarley heard Jessamine ask Nixus and Auri.

But Tarley couldn't concentrate on their answer. For the life of her, she couldn't rationalize why Lachlan would change his mind about sharing, unless he'd changed his mind about marrying her. The thought made it suddenly hard to breathe, which made her angry.

"In the woods," Auri said and turned to smile up at Nixus.

"Magical woods," Lachlan replied, and his eyes skipped back to her.

"Very," Nixus said, looking at Auri.

Being out of control was unsettling. Tarley couldn't get herself back together, sitting there trying to be calm and collected, to smile and behave as if nothing about what was happening at that table was out of the ordinary when her world suddenly felt like it had tilted, and she was sliding away toward a calamity.

Why had he changed his mind?

And why did she suddenly care? She hadn't wanted to get married, remember?

Dinner progressed at a snail's pace, considering she wanted to be anywhere but there, but Tarley did her best to keep herself together. Lachlan was being his usual charming self as if nothing had changed between them.

She wanted to both scream at him and clutch him against her.

After helping to clean and sitting politely for too long, eventually he asked her, "Are you ready? To walk back?"

"I'll hitch up the wagon to drive you," her father said, moving to stand.

"No." She reminded herself to look normal. "I could use the walk. And I'll be with Ollie. Is that okay with you?" she asked Lachlan.

Just then, she wanted to get into a giant fight, and after, she wanted to fuck him, which was ludicrous. She was losing her ability to think clearly.

He glanced at her, a look that connected with the base of her spine, sending warmth right up into her shoulders. Her skin heated, her face reddened, and she was convinced he knew what she was thinking, because he straightened, the tension between them becoming something writhing and alive.

He swallowed, offered her father a tight smile, and nodded.

"But it's dark," Tomas said, confused. "I always drive you back–"

"We'll be fine," Tarley said.

Her father frowned, but she ignored him.

Auri giggled.

Tarley ignored her sister. "We'll be fine," she repeated. "Thank you."

Her father balked, but Tarley's focus was completely on Lachlan and the bigger question: why had he changed the plan?

After Lachlan helped her into her cloak, with what seemed great care not to touch her, Tarley offered each of her family members a hug and a kiss on the cheek, exchanging words and laughter as she did. Lachlan expressed his gratitude. And finally, the door closed behind them.

Rather than turn on him there in front of the cottage and demand an explanation, she retraced their steps to the hedge past the barn and across the meadow. She heard Lachlan's steps right behind her, felt the heat of his presence at her back, both longing to feel his touch and wanting to push him away.

She ducked into the darkened archway of the hedge, the fragrance of the white flowers overpowering. Unable to wait, she turned to face Lachlan, and the moment he entered the shadow of the hedge she grabbed him by his jacket and pulled him forward—but instead of yelling at him, she pressed her lips to his.

His hands framed her face, and he said her name against her mouth.

She pushed him away, bumping against the wall of the hedge with her back. "What the hell, Lachlan. We were supposed to tell them! Why did you do that? You changed your mind?"

"No." He grasped her hips, pulling her back against him, his lips connecting with her cheek, then sliding back toward her mouth. "Yes. No."

She let his lips work over her skin, turning her head to meet his mouth while saying, "Which is it?"

"I can't marry you–"

Her heartbeat suspended, waiting for the rest of her world to be torn away when he admitted it had all been a mistake. Grasped his face, she pushed him away. "What?"

He sighed and stepped back, giving her more space, but his hands remained on her hips. "I want to marry you, Tarley, but I can't if it means forcing you to marry. Forcing you to choose me because of a treaty, that sacrifice, it's wrong. You have a life, a family, and what kind of monster would I be to force you into—" He stopped and disconnected, running a hand through his hair as he sighed.

She wished she could see him more clearly in the dark. "You still want to be with me?" she asked, her heartbeat changing from fear to something more vital.

"More than anything. But as you and me. Tarley and Lachlan. Not Kaloma and Jast. I want you, Tarley, just like this. I want your anger, your passion, your stubbornness, your pride, your arguments, your kisses. I want your love. Because that's what I know—and maybe I don't deserve it—but I fucking love you." He grabbed her hips with a hand, then stood there in the darkness, silent and waiting.

Her heart began beating faster and more frenzied, the anger and fear gone and making way for need and longing, for that vitality she had yet to identify. Rather than ponder it, she closed the distance between them.

"Say something," he said. "Put me out—"

She hushed him with a finger pressed to his lips. "Not yet." Sliding her hands into his hair, she pushed him up against the wall of the hedge and pressed her mouth to his.

He moaned her name into her mouth.

"I said to be quiet," she ordered him. "I need you to understand my answer." She wanted this moment with him. "Behavior speaks the truth, yes?" She slid her tongue across his lips and ran her hands over his shoulders, down his arms as she tilted her head.

He groaned, his hands leaving hers and jerking her against him. His mouth opened wider, and his tongue collided with hers. His palms found her face, framing it as he kissed her first with fire, then with tenderness.

"I need you," she said between kisses, reaching between them, grabbing at his pants to unfasten them. "I want you."

"Here?" he asked, but didn't wait for her answer, pushing her hands away to unbutton his trousers, mouth pressed to hers, walking her back until she was pressed against the hedge once more.

"Yes. Here." She pulled up her skirt, the rustle equal in sound to her panted breaths. "Please—I want this. You and me. Lachlan–"

"Tarley. You mean it? You choose me? This?" He reached down, grasped her ass, and lifted her. She wrapped her legs around his hips, wishing her dress away, her skirts pushed up, an explosion of fabric between them.

His erection pressed against her core, and she moaned. "Yes. Lachlan. Please. Don't make me wait."

"Fuck, Tarley," he said, his hand sliding between them over her underclothes, finding that place that made her gasp. "Hold on," he said against her mouth.

"There," she gasped and gripped his shoulders, tilting her hips toward his touch. "There."

"I've been fantasizing about this all day." He tore through her undergarment, ruining the fabric.

Under different circumstances, his forcefulness might have bothered her, but not then, not with him.

She loved it. Loved that Lachlan's need met her own. The wildness was consuming them both, burning through what was between them like a wildfire, and Tarley wanted more, moaning, moving against him, holding the nape of his neck with one hand and a shoulder with another. "Make me yours, Lachlan."

He groaned at her words. "Mine," he ground out. His body pressed against hers, holding her in place, though there was much to be desired in the hedge's support. "You're mine, Tarley." As the silky tip of his cock pressed against her entrance, he slid the head up to connect with the origin of her pleasure. "What do you feel?"

"You. Gods, Lachlan. Inside me—"

"What do you feel?" he repeated, sliding his head back and forth.

"Stars," she breathed into his ear and tilted her hips into the sensation. Images of Lachlan flashed in her mind's eye as pleasure rolled through her like rapids on the River Grimz. "So much. Too much."

"Tell me," he ordered.

"Don't leave me," she said. "I'll follow you—"

"I'll follow you."

She cried out against the skin of his cheek.

"Come for me, love."

Lachlan continued to use his cock on her until she gasped, "I'm coming, Lach. Please!"

Then he reached around to grip her shoulders and pressed her down onto him, burying himself all the way until the skin of his hips met hers.

Tarley cried out, and he captured her cry with his mouth, grunting as he moved inside her.

"I said to hold on," he growled. "Hold the hedge."

Tarley reached up and grabbed onto the branches. Lachlan held her hips, helping her ride him as he thrust into her again and again. She held onto him with her legs and panted as he rammed into her, reveling in the feeling of him filling her, at the sensations alive inside her like a coiling creature needing to break out, filling her to overflowing.

"I love to feel you inside me," she gasped. "I love that we fight. I love that you listen to me. I love your smile." Her words wouldn't stop, panted out as Lachlan fucked her. "Your smile. I love this. Lachlan. Oh. Lachlan. I love you."

And suddenly she understood what was most vital: love.

It wasn't a sacrifice, it wasn't weakness, because she loved him. Tarley's heart pinched with the awareness, the acknowledgement taking her by surprise. She sucked in a breath as heat exploded from her chest to her extremities. A tingle twinged at her wrists, increasing in intensity before driving back through her body to her heart. And she came again, crying out.

He covered her sounds with his mouth on hers. A deep, guttural sound escaped him followed by a raspy, "Fuck, Tarley," ground out through his teeth, still pumping into her until he panted against her lips, "I'm coming." And with a final thrust, he grunted and shuddered against her, still holding her up against the hedge, gasping for breath as he did.

Tarley released her wobbly legs, Lachlan's body easing from hers, and she held him while they both caught their breath.

"Tarley." Lachlan lifted his head, and though she knew he couldn't see her in the darkness inside the hedge, she pictured his eyes taking her in. "I love you," he said, grabbing her face between his hands. "So fucking much." He kissed her, only it was sweet and filled with something new.

Tarley's heartbeat was loud in her ears as she threw her arms around him. "I was afraid…"

"I was too," he admitted, kissing her neck. "But I'm not afraid anymore," he said against her skin. "You make me brave."

Her heart rate increased, echoing in her ears.

"What does this mean? We're still getting married, right?"

"Now you don't have a choice," he growled and pressed his mouth to hers. "You're mine, Tarley. Always and forever."

She kissed him back, her heart thundering in her ears.

Suddenly Lachlan drew back, and though she couldn't see his face, she watched his shadowed head tilt. "Do you hear that?"

The thundering echo of her heart echoed the galloping horse moving quickly down the road. With a flurry of movement, they righted themselves. Tarley smoothed her skirts and made sure her hair was in place as much as she could as Lachlan refastened his trousers, shoving his shirt into the waistband. They rushed from the hedge back toward the cottage as the rider dropped from the saddle.

"Mattias?" Tarley called out.

Her brother turned, just as the rest of the family burst from the cottage, golden light bursting out behind them. He looked different—older and more worldly somehow, as if he'd been touched by magic to make him… more.

"Mattias!" Scarlett moved through the bodies. "You're home!" She rushed to him and wrapped him in a hug. "I was so worried. You must be hungry. There's some dinner."

"I can't stay," he said, even his voice deeper, though more strange than different. He searched each face, and when he saw Lachlan he stopped. "Trevis said you'd be here."

"Did you get the message to her?" Tarley asked, referring to Princess Meera.

"Yes," he replied, his eyes still stuck on Lachlan.

"Then what took so long?" Scarlett asked.

He turned to look at her. "I couldn't leave her with them. They were already on their way to Sevens when I found her."

"Where is she now?" Lachlan asked.

Mattias turned once more to Lachlan, his eyes narrow and hard—a look Tarley didn't associate with her brother. "The Copper Pot. Only they're not the only royals there. There's a group from Jast," he said, his eyes landing on Lachlan once more with accusation. "Including someone claiming to be Ollie Berkman."

Lachlan

Lachlan's heart, already overflowing, threatened to burst. A group from Jast! They'd come!

Tarley's fingers twined with his.

"Are you certain?" he heard himself ask, though he wondered if he was still connected to his body.

Tarley squeezed his hand, bringing him back to earth.

He squeezed hers back. "I need a horse." He couldn't rein in his thoughts. He was a bundle of emotion. First Tarley and her love. Now his people. Ollie!

"Why is there an Ollie Berkman waiting at The Copper Pot?" Tomas asked. He was scowling, the family's faces varying between shock, trepidation, and mistrust.

Lachlan opened his mouth, but Tarley stepped forward, between them. "I lied."

"We lied," Lachlan said, drawing her back to his side. "We thought it would be best."

"Why would it ever be best to lie?" Mattias asked.

"Someone tried to kill him," Tarley said. "Like the queen." She paused, glanced at Lachlan before adding, "So it seemed like the right thing to do—to protect him."

"We?"

"Us. The queen."

Her family looked at one another, and Scarlett asked, "The queen knows? What is the truth? Who are you?"

"Lachlan Nikolas, Mrs. Fareview," he admitted, dipping his head toward her.

Brinna squealed, "The Crown Prince of Jast?"

Nixus snorted. "Is that all?"

"Nix." Auri bumped against him.

Lachlan looked at Tarley. "You did say Brinna would be excited."

"See?" Tarley grinned.

"I don't see how this is funny," Scarlett snapped, facing Tarley. "You knew this whole time?"

Tarley nodded, gripping Lachlan's hand tightly. "There's more to tell you–"

"More?" Tomas asked.

Lachlan cleared his throat. As much as he wanted to tell them, to reveal the wonderful news, he knew he was needed immediately. "I need to get back to the inn as quickly as possible. There's so much to say." He looked at Tarley, hoping she'd understand his duty. "And—"

"The queen." Tarley nodded.

"Take Ferdi," Mattias offered, holding out the reins to the gelding.

Lachlan took them. "Thank you, Mattias."

Tarley stepped back, toward her family. "I'll be right behind you. I can tell them."

Lachlan hesitated, not wanting to be apart from her for that announcement. Needing her with him because he didn't know what he was riding toward at the inn. He stepped toward Tarley, wanting to grab hold of her and keep her with him but also aware he needed to honor her needs in addition to his own.

She seemed to sense his indecision. "Do you need me with you?"

"I'd like you with me," he said.

Brinna audibly sighed behind them.

"We should tell them," Tarley said, stepping closer.

"Tell us what?" Tomas asked.

Lachlan helped Tarley onto the horse, then climbed up behind her.

"We're betrothed," Tarley said.

"What?" Auri exclaimed.

"Wait!" Scarlett rushed forward and grabbed the bridle. "Look at me," she demanded, her eyes assessing Tarley shrewdly.

"What is it?" Tarley asked, confusion shaking her

voice.

Scarlett grabbed Tarley's right hand and pushed up her sleeve. "This was here this morning—it's done?" Scarlett's gray eyes bounced between them.

"What is it?" Lachlan asked, confused by what was happening and even more disturbed he couldn't seem to track it.

"Oh my stars," Auri said. "Like mine." She held up her wrist.

Tarley was still in front of him, the shock apparent in the tension of her shoulders. "Oh." She grasped her wrist and looked around, then held it up for Lachlan to see, twisting in front of him. "My ribbon. It's gone. I lost it." She looked at her mother. "I refuse to stay in the cottage."

"I'll get you another one," he said, taking hold of the reins.

"You don't understand," Scarlett cried, panic in her tone and written on her face.

"This should be interesting," Nixus said from somewhere in the mix of people.

Scarlett turned to Tomas. "She's exposed," she said, clinging to the horse. "If she leaves here. He'll come for her–"

"He?" Nixus's voice captured Lachlan's concern.

"What?" Tarley snapped. "Who?"

Auri grasped Scarlett's shoulders. "What's going on? What aren't you telling us?"

But rather than answer Auri's questions, Scarlett burst into tears and turned into Tomas's embrace.

"You need to tell them. You've done your best," he murmured. "They're grown, now."

"But it will change everything—"

All the Fareview children exchanged glances, and Auri moved next to Nixus, who wrapped an arm around her. "You were right," she said.

"I usually am, Auri," he said.

Lachlan didn't understand what was happening, but he couldn't focus on it, not just then. "Would you like to stay, Tarley?" he asked. "I understand. I just can't—" He paused, not wanting to leave her, but knowing that whatever this was with her family was important. "I need to go. I can—"

"I'm coming with you," Tarley said.

"Please, Tarley," her mother said, tears staining her face.

"You've had time to tell us the truth, Mother," Tarley said. "How can I ever trust you to offer it now?" She turned her head to look at Lachlan over her shoulder. "I go where you go."

"Tarley—" Lachlan started, wanted to temper her anger with reason. "Maybe—"

She shook her head. "Let's go."

He'd reason with Tarley and return after he got to the inn and understood what he was facing. So he said, "She's safe with me. I'll bring her back—" Then he pulled the reins and pressed his heels into the horse's flank to urge the gelding forward until they were racing down the wooded lane, now pitch black.

By the time they careened into the courtyard, it was

filled with horses—both Trevis and Horance working with soldiers to get them stabled—carriages, wagons, and people. He brought the gelding to a stop, tied him to the hitching post, and helped Tarley down.

With her hand in his, he dragged her toward the entrance of the inn, but she pulled him to a stop. "Lachlan!"

He turned to look at her.

"I…" Her hands went to her hair, which was mussed from their sex in the hedge. "I look a fright!" she whispered at him. "And my underthings are torn," she added, her eyebrows arched high over her wide eyes. Her skin darkened with a blush.

Lachlan smiled, thinking her the most beautiful, most marvelous woman he'd ever known. "Do you know how excited it makes me, knowing you're standing next to me wearing underthings I've ruined?"

Her blush deepened. "I need to change before–"

"Tarley. You're beautiful." He pulled the ribbon from her hair so all of it fell down her back, then smoothed it and grasped her face. "No one will know except me, and I'm going to be fantasizing about it. I plan on completely removing them later. And then you can fight me on it then until you're screaming with pleasure." He grinned before kissing her chastely, then searched her face. "Hold your head high like you always have, my queen." With her hand in his, he drew her through the doors.

Every head in the room swiveled toward the noise, and half the room dropped to a knee, *Your Highness* the words uttered as they did. Only one figure remained standing—aside from the contingent from Kaloma— his father. His father had come!

Cutting an imposing figure, he wore his armor without the Jast marker, which Lachlan presumed was a precaution for would-be assassins. His white hair was overgrown, thick and wavy, and his face sported a beard, which was unusual. He looked older, his hazel eyes tired, whether it was from travel or worry, Lachlan couldn't be sure.

"Father." Lachlan stepped forward and kneeled. Tarley dipped into a curtsey next to him.

"Lachlan?" he asked. "Is that really you? The message–" The sound of his voice was less imposing and more filled with disbelief. He wove a path through the kneeling people, and when he reached Lachlan, he grasped his arms, pulling him back to his feet.

Lachlan wondered when he'd gotten taller than his father. It wasn't as if he'd grown, suddenly.

Then his father embraced him roughly. "The message—Captain Johesha saw you go over the cliff. They scoured the river for days before returning to Jast." He drew back, holding Lachlan out in front of him. "You're alive." He pulled him back into his arms.

Tears pressed against the back of Lachlan's eyes. His father had come for him. And now as others began to stand, he noticed Ollie, Captain Johesha, his personal guard, along with several others he'd worried about.

Lachlan pulled away. "There's so much to tell you,"

Lachlan told his father, then looked at Ollie. "I'm so relieved to see you."

"And I you." Ollie smiled. "You lead a charmed life, my friend. First you escape marriage and then death. Always getting out of your responsibilities–"

Lachlan laughed and embraced Ollie.

Captain Johesha, stood stoic, a hand on his sword and the other fisted at his side, his dark brown eyes were downcast. Johesha had been Lachlan's primary guard for many years, the rock keeping Lachlan safe through all of Lachlan's ridiculous exploits for the last sixteen years, never complaining, always challenging, but never abandoning. And now, Lachlan could see the pent-up emotion in this man had who never allowed emotion space.

"It wasn't your fault, Captain," Lachlan told him.

"I should have–" Johesha clamped his mouth shut and pressed his teeth together.

"You couldn't. The fall was an accident. Goldie spooked," Lachlan explained.

Johesha's eyes rose to Lachlan's for just a moment, and Lachlan could see he wouldn't absolve himself but he would resolve to continue to do his job even better than before. He offered Lachlan a nod. "With my honor," he recited, the opening of his oath for Lachlan, who nodded at the renewal.

"We must talk but not here," his father said and glanced around at the Kaloma contingent, which Lachlan finally studied. They were mostly men, guards, a contingent in robes, and one young woman among them who looked strikingly like Keyanna. Her sister, Meera. When he looked back, he met his father's gaze with a nod.

Then his father's gaze found Tarley and faltered. "Who are you?" he asked.

"Father." Lachlan stepped back to draw Tarley to his side. "I'd like to introduce you to Miss Tarley Fareview of Sevens, Kaloma."

His father tilted his head, but Lachlan didn't like the way he measured her with his gaze. Lachlan dismissed it as his father's mistrust given what his father knew of Kaloma; he had thought his son assassinated, after all.

"Miss Fareview, this is my father, the benevolent ruler of the peoples of Jast, King Mallor Nikolas."

"Your majesty," she said and dipped into a curtsy once more.

"And this is what you've been doing?" Mallor's voice, though lowered, was filled with censure. "Sewing your oats. Allowing your mother to grieve—"

Lachlan was taken aback by his father's condemnation, though he knew he probably shouldn't have been. Lachlan's prior behavior, he was sure, was fueling his father's assumptions. "What?"

Tarley's hand tensed in his.

His father's eyes burned bright with anger. "Rather than come home and ease our fears that you were in fact alive, you've been cavorting with a Kaloma whore?"

Lachlan's thoughts locked up, along with his

words. "I sent a message–"

"That we couldn't verify was true," Mallor snapped.

Lachlan slid back into the way his father made him feel small. Mallor's reproach about everything. His accusation and condemnation of Lachlan being a disappointment. All the reasons he'd been underhanded rather than facing his father—just like Ollie said—because his father failed to hear him.

"Your Majesty." Ollie stepped forward like he always did. A bridge.

But Lachlan refused to need the bridge anymore and held up his hand. His father needed to see him as he was, like Tarley had. Mallor could accept him or not, but Lachlan couldn't make that his issue any longer. He was Lachlan, the Crown Prince of Jast, betrothed to Tarley Fareview of Sevens, Kaloma. He would be the king one day, but on his own terms. He alone knew what was in his heart, and his behavior would exemplify that from this day forward.

Except as he worked through the paralysis to defend his betrothed, defend himself to his father— Tarley's hand slipped from his grip. He hadn't been fast enough. She turned, looked at him—tears bright in her stormy eyes—and she walked out.

Lachlan spun on his father. "That's what you think? That I didn't return home because I was on some pleasure vacation from my responsibilities? I almost died, and if it hadn't been for her–" He swiped his hand over his forehead, then looked at his father, seething. "You'd be mourning me instead."

The rebuke on Mallor's face softened slightly.

"Did it ever fucking occur to you that I was stuck?" Noticing the looks from the Kaloma contingent, Lachlan lowered his voice. "That there wasn't a way to get home. And that woman" —he pointed at the door where Tarley had disappeared— "the daughter of a gentleman and a favored family of Sevens—is the reason I'm alive." He searched his father's expression and noticed the momentary regret followed by the mask of pride. Lachlan shook his head and turned away to go after Tarley.

But Ollie waylaid him with a hand on his arm. "She'll wait." His eyes shifted to the Kaloma contingent, and Lachlan noted the tension in the room. "There are things that can't."

"Jast has been in Kaloma for some time," one of the robed men said from the Kaloma side of the room. "It is rumored our queen was assassinated by marauders from Jast."

Lachlan glanced at the doorway across the room to the kitchen, at Credence and Genevieve attempting to placate the Kaloma officials with food and drink, standing still among them. Credence stared at him, shocked.

"Jast didn't kill your queen," someone said.

The room exploded as accusations flew.

While he wanted to go after Tarley, Ollie was right. Lachlan had responsibilities that needed to be addressed immediately, including the fact the queen was alive. "Father only," he said and led the king and the guards from the room up the stairwell until he was standing outside Keyanna's door.

He knocked. "It's me."

The door opened.

Lachlan stepped inside with his father in tow, leaving the guards outside the door.

Mallor stopped, his eyes connecting with the queen, then looked back at Lachlan. "How?"

"You did come for him," she said, her tone laced with her own version of condemnation. "I was beginning to wonder. Took you long enough."

"Of course I came for him. We couldn't verify the message." Mallor looked from Lachlan to Keyanna and back again. "What is this? They just said you'd been killed—"

"Well, Uncle Mallor," Keyanna replied and went to sit on the edge of her bed, leaving the chair for the king. "What you see before you is the product of two assassination attempts. One against your son and one attempted against me."

"By who?"

Queen Keyanna glanced at Lachlan, then to his father. "I suspect someone down in that hall," she said. She looked at Lachlan. "What of my sister?"

"She's here. Safe. Mattias got her your message and trailed her here."

Keyanna took a deep breath and closed her eyes, her features relaxing with relief.

"They don't know you're alive," Mallor surmised.

She shook her head. "Neither of us, well, now they know Lachlan is–" she said, glancing at him with a short smile. "But as far as they know, I perished in an attack and a very piss-poor attempt to frame Jast for it."

"Jast? Why would we be stupid enough to start another war? Besides, we wouldn't need to. Kaloma is poor in might, niece."

Keyanna bristled at Mallor's arrogance, but Lachlan knew she could admit he was right. "Then why not come for us if we are so poor?"

"I don't want that. Never have. The war waged by my father was nothing more than revenge for his ineptitude when it came to my sister."

Keyanna stared at Lachlan's father without flinching. She tilted her head and said, "We have settled on a treaty."

"Who?"

"The Crown-Prince and I." She stood and walked to the window; her hands clasped behind her back. When she turned, she said, "I expect you to honor it."

"And what is it I have agreed to?" Mallor's eyes hit Lachlan with accusation.

"This is what you asked of me–"

"With Ollie's guidance."

Lachlan narrowed his eyes. "The queen and I worked with what we had given the conditions. She trusts my word," he said. He could see when the added meaning struck his father.

"The conditions?" Mallor asked.

"Open trade to the Dauntiss. No tariffs, provided Jast gives military support to back my position as the leader of my kingdom."

Mallor turned his head to study Keyanna. "That is all? Did we need the meeting for such a simple agreement? I was prepared to offer reparations for what befell your mother."

"That, and the betrothal of your son to a bride from Kaloma."

His father's eyes snapped to Lachlan's.

Lachlan dipped his head in acceptance of the condition. "The treaty is in the best interest of both our kingdoms."

"Who are you betrothed to?"

Lachlan met his father's gaze with a steely one of his own. "The woman who saved my life."

Mallor sat back in his chair, in which Lachlan could only describe as unsteady. He swallowed and said, "It would seem there isn't much to be done then–"

"On the contrary, Uncle Mallor," Keyanna said. She walked toward the door. "It's time to bring me back to life with Jast by my side. Now the hard work begins."

Into the Fire

Tarley

With tears blinding her retreat, Tarley hurried up the stairs to her room, chastising herself the entire way. Why had she let her guard down? She burst through the door and shut it behind her, leaning against it as the tears fell, angry there were any tears at all. Swiping at the drops on her cheeks with stiff movements, Tarley knew she was angry, but more than anything, she was hurt. She'd opened herself completely to Lachlan, only to be crushed.

His father had called her a whore.

Like any Kaloma man.

Had she thought because Lachlan had been different—until he hadn't been—that Jast would somehow be better?

Lachlan hadn't defended her to his father. They'd exchanged *I love yous* in the shadow of a hedge, but when he'd had to admit their arrangement to his father, he'd remained silent. Embarrassed by her, she could only guess. She felt like a fool.

She wouldn't waste time crying and allowed herself to the count of three.

One. Wipe the tears.

Two. Deep breath.

Three. Go.

She moved. Her heart might have been punctured, but she wasn't going to wallow. She needed time and the space the woods provided. She hurried about the room packing items, wondering if perhaps her mother had always been right. To hide them away behind a hedge. Remaining protected and safe. She reached for her wrist to find comfort in the ribbon only to encounter bare skin, remembering the ribbon had been lost somewhere. Like her. Tarley felt like she'd sloughed off her old skin and was now exposed, raw and new. Being with Lachlan hadn't felt wrong, only now the hurt was scraping away new growth leaving her exposed once more.

But she wasn't sure her mother was right either, a strange extreme that felt isolating. Tarley pictured Auri, and her pain trapped inside the hedge. And their mother had lied. How could Tarley justify that?

Lachlan had.

To protect himself, she reminded herself.

Which begged the question: why had her mother

lied?

Once packed, she shimmied out of her dress, dropped it on her bed, and donned her disguise.

You're running, that little voice inside her chastised. *I thought you were done running.*

Tarley ignored it, hurrying through the dark courtyard where Lachlan had tied Ferdie, the horse still connected to the hitching post. She was lucky the courtyard was both dark and chaotic. Servants walked between wagons and the inn, unpacking. Men in armor stood in circles, talking, unconcerned by her—or the young boy they offered cursory glances to as she passed—moving through the courtyard to her horse. She looked around for Trevis and Horance, who'd both been out earlier, but didn't see them.

"Here, Ferdie." She offered the gelding an apple swiped from the kitchen. "I know you need rest, but can we just go a little bit further today?"

Ferdie nickered and stomped, enjoying both the apple and her voice.

After securing her things, Tarley mounted the gelding and pulled his reins to turn him toward the woods. She stopped to look back.

Don't go, her inner voice said. *Stay and fight.*

Only she didn't feel the fight, but rather the pressing weight of sadness. She loved Lachlan with every part of her. He'd said the right things, and she'd believed him. Now, she felt sad in a way that crushed her heart as if it were under a mountain. Maybe if he were there, if he told her it would be okay. She willed

Lachlan to appear, to offer her an explanation she would accept. Because she loved him. Rationally, she knew this already, but if today had proved anything between Rufus's threats, Lachlan's declaration, her fear, her mother's lies, Tarley wasn't feeling secure in her abilities to navigate her feelings.

He didn't appear.

And Tarley knew then that she'd come back, face him when her mind was right. She needed clarity. No matter how hurt she was, leaving Lachlan was an impossibility now. She just needed the space to think, and the woods was where she did that best.

She turned in the saddle and spurred Ferdie forward. The gelding lurched, unsteady on his legs, so she kept him at a walk, knowing it would still take her hours to get to her spot in the woods. The dark made it more dangerous.

Then what are you doing? her mind chastised. *You know better. You're smarter than this.*

She considered the cottage instead. She could crawl into bed with Jessamine and find comfort in her sisters, but Tarley was so angry with her mother, she wasn't sure she could face her just yet. There wouldn't be clarity there. She pushed Ferdie deeper into the woods.

It took her several hours to reach her usual place. When she stopped, she fed and watered Ferdie, and instead of pitching the tent, she lit a fire and wrapped up in a blanket to lay under the stars shining overhead.

On her back, she watched the winking spirits in the sky overhead, thinking about Lachlan. She wished on those that darted across the dark expanse to new homes in the universe, recalling Lachlan's story he'd shared at the campfire all those weeks ago. "As the story goes," he'd said with a wink., "there were two lovers, forbidden from being together by their parents. Only they didn't listen—"

"Because whoever listens to their parents," Tarley had said with a half grin, letting her guard down with him. "Why couldn't they be together?"

He'd shrugged.

"Come on. You can't expect me to believe that these lovers were forbidden to be together just because—"

"It's been lost to the time of legends."

"Convenient."

"Do you want the story or not?" he'd asked.

She'd waved a hand at him. "Go."

He'd grinned. "When their continued love affair was discovered, both sets of parents had a spell cast on the lovers, hurling them into the sky to forever be forced apart."

"That's a terrible story."

"You didn't let me finish it," he'd said, poking at the fire. "The legend is that every time we look up into the night sky and see a traveling star, we are witness to their union having found one another once again. And, for that moment, we can rest in the knowledge that even though they were forced apart, they have always been able to find one another across time and space."

She'd told him that was a ridiculous story, even

though secretly she'd loved it.

Now, she smiled, remembering, and took a deep breath of the cool, crisp, forest air. It moved through her chest, but it didn't have the same cleansing effect is usually did. She knew why. Lachlan. Even angry and hurt, she missed him.

She blinked up at the sky, her eyelids feeling heavy with exhaustion, and when the stars suddenly shifted, moving quicker, spinning, it made her dizzy. She blinked once more, only the stars continued their race across the sky. Then the stars converged into moving pictures in the night sky. Enraptured, Tarley watched a man embrace a woman, but the woman stole his fire and ran. The man wandered, searching the universe for the woman and the fire. When he found her, he sent star birds to watch her. At first, it seemed romantic, only the birds eventually pecked her and consumed her, leaving the man with the fire once more.

Tarley opened her eyes, realizing she'd fallen asleep and had collapsed into a dream. Only now her heart was pounding in her ears, making it hard to hear beyond it and the crackle of the embers in the low fire. It was still dark, a few hours before dawn. Ferdie snuffed a noise at something.

Tarley tensed.

Someone or something was in camp.

Having spent so much time in the woods, Tarley didn't frighten easily. She knew how to avoid dangerous animals, how to track, and how to keep to herself. Nothing had truly given her cause to be afraid, but an animal wouldn't cause that reaction in Ferdie. Only a person would, and that was terrifying. Gan's horrible grin accosted her thoughts. A part of her hoped it was Lachlan, but Lachlan wouldn't have made it to her so quickly.

With a deep breath, Tarley counted to three and considered a weapon. Her bag with her dagger was an arm's reach away; she wouldn't get to it in time.

Thoughtless, Tarley.

A whisper cut the silence of the night, followed by the light crackle of someone walking through the scree.

Shit.

She needed to move.

Being as quiet as possible, she rolled.

The steps halted.

"There," someone said; it was a voice she didn't recognize.

"It's her."

Tarley knew that voice—Dr. Allean Rufus.

A different voice said, "Seems stupid to wander unprotected in the woods," the volume barely a breath in the darkness but enough of a difference from the forest to hear it.

"She's so bright," Rufus said.

"What's that supposed to mean?"

"You said she's been whoring it up with Jast?" a third man asked.

"Traitorous bitch." A fourth.

The whispers dropped away.

Afraid they knew she was awake and aware, Tarley

remained still at least until she realized this was her only chance. She flung the blanket off and scrambled to her feet to run, but she didn't get very far. The weight of a body slammed into her back and took her to the dirt.

She screamed and fought against the added weight as Ferdie, whinnying with distress, stamped his feet.

She threw an elbow and connected with the man on top of her, as pain shot up her arm and through her shoulder.

He grunted. "Fuck," a stranger's voice, deep and raspy, said. "Bitch is feisty."

His hold relaxed.

She scrambled through the dirt.

"Hold her!" another voice yelled.

Her captor doubled down, dragging her by the legs as someone else secured her arms.

"Let me go, you pricks!" Tarley screamed, struggling and looking for an opening to free herself. Her father had taught her methods to defend herself, but these men must have known them too.

"Tie her up. Stupid bitch." The man wiped his face.

Tarley was bound and lifted.

The birds were starting to sing in the trees as the sun began to rise, the sky a less intense shade of dark. The three men she didn't know were shadows, but she could make out Rufus's bright, blond hair shining in the weak light as he walked toward her. He stopped so they were toe to toe, and if she could have kicked him, she would have.

He smiled and tilted his head. "What happened?

You're so shiny now." He pinched her chin and moved her head back and forth. "Tell me."

"Tell you what?"

"Why you're so bright?"

"I don't know what the hell you're talking about."

He clicked his tongue behind his teeth. "I tried to warn you, little Fareview, but you insisted on denying me." He ran his thumb over her lips, and she jerked her head back against the chest of her captor. "I was always going to win. I'm stronger, faster. Even with all your prince's threats, there's nothing to stop what's coming."

"What are you rambling on about?" one of the men said. "She's our prisoner. You said you'd lead us to her. She's going to tell us everything she knows."

Rufus's eyes flicked to the owner of the voice, then back to her. "You've made this so much fun. The chase is so satisfying." He grinned.

She spat at him, catching him in the eye.

Her captor shook her. "Calm yourself."

Calm herself?

Rufus removed a cloth from his pocket and wiped his eyes. "Yes. A chase to satiate. But not when I'm this hungry. It won't do." He looked at the man holding Tarley's captor and licked his lips.

"So go. Bock has your coin. You can go buy your damn dinner, but she's coming with us," her captor said, tightening his grip. "Romis will want to question her."

"So this is your revenge for telling you 'no.'" Tarley

said through clenched teeth. "Collection? Why go to all this the trouble?" she asked Rufus, focused on his strange words rather than the man at her back.

Rufus grinned, his white teeth suddenly sharp in his mouth. Tarley blinked to restore the proper image, and his awful grin returned to normal.

"A good question," Rufus said. "I made a promise. Find you for him. I was looking for the green one, but I get the purple one." His gaze roamed her outline. "I'm collecting you. And your two sisters. And your brother. All of you."

Tarley wanted to correct him—she had three sisters—but didn't. "They hate you."

"Enough chit chat," one of the men said. "Sun's coming up. We need to get across the river."

"Hate is tasty," he told her, leaning forward and sniffing her, ignoring the man. "I was promised you would be... rich. You're so bright." He licked his lips, and Tarley shuddered. "But I need to eat first."

"Just take your coin and be on your way," her captor repeated, his impatience giving way to something more wary. Tarley understood. Rufus seemed... off.

Rufus ignored the man and said to Tarley, "He said he'd give me a plaything. I choose you."

"Who said? Romis?" Tarley asked.

"I waited, chasing." He moaned and Tarley leaned against the man at her back, who suddenly felt like less of a threat. "I'm so hungry. You have disappointed me with your prince, giving yourself to him. Innocents are so much sweeter."

Oh, no. "I'm not having sex with you, Rufus. I'm..." But she stopped speaking, not wanting to reveal she was betrothed to Lachlan to these men who'd captured her for information about the royals.

"Sex?" Rufus laughed, a horrible sound. "This isn't about sex. It's about Satiation. My kind can't undo the bond to move on until satiation occurs."

"I don't know what you're babbling about," she snapped. "Your kind? Doctors?"

He chuckled and said, "Satiation or death, that is." Rufus paused, his fingertip running lightly down her cheek. It felt sharp, as if his nail was now a claw. "I can't wait to taste you. To turn you–" He looked up at the sky. "But we'll have to wait until I've eaten. And the sun is coming."

"Yes," one of the men said. "We should get going."

She jerked away from Rufus's touch, her head slamming up against her captor. She struggled against his hold. "Don't touch me."

As the sun rose, the sky changing from dark blue to a shade lighter, Tarley could see Rufus's features were more angular that she remembered. But the strangest sight she couldn't explain away were his usually bright blue eyes, black all the way through.

"What are you?" she breathed.

Rufus swallowed and grinned, his teeth sharp. "Now that is the perfect question."

"Hey. Let's go. Just take her," one of the men said.

"This guy's cracked." The man behind her started

moving away from Rufus. "We're going. Toward the river," he ordered the others.

Rufus's horrible eyes flicked over her, and he sniffed her again. "You ready to see what your future holds?" he asked her, then turned to the men and said, "I'm so hungry."

"We had a deal."

Rufus's eyes moved to her captor. Without warning, Rufus snapped forward and latched on. Her captor tensed, gurgled, and fell with a thud like a tree chopped down, releasing her.

The other two men screamed and ran, disappearing into the woods.

Ferdie screeched in terror, yanking at his tether until the branch cracked, and the horse galloped away.

With her arms and legs bound, Tarley couldn't run, helpless in the dirt as the captor jerked next to her. She was afraid to look at what Rufus was doing. But she couldn't wait, scooting over the ground like a caterpillar to get away. She inched away from the awful noise—the slurping and sucking, the gasping and the gurgling—coming from the man and Rufus as she worked her bonds. When she chanced a look in their direction to see how much time she had, Rufus was attached to the man's neck. And there was blood. So much blood.

Overflowing with terror, she knew she was about to freeze with it.

The woman's body had been mutilated. The story surfaced like a branch bobbing in the river.

Her gaze jumped back to Rufus, doing… something with all that blood. She couldn't be sure and didn't want to take the time to figure it out.

Get away! her inner voice screamed.

With additional fervor, she worked on the bond at her ankles, sliding her feet back and forth to loosen the binding. She knew she couldn't get the boots through, so she worked one of her feet free of its boot. Then the other. She stood, ignoring what was happening behind her, afraid that if she looked, she'd freeze. So she ran, darting into the dark woods for the river.

"Tarley!" the monster that was Rufus roared, the birds in the trees taking flight at the terrible sound.

She didn't think about her bare feet, the rocks and sharp sticks biting her skin. The river. She needed to get to the river. The river, she chanted as she ran. Then she thought of her family and chanted for them. *Father… Mother… Jessamine… Brinna… Auri… Mattias… Lachlan.* Tarley thought of each of them, picturing their faces, recalling their smiles, feeling the deep way she loved each of them, even Lachlan. Especially Lachlan. *Help me.*

An unnatural sound of wind snapping against branches like a horrible storm echoed behind her. Terrified that Rufus—or whatever he was—was going to catch her, she didn't stop. Her arms were still bound, but the water seemed her best option, the swift moving water to carry her away. She'd much prefer to drown than to face whatever kind of monster was chasing her through the woods.

Brinna

rinna sat up in her bed, coughing and clutching at her throat, the horrible dream sticky in her mind. Tarley was in trouble. Brinna had heard her cry out for her in the dream and shuddered now in the aftermath. Every fiber that made her—even if her dreams weren't exact—told her Tarley was in danger. Her gut rolled, telling her to trust her instincts.

"Jessamine? Auri?" She pushed Auri in the bed next to her.

Auri roused slightly, groaning, and rolled away. "It's not morning, Brinna."

"Tarley's in trouble."

"What?" Auri rolled back. "What do you mean?"

"I had an awful dream."

"What is it?" Jessamine asked from the next bed over.

Brinna turned to look at her sister's shadow, propped up on her elbow. "Tarley was in the woods being chased."

"She went with Oll–I mean, Lachlan," Jessamine said. "He said–"

"I know that." Brinna flung the covers off and got up.

"She's not in the woods. She's at the inn," Auri said. "What are you doing?"

Brinna pulled the nightshirt from her body and slipped into a chemise. "There was something after her. Remember what mother said? 'Him.' That he would find her—without the ribbon."

Auri sat up and took a deep breath, like she often did when she was thinking. "Who can make any sense of what Mother says?" Auri asked.

"Listen," Brinna continued. "In the dream, Tarley was in the woods by herself. Then there was a wolf— I think it was a wolf. I didn't get a good look at it in the dream—and it was hunting her. Tarley was running, but it caught up to her, leapt and–" Brinna shuddered but resumed buttoning her dark blue skirt. "I can't get the beast's horrible snarl out of my head."

"Okay. Okay." Auri scooted from the bed and stood.

"What do you think Mother meant when she said 'he'd find her,'" Jessamine asked.

Brinna shrugged, tucking in her tunic into her waistband of her skirt. "Does it matter? If Tarley's in danger, we need to help."

Auri shrugged out of her nightgown. "You're right. And now that you say it… I, don't know, I feel something. Right here." She pressed a hand to her belly.

Jessamine lit a lamp. After she replaced the glass chimney and turned up the oil for a more expansive glow, she also left her bed and began to dress. "Do you think she's hurt?"

Brinna turned to her sisters as she haphazardly braided her hair. "I hope it's one of those dreams that means nothing. But if we go to the inn, and she's there, at least we know she's okay."

"What if she's not?" Auri paled, her hands still at the buttons of her shirt.

"That's why we have to go," Brinna said. "In case…" She stopped not wanting to believe there was something wrong but feeling it as concretely as the bow she was tying in her hair.

Auri secured her hair in a hastily wrapped bun on top of her head. "I'll call for Nix."

"Call? How?" Jessamine ducked into the yellow skirt and pulled it into place. "Where is he?"

Auri grasped Jessamine's hand. "Don't worry about it," Auri said. "I just know he'll be here."

Jessamine tucked the ivory shirt before buttoning her skirt. "There's something strange–"

"Yes, Jessamine," Auri interrupted. "There's a lot

of strange around here. Nix is just one of those things. And I promise to tell you everything soon."

Jessamine stilled and leveled her brown gaze on Auri. "What are you talking about?"

Auri sighed, fastening the final button on her dress. "Trust me for now."

"You sound like Mother," Brinna said.

Auri stilled. "You're right."

"We don't really have time right now. Not if Brinna's dream is a prediction," Jessamine said. "I'm holding you to telling though. When we find Tarley safe and sound at the inn." Jessamine tied back her dark brown hair with an ivory ribbon.

"Same," Brinna said.

From the doorway, Jessamine turned. "So you call for Nix, Auri, and I'll get Mother and Father."

"And I'll get Mattias to hitch the wagon," Brinna added and followed Jessamine, hoping that her dream was nothing more than her imagination but terrified it was so much more than that.

Lachlan

Lachlan took three stairs at a time to Tarley's attic room. He'd hated he hadn't been able to go to her immediately, but establishing the treaty for the safety of Kaloma, Keyanna and Meera, and Jast had taken precedence with the tension claiming each kingdom's factions. They hadn't needed to reignite a war in the dining room of The Copper Pot. While he knew he had to apologize for hesitating after what his father had said, he was confident she would listen to his explanation. They had reached a new level of understanding, he hoped. She loved him. He loved her, and he would spend the rest of his life proving it.

Except when he knocked on the door, there was

only silence behind it. Unsure and suddenly concerned, Lachlan let his impatience to rule and opened the unlocked door. The room inside was dark and empty. Cold. She'd never started a fire, and upon closer inspection, her dress was tossed on the bed, the room disheveled, as if she'd rushed in and out.

The woods. She'd run to the woods.

Damn it, Tarley.

He slammed the door shut and raced down to the stable, anxiety swirling inside him. How long had he been busy? Two hours? Three? Maybe she was just inside with her horse, except when he burst into the stables, he found Trevis finishing with the new horses and resting Jast guardsmen rushing to stand, snapping to attention when he entered.

"Where's Tar-" He stopped as soldiers bowed to him.

Trevis measured the soldiers' response to Lachlan with his eyes, then looked back at Lachlan. "It's true, then?"

"What?"

"You're a prince. Of Jast."

Lachlan nodded, but he couldn't take the time to assuage Trevis's curiosity. "Have you seen Miss Fareview?" He shook his head. "Tarley."

"What am I to do, my lord?" Trevis lowered his head.

"First, I'm not your lord, Trevis. And I just need to find Tarley."

"It's 'Your Highness'," one of the soldiers

provided the boy.

Lachlan held up a hand. "Trevis. Look at me."

Trevis looked up and met Lachlan's eyes. Lachlan could see that the boy felt lied to, probably hurt by Lachlan's omission, which gave him pause, but he said, "Just Lachlan to you, Trevis. I mean, we've been sleeping in the horse loft like brothers, haven't we?"

The soldiers exchanged surprised glances.

"I wondered why you were so terrible at mucking the stalls, Lachlan. It all makes sense now."

Lachlan smiled. "Not a ton of practice in that regard. What about Tarley?"

"Saw her take Ferdi a few hours ago."

"Home?"

"Didn't talk to her, but she had her gear with her."

"At night?" Anxiety rose like a flooding river. While he knew that Tarley could take better care of herself than he could manage of himself, it didn't keep his gut from churning with trepidation. The danger was significantly higher now with their betrothal and unknown assassins. And if there were hunters out there. What if she was abducted. He knew he'd rip Kaloma apart to find her, but he didn't want to think about what could happen in the meantime.

The sound of boots scuffing across the cobblestone made Lachlan turn toward the doorway, hopeful that it was Tarley, but it wasn't. It was Captain Johesha. The acid in Lachlan's gut swirled, making him feel slightly ill.

"Your Highness!" Johesha's brow collapsed over

his brow. Guards Jude and Brendsen were right behind him.

"Is my father alright?" Lachlan asked.

The guards dipped their heads in acknowledgement. "He's fine. Major Urik is with him, and I'm not his guardsman," Johesha said. "I'm yours and you keep disappearing… Sir." The captain's dark eyes bounced around the stables, shrewdly taking in information. Lachlan watched him assess the soldiers, who were standing at attention and Trevis, who was eyeing Johesha. The captain's eyes returned to Lachlan. "Forgive me, Your Highness." He tilted his head.

"Johesha. It's fine."

"I suggest we return to the inn. We aren't sure who instigated the assassination attempt–"

"I can't, Captain–"

He sighed. "Your Highness."

Johesha was familiar with Lachlan's shenanigans and had followed him often under duress in Jast on many hairbrained adventures. Lachlan knew, however, that the stakes were higher in Kaloma. Tarley was at risk. Johesha and the guard weren't familiar with the terrain or the place. There were so many things that could go wrong and had. But something in Lachlan's gut was warning him he needed to get to Tarley. An hour ago. He wouldn't be at ease until he saw her. Until he could apologize, kiss her, hear her reassure him nothing had changed between them, he couldn't rest.

"Johesha… I must find Miss Fareview."

"Your Highness. A woman?"

Lachlan bristled. "Your future queen, Captain."

Johesha's eyebrows rose.

"What?" Trevis said.

Lachlan glanced over his shoulder, then back at Johesha. "She's gone to the woods. I'll have to track her, but I'm going to find her. You can either accompany me, or not–"

A clatter rose beyond the stables, and Lachlan's guards went for their swords. They swung around, and the soldiers at his back pressed in closer. Lachlan had gotten used to being able to function in the anonymity of being Ollie and was suddenly wishing for it once again. The voices talking, loud for that time of night, were… familiar.

Lachlan walked from the stables surrounded by his guard to find the Fareviews climbing from a wagon. Johesha, Jude, and Brendsen stepped between Lachlan and the family. Scarlett started across the courtyard at a brisk pace, and Lachlan could see she was pale. "Tarley?" She took in the scene and stopped, looking through the three men.

Obviously, Tarley hadn't gone home, which had been the best-case scenario. Lachlan's hope that was where she'd gone was dashed, and it was too clear in his voice when he admitted, "She's not here."

Brinna grasped onto the wagon. "The woods." Her eyes were slightly glazed and wholly terrified.

"What is it?" Lachlan asked.

Tarley's mother shook her head and whirled on Tomas behind her. "She doesn't have her ribbon." She grabbed hold of her husband's jacket, and his arms wrapped around her. Tomas bent forward and whispered something Lachlan couldn't hear, but what he did see was a husband offering comfort.

Jessamine, followed by Brinna, Auri, and Mattias appeared around their parents. Lachlan noticed each of their ribbon's—all but Auri. He wondered about what they meant.

"What about the ribbon, Mother?" Brinna asked, inadvertently grasping hers with the opposite hand. "What does it matter?"

Auri looked down at her own wrist, naked of the red bow. "They're spelled." Auri looked at her mother. "A protection spell."

The siblings looked surprised. "What?"

Scarlett straightened her spine as if reinforcing her body for what needed to be done. "Now's not the time. We need to find her. I felt uneasy, but now I feel danger." She pressed a hand to her stomach. "Brinna, the dream. What did you see? Mattias, listen."

"I don't need that. I know where she'd go if she's gone to the woods. She doesn't deviate from her spot, so I can always find her."

Lachlan couldn't make heads or tails of what was happening between the family, about spelled ribbons, but danger was enough of a warning to speak to the anxiety already swirling through his body, though he recognized Mattias's surety. "The one near the river, where she found me–" was all he seemed to be able to say, his thoughts racing through the woods after her.

"Yes," Mattias said.

Lachlan rushed back into the stable. "We're wasting time–"

Trevis jumped to get him a horse.

"Captain." Lachlan turned to his guardsmen. Johesha drew his gaze away from the family and focused on Lachlan. "Prepare your men. We're going after her." He turned to Trevis. "A horse for Mattias."

Trevis nodded and disappeared into stables. Mattias followed to help, as did Jude and Brendsen.

"And me," Jessamine volunteered, stepping forward.

"No–" Scarlett grabbed hold of her oldest daughter's arm. "Let Mattias. The rest of us stay together."

"I can–" Auri started.

"No. No ribbon," Scarlett said, refusing any opposition.

"Mother, you're needed here. In case she comes back. And I have my ribbon," Jessamine held up her hand. "If she's hurt? She'll need one of us, and you aren't thinking clearly." Jessamine hurried to the wagon. When she returned, she had a small leather satchel over her shoulder.

The sensation occurred again, that Lachlan hadn't really stopped to notice Jessamine, as if he could see her, but his eyes would slide past her. She looked so much like her mother except for her dark hair and dark eyes. The sensation of seeing her was strange, and gave Lachlan the feeling he needed to shake his head to clear the cobwebs away.

"We split up," Jessamine demanded.

"Take weapons," Brinna said, the bouncy bubbly woman from earlier only a shadow now. She looked frightened.

"What?" Lachlan asked, his stomach seizing.

Brinna's gaze locked on his. "Just to be prepared."

The clattering of horses announced the party was ready to ride. Lachlan mounted a horse handed over to him by Trevis, the guardsmen and soldiers doing the same.

Mattias assisted Jessamine onto a horse and started up after her, but Captain Johesha stopped him, grasping the bridle. "You're leading?" the captain asked.

Mattias nodded. "I know the woods the best–"

"Then she shouldn't ride with you. In case–"

"I can take care of myself, sir," Jessamine bristled.

Captain Johesha shook his head. "It isn't a comment on taking care, ma'am. It's dark. And his mount has much to contend with besides carrying double the load. Can you ride?"

Jessamine nodded. "Of course."

"I'm sorry, Captain, there aren't any more mounts," Trevis said.

"You'll ride with me," Captain Johesha said.

"But–"

"If it were Ferdie or Wilhemina, then we'd be fine," Mattias said. "But the captain is right. I don't know this horse. And I wouldn't want anything to happen to you."

"Fine," Jessamine said and slid from the horse, Captain Johesha catching her waist on the way down.

The captain released her and stepped back, returning to his mount.

"Lachlan?"

Lachlan turned in the saddle as his father, surrounded by his guard, appeared in the courtyard.

"What is the meaning of this?"

"I apologize for the lack of ceremony, Father, but these are the Fareviews—your future in-laws. They are responsible for saving not only me, but Queen Keyanna."

"Where are you going?" his father demanded.

"I'm going to find the woman who is to be my wife," he said, "and I swear to all that is holy, if anything has happened to her, I will raze these woods to the ground." He spurred his mount forward, leaving Mattias to catch up to lead the way.

Tarley

A gust of power toppled Tarley against the rocks, just short of the water sliding past. "No!" she screamed, the weight of monster Rufus was pressed against her back, trapping her on the shore. With her arms stretched out, still tied at the wrists, she could almost touch the water.

"I told you the chase is what gets me going." His hands—cold and dry—drifted up over her thighs and stopped at her shoulder blades. He pressed his thumbs into her back, his fingers wrapped around her ribs. "I've imagined this. Chasing you. Catching you. Fucking you. Biting you. Tasting you. Then doing it over and over again. He promised me a plaything–"

She struggled against his weight and felt him harden against her.

"The human form is so delightful."

Tears flooded her eyes. She was trapped, truly powerless, and hope shifted inside her, collapsing.

"The smell of your fear is…" His nose pressed against the skin at the back of her neck, and she felt the scrape of his sharp teeth.

One. Stop fighting, she thought, *since that's what he wants.*

Two. Stop running and face your fate, she decided. She'd go down without fear.

Three. Tarley took a deep breath.

"Just do it," she told him. "Kill me, if that's what you want."

He hummed, his mouth near her ear. "So resigned? That doesn't seem like the Tarley I've come to know." His tongue ran over her skin, and he hummed. "I don't want your death, not really."

"I won't be your 'plaything.'"

He laughed. "But you already are." The vibration of his laugh, his words, were an ugly thing that reverberated from his chest through her back. "Why can I see you now?"

"You saw me perfectly fine before—" Tarley tried to inch forward. "You stalked me daily."

"Stop moving," he growled against her skin, and she felt his teeth press down between her neck and shoulder. "I'll only catch you again." He licked the spot of skin where he'd pressed his teeth into and moaned.

"Satiation is going to be good."

He seemed content to talk for the time being, so Tarley stalled. "What do you mean you couldn't see me?"

"You were hidden—your power was hidden." He flicked her braid away from her neck.

"Power?"

He ran a finger along her spine from the top of her neck down. "Like one of those rocks you crack open to reveal the gems inside—the purple one. He said you'd have it–"

"Who?"

"My master."

"You aren't your own master?"

"I'm the master of some, but I answer to one, and he's been looking–"

Then suddenly, Rufus's weight disappeared. He snarled and fell with a thud, draped across her legs, which allowed her to twist out from under him.

"Get up," a deep voice ordered. "Hurry. That won't hold him–"

Tarley scrambled as whoever was behind her bashed Rufus once more with a grotesque, squelching thud.

Tarley glanced at Rufus, his face covered with blood, his mouth slick with it, and his head sunken in by a man she could only see in her periphery. She couldn't look away from the gore, sick with it. Rufus blinked those terrible black eyes but didn't move. Granules of black dust drifted from his bodily form and disappeared into the air around him as if he were breaking apart.

She swiped at her neck, slick with blood that wasn't hers, and shuddered, a scream working its way up her throat.

The man who'd hit Rufus stepped forward and pulled her up to her feet by the binding around her wrists. "Come on, girl."

She struggled up and scrambled after him. "Where—"

"No talking. We don't have time for tea." He led her through the brush away from the thing that had been Rufus. "That monster will heal itself and come hunting. It's got you in its sights." Tarley, forced to follow the man into the forest, limped as she went, knowing her feet were leaving a trail of blood. They stayed along the river, walking upstream, until they came to an inlet Tarley had fished in before.

"What was it?" she asked.

The man uncovered a small canoe. "In." He assisted her into the boat, his touch surprisingly gentle. "It's a darkling. Enough chat."

She'd never heard of a darkling. "A vampire?"

The man climbed into the canoe behind her, shoved off from the shore, and started down the river. When they passed the inlet where she'd been trapped with the Rufus-monster, his body was still there, only partially disintegrated, the darkness more present, and floating like pollen in the sunshine as it peeked over the trees.

Darkness coalesced at the edge of her vision, then rushed toward her like a heavy curtain obscuring her sight and swallowing her whole. She heard crying and screams. When she blinked, she was back in the canoe on the river. Another vision but no headache. One small favor, it would seem.

"Like a vampire in some ways. Different in others. They heal themselves," the man said after they'd passed. "You can incapacitate their human bodies when they're in human form, but if they shift, you're fucked."

"How did you–"

"Know? Where I'm from, the darkling is feared above all."

"Where are you taking me–"

The man didn't answer, just rowed the canoe downstream.

Tarley wasn't opposed to it. The stranger, who she knew she couldn't trust since he'd left her tied, had saved her from the creature she'd once known as Rufus—at least for the moment—and he was taking her closer to Sevens. Closer to her family. Closer to Lachlan.

Why had she ever run? She should have stayed and fought.

When the stranger directed the canoe to the opposite side of the river, he pulled it ashore and forced her out. He grasped the rope and jerked her along with him. Tarley glanced over her shoulder taking stock of where they were, but it looked so different on this side of the river. She was confident they were just before the rapids.

"Keep up," the man said.

"Do you have a name?" she asked.

"None that means anything to you."

They walked, Tarley limping along behind him. She slowed, her feet slick with blood now. The man jerked her rope again.

"Hey. My feet."

He shook his head. "Nothing we can do about it now." He continued walking. His stench was atrocious, as if he hadn't bathed in weeks. Probably hadn't; it was a good way to hide in the woods from animals and was perhaps why the man had been able to attack Rufus at all.

After what felt like hours because of her feet, they walked into a clearing. The fetid aroma hit her like a slap to the face. She coughed, gagged, and pressed her tied hands to her nose. Death lingered. Carcasses strung from the trees hung around the encampment. Whoever she was dealing with weren't Whitling woods folk. The stench would draw feral creatures. She was surprised they hadn't already. But it was also a good way to hide your own stench. Keep people away. The question would be, which was more important?

She needed to get to the river somehow. She'd follow it downstream, where it would spit her out near Sevens after the rapids but before the waterfall. Getting free of her bindings was priority number one. Slipping into the woods bound wasn't going to do her any favors especially if she was trying to avoid that darkling thing.

And shoes. She needed shoes.

The dark of night had long been chased away by the dawn. Goldenrod streaked across the blue sky high above the trees, which then melted into the barely blue sky of a warm summer day. Not ideal weather in which to hide once she escaped, but she'd figure it out, hope blooming in her chest once more.

Her captor stomped them toward a large tent across the camp.

A man stepped toward them from the front of the tent. He looked dingy from a life in the woods, but not hungry. His body hinted he was well fed and his clothes and shoes that he was well paid. There was a weapon—a rope with several stones—at his hip, and a dagger tied to a leg. "What you got here, Hep?"

"The project that Snell and Bock ran from. Found Klem ripped to shreds by a darkling."

"Who is she? A whore?"

"Dressed like that?"

Tarley bit her tongue. King Mallor's earlier comment hit her. Only then she'd been dressed as a lady. She might have been standing there with her under clothes ripped after being with Lachlan earlier, her heart racing at the knowledge of sharing that secret with him, but no one else had known. Then she'd been called a whore. Kaloma stripped women of their autonomy, but it took Lachlan's father to strip her down to her insecurities.

Perhaps that was always what her problem had been? She'd worked so hard to lock those insecurities about her womanhood in a small trap inside her and keep them hidden. Only the more time she spent with Lachlan, even loving him, her fears of being inadequate broke open and spilled out. He'd made her feel safe and desired. Loved and cherished. Accepted as she was. But when he hadn't stood up for her, her heart had cracked open, giving those insecurities power.

And she hadn't waited.

She should have waited.

Instead, she'd fled like she'd always done.

She raised her head. "I'm no whore, and even if I were, I'd have more standards than what could be had here."

"You're a mouthy bitch." The man who wasn't Hep stepped forward menacingly. "A woman needs to know her place."

Her captor—Hep—jerked her closer to him and swiveled her bodily so he was between her and the other man. "Now none of that. She's here because boss-man paid for it."

Hep pulled on Tarley's wrists once more. "Let's go." He dragged her just outside the large tent.

"What the fuck?" a voice snapped from inside the structure. It sounded familiar to Tarley somehow, but she couldn't place it. "How could they screw that up?"

"Hep went after her. He's back," another faceless voice said from inside.

There was a stretch of silence followed by the

murmur of voices.

Then the flap on the oversized tent slapped open, and a giant man ducked out through the opening. When he straightened, Tarley shrank back against Hep now behind her, his grip tightening on her shoulder.

"You," Four Tankards said and grinned. He glanced around. "Where's your bodyguard?"

Tarley clenched her teeth together and tried to keep the rest of her face impassive even though her heart tripped about in her chest. That, she hadn't seen coming, but maybe she should have.

"What? Someone cut out that razor tongue of yours?"

"Why have I been abducted?" she asked.

"Sir–" Hep started but Four Tankards raised his hand.

"Abducted? Is that what you call it?" Four Tankards asked. "I call it monitoring your welfare." He stepped forward. "You're a woman, all alone in the woods without the covering of a male to keep you safe. This is perfectly within the law of the land." His hand, palm up, pointed at the ground. "Look at your feet."

She knew they were a bloody mess. She could feel it every time she took a step.

"There's a darkling after her," Hep interrupted. "Stunned the fucker, but it will be after her soon enough–"

Four Tankard's eyes jumped to Hep behind her. "And you brought her into camp?" He obviously knew what a darkling was.

"The carcasses should mask the scent—"

But not her bloody footprints that led her here.

Tarley glanced around, taking in the space. The number of tents lined up in neat rows, the number of men dressed in nice clothes and boots, no want for supplies, the smell of food, the horses. This wasn't a random encampment of hunters. This was something else.

Tarley wondered if he might bargain. "You can just let me go. Then that creature won't even come near this place. Untie me, give me some boots, and I'll be on my way."

Four Tankards laughed. "Now what kind of man would that make me—to allow a woman to get lost in these woods? Women have no sense of direction, no survival skills. Besides, I wouldn't ever give a perfectly good woman to a monster." His eyes raked her bedraggled form. "Even one as used up as you."

Tarley ground her teeth.

"Take her into the tent, Hep. I'll make sure she's taken care of until we can deliver her."

"Deliver me?"

"Yes, sir." Hep pushed her forward, and Tarley ground her feet against the dirt, fighting him.

"Deliver me where?"

"To the convent, of course. After we talk about the royal party that arrived at the inn. Then we'll take you to the convent south of here, there's one outside Lilim. You'll be kept clothed and fed and sheltered until the end of your days. Provided we can keep you free of a darkling." He looked at the men around him. "Maybe if you're lucky, you'll get chosen by a husband who comes to the convent looking. Heard that's rare." He laughed. "Slaver, more likely."

What the hell?

Tarley contested Hep's hold. "I have a father and a brother—"

Four Tankards looked around. "I don't see them." He looked back at her, his dark eyes narrowing. "Can you produce them?"

She couldn't. Other than her family aware of her usual camping place, she hadn't told a soul where she was going. Had it been her arrogance that made her feel safe enough? What had she done?

Lachlan

An hour into the woods—which felt slow on horses as they plodded through the thick landscape—they came across the Fareview horse grazing, his halter broken and no saddle. The care the gelding received from Mattias and Jessamine was honorable, but Lachlan was beyond impatient, then relieved when they tied the horse to Royal Guard Jude's mount so they could continue on. When they reached Tarley's camping spot at dawn, his anxiety turned to turmoil.

"Tarley?" Mattias called, jumping from his horse. Jessamine echoed him.

Tarley's things were in disarray around the

grounds, the tent never even assembled, all of it in a heap near a blanket strewn away from the firepit bright with waning embers. This wasn't Tarley, and perhaps he didn't get to be an expert in Tarley in as little time as he'd known her, but he'd learned, observed, and had been taught by her. He knew without a doubt, she wouldn't have ever left her campsite like this. Something was wrong, which was confirmed when several feet from the blanket they found a body—a man—coated in in blood, eyes wide, and mouth open in a silent scream.

"What the–" Jude said, kneeling to get a closer look at the dead man.

Brinna's comment echoed in his mind: *bring weapons.* What had she known?

"How did you know to come looking for Tarley?" Lachlan asked, attempting to focus on something other than his rising fear that Tarley was in worse danger than he'd realized. He turned to look at Mattias who stood slightly back, eyes fixated on the body, face pale.

"Mattias. Look at me," Lachlan said. He was equally terrified but needed to hold himself together. He needed Mattias—their guide—focused too. He stood.

"Mind your steps," Captain Johesha called.

Mattias's eyes jumped to Lachlan's. He swallowed and sputtered, "Brinna dreams." He looked over at Jessamine standing at the edge of camp holding the horses, then back at Lachlan. "She'd had one, about Tarley. That's why we came to the inn. To make sure she was okay."

"That's why we're here. For Tarley," he reminded Mattias, who nodded and took a deep breath.

Once Mattias appeared more cognizant and focused, Lachlan slowly moved past the horrifying spectacle, taking in everything as he did, careful where he stepped, hoping to find something that would lead him to her. "What do you think could do that?" he asked Jude. "A bear?"

"No," Jude replied. "The body would be more mauled. This is—" But his words dropped away. "I don't know what this is. I've never seen anything like it."

"A wolf?" Lachlan asked.

"Wolf attacks are rare," Mattias said moving toward the tree line. "I'm not sure—if it were a wolf pack—they'd leave the kill like this."

"Oh fuck." Lachlan stopped moving and took a breath. He closed his eyes, then opened them to be sure he was seeing what he thought he was. "Tarley's boots." They were tied together with a rope. His throat closed. Someone had tied her up. Someone had killed a man. His heart was water-logged, swelling with horror and anger, slowing under the strain of his fear.

Jude joined him. "This." He pointed at smudges in the dirt. "Someone sliding here." The tracks stopped a few feet from the boots.

"Her hands are tied," Lachlan guessed.

"Good bet."

Lachlan pointed at the boots. "She couldn't get

them out, so she removed them and ran?"

"Worked her feet out." Jude stood and looked back at the body and then over his shoulder. "The river?"

Mattias walked past them further into the brush. "Tracks," he confirmed. "Not only hers."

"There were others," Johesha said. "Here." He stood on the other side of camp near Jessamine and the horses.

"How many?" Lachlan stopped, his gaze zeroed in on a set of tracks, a slide through the dirt. He pictured Tarley putting up a struggle—he knew she would and his heart drained, squeezing itself dry in his chest, then aching as it raced with trepidation.

Johesha trailed the tracks he'd found, his steps slow and precise. "Best guess—two or three, maybe a fourth."

"One dead." Royal Guard Brendsen pointed at the body.

"Tarley," Jude added. "The others?"

"Two sets disappear this way," Johesha said in the opposite direction Tarley went.

"Should we split up?" Brendsen asked.

"No," Captain Johesha said. "We track Tarley."

Leaving their mounts tethered at the camp, Lachlan and the party walked the trail to the river. His mind vacillated between frustration to awe to fear. First because he just wanted to go back in time, fix what had happened with his father, and ask her to wait. He also recognized the futility in it. He couldn't slip back in time. And Tarley was her own person. He should have known she'd run. She was wired to act. The woman was a force. That pride gave way to fear, afraid for her should she decide to do something that might endanger her, his fear alive and writhing inside him.

When they finally cleared the tree line, bloody rocks, slick with footsteps, led them to the river's edge.

"Think she went into the water?" Mattias asked.

"Not unless she jumped the last six feet," Johesha said. "Look. The last footprint–" He walked in a line between the last footprint and the water's edge. "What is this?" He crouched down.

At his feet was a bloody mess. Bits of unidentifiable matter, as if a mound of viscera had been left behind, but from what was anyone's guess.

"That's not–" Jessamine started but stopped.

"No." Lachlan shook his head. It wasn't. He refused to believe it, though his heart hurt looking at the gore. Bits of black dust coated it, some of which floated into the air, drifting toward the shadow of the woods though there wasn't a breeze to carry it.

Lachlan's pained heartbeat quickened with stark awareness that there was something terrible in the woods—a sharp awareness like a knife in his gut. He didn't want to follow the floating dust but asked, "Do you think Tarley's there?"

"Look!" Jessamine cried out, upstream, leading away from them. "Look! Tracks here. Bloody footprints. Tarley." She looked up at Mattias with a tentative but hopeful gleam on her face.

Relieved for a trace of Tarley that wasn't whatever

had been left on the shore, the party followed her tracks until they disappeared altogether at the edge of the river.

"She went into the river?" Brendsen asked this time.

"Or on it." Johesha was crouched down next to a patch of depressed grass along the shoreline.

"A boat," Jude said and turned to look downstream.

"How do we know they didn't go upstream," Mattias asked.

"We don't," Johesha said as they backtracked to the horses, "but if you were afraid of being killed, would you fight the current?"

They grabbed the horses, and once mounted started downstream along the river, back toward Sevens.

Each of them focused on the landscape looking for footprints, depressions, anything to tell them they were going the right way. Only most of it was looking at the woods, the river, the bushes, the grass unsure and afraid.

Lachlan tried not to be afraid. He did. Only when he wasn't afraid, he was angry that she'd run, and he didn't want to be angry either. He just wanted her. So he distracted himself by asking, "What's with the ribbons?"

Jessamine, riding in front of Captain Johesha next to Lachlan, glanced at him. "Our mother gave them to us when we were babies."

"Did you get new ones each year?" Lachlan asked.

Jessamine shook her head and looked at the ribbon. "No. Actually–"

"They've grown with us," Mattias said.

"Where's Auri's?" Lachlan asked.

"She lost it in the woods."

"Tarley did too," Lachlan said, but he didn't know when. She'd had it, then it was gone. "Why did Auri say they were a protection spell? What would you need to be protected from?"

He watched Mattias look over his shoulder at Jessamine then face forward. He shrugged and Jessamine said, "We don't know."

"That's why Tarley said your mother lied?"

"We know about as much as you do," Jessamine said, her voice tight with irritation.

So Lachlan let it drop but hated that his mind wouldn't stay where he wanted it, on the landscape.

"There," Mattias eventually said, pointing across the river at a canoe dragged up onto the shore.

"Two lira that we'll find bloody footprints and at least one more set with them," Johesha said. "Safe to cross here?"

"No," Mattias answered. "But there's a spot downstream a bit further, and we can backtrack on the other side."

With a squeeze of his legs, Lachlan urged his mount to go a touch faster. They hurried through the forest, crossed the river, and backtracked until they reached the canoe. By this time, the sun was shining, and the warmth of the day was rising. Sure enough, there were bloody tracks easy enough to follow through the woods.

Captain Johesha with Jessamine and Mattias's council pushed their party quickly. It was less than an hour later that Johesha pulled them all to a stop, his hand raised, and dismounted. They followed his lead, and Lachlan searched the woods to see what Johesha had seen. He caught sight of movement several hundred yards ahead of them. Johesha signaled Jude and Brendsen forward, and Lachlan watched them move through the forest in the opposite direction, to scout.

"Your Highness, I'd like you to say here, with"—Johesha cleared his throat—"Jessamine."

"No," Lachlan said at the same time as Jessamine answered, their fierce whispers a matching set. Their gazes collided, and Lachlan noticed the stubborn set of her dark eyes, so different from Tarley's but the same stubborn streak.

He understood her emphatic refusal. "I won't sit by."

"I can't protect you and attempt to rescue her."

"You won't need to. Protect–"

"Lachlan," Johesha snapped, dropping any pretense of propriety between them. "You are the future of Jast—the future king. Think on that for once and allow me to do my fucking job!"

Jessamine cleared her throat, and Johesha glanced at her, then back at Lachlan "I failed you once, failed

Jast. Never again. We lost you."

"I wasn't lost, Jo." Lachlan's gaze skimmed the stubborn-set features of his guard, his friend, begging for his understanding. "I love her."

Johesha's dark eyes studied him. "On me, then," he relented. "But you do as I say."

After securing the horses, they pressed quietly through the woods on foot until they reached the edge of a clearing. The first thing that hit him was the awful stench. He held his arm up to his nose and mouth. Jessamine and Mattias were doing the same. It made his eyes water. The second thing he saw was Tarley. Alive. Her nose pressed against her shoulder as she limped across the clearing, her hands were tied. She was being led by a horribly, filthy man, dressed as if he were wearing the forest. That, Lachlan decided, was probably a Northman.

He looked a mess.

So did Tarley, though despite dark stains on her haphazard attire, missing shoes, and the mess of her hair, she looked unharmed. But then she turned to look around, he saw blood streaked along the skin of her face and neck.

Lachlan lurched only to be dragged down into the brush. "She's hurt," he snapped at whoever had him.

"Lachlan. Think!" Johesha. "Impulsivity isn't going to get Tarley to safety."

He looked at Johesha, then.

"Focus on the end, not the now." Johesha nodded at him, his eyes wide and waiting for Lachlan's acquiescence. When the tension in him eased, Johesha's grip did as well. "First things first. We're waiting on Jude and Brendsen to bring back their report."

Lachlan knew this. He'd learned it. He took a deep breath. They needed to know the numbers, weapons, guards, orientation. To get Tarley, Lachlan knew they needed to know what they were up against to counter with the appropriate move. But his emotions weren't letting him think clearly. He took another breath and turned back to watch Tarley. The man escorting her stopped as another man appeared. The Northman moved behind Tarley, blocking her from Lachlan's view.

Then a mountain of a man appeared from inside the tent and started toward Tarley.

Movement in his periphery caught his eye. Two men from the camp moved along the tree line toward their hiding spot. Suddenly, they dropped and were dragged into the underbrush. It happened quickly, silently.

"I've seen him before. At the inn," Mattias said.

Lachlan looked back across the camp. The man spoke but was too far away to hear what was said.

"Who is he?"

"I don't know him. Just know he's been around Sevens."

"He seems to know Tarley," Jessamine whispered.

The large man's laugh drifted across the clearing. It wasn't a comforting sound.

"But he hasn't freed her," Johesha said. "Not sure she's out of danger yet."

The large man took the rope from her first captor and led her into the tent.

"Shit," Lachlan said, the tension to move bursting through his limbs.

"Report," Johesha whispered to the bushes.

"Forty or fifty. Look organized." Jude's voice drifted from somewhere Lachlan couldn't see.

"All armed, but they aren't at the ready," Brendsen added. "Paired guards at fixed intervals. We took care of the entry point, sir."

Johesha unbuckled his leather breastplate.

"What are you doing?" Lachlan asked.

"Going in. Can't go in with Jast insignia."

Lachlan unbuckled the one he was wearing, offered by a soldier at the inn, bare of any unearned sigil. "Take this one—"

"Your Highness," Johesha started.

"I'll put yours on," he said.

They traded.

As Johesha slipped back into the unmarked breastplate, he offered orders. "Do not come in, no matter what you see. Understand."

Lachlan nodded.

But it seemed Johesha didn't trust him, because he said, "Jude. Brendsen. The prince isn't to move."

Both guards offered a noise of affirmation.

"I'll get her," Johesha said to Lachlan. "On my honor."

"Jo-" Lachlan started.

"On my honor." Then the captain slid from the hiding spot and disappeared through the bramble. He reappeared where the two guards had once been, stood at the edge of the tree line, then walked right in as if he wanted to be caught.

"What is he doing?" Jessamine exclaimed, though her tone was hushed.

"What should we do?" Mattias asked.

Worried about interfering with whatever Captain Johesha had planned—because he clearly seemed to have one—Lachlan looked at Mattias, and with as much wisdom and patience as he could muster, said, "We wait."

"And be ready," Brendsen added from somewhere in the brush. "We'll need the horses when they get her out."

Lachlan hated sitting on the sidelines. His body began to twitch with anxiety. When Jessamine's hand closed around his arm, he stilled.

She stopped him with her whisper. "Tarley won't want anything to happen to you."

"I don't want anything to happen to her."

"Your guard is capable?"

Lachlan nodded.

"You have other duties. Let them do theirs."

He hated that she was right and hated that he felt ill with his impatience, but he understood. There was a time to act and a time to be patient. A time to fight and a time to relent. The wisdom was understanding the difference and acting accordingly. He took a deep breath, closed his eyes, and despite everything in him wanting to act, trusted Johesha to do what needed to be done. For Tarley.

Tarley

Four Tankards dragged her forward toward the tent.

Digging her injured feet into the dirt, she screamed, "No!"

"Dramatics won't change your circumstances," he said, yanking her harder.

Tarley planted her feet and dropped down to her knees, but with her hands bound she couldn't control anything. Four Tankards just dragged her through the loam anyway.

Hep rushed forward to help her.

"Leave her," Four Tankards snapped, then yanked her to her feet, nearly pulling her arm from her socket as he did. "Calm the fuck down."

She ignored the pain in her shoulder. "I won't! I will make your life a living hell." She spat the words with vehemence. "That's a fucking promise."

Four Tankards backhanded her, his thick, meaty hand catching her squarely across the face. There was a ring on one of his fingers, slicing her cheek. "You don't fucking calm down, you'll arrive at the convent ridden and broken." The man pulled her through the flaps of the tent and shoved her so she fell face first in the dirt, everything on fire. "That's a fucking promise."

Having bitten her lip, she tasted copper and iron and spat bloody spittle into the dirt.

"Now. Let's reacquaint ourselves." He walked past her and poured himself a drink, then threw it back before pouring another. "We have unfinished business, you and me."

She bit down a curse and spat more blood instead. She wanted to fight, but she didn't have what she needed to win, and inflaming him might be worse for her if he was willing to hit her. *Ridden and broken.* Besides a horrific creature called a darkling, this was the worst-case scenario; it didn't stop her from casting an angry look at him.

Four Tankards chuckled, but it wasn't a pleasant sound. "What? Nothing to say?" He poured himself another drink. "That I highly doubt. I've met you."

She ignored him, struggling to get to her knees. She

needed to think, but it was difficult. She was panicked and hurt, blinking to correct the way she was suddenly seeing double. Tears stabbed her eyes — pain, but also frustration, wishing she could do more.

As she pushed off the ground, she wasn't in the tent anymore, but on the forest floor, her hands in the soft loam of moss and leaves. The earth trembled around her, and she looked up to see horses rushing past her, carrying shadowed riders.

She shook her head, in the tent once more.

A vision.

Four Tankards stalked forward, grabbed her hair, and yanked her head back, forcing her to look up at him. "Exactly where you should be. On your knees." He took a sip of the drink in his other hand. "No champion this time. I owe you for last time."

Darkness blinded her, but she hadn't moved. A horrible voice spoke to her from the pervasive gloom in her mind. "Azleah," the unnatural voice hissed from the darkness. "I'm coming for you–"

She tried to pull away, only she was still in the tent, her hair in Four Tankard's grip. Her scalp smarted as he wrenched her head.

The giant man bent forward so they were nearly nose to nose. "I can't wait to fucking break that spirit." Those words were a promise.

Tarley shivered.

Then she descended into another vision, falling against a wall, only it wasn't a wall, but a chest, a breastplate stamped with a tree—the tree of Jast—but then the image faded into nothing. She tried to focus on the face it belonged to, but the vision drifted away just as quickly as it began.

She felt sick, suddenly and pressed her bound hands to her belly.

Four Tankards released her hair. "I reported you to the Sevens' priest. You and your bodyguard. The acolyte tried to claim you were protected." He took a few steps away to the table where the bottle of spirits sat, pouring himself another dram. "It makes me wonder why you're here at all if that priest did his job."

Tarley didn't respond, sure it wasn't really a question, swallowing her nausea.

He took another gulp of his drink. "That priest is probably corrupt. Which is what we're fighting against."

We're? Tarley caught the word.

"Well?" Four Tankards asked.

"Oh. You were expecting an answer? How would I know? I'm just a woman."

The man narrowed his eyes. "This is why we do what we do." He pointed at her with his glass, then thought better of the passive action and stalked across the space to her, grabbing her face with his hand and squeezing her cheeks between his fingers. She tried to yank her face from his grasp, but couldn't, the pressure of his grip biting into her skin and bones. "Keep you in your place. Like that bitch queen." He pushed her face away, knocking her back to the ground.

His comment struck another note of familiarity,

but Tarley wasn't hearing the song yet. "The queen?" she asked, struggling back to her knees.

He grabbed the drink and sucked another gulp, then smacked the glass down on the table. He was in a fair way of finding himself drunk as fast as he was drinking it. Tarley wasn't sure if that was a good thing for her or a more dangerous one.

"She had to die. Her and that idiot prince."

"What do you mean?" Tarley breathed, her eyes drifting down to the ground as if the final pieces to this puzzle might be found there. The assassinations. She lifted her face and looked at him. "You?" And she knew it as clearly as she knew she was bleeding. This wasn't an encampment of random thieves or a clan of hunters. There was structure here. Piecing together what she'd heard and observed, she was positive she was in the middle of Fiedel—the group Queen Keyanna believed was behind her assassination attempt, and the most likely to have made the attempt on Lachlan as well.

Indignant anger rose inside her.

"Who's at the inn?" he demanded. "We know you have information about the groups that arrived."

"I don't know anything," she said.

He moved quickly across the space, yanking her head back once more. "I'm not an idiot, wench," he said and raised his hand.

Tarley flinched, but the blow never hit because someone entered behind her, catching his attention.

"Romis."

"I said no fucking interruptions," Four Tankards growled. "I'm interrogating the prisoner."

"I know, but–"

"It better be something very important."

"A messenger's arrived."

"The courier?" Four Tankards—Romis—asked, and stepped back, releasing Tarley's hair and shoving her back so she lost her balance once more.

"He says he has something for you."

"Bring him in. The Patriarch must have sent word." When they were alone again—or Tarley assumed it was so—Romis measured her. "Don't get comfortable."

Barely a breath later, the flap shifted and there were footsteps, until a man appeared at her side.

Tarley stared at the stranger. He was handsome: dark-skinned, dark-eyed, his hair shorn close to his head, a beard framing his face. A frown sharpened his features and made him seem as if he'd been hewn from dark granite. He was tall and muscular, the sinew of his arms a study in peaks and valleys. Intimidating.

Tarley looked down at the dirty floor inside the tent where she'd been dragged, relieved that he'd arrived, but wary to know what it could mean. Suppressing a shudder, she hated to imagine what might have happened if he hadn't interrupted. She had to get away.

"Well?" Romis asked of the newcomer. "The message?"

"It's time," the man said and glanced at Tarley. When his eyes met hers for a fleeting moment, she felt as if he was talking to her. In the next instant, she realized she recognized him. He'd been at the inn, a part of the Jast contingent. Lachlan had touched him—clapped a hand on his shoulder. The relief this man had worn on his face the moment he'd seen Lachlan alive was what she remembered; a look as concrete as the plain leather breastplate sans sigil covering his wide chest. She looked at it closer, feeling the warm rush of familiarity.

Her vision.

Her eyes flew up to the man's face.

Was he a traitor? Had he sold out Lachlan and Jast? The one who'd provided the means to assassinate Lachlan and frame Jast for the queen's death? The thought burned through her. But her vision hadn't made her feel fear or anger. She'd felt relief. Safe. Tarley wasn't sure what to trust.

"We're to move on them? When?" Romis asked and crossed his arms over his chest.

"Immediately."

"Verify it with a name."

"You know I can't tell you. Anonymity and deniability." The man's hand rested on the sword at his hip. "But you may know my name—Johesha."

Suddenly Tarley didn't want to run away or hide in the woods anymore. She didn't want to run from Lachlan. She wanted to run toward him. To protect him. To fight for her home, for Keyanna, for her sisters and every other woman in Kaloma subjected to injustice based on her sex. She'd twistedly thought hiding and living her life hidden had been an act of subversion, but revolution meant action. She was ready to fight.

As if the man next to her—Johesha—heard her thoughts, he moved. He was a blur, the stealth, speed, and power of it—so quick—Tarley barely had time to blink, before Johesha held a blade to Romis's throat.

"Untie her," Johesha said to the other man in the tent near the entrance.

"What the fuck is this?" Romis asked, his hands out in front of him.

"Your reckoning."

"You fool!" Romis yelled at the other man, then hissed as the blade pressed deeper into his throat. "Not the courier! You didn't check?"

"Are you willing to die today?" Johesha asked, his voice even and calm.

Romis—eyes flashing with panic—looked at whoever was behind Tarley. "Untie her. Untie her."

Suddenly Tarley's hands were free, and she stood, turning to the other man, and snatched his weapons.

"Your Highness–"

"Highness?" Romis asked.

Tarley turned to look at Johesha. "What? I'm not..." She stopped. "How do I know you're not a traitor?"

"The Crown Prince of Jast has claimed you as his future wife. I serve the crown. I serve you, but for the moment, I need you to do everything I tell you to do."

"Is he–"

"Waiting on you," Johesha said with a slight nod.

She knew in her gut she could trust this man, not so much by his words, but by his actions. By the vision and its impression stamped on her own heart. Lachlan was here! He'd come for her. She needed to see him.

"Tie him," Johesha nodded at the man she'd just relieved of his weapons.

"The prince?" Romis spat the words but they were cut short. "How is he alive?" Blood appeared at the tip of Johesha's blade pressed deeper into Romis's neck.

"My prince is a fighter, and if you want to live to see a trial—or whatever it is you do in this ass-backward country—you will choose silence and do everything I say to keep your head."

Romis swallowed against the blade but didn't attempt a nod.

Tarley faced Romis. "How did you get the Jast armor and arrows?"

Romis smirked, then frowned when the force of Johesha's blade pressed deeper. "I give you leave to answer the lady's question."

"Stolen from the dead bodies after the attack on the prince."

"Behind me," Johesha told Tarley, then pushed Romis forward saying, "Tell your men to stand down, and you might make it out alive. The camp is surrounded."

Surrounded? Tarley followed Johesha from the tent.

"Make way," Romis said to each man moving

forward, hands on weapons. "Let us pass—"

The men—faces dark with anger—made way for them to walk through, but the swath closed behind them, so Tarley turned to watch their backs. She held up the knives she'd taken and hoped Johesha had been telling the truth, that beyond the tree line the calvary awaited. Otherwise, she wasn't sure they would make it out of this meadow alive.

Lachlan

From the cover of the trees, Lachlan with Mattias and Jessamine, along with Jude and Brendsen somewhere in the cover of the wood's shadows, watched as Captain Johesha walked into the center of camp as if he belonged there.

"What is he doing?" Jessamine asked, her voice slightly elevated with surprise and concern.

Lachlan's chest compressed, though he knew Johesha never did anything impulsively. He was thoughtful, conscientious, serious, and very skilled. "Whatever he needs to," Lachlan said.

Tall and imposing, Johesha looked like a man with a purpose. Men stood near their tents and fires and watched him pass. The camp—despite the awful smell—was surprising when assessed beyond that fact. Top-shape tents constructed of excellent materials that would withstand the first frost. Lots of young, skilled men. Horsemen working with quality animals. Excellent leathers on the animals. Men practicing with a variety of well-kept weapons. They were well-fed and their humor was good, a laugh drifting across the meadow every so often. And in the far corner he noted the roof of something constructed—perhaps a pen for animals. This didn't appear to be a random group but rather an organized one, funded well.

Lachlan's breath caught when a man finally stopped Johesha's progress—much too long had he been walking through a Jast encampment. They spoke. Lachlan could only imagine what about, but a few seconds later, the men started moving and Lachlan resumed breathing.

"What do you think he said," Jessamine asked.

Lachlan tracked the captain's progress. He was free to maneuver without restraints and still had his weapons, which suggested whatever he'd told the other man had been the right thing. Lachlan could take a guess and knew it probably would paint the captain as a traitor to Jast.

"Spy stuff," Mattias answered, not far off base. "That's... wow."

"Mother would kill you first," Jessamine said, as if to stop any ideas Mattias might be getting.

"I'm a grown man," he groused.

"She'd argue with you."

"She'd argue about everything."

"Don't worry," Brendsen whispered from somewhere unseen. "The captain is the best."

Lachlan knew that was true, but Captain Johesha's abilities didn't stop the way Lachlan's gut churned even more when the captain disappeared into the tent. After a minute—which felt like ten—Lachlan started twitching. After another, he knew he couldn't stay in his skin.

"Your Highness," Jude said from his hiding place. "Stop moving."

"I can't. I can't." Lachlan lurched to his hands and knees, ready to bolt, when all the air was knocked from his chest.

"Forgive me," Jude said, his gruff voice near Lachlan's ear, his heavy body draped across Lachlan's back.

"Me too, sir," Brendsen said, his wiry frame locking down Lachlan's legs. "We have orders."

Lachlan pressed his forehead into the loam, angry with himself. He knew better and still hadn't reined himself in. They were right, and he'd failed the test. He hadn't considered running into the camp for the good of Jast, but for himself. "Fine," he grunted in acquiescence. "I'm good. Let me up. On my honor."

Those three words were enough for the two guards holding him down. They released Lachlan but watched him warily.

Lachlan held up his hands. "Just keep my mind engaged." He turned to Mattias and Jessamine.

"Keyanna told me Kaloma doesn't have a standing army, but this looks—"

"They don't," Jessamine answered. "This isn't a Kaloma army. But each community does oversee a group of militia volunteers. Sevens has three or four if there was a call to arms."

"Father said the coffers were decimated after the war with Jast," Mattias said.

"Which led to the Law of Means," Jessamine added.

"But not for an army."

They both shook their head.

"Mattias, you've been out in the woods a lot?" Lachlan asked.

The young man nodded.

"This look like a typical hunting party to you? Tarley and I met a hunter before she brought me back. He didn't look like these men. He'd been filthy and hungry."

Mattias skimmed the glade before looking back at Lachlan. "Not really. Father and I have come across a few. I've never thought of them as organized."

"Makes me wonder where this group's money came from. Know where the Law of Means collection goes? Doesn't the government get it?" Lachlan asked.

"Supposed to, but like everything, the Rayoran— the church—receive their portion off the top," Jessamine said.

"How much?"

"I'm not sure, but the normal tithe is big. At least

half."

He couldn't keep the shock from his voice. "Half? To the church?" He looked back at the meadow filled with what looked to be an army. Keyanna suspected that those in her cabinet were behind the attack, because of her desire to change the laws, but she'd thought it had been about the subjugation of women. Perhaps it was on one level, but not completely. It was about money. "If the government isn't funding a militia like this one, who could afford it?" Lachlan asked, though he was pretty sure he knew the answer.

"The church," Mattias and Jessamine said simultaneously.

"Then what's funding the collectors? The hunters? The convents?"

They both shrugged. "We've always thought it was the church."

"Know what happens when a woman gets turned over to one of those convents?"

"She's supposed to be cared for," Mattias said.

"But?" Lachlan asked, hearing the unfinished thought in Mattias's voice.

"If rumors are true, women are being sold–"

Lachlan shook his head with disbelief. "To whom?"

"Whoever can afford it, I suppose: skin houses in the capital, lords, other kingdoms. Jast isn't–"

Lachlan shook his head. "Absolutely not. Refugees have crossed the border, but we didn't know this." But did he know that for sure? What did happen to refugees after they crossed? He looked at the other two men. "Did you map the whole camp during your reconnaissance?"

"Yes, Your Highness," Jude nodded.

"What's in the pen? The opposite side of the camp?"

Jude's eyes flashed with rage, but he shuttered it for duty and said, "Women, sir. And children."

"Children too?" Jessamine paled. "You left them?"

"Couldn't raise the alarm. Not yet," Brendsen explained. "Not if we want to get your sister out."

Jude and Brendsen stilled, each of them holding up a hand. They moved, placing themselves near Lachlan.

"Someone's coming," Jude whispered. "Get down."

Brendsen lifted his bow and notched an arrow.

They heard the rustling of footsteps, though the shadows under the trees concealed whoever was approaching. Lachlan's fingers flexed around the cutlass at the ready, grateful this was an area he was skilled in thanks to Johesha. His heart raced, pounding the rhythm in his neck and ears. Then, as if a shining sun in the dark forest filled with dark circumstances, a Jast soldier appeared, followed by another, then another, their movements as measured and stealthy as possible in a mass of people.

Jude rose.

"Stand down," one called. "We've come to help."

And from the throng, Lachlan's eyes connected to one he recognized.

Lachlan stood. "Father?"

Mallor's gaze connected with his. "We saw..." He stopped, clearly shaken. "The horses."

Tomas Fareview stepped up to Mallor's side, strangely quiet for such a large man. His pallor hinted at his fear for his daughter.

"Father!" Jessamine hurried through the thicket to meet him.

"Have you found her?" Tomas asked as he folded Jessamine in his arms. "We saw the body–" He tightened his hold around her. "It isn't–"

"Tarley's here," Mattias told him.

Tomas blew out a breath. "Alive?"

"Yes."

"We tracked her here," Lachlan told him. "Watched her taken into a tent."

Tomas's relief was palpable, his rigid posture melting around Jessamine with an audible sigh. "What's been done?"

"Captain Johesha's gone in to get her," Mattias explained.

"What do we know?" Mallor asked.

Lachlan looked at his father, studying the face of the man he'd spent so much time at odds with, relieved to see him. "You're here."

"Of course I'm here," Mallor replied as if there weren't any other alternative. "My son is here. His betrothed has been——abducted, it would seem. This is an attack on Jast."

Lachlan swallowed, looked down, and nodded, his

throat suddenly struggling to operate. He wasn't exactly sure why his father being here moved him in such a way. Lachlan knew his father loved him—despite their epic arguments and failures to communicate with one another—his father's love hadn't ever been in question.

"Why do you doubt me?" Mallor asked quietly.

Lachlan was taken aback at the question. Had he doubted his father? "I don't doubt you, Father. I felt you doubted me."

Mallor reached out and grabbed the side of Lachlan's face, his fingers curled around the back of Lachlan's head. "I have always believed in you, Lachlan. Even when you didn't believe in yourself."

He hung his head. "I didn't give you a reason to. Before."

"Do you think any of us have given our fathers reason to think we'll rise to the occasion." Mallor grinned, pulling Lachlan into his embrace. "I shouldn't have promised you to Truisante that way."

"I should have spoken to you–"

Mallor pulled away to look Lachlan in the eye. "What is done is done. On my honor," his father started and stopped, filled with the emotion and weight of those words. He swallowed. "On my honor, I will strive to be a better father."

"On my honor, I will strive to be a better prince."

When Mallor drew back, he took a moment to search Lachlan's face, offered him a wan smile, then repeated his question, the mantle of king on his shoulders once more. "What do we know?"

Lachlan took a deep breath, centering himself. "Organized group. Forty to fifty strong. Armed." He paused. "I suspect this is the group Keyanna's spies uncovered."

"The assassins?" Mallor asked.

Lachlan nodded and looked at Jude and Brendsen. "Anything else?"

They shook their heads.

"If they find out Miss Fareview is your betrothed…" Mallor's brow creased deeper than it already was. "What's been done?"

Lachlan filled his father in.

"They let Johesha in?"

Major Urik, the leader of the King's guard, moved through the ranks to Mallor's side.

"What is it, Urik?"

"Movement, Your Majesty."

Turning to look, Lachlan saw a mass of bodies moving through the encampment. The cluster of men broke apart as Captain Johesha, held the man who'd taken Tarley into the tent at knifepoint in front of him, walked through the throng of men allowing him to pass.

"Where's Tarley?" Tomas asked.

"There," someone said. "Behind the captain."

Barely visible behind the captain, Lachlan caught the movement of her head, just over his shoulder. The closer they drew to the tree line, Lachlan could see she was wielding a set of daggers, one in each hand, protecting Johesha's back.

Lachlan's chest expanded with pride.

As much as he wanted to rush the field toward her, he checked his impulse, and his eyes jumped to the roof of the pen. Tarley wouldn't forgive him if there were others to save, if they had the opportunity to bring this group to justice and hadn't–

"There's a cage of women and children in the southwest corner of the camp," Lachlan stated, swallowing any trepidation he had for Tarley and trusting Johesha. "And if this is Fiedel, we are duty bound to respond not only for Jast, but for the new treaty with Kaloma."

Mallor straightened, his features relaxing a touch as he looked at Lachlan. "What are you suggesting?"

Lachlan looked around at the group. They were twenty strong. Capable soldiers with horses. "We take them all."

Mallor turned to Major Urik. "Assessment?"

"With horses, it's possible, Your Majesty."

Mallor nodded, turning back to Lachlan when a crack beyond rang out in the woods like a shot. The entire group swiveled toward it, swords and bows raised.

"Whoa," Nixus Uraiahs said, stepping out from behind a tree, hands up and empty. He was dressed in a black suit as if he were off to a dinner party. "Not the enemy. Not today, at least. I've come to offer my aid."

"Stand down," Lachlan said and pushed through the soldiers between them. "Dressed like that?"

Nixus smirked. "As you see."

"How did you—"

"Auri told me."

Lachlan glanced around looking for a horse, "But, how—"

Nix stepped forward and leaned a touch closer to Lachlan. "It's probably best to just suspend your questions, young prince. The answers might be more than you're ready to consider at present." He smiled a dark smile. "But our goals are aligned."

Lachlan frowned but said, "My thanks."

"Thanks aren't unnecessary. I would destroy the universe for Auri."

Lachlan couldn't fault him for it, though the sentiment was rather dark. "Do you need a weapon?"

Nix smiled another of his unnerving smiles. "I've an arsenal at my disposal."

Confused, Lachlan couldn't see any.

Nix chuckled again. "My weapons are best showcased in action."

Unsettled by Auri's strange suitor, who rarely made sense, Lachlan turned back toward the meadow, and his father.

His father's eyes met Lachlan's. "The prince makes this decision," Mallor said, his gaze never wavering.

Lachlan offered an imperceptible nod to his father, a way to communicate that he accepted his trust, and said, "Here's the plan."

Tarley

arley held the daggers at the ready, each step backward feeling too slow, too clumsy. Romis—Captain Johesha between them—was yelling at the men to "stay back" and to "make way" creating a wide swath allowing them to pass, but the passage collapsed around them as she and Johesha moved through it.

"Captain," Tarley said, beginning to panic, her heart racing in her chest and her muscles tight with tension. She gripped the daggers tighter. The men behind her pressed in closer, their faces twisted with an appetite to destroy. She raised her daggers, forcing herself to appear as if she was confident to use them, but knowing she was completely unprepared. Her father had taught her to defend herself, but not to go to battle with weapons.

"Focus, my lady," Johesha said.

"But—"

Suddenly one of the men lunged toward her. She yelped and a "thwack" snicked past her, the man dropping to his knees with an arrow protruding from his head.

Johesha whistled.

With Tarley's next breath the forest came alive. The ground trembled as a company of men on horseback, weapons at the ready, streamed into the grove from the forest. Her vision! A shout went up around her as the band of men beholden to Romis roared, surging toward them.

Johesha released Romis, grabbing hold of Tarley. "My lady. To the forest," he said.

Only Romis, with murder in his eyes, stood between them and the trees. They were surrounded everywhere else. Romis picked up a sword from a fallen comrade. "You should have killed me," he shouted as a battle waged around them, lifting the sword and rushing Johesha's back.

Tarley screamed, grabbing hold of the captain, and yanking him out of the way, but her efforts were unnecessary as a dark shadow whirled between them.

Romis stopped. "What—"

Tarley was equally confounded.

Like a stretch of shade under a tree, the shadows

swirled, combining, until they coalesced into a well-dressed man.

"Mr. Uraiahs?" Tarley said.

He turned his head and winked at Tarley before facing Romis, whose jaw was slack with shock. After blinking several times, he said, "You."

"In the flesh." Nixus straightened the cuffs of his stark white shirt under the black jacket. "I had hoped our last encounter left you with a lasting impression. It would seem I've grown too merciful from my confinement."

Romis backed up a step, sword slumped, and looking as if he might run.

"Please do it," Nix urged.

Romis raised his sword, looked at it, and grinned. "It seems I have the upper hand today."

"So tiresome," Nix said, then followed up the observation with a deep sigh. "You should know before you try it—I don't give second chances."

Romis yelled, sword raised, and rushed Nix—but Romis crumpled to the ground, his face a bloody mess, sliding to a stop at Nix's feet.

Nix hadn't even moved, just looked down at the man before he straightened his sleeves again. He turned to Tarley and grinned. "Well, that was rather easy. Shall I end them all?"

"End all of whom?" she asked.

Nixus glanced around the meadow, and she followed his gaze.

"The men?"

"Allow me to demonstrate once more," Nix said and pointed at a man with an ax high over his head. The ax began its descent toward a Jast soldier, the traitor froze, blood blooming from his eyes, his nose, and his mouth and the ax dropped from his hands before he crumpled to the ground at the Jast's soldier's feet.

"Humans are so fragile," he said. "I forgot that."

The battle raged around them, though it was clear that the soldiers of Jast were gaining the upper hand. Men fighting near them noticed Romis's dead body and stopped, laying down their arms and falling to their knees.

"So?" Nix turned and looked at Tarley once more. "End them? Or do you feel mercy is appropriate? Which would Auri prefer? I don't often choose mercy, but I find I'd rather not face Auri's wrath."

Tarley looked at Nix—obviously not a man—named after the god of night and darkness and asked, "Who are you?"

He grinned. "Ask Auri. I would be diverted by her answer."

"Are you a—" she swallowed, "a darkling?"

"What?" He straightened looking insulted. "A darkling. Absolutely not. A darkling is a parasite! Why would you—"

But a shout across the meadow cut off his question. He dematerialized, becoming a shadow once more, then disappeared altogether.

Johesha—who Tarley was sure was rarely surprised

by anything—looked dismayed, his face slack with shock, before asking, "What just happened? Was that real?"

"I wish I had an answer for you, Captain, but it is only one of the strange things I've witnessed today," Tarley pulled on his sleeve to get him moving.

"Tarley!" a voice yelled.

She looked up to see Jessamine, followed by Mattias and their father, rushing from the woods.

"Go," Johesha said, raising his sword and disappearing into the throng.

Tarley raced across the grove, closing the distance to her family, and they swarmed her. Inside their collective embrace, she relaxed into them as they all spoke at once. Angry with her, relieved, warning her of Scarlett's impending wrath, but the discontent meant so little now when before it had meant everything, because they loved her. They'd come for her.

But she needed Lachlan and pulled away. "Where is he?"

Her father—seeming to know—nodded toward the meadow beyond. "Doing what needs to be done."

Tarley followed her father's gaze and found Lachlan astride a horse, moving through the mass of people, his countenance assured and in command. It was clear Jast had control of the camp, the traitors restrained, strays being subdued. Lachlan stopped his horse when he found Captain Johesha and leaned forward as they spoke.

The captain gesticulated in her direction and

Lachlan looked up. His eyes locked with hers. Tarley raised her hand, and his body seemed to sag with relief. He nudged his horse in her direction, pushing it into a trot so he could reach her faster.

Suddenly, an awful screech rent the air.

Tarley—along with everyone else in the meadow—covered her ears, crouching down. Lachlan's horse cried out, rearing. The horse yanked against Lachlan's lead, sidestepping, but Lachlan remain seated.

A horrifying darkness appeared, floating between Tarley and Lachlan—an entity of corporeal form—spooking the animals and terrifying everyone in the glade. Unlike Nixus's appearance from the shadows, however, this being's countenance seemed both slick—like black liquid—and simultaneously matted like granular sand. It had a pale, gray face, red eyes, and a wide grimace filled with sharp, pointy teeth. Its face turned Tarley's way, tilting its horrible head at an unnatural angle, and floated across the meadow toward her with a terrifying grin. It lifted a clawed hand and pointed at her.

"I see you, Tarley Fareview," it hissed. "So shiny." The horrible voice scraped along her nerves, and she shuddered. "You cannot hide. You're too bright."

"Tarley!" Lachlan yelled, sliding from his horse and rushing toward her.

"No!" she screamed, afraid for him, knowing what that thing had done at the campsite. Lachlan scrambled forward anyway, only Captain Johesha tackled Lachlan to the ground as the dark thing folded in on itself in the opposite direction without turning at all.

"Mine," it seethed, the sound stretched out.

On shaking legs, Tarley stepped forward. "Not yours." Someone grabbed at her arms to keep her in place.

"That, Miss Fareview, is a darkling." Nix's voice—unexpectedly next to her—startled her. "And technically, it would seem in its way of doing things, you kind of are."

She turned her head and frowned at him. "Nixus!"

"First names then? Got it. Tarley!" He mimicked her frustrated tone.

"Where have you been?"

He crossed his arms. "Here and there," he said and nodded at the creature who'd stopped. "And as you can see, I'm nothing like that. I'm quite put out by your comparison. You should take it back."

"Can't you just snap your fingers or something. 'End him,'" she lowered her voice to Nixus's octave.

"Terrible impression, Tarley. Sorry. Can't do it with this. There are other factors at play. I could steal and control its darkness momentarily, but–" He shuddered. "Gross."

The creature screeched again.

Her gaze snapped back to the monster undulating over the meadow, staring at her once more with its mouth distended in its awful scream. "Mine! Mine!"

"That's Rufus?" she asked, more to herself than to Nixus.

"Is it? I don't know what a Rufus is. Horrible

creatures. Difficult to kill, but not impossible."

"Why can't you?"

"The magic that created it isn't the kind of magic I can wield. We need magical light and fire. But I know a couple of gods." Nixus made a disgusted noise, and Tarley had this strange sense she was in a weird dream.

The bored indifference of Nix was a strange juxtaposition to the terror of what was pulsing around her in the glen. Though perhaps Nixus's countenance was exactly what she needed to remain calm. Everyone else aside from Lachlan, struggling against Captain Johesha's hold, was frozen with fear.

"Did you say gods?"

"I did."

Tarley turned to him, mouth agape. "Nixus. As in god of night?"

He turned at looked at her, a true smile blooming on his face. "I'm so honored, Tarley. Auri said you Fareviews aren't believers in the old gods."

"Mine! Mine! Mine!"

They both turned back to the creature screaming and floating back and forth in front of them.

"I think it's screaming at you, Nixus."

"Seems a bit preoccupied with you though, Tarley." He unfolded his arms. "Did you speak with it?"

The darkling moved hesitantly toward her, though skirting opposite Nixus.

"I didn't speak to that!" She pointed at it, incredulous.

"They can shapeshift. In a different form, maybe?"

"A man? Rufus."

"Ah. Right. A Rufus." Nix paused, considering it. "It would seem it's imprinted on you. Won't stop looking for you—ever—until you're either its blood-slave or it kills you."

Tarley paled.

"Though if you die, the bond will break, or so my sister once told me." Nix glanced at her with a grin. "So which will it be?"

The darkling lurched, then stopped, wary of Nixus.

"Tarley!" Lachlan yelled.

"None of those options work for me, Nixus."

"Figured as much."

"But it seems like it wants to avoid you," she said and turned to look at Auri's suitor, who also happened to be a god, but he was gone.

Her heart slammed against her chest. "Nixus?"

No answer.

Without Nix by her side, the creature moved toward her once more.

"Tarley," Lachlan shouted. "Run!"

Only she knew she couldn't. She'd tried it and failed. She was only alive because of Hep.

No. She had to stand her ground.

Tarley watched as the monster's form shifted. The shreds of its cloak became legs wrapped in dark trousers with dark shoes on its new feet. Its torso morphed into a chest with arms covered with a dark jacket, buttoned over a white shirt. Normal limbs, shoulders, neck, and its horrific face shifted into one she recognized. Rufus, blond hair and all, completely back together once more, only not as substantive.

"Oh gods." Jessamine's grip around Tarley's arm tightened, and her sister tugged her backward.

Rufus drifted slowly across the meadow toward her, his form nearly whole as opposed to how she'd seen him earlier with his head bashed in. "Tarley. Tarley. Tarley." It clicked her name. "You can't escape. It's time to satiate."

"Enough," a powerful voice echoed across the meadow, startling the darkling back into its monster form.

Horses screeched and yanked at their bridles. Birds alighted, taking flight from the trees. Every person in the meadow looked up at the sky. Meanwhile, the creature hunched in on itself in supplication and hissed out, "Master."

A raven landed in between the darkling and Tarley. Then another. And another, until there were three birds hopping between them. One bounced toward the darkling. "You disobeyed me–" the raven spoke in that powerful voice.

"What the–" Mattias breathed behind her, holding onto the arm Jessamine wasn't squeezing.

"You said I could have one–" the thing rasped.

"I said to find them. Nothing more."

"But she invited me–"

"You deserve punishment."

"I need to eat," the thing whined.

"You were given leave to feed, but the Fareviews were to be unadulterated."

The raven hopped closer. "I can give you relief, however. I feel your pain."

The pitiful monster lifted its head, and its horrible red gaze hit Tarley's. "Mine," it sneered.

Tomas stepped forward, next to Tarley. She grasped her father's hand.

One of the ravens turned its head at Tomas's movement, tilting its head and watching with beady black eyes. The bird hopped forward, then took flight, landing a few steps away and looking up. "Ah, Tom," the raven said in the same voice as the raven that had spoken to the darkling. "I almost didn't recognize you. Bigger than the last time I saw you."

"Who are you?"

"Where's Azleah?" it asked.

Tomas retreated a step, and Tarley could see by her father's shocked face that whatever this creature was saying was something familiar.

The raven hopped around, its wings spread, then it settled. "She knew I would find her eventually, hence the spell. The darkling helped me see." The raven hopped. "She has what's mine. I want it back."

"Never," Tomas said, plainly, shaking his head.

The raven blinked and made a humming sound. "I don't think you understand the gravity of denying me. I see your children. My pet wants the one who's lost her protective spell. I can just as easily allow the imprint to remain as I can break it. And the other one—he's faint, but now that I know the spell, I can find them. And I will take them, just as Azleah stole from me. She will pay."

"Who's Azleah?" Tarley whispered to her father.

Tomas tensed, his hand tightening around hers. "Leave my children out of it—"

"Then give me what's mine!" the voice coming from the ravens roared, only it reverberated across the meadow like the deep guttural bellow of a thousand bears all at once. The sound climbed up Tarley's skin and sank its teeth into her skull. The three birds took flight and rushed across the space, attacking Tarley and her family, pecking, clawing, and yanking with their savage beaks and claws.

Then suddenly the barrage stopped.

The ravens sank back to the earth. "Darkling rise," the voice ordered.

The darkling uncurled its form and floated high, it's shadow long and thin, wispy and awful.

One of the ravens jumped, spreading its wings, and took flight.

"Open your well," the voice ordered the darkling.

The creature lifted its head and tipped it back as the center of its greasy form spread apart. At its core was a darkness so wrong, Tarley couldn't identify where it began and where it ended. She wanted to look away but didn't. Blood seemed to coat it, but she couldn't be sure, since she'd never seen anything like it.

The raven, flying above with something Tarley

couldn't identify in its beak, started to speak, chanting words she didn't recognize. The bird flew into the monster, the opening closing behind it, swallowing the bird whole. And then everything was still.

The two remaining ravens fluttered above the darkling now floating silently in the meadow.

"See. A good faith effort," the voice said. "I have broken the imprint. I have saved your daughter, Tomas. Am I not merciful?"

"There is never mercy where you are concerned," Tomas answered.

The voice made a disgruntled noise. "So be it. Here is my vow: I will unleash the darkling and everything else I have to hurt what you love, until Azleah gives me back what's mine. I will take everything from her, just as she did to me."

"Master," the darkling hissed. "The gods—"

The darkling and the ravens effervesced into nothing, leaving behind only a single sound carried across the meadow: "Everything."

Nixus reappeared where the darkling and ravens had been. "So? What did I miss?" He was facing Tarley. "Oh good. You're still alive." He made a relieved sound. "Auri would have been very angry." He turned in a tight circle assessing the meadow. "Wait? Where is it?"

The flutter of giant wings and a massive shadow overhead made everyone in the meadow duck down, yelling in terror. Tarley had a horrible fear that thousands of ravens had returned as a strong wind pressed against her skin made it difficult to remain upright, while an updraft of dirt and dust flew, biting at her exposed skin. When Tarley peeked out from behind her arm shielding her eyes, she watched a red dragon land its hulking form in the meadow.

A fucking dragon!

And it was fearsome. Scaled with sleek, shiny red scales that shone in the sun, some rimmed with gold so light reflected, glinting in the sunlight.

The creature blinked at Nix, yellow eyes narrowed with black slits. "Nixus? Where's the darkling?"

"Sorry, sister. It's…" Nixus looked perplexed and looked at Tarley.

"Sister?" Tarley yelled.

"How is it not here and you still are?"

"A dragon!" Tarley pointed.

"You dragged me here for nothing," the dragon snapped. The fearsome creature swiveled her head around, looking at the meadow. "But at least there's snacks."

"Nope. Nope." Nix walked to her and placed a hand on her long neck. "No snacks. Just the darkling, Lex." He glanced over his shoulder at Tarley, his brows drawing together with concern. "Where is it?"

Tarley looked around. Her father's and Mattias's faces were both cut and bleeding. She knew hers was as well, the cool mountain air biting against the slick heat of blood dribbling down her skin. Jessamine was thankfully unharmed. "I don't know. It just was here and then… not."

"Darklings don't just disappear." The dragon shrank down, morphing into a beautiful woman with sleek dark hair, tanned skin shimmering with gold dust in the light. She wore a red suit. "Not if they've imprinted on a victim."

"Tarley." Lachlan rushed past the dragon-woman until Tarley was in his arms. His hands were all over her face. "You're hurt."

Johesha rushed, flipping around between Lachlan and the dragon-woman

"You're here," she said.

"Of course I'm here." He ran his hands through her hair and pulled her back to look into her eyes. "I told you I would follow you anywhere." He cataloged every wound.

"Disgusting," the dragon-woman groused. "Where's Aurielle?"

"Mr. Uraiahs?" Tomas asked.

"I guess the dragon's out of the bag now," Nixus said. "Where's the darkling?"

"A conspiracy of ravens showed up after you disappeared and left me to die," Tarley snapped, stepping toward Nix, angry that he'd left them.

"Tarley," Lachlan said. "Maybe best not to upset a man with a dragon."

"A conspiracy of ravens?" Nixus clarified. "I sense a conspiracy." He looked at the dragon-woman, then back at Tarley. "And?"

"The ravens were its master," Lachlan added, then shook his head, looking confounded at the words he'd just spoken.

"Master?" Nix frowned.

"It broke the imprint," Mattias said. "Some spell."

"Please tell me, Tomas, that this voice wasn't the infamous *him* we've heard about."

Tarley turned to look at her father, who looked down at his feet, but didn't say anything.

"We need to get back to Sevens." Nixus's tone urgent. "Auri doesn't have her ribbon."

Tarley looked at her wrist, empty of its ribbon.

"You promised me a darkling, not a reunion, Nix."

The forest seemed to disintegrate around them, the whole of the meadow like dripping clay under the weight of water. Nixus and his sister stood at the center of it, arguing, and with a strange sensation that was a cross between floating and falling, Tarley grabbed hold of Lachlan and squeezed her eyes shut. When she blinked them open a moment later, the whole of the encampment, the tents, the soldiers, the horses, the prisoners, the freed women, and children stood stunned at the center of Sevens. Tarley watched Nixus—the dragon-woman no longer with him— walking toward the inn.

"Am I alive?" Mattias asked, his voice uneven and uncharacteristically subdued. "Because I think I've died, and I'm in some afterlife where there are dragons, and talking birds, and feral creatures with sharp teeth after my sister."

"Then we must all be in the same place," Lachlan said.

"Why doesn't that bring me comfort?" Mattias asked.

The Wizard

In a great burst of power, the wizard, now whole, along with the darkling in tow, landed in the room. With a shout, the wizard swiped the nearest table with both hands, and everything on it flew off with a great crash against the stone wall.

"You!" He turned on the darkling huddled in the corner and pointed, a spell on the edge of his mind to destroy it. "You nearly ruined everything!"

"Master," it hissed. "It was so shiny."

"Silence," the wizard raged, and the creature curled into a tighter version of itself.

He hated it, longing to destroy it to put the accursed thing out of its misery. Only they were bound, and he needed the pitiful thing for its tracking abilities and magical sight. For now, anyway.

The darkling hissed. "So hungry."

The wizard sighed. The creature had accomplished its task: find the girl from the woods, only the monster had exceeded the wizard's hopes, leading him to Tomas. Where Tomas was, Azleah was nearby. The wizard couldn't undo his bond to the darkling yet; he might need the creature still.

"I did promise you a plaything, didn't I?" He had made it a promise.

"Blood," the darkling moaned and sniffed the air.

With a sigh, the wizard muttered, and the wreckage from the table rolled across the floor collecting into a pile of refuse. Next, he muttered another spell and burned the offal with a snap of his fingers.

The darkling screeched in terror at the small flame.

"It isn't for you," the wizard said, glancing at the pitiful darkling once more. "Up," he commanded.

The darkling unfolded, rose to its full height taking up the room from floor to ceiling, and hovered in its grotesque form.

"Change," the wizard ordered. "I hate looking at you like that."

"Yes master," the creature rasped, and its form morphed. The wispy black tendrils of its outline smoothed into a clear line as it shrank. A body formed—one of a woman—clothed in a black dress. Its skin was pale, eyes black until it blinked, and the eyes shifted to a bright, clear blue.

"Better."

"Does this please you, master?" the darkling asked, its voice sweet and lilting now. Alluring if the wizard was interested, but he wasn't. He had another purpose and that would remain his focus.

"Yes," he told it. "I am pleased." He felt the creature vibrate at his words. Luring and binding himself to the creature had been a lesson in patience and power. The binding had proved bothersome. Casting a spell to keep the darkling from seeking him had been necessary. Additionally, he had to feel its ravenous hunger which was horrid and often painful. The wizard hadn't realized the darkling's need to imprint and satiate would become such a problem. When the creature's hunger grew so intense, the darkling ignored the tether between them.

But the binding had been fruitful as well. He'd siphoned some of his own powers to the darkling to enhance its ability to see through spells more clearly, though unfortunately not all. But in looking for the girl, it had led him to Tomas.

He was one step closer to Azleah. He would find her and break her. And she would break.

Just like she broke him.

"I have something for you," the wizard told the creature.

"A present?" it asked, grasping its hands between its ample bosoms. "I am so hungry," it moaned.

"I will end this pain for you."

"Tormented," it cried.

"Follow me." The wizard led the darkling from the room, through a doorway, and down a spiral staircase which wound into the darkness below the manor. When he reached the bottom, he lit a torch and led the creature though a dark corridor to a small wooden door. The wizard touched the lock and it clicked, but he didn't push it open.

"Hello?" someone called from inside.

The darkling sniffed. "A plaything?"

"Do you promise to help me?"

"Yes." The thing drew out the last sound, it's desire for whatever was beyond the door creating both ecstasy and pain.

The wizard pushed the door open. Huddled inside a dark cell littered with bones of other feedings was a chained woman. The darkling started through the door.

"Oh. You poor thing," the darkling in its new form said.

"Are you here to let me out?" she asked.

The wizard shut the door, listening as the darkling coerced its next meal, playing with its food. The screaming started as he reached the bottom of the staircase, but the wizard disconnected from the horror of it. He had more pressing things on his mind. Now that he knew where Azleah was, he could plan his revenge. He could restore what was his.

He grinned as he walked up the spiral staircase.

As he retraced his steps through the corridor, he considered the gods, knowing that was a complication he would have to consider. Their power was greater than his, but if he could only get back what Azleah had stolen… He'd determine a way around them.

As he climbed the stairs, he thought about the look Tomas's had given him when the man realized who he was. The fear on the man's face was perfection.

The wizard smiled. The darkling had found a different woman—her ribbon gone now—Tomas, and a son—nearly transparent with the ribbon spell still working.

When the wizard closed the door behind him, cutting off the screams, his smile faded. Something about the meadow wasn't quite right.

He'd missed something.

Tomas, the daughter he called Tarley, and the transparent son. He worked though the tableau in his mind, focusing on the details. When he returned to the main room, he sat down in his favorite chair and closed his eyes. Tomas, unprotected. Tarley, unprotected. The boy, protected, his ribbon glowing with golden light on his wrist holding onto the one named Tarley. The boy was faded from sight, difficult to see because of that spelled ribbon, but now that the wizard knew what he was looking for—thanks to the darkling—seeing them was clearer.

But he was missing something.

How did he know?

He could feel it in his being, like the blood running through his veins, only it was clotted and slow. There was nothing to indicate he'd missed something had other than his feelings. A sixth sense which he'd trusted all but once. Tomas. Tarley. The boy. The ribbons. Tomas. Tarley. The boy. The ribbons.

Then his eyes flew open.

Ribbons.

There'd been two!

Who had been wearing the other one?

Lachlan

Lachlan was never letting Tarley go. Not again. So as she rushed across the green toward the linn after Nixus, he kept hold of her hand.

"We need to find out what's going on."

Lachlan yanked on her hand to stop her. "Wait." He grasped hold of her face with his hands and pulled her to him. His mouth met hers with a force that spoke of his fear and desperation. She melted against him, kissing him back. "Don't ever leave me," he said against her mouth. "I was so afraid I'd lost you–"

Her hands gripped his shoulders. "I won't. I'm so sorry–"

He shook his head, his lips still connected to hers. "I'm sorry I wasn't quicker to defend you."

She leaned back to look at him, her finger skimming his hair away from his eyes. "I should have stayed to fight."

He smiled and pressed another kiss to her lips once more. "You should definitely always stay to fight." He squeezed her tighter. "Because then we can make up," he whispered in her ear.

A throat cleared behind them.

Tarley turned her head, and Lachlan swiveled to look over his shoulder. His father stood an arm's length away. Though she hurriedly stepped away, Lachlan didn't let her go, drawing her back to his side.

Tarley tried to straighten and smooth horrifically soiled boy's clothing, then looked down at the ground. Lachlan could imagine her trepidation, considering she'd been worried about facing the king in a normal dress. He squeezed her hand, hoping she knew that was the only place she would ever be from this point forward, in boy's clothing or not.

His father's eyes jumped to his, then back to Tarley. "It would seem, Lady Fareview, I owe you an apology." When Tarley moved to speak, he held up a hand. "I misspoke, and my son has set me right about the matter." His eyes connected with Lachlan's once more, giving him a nod.

"Your Majesty." She started to dip into a curtsey, but Mallor stopped her with a hand on her arm, drawing her back up.

"Let's forgo the formality, shall we. Fields and forests make for terrible places to be beholden to such strange protocols, wouldn't you say?" He offered her a smile, then cleared his throat. "I understand it is not only an apology I owe you, but my sincerest and humble gratitude for saving my son's life. And not only have you saved his life, but you also found the assassins to bring him and Jast justice."

Tarley looked at Lachlan once again and remained looking at him when she said, "Perhaps inadvertently."

"Forgive me." Mallor cleared his throat. "I find myself… unsettled by what we witnessed in the wood and what has transpired since." He glanced around, disturbed like everyone else about being in the meadow of the woods and within a heartbeat standing in Sevens.

"Only unsettled?" Tomas asked.

Lachlan looked at Tarley's father, his hair standing on end, worry etching his eyes.

Mallor gave him a short smile. "I might have understated that slightly."

"Pardon me. I need to find my wife." Tomas nodded then hurried past. "Tarley, Mattias, Jessamine," he shouted at them, forging the same trail Mr. Uraiahs took. "I think it's best you come with me."

"I'm not going behind the hedge! Father!" Tarley yelled after him. "Excuse me, Your Majesty." She curtsied, kissed Lachlan's cheek, and hurried after her father.

"Lachlan—"

"You don't like her?" he asked at his father's tone.

"She seems a wonder," his father said, "though I

can't say my first impression is one on which to base a formulated opinion. And I fear based on all that has occurred since, it might be jaded."

"I'm marrying her," Lachlan said. "That's... there's the treaty."

Mallor raised his hand. "I don't want to argue with you. I only wish to tell you that we can find a way to secure a treaty without a marriage. If that is what you want."

Lachlan took a deep breath, relief at his father's willingness to include him, to value what he might say. "I appreciate that, Father, but I would marry Tarley, treaty or not. I love her."

His father offered him a nod chased with a smile. "Well then. I am content with that." He cleared his throat. "You should probably go after your intended. It would seem there are some family matters to attend to." He looked around the chaos of the green. "I'll make sure this gets taken care of. I've already sent for the queen." Then his father grabbed hold of Lachlan and pulled him into his embrace. "I am so proud of you. You will be an amazing king when it is time to take up that mantle."

Lachlan returned his father's hug. "I love you," he said.

Mallor squeezed him, then drew away, tears shining in his eyes. "Go."

Lachlan nodded, turned, and followed Tarley. By the time he walked into the kitchen of The Copper Pot, Scarlett looked as if she'd been cornered in the kitchen by a pack of wild dogs, Tarley among them. Though Tomas stood at her back, his large hands on her slim shoulders, the Fareview siblings squared off with their mother. Mr. Uraiahs stood near Auri. When Tarley saw Lachlan, she held out her hand for him to join her.

"No more se—" Auri's voice got caught on the word, and though Lachlan was sure he knew the word Auri had been about to say, it slipped away from his mind. "Lies. No more lies," Auri finished.

"You might have been trying to protect us, Mother," Jessamine stated, "but full knowledge might be what keeps us safe from here on out."

Scarlett nodded, her gaze jumping to Tomas. "I was only trying to protect you." She turned and looked at Tarley.

"Then tell us the truth," Tarley said. "Who's Azleah?"

"Tell us who *him* is," Mattias insisted.

The siblings erupted, all speaking at once. Lachlan noticed the room was warm. Too warm. And it was too small with all the bodies inside the kitchen. With all that had happened, this wasn't the time or place for this conversation that needed to be had.

"Stop," Tomas said. "Enough."

The room went silent.

"There is much to be said," he said, his hands tightening on Scarlett's shoulders. "Though both of us can understand your anger"—he tilted his head to glance at Scarlett—"it won't serve the greater need, which is to learn the truth." He took a deep breath.

"Yes, your mother and I have kept information from you."

"Why?" Brinna asked.

"It didn't seem right to tell you as children," Scarlett admitted.

"And when we were older?" Jessamine asked.

Scarlett searched her oldest daughter's face. "Later, it just never seemed like the right time."

"But Jessamine is right," Tomas said. "Knowledge is what will keep you safe now."

Scarlett opened her mouth as if to argue, but Tomas leaned forward and pressed a kiss to her cheek.

"It's time," he said quietly.

She closed her mouth and nodded. "Not here. Not now," she said, echoing Lachlan's thoughts. "There are things to be done."

Auri stood. "I refuse to be a prisoner behind the hedge."

Mr. Uraiahs slid a hand from her shoulder down to thread their fingers. "I would like her to come home with me," he said. "As my wife."

Auri leaned back against him.

"She would be safe there—"

Lachlan blinked, sure Auri and her suitor were outlined in a golden aura, together, though that seemed incomprehensible. Though after all he'd witness this day—he blinked again, and the golden outline was gone. He was imaging things, now.

"No," Scarlett said, shaking her head. "She won't be!"

Surprise slipped through Lachlan's chest like a breath held too long at Scarlett's refusal, considering she was talking to a man who could materialize from nothing and move groups of people from one place to another by thinking it. He'd seen Mr. Uraiahs cut down a man with nothing more than a touch. There was also the dragon. But there wasn't an ounce of fear on the woman's face, and Lachlan recognized that determined bravery so often exhibited in Tarley.

"Mother," Auri warned. "This isn't your choice. It's mine. And I will go with or without your blessing—"

The Fareviews burst out in loud chaos once more.

"After Tarley's wedding!" Scarlett yelled, her hands up in acquiescence. "I'll tell you everything after the wedding!"

Everyone's eyes jumped to Tarley and Lachlan. He leaned forward and whispered in Tarley's ear, "We're still getting married, right?"

She turned her head. "After witnessing this, I can see why you might run for the border."

Lachlan smiled. "Not a chance."

She turned slightly. "Even after all that's happened?" she asked. "Monsters, talking ravens, dragons? This chaotic family?"

"We'll fight them together," he whispered.

"After the wedding," Scarlett repeated, and her gaze connected with Auri. "And if this is still what you want, after—I will support your choice, Auri."

"Why wait?" Mattias asked.

Scarlett took a deep breath. "The story is... a lot.

Besides your ribbons, there are spells protecting the story that need to be unraveled, and that's before I tell it. Remembering it will hurt me." Tomas wrapped his arms around her from behind, and she leaned into him. "I don't wish that unhappiness during a time in which we should be celebrating. When there is much work to be done." She offered a wan smile to Tarley, then to each of them.

"After the wedding," Jessamine said and looked at each of her siblings. Even though there were mixed emotions on each of their faces, they all deferred to their older sister and nodded in agreement.

Scarlett turned and looked at Tomas. "Take me home."

Tomas nodded and led his wife from the room, each of their grown children finding it in their hearts to follow.

Lachlan stood in an alcove of the meeting house, dressed in his Jast finery of purple and gold, feeling like a trussed-up peacock. Ollie stood with him, staring out a window at the people walking in.

"Your brother looks bored," Ollie laughed.

"Loam is bored at everything."

"We were never like that."

"Of course not." Lachlan smiled, but his heart was

fluttering with the nerves dipping into his stomach. "I definitely don't feel bored right now." He took a deep breath and let it out slowly.

Ollie turned from the window. He, too, wore Jast regalia, a rapier at his hip and his auburn hair pulled back at his nape with a bow. "Nervous?"

Lachlan nodded.

"Still happy to be going through with this?"

"Won't change my mind about that. Tarley's the best thing that's ever happened to me."

Ollie lifted a brow—an action that Lachlan hated because he couldn't replicate that unnerving look. "Then what are you nervous about?"

"What if she does?" Lachlan had had a nightmare that he'd been standing at the altar of the meeting house waiting, and when the door opened for Tarley's procession, it wasn't her. In her place, Beaknose Truisante.

Ollie clapped him on the back. "Deep breath so you don't faint. Otherwise, your bride might have to give you smelling salts to revive you."

Lachlan chuckled.

It had turned cold in Sevens—a month since the wild day filled with assassins and monsters and a dragon. Nothing so intense had occurred since, other than wedding planning. It was technically late summer, but a bite in the air had turned the leaves in the trees from green to gold with dashes of orange and red among them.

Scarlett had been right about the wedding

becoming the center around which everything else swirled. From clothing, flowers and decorations, party planning fit for a royal party that she refused to relegate to someone outside of Sevens, food, cakes, and drinks along with the million other details Lachlan didn't consider, this royal wedding to a commoner had become the event of both countries.

Sevens was alive with people near and far. The Copper Pot Inn had become royal headquarters. The cottage was Fareview headquarters, where Tarley had retreated after their row at the inn. While he'd spent as much time as he could with Tarley, they hadn't much time to be alone together beyond the hedge. There was a pall still hanging over the family that needed closure.

Now he understood Nixus's scowl.

"Divert me then. What is New Taras like?" he asked Ollie.

"Old."

Lachlan laughed. "Opalant is old."

"Not the same. New Taras overlooks a river like a fortress. The castle is situated at the top and the streets meander around and around until they reach the river valley below. Its rock and plaster, brick and mortar, arches and pillars painted various shades of a sunset."

"Poetic, Ollie."

"You know me. Always wanted to be a writer and got stuck with this job." He grinned.

"And Queen Keyanna?"

Ollie arched his eyebrow again. "Infuriating, but brilliant."

"Thinking of joining her harem?"

Ollie scoffed. "I plan on remaining in Kaloma only as long as your father insists to help her with her cabinet. Hopefully that archbishop will be found. Then I will look forward to my return to Jast."

"Spoken like a true Jastian if I've ever heard one. I must admit, I'm looking forward to spending the year with Tarley there."

Ollie grinned. "Don't want to return immediately to Jast with your family then?"

"Absolutely not. I plan on…" Lachlan stopped and swiped a hand down the placard of his jacket, checking each of his buttons. "Let's just say, what I plan to do isn't fit for my mother's ears."

Ollie laughed loudly. "Perhaps we'll have a new heir before the month is out."

Lachlan furrowed his brow. "Let's not be too hasty. I'd like some time with my wife first. Maybe by the time we're thirty-five. No. Forty." He smiled.

"Lachlan." Trevis poked his head inside the small space. "They're ready."

"Thank you, Trev," he said to the boy who'd become enamored with his seventeen-year-old sister. Of course, Lea couldn't see past the tip of her nose to notice. His siblings weren't exactly enamored with Sevens and had grumbled repeatedly about wanting to return home.

Lachlan joined his family also dressed in their royal garb standing on the dais that Tomas and Mattias had built at the front of the meeting house. It was a beautiful recreation of the tree on the green. His mother reached out as he passed, grabbed his hand, offered a quick squeeze, and released him. As he turned to face the front, Lachlan tracked Ollie across the room and watched as he took a seat next to Queen Keyanna. The Queen offered Lachlan a smile and a regal nod.

Lachlan took his place near Horance, who held the binding cloth for the ceremony. Tarley had refused to allow the Rayoran priest to marry them, though Acolyte Primson was still present, watching from the gallery, to confirm their vows as was still necessary by Kaloma law until the laws were changed. And surprisingly, Horance had agreed to do the honors of leading them through their vows.

The meeting house was decorated in sprigs of pine and berries, late flowers still in bloom, ribbons, and candles—a recreation of the Green. An array of forest colors throughout the hall made Lachlan smile, remembering their time alone in the woods when he fell in love with a woodland fairy named Tarley.

When Tomas and Scarlett appeared in the doorway at the opposite end of the building, Lachlan's breath caught in his chest, knowing Tarley was on her way. The guests began tossing flower petals as soon as they stepped into the aisle. By the time Tomas and Scarlett, arm-in-arm, climbed the dais where Lachlan stood with his family, he was eager to see his bride. Jessamine followed them first, then Brinna, then Auri, and finally Mattias.

His heart stopped then decided to race forward,

lurching in his chest when Tarley appeared in the doorway. His woodland fairy. She wore a dress her sisters had made, of mauve silk and sparkling with gems the queen had sent. The fabric skimmed her like a dream. As she walked forward, the silk moved with her steps, drifting around her like a cloud, flower petals raining around her. A crown of greenery circled her head. Lachlan was sure he was standing in a woodland glen, watching his fairy-queen wife who'd stolen his heart.

Her eyes jumped to his and curled with joy as she smiled at him—a smile that stole his heart one more time and he knew would for the rest of their lives.

Ever After . . .

Tarley

Lachlan carried Tarley over the threshold of the room in the inn. It was the first time they'd truly been alone, aside from a few stolen moments at the cottage over the last four weeks. Scarlett had insisted Tarley return home to the cottage where it was safer, and while things had been strained, planning a royal wedding in a place like Sevens had proved all encompassing.

Now, though, in her husband's arms—her husband!—Tarley's heart was knocking against the inside of her chest with an excited rhythm.

Lachlan kicked the door closed behind him, set her down, and leveled a dark look full of promise. "Clothes off," he ordered.

A thrill went through her as she took a step away

from him. "Is this how it's going to be? You ordering me about, Your Highness?"

"That is not all I plan to do to you–" He took another step toward her while undoing the gold buttons of his purple jacket. He looked divine. As she'd walked down the aisle, when she saw him in his royal finery, the weight of marrying him carried crashed into her. She'd only ever known him as a man, and how wonderful a man he was. He was going to be an incredible king. The king of Jast!

"When I get these hands on you, Tarley," he promised, holding up his hands for a moment. She tracked them as he returned to working the golden buttons of his jacket loose. "Clothes."

"The guard is right outside," Tarley whispered, retreating a step as Lachlan stalked forward.

"Now you're shy?" Lachlan asked. "You weren't exactly opposed to going at it in the hedge outside your parents' cottage where everyone could hear us."

She grinned as heat spread across her cheeks. "Hush."

"And you'd do it again."

She grinned at him.

Currently, their guests were in the Inn's courtyard and the dining room for the reception. She could hear the faint threads of music and raucous voices deep in drink by now. She imagined her family dancing with the rest of the community that had raised her, along with the Queen and her sister, as well as her new in-laws celebrating.

There was a lot to celebrate. The treaty, the capture of the Fiedel leaders, and the removal of the treasonous Rayoran from Queen Keyanna's council. Things had moved so quickly and so successfully that when the Queen informed Tarley that she didn't have to marry Lachlan if she didn't want to, Tarley knew without a doubt that marrying him had never been about duty. When the same had been posed to Lachlan, he'd looked at Tarley, and said, "I will fucking want you until the end of my days—if you're willing to make me yours?"

That had been it.

Now, he stalked another closer. "There will always be guards around, Princess. Clothes," he reminded, shirking out of his jacket with two jerky movements. "I think they secretly get off on hearing it. I mean, who wouldn't." He grinned and yanked the tunic from his breeches, then hopped toward her, pulling off his boots one at a time. "Do you think you'll be loud, my queen?"

My queen.

Her heart squeezed with joy, and with trembling fingers, she unfastened the diamond clasp at her throat—a gift from her new mother-in-law—loosening the heavy fabric of the cloak. "It's a distinct possibility. I've been fantasizing–"

Lachlan groaned and pulled the shirt over his head, his gaze intense with want when they came to rest on her once more. "If you don't move faster, I'm ripping that dress from your body." He continued forward as

Tarley backed toward the bed. "I have been fantasizing too, and I'm so fucking hard, Tarley." Lachlan took himself in hand over his trousers.

She stopped moving, her throat suddenly dry. "Gods, Lach."

He stopped in front of her, and she grasped his hips, then tugged at the fastening on his trousers, struggling to get them open, until finally, she released his erection, and it sprang free of its confines, glorious, hard, and perfect. "I've been dreaming about this, about you." She wrapped her hand around his girth, his moan filling her ears with power. "In my mouth."

"Tarley. Oh gods–" His breath caught, and she tugged on him, root to tip, then repeated the motion. He grasped her hand. "Stop." He leaned forward and nipped at her lips, groaning as he did. "As much as I want to be in your mouth, let's save that for later." He ran the pad of his thumb over her bottom lip. "Why are you still dressed?" He grabbed her bodice and tugged on it, pulling several buttons at her back loose to rain on the wooden floor.

She gasped. "Lach!" she admonished, but her heart wasn't in the complaint. Rather, the weight between her thighs, the heaviness of her breasts, as she anticipated Lachlan's touch, his tongue, his cock was more adamantly on her mind.

"We'll get it fixed." He grabbed her face, his fingers diving into her hair, and pulled her in for an all-consuming kiss, his mouth taking more than it was giving, until he seemed to remember himself, pulling away and trailing kisses over her skin. "I find," he said between each kiss, "I'm extremely impatient, my dear."

He turned her and began releasing buttons one at a time, until he pushed the fabric down her arms. Tarley helped him, pulling free of her dress until she was just in her chemise and the slip, and turned to face him. She reached back to find the button fastening the slip at her waist and made quick work of it. The fabric loosened around her hips, and Lachlan pushed it down then lifted her out of the pool of silk.

She wrapped her legs around his hips, meeting his mouth once more as his tongue swirled with promise against hers, a beautiful dance that pushed her pulse and emptied her mind of everything but him. With a sigh, she tightened her legs around him to move against his hard length between them, reveling in the friction, moaning into his kiss.

"I want you," she said.

"You're still dressed." He set her down.

"So are you." Her eyes flicked to his open pants, still riding the curve of his hips even if his cock was free. She licked her lips.

"I'm going to rip them," he warned, gripping the fabric so it tightened around her body, creating amazing friction against her skin.

"They're my nicest set." She hurried to remove them.

"I plan on you not wearing much of anything for a while." He wiggled his eyebrows at her and grinned as he helped her remove the chemise, drawing it over her head until all that was left were her stockings. Then he grasped her hips, pulled her across the bed toward him, pressed her onto her back, and placing each of her ankles on his shoulders.

"I'm not sure that's going to be appreciated by everyone else."

"Oh. I think they would appreciate it very much." He paused, considering it. "You'll never leave our rooms."

She laughed. "That doesn't seem very practical."

He pushed one stocking down her leg. "I should warn you." He pulled the fabric free and dropped it.

"Warn me about what," she asked, tilting her head.

"I'm about to make you scream, Tarley. I want everyone to know you're mine." He kissed the arch of her foot, before setting it on the bed at the edge. Then he turned to the other leg and removed the other stocking, exposing her skin, kissing, licking her leg as he did. "Then I'm going to do it again."

Tarley shivered.

He set the other foot on the bed, her legs spread for him. Lachlan dropped to his knees and kissed her inner thighs. "Stars, Tarley." He assessed her a moment before she felt the warmth of his tongue slide along her slit. Then he pressed a kiss over her clit—a caress and a kiss to cherish. "I've been dreaming about this." He licked her again, his tongue flat and gentle. "My dreams are not enough," he moaned and buried his face between her legs.

Tarley sucked in a breath. "Oh," she said and tilted

her hips toward him. "That's—"

He looked up at her, his mouth still indulging, his hands sliding up her thighs, holding her legs open and pressing her hips in place. He stopped a moment and said, "Don't move." Another order, and she loved it. "Or there will be consequences."

"So bossy," Tarley gasped, the words stolen, when Lachlan's tongue slid through her essence until he settled on her clit, focusing his attention there, then driving down and inside her. She gasped but tried not to move, tried not to buck her hips against his mouth, panting as he drew her closer to a precipice of release. Slow and sensual, his tongue swirled and savored, relishing her, until she was crying, "Please. Please. Lach." Finally, unable to contain herself, she grabbed his head.

He stopped.

Tarley cried out, her pleasure drawn to the point of a sharp edge and held aloft there. "No!" She moved her hips, looking for that satisfying friction.

"I said there'd be consequences." He trailed kisses up over her pelvis, stopping to nip at her hip bones, before working his way up her stomach, his hands roaming over her breasts, teasing her nipples with his fingers, until one was his mouth. "Didn't you believe me?" he asked around it and sucked.

"Please, Lach," she said, rolling her hips against him, seeking completion, her body connecting with his erection.

He groaned. "Gods, Tarley. You're making this

difficult." He drew the opposite nipple into his mouth and added pressure with his teeth.

Tarley cried out again, a sharp whip zinging through straight to her aching core. She arched her back into him. "Yes."

Lachlan rose over her, his hands on either side of her head. She wrapped her legs around his hips and pulled him toward her with her heels, though he resisted and smiled, but it seemed to be an afterthought, because his eyes, filled with a dark hunger Tarley recognized, raked over her.

"I wish you could see what I see," he said. "You're so fucking beautiful."

"I want you in me," she bit out, gasping, needing, grabbing his hips.

He leaned down and kissed her, grinding against her hips, then pulled away, pressing his forehead to hers to release a heavy breath himself. "I want this to fucking last," he said, "but fuck, Tarley." He rolled his hips again, until he reached between them, took himself in hand, and slid the head of his cock through her slick center to meet her clit. "You fucking undo me."

She gasped. "Yes," she breathed. "There." She tipped her hips toward the sensation.

"Come for me," he said. "Come, my queen."

And with a few more strokes, she tensed, her gasps and cries unrestrained as her seams came apart, chanting incoherent worship of the man who'd become her husband. Her body arched toward him, and Lachlan pushed into her, deep and unmoving, his body rigid and controlled as every part of her clenched around him. She melted, her body relaxing as her release ebbed, and when she opened her eyes, Lachlan was watching her, his face filled with awe.

"Watching you come will be the single most amazing image I carry with me." He moved his hips, pulling out a fraction before thrusting back in. "You feel so good." He grunted the words, repeating the movement before grinding back into her. "Fuck–" He repeated the motion, over and over, a controlled rhythm.

Mine.

Mine.

Mine.

Tarley rode through the pleasure, satiated, until suddenly her body wrapped around the desire inside her once more, a silky ribbon tightening as her body responded to Lachlan's penetration. Her panting and cries grew in volume, mingling with his heavy sighs and grunts that went straight into her head and heart. "Yes." She encouraged him. "You feel so good inside me," she said. "Please, Lachlan."

"Are you?" he asked. "Again?"

"Close," she said. "Oh–"

"Tarley." He ground his hips.

She tilted her hips toward him and sought a rhythm to add more friction to his. Things between them sped up, and his rhythm grew haphazard as Tarley begged. "Oh. Yes. Please. Please, Lachlan." He wrapped his arms under her legs, grinding into her with a gorgeous unrestrained fervor.

Suddenly, she was unraveling with her second orgasm, crying out, louder this time, as it rocked through her whole body, and she bucked wildly against him. Lachlan drove one, two, three more times into her, growled out her name as if it contained a magic spell to keep him contained, and repeatedly grunted "mine" on each panted breath as he became undone with his own orgasm after hers. When it passed, he melted against her body, chest to chest, and she swallowed him with her arms, his weight welcome.

A few breaths later, Lachlan rolled to his side, drawing her against him so they faced one another, and though his eyes were closed, he was smiling.

Tarley skimmed his smiling face with her fingertips. "Well," she said, pushing a sweaty lock of hair from his forehead, "I think we might be pretty good at that."

One of his eyes opened. "Just pretty good?"

She smiled. "Oh. Did that damage your pride?"

He closed his eyes. "Give me a few minutes. Rather than pretty good, it's going to be fucking great." He grinned, then planted a kiss on her shoulder.

Tarley laughed. "That's what I love about you. You never give up."

"Where there's a will, there's a way."

An overwhelming feeling crashed over her, and she tightened her hold on him. "I love you."

He pulled her closer. "I'm going to spend my life

earning it."

"My love is yours not because of what you do, Lachlan," she said, running her hands over his skin, grateful to be able to do it, "but because you're Lachlan—my Lachlan."

He opened his eyes to study her, skimming her face, then moving forward until she was on her back again, and he was seated between her thighs. "I know something I'm really good at, and I'm only going to get better with practice."

"What's that?" she asked, knowing he was about to say something cheeky.

Only he said, "Loving you," and leaned forward meeting her lips with his. He rolled onto his back, pulling her with him until she straddled his hips. Then he laid back and looked up, his eyes roving over her. "I think it will be the single greatest thing I have ever done in my entire life."

Tarley's heart answered with a jolt. She smiled—completely open and content—then she leaned down, pressing her lips to his to show him just how much.

King Thrushbeard

A Grimm's Fairytale

Once upon a time there was a king with a very arrogant daughter. When it came time for her to marry, he brought all the eligible husbands to the kingdom. The princess, rather than choose from among them, decided to mock each with loud jests to the court. The suitors were too fat, too short, too red-faced, too old. One she even ridiculed saying he had a chin like a thrush's beak, and from that moment on was called King Thrushbeard. Her father, angry and embarrassed by his daughter's behavior, decided to teach her a lesson, and told her that the very next beggar to their door would become her husband.

A few days later, a traveling minstrel arrived to sing under the window at the palace, and the king invited him in. The singer entered the palace in tattered rags. The king announced, "Your song has pleased me so well that I will give you my daughter as your wife."

The princess was horrified, but the king reminded her, "I made a vow. This is your husband." The priest was fetched, she was married to the beggar-man, and without further ado, the princess left the castle with her new husband.

As they traveled, she marveled at the breadth of the forest, she noted a fine meadow and livestock, and a great city they passed through. To each compliment, the minstrel told her they all belonged to King Thrushbeard. The princess grieved, "He could have been my husband," to which the singing beggar replied, "I don't like you wishing for another husband. Am I not good enough?"

Eventually, they arrived at a very small cottage, and in shock, the princess learned she would need to cook, clean,

and care for the beggar-man herself. Only she had no skills, so he taught her what he knew. When she had managed to learn how to build a fire, cook a meal, and keep the cottage, the beggar said, "It is time for you to earn your keep." He told her she would make baskets, only she couldn't manage the willows. He told her she could try spinning, but the spindle and thread cut her fingers until blood flowed. So he determined she would sit in the marketplace and trade and sell pots. Afraid members of her father's kingdom would see her and mock her, she balked, but it was yield or starve.

The first day at the market went well; she was beautiful, and people wanted to buy wares from her. On the second day, however, a drunkard smashed through her clay pots, breaking them all. Afraid what her husband would say, she hurried home to tell him of her misfortune. He was kind and told her not to worry, indicating he'd been asking at her father's castle for a job she might acquire. So she returned to her father's castle as a kitchen-maid. One evening she was forced upstairs and as guests arrived for the myriad of celebrations at the castle, guests more handsome than the next, she lamented her haughtiness and pride, then returned each night to her small cottage with her beggar husband and the food she'd earned.

On one such night, the royals gathered to celebrate the wedding of a prince. The prince, she realized, was her former suitor, the one her horrible comment had coined King Thrushbeard. As she stood in the doorway, he passed by dressed in his finery, handsome and admirable. He noticed her standing in the doorway, her pockets full of food she would take home with her. He asked her to dance. Afraid, she declined because she was ashamed of

how she had treated him along with her current circumstances. Only he insisted and pulled her to the dance floor. The food scraps in pots she carried in her pockets fell out onto the dance floor, cracking, and spilling at her feet. The other party-goers mocked her for her appearance, so she fled.

King Thrushbeard chased after her, catching her before she could leave the castle. "Do not be afraid," he told her, "I am your husband. The beggar-man and I are one in the same. For great love, I disguised myself. It was I who taught you, I who broke the pots in the marketplace, and I who brought you home. I only wanted to help you recognize your proud heart."

She wept bitterly, "I have done you great wrong and am not worthy to be your wife."

"Take courage," he said. "Leave that behind us, for our wedding celebration is here."

Then came her ladies-in-waiting to prepare her. She was brought to the wedding celebration, restored to her place as a princess, to meet her true husband, King Thrushbeard. And her father, the court, all in attendance for their wedding feast wished her joy with King Thrushbeard, and she was happy.

And they lived happily ever after.

PLAYLIST

Lovely	Billie Eilish, Khalid
Sad Tune	AK
Famous	Hailaker, Lowswimmer, Jemima Coulter
A Great Longing of an Unquiet Heart	Luke Howard, Budapest Art Orchestra
Temporary	Tim Schaufert
Against My Skin	Liam Thomas
The Chase	Emmit Fenn
Feel	Two Lanes
Softer Still	Emily Nance, kinnship
Breathing	KIDSO
Lose My Mind	Arrient
Hollow	Emmit Fenn, Shallou
All I See	Tim Shaufert
Deep	Peter Sandberg
Stoned on You	Jaymes Young

My Poor Heart	Andrew Belle
Talk to Me	Dave Thomas Junior
You're All I Want	Harvey, Oscuro
Gwythian	JJ Draper
See Me Through	John Metcalfe
Wherever You Go	Tim Shaufert, CASHFORGOLD
Home	Ben Bohmer, JONAH

ACKNOWLEDGEMENTS

There are so many people to thank—READERS most of all. Look, I wouldn't get to do this over and over again without YOU. You're the ones who buy the book, talk about the book, share the book, champion the book. To my street team, The Red Ribbons, to the librarians and indie booksellers taking chances on new authors to get the word out about the stories. Without each of you, I'm just writing stories and hoping someone is interested in reading them. So, thank you, thank you, thank you.

I should also take a moment to thank some magical people in my life. These are the voices casting spells to help me combat imposter syndrome, to tell me I can when I'm sure I can't and commiserate when I need to vent. Thank you, Mae, Maggie, Willow, Leisa, Lindsey, Kara, Rachel, Robin, my Carpe Diem crew, Stephanie, and Lavinia. A big, hefty thanks belongs to Beth Stedman, who talked me off the ledge when I thought I would burn this book. She helped me see the forest for the trees. Thanks as always to Kate Lamoureux, editor extraordinaire and keeper of all magical knowledge to keep the words coherent (any mistakes are mine!). And always, Sara Oliver, cover magician. I'm so grateful for the forged partnership with you. The magic you create with your covers enchants me.

To my grown-up kids—my own version of the Fareviews—thank you for your support. When I asked if you would be embarrassed if I wrote spicy fiction, you both offered me an impatient look and said, "No. Write what you want, Mom." It means so much that you've got my back. I've got yours and I love you.

To my partner, Vince: As I wrote Lachlan, I kept thinking about how much you make me smile. There's something magical about a partner who can make you laugh, to find the good things in each moment, each day. Like Lachlan. Thank you for being my prince charming. I love you.

To my Creator—Praise God, from whom all blessings flow// Praise Him, all creatures here below// Praise Him above, ye heavenly host// Praise Father, Son, and Holy Ghost!—Thank you.

A Fareview Fairytale
Book 3 coming soon

An excerpt from

In the Shadow of a Dream

By Maci Aurora

Brinna

Brinna, third daughter of Tomas and Scarlett Fareview, stood near a wall in the courtyard at the Copper Pot Inn, the crisp, clear air of the autumn night caressing her exposed skin as she watched the wedding revelry. Happy. Her older sister, Tarley had disappeared with her new husband some time ago, but the celebration continued, and it was a sight to behold.

There were so many people in Sevens—strangers, most of them—dressed in an array of colorful finery, glimmering in the flickering candlelight. Tall spires of fire offered both heat and light, and glasses filled with spirits glinted like fairy lights flitting through the forest as people moved, the din of their conversations and laughter carried like notes swirling with the music over the cobblestones. The dancers moved in a flurry of movement, like snowflakes riding a breeze.

The spectacle was beautiful.

It was romantic.

Brinna loved it and pressed the fingers of one of her gloved hands against her fluttering heart.

Scanning the crowd for her family, she found her parents speaking with Tarley's new inlaws. A king and queen! Unable to contain her awe, she grinned. Who'd have ever imagined her mother and father would be speaking to the King and Queen of Jast! In Sevens! She saw her sister Jessamine dancing with one of the Jast soldiers, though she wasn't sure which one since there were many and their mother had kept them busy at the cottage with wedding preparations. No time to make new acquaintances.

"It's too dangerous," her mother had warned, justifying the isolation.

Brinna's brother, Mattias was across the courtyard, frowning at something—or someone—though at her distance, she couldn't tell, since he just seemed to glower at the dancers in general. Mattias had been more reserved since returning from his errand for the Queen of Kaloma, and Brinna had wondered if perhaps he needed to talk about it. There'd been so little time to debrief any of the recent events, Brinna had barely been able to make sense of them herself.

A few steps from Mattias, Auri and her suitor, Nixus Uraiahs, danced together, twirling with the rest of the revelers. Nixus bent to say something in Auri's ear. She threw her head back and laughed, pulling him closer, and they lost all semblance of the dance steps and just held on to one another. Given Nixus's announced intentions, Brinna suspected there would be another wedding soon.

With a quick scan, she looked for Nix's infuriating brother, Lucian. She knew he'd attended the wedding, since he'd deigned lower himself to incline his head in a greeting. The haughty ass. She would deny looking for him if asked, but he was definitely worth ogling even if his personality left much to be desired. Given his height, he should have been easy to spot, but he was nowhere to be found. Typical.

She sighed, content to enjoy the moment considering the chaos of late. With both Tarley and Auri losing their protective ribbons, the revelation that Nixus was the actual god of night and darkness, and that the horrid Dr. Rufus revealed as a darkling hunting Tarley for her blood, things had been stressful. Brinna had so many questions. Grabbing hold of her own ribbon as if to ground herself, she twisted it around her wrist so the bow was outside. Their mother was the only way they were going to get answers, and she'd promised to provide them after the wedding.

Mattias caught Brinna's attention, skirting the dancers as he moved toward the in. She didn't like that her brother looked so unhappy, especially on such a night when celebration was in order. He was only nineteen, which might have been a factor. At twenty-five, Brinna remembered the morose way Sevens and the Whitling Woods had sunk their teeth into her thoughts at his age, that horrible feeling that she might be stuck there forever with other options. And yet, the vibrancy of the party around her, the crowd of strangers spoke to a world beyond their small village.

There was hope.

She started after her brother, if not to change his mind, but to offer her moral support. That was who she was, after all: the sweet one. The romantic. The dreamer. Jessamine was the healer, Tarley the sour to Brinna's sweet, Auri the realist, and Mattias the baby and the only boy. Slipping into her role as the nurturer, Brinna went after her brother. Bypassing the throng of people, she walked into the dining room where the feast had been held and scanned the room. But Mattias was nowhere to be seen.

"Evening, Miss Fareview."

Brinna turned her head and smiled at the barkeep, one of the proprietors of The Copper Pot Inn. "Hello, Horance. A lovely wedding, though I think we're long past evening."

He nodded. "True enough."

"Have you seen Mattias?"

Horance glanced around, then shook his head. "Not for some time. Not since dinner."

Brinna frowned. She was confident Mattias had only just walked in. Looking around once more, she thanked Horance, then returned to the courtyard. The night's chill suddenly felt colder as she spun in place, finding no sight of her giant brother, who she certainly should have been able to see in the crowd. Worry climbed into her chest, weighting the buoyant happiness. Might he have left for the cottage. Considering it would snap their mother's already-taut nerves, she couldn't imagine him doing so. Their mother had expressly forbidden the family to be without one another for the sole purpose of safety— or so she'd said.

Mattias wouldn't have just left, would he?

Brinna glanced at her parents, but they were dancing, her mother was smiling, so Brinna didn't dare interrupt. It seemed such a long time since Scarlett had smiled.

Turned to the darkness beyond the fire, Brinna considered the danger. She knew she shouldn't leave but worry for her brother nullified any rationale she remain within the light. Mattias shouldn't be alone.

Decided, Brinna left the celebration for the darkened village, calling her brother's name and wishing they'd lit the lanterns along the main thoroughfare of Sevens—but every lamp was currently being used at the inn. Her voice sounded muted, as if it had hit a wall and dropped back into the dirt before her with a thud. She wasn't afraid so much as concerned for her brother—and slightly annoyed at the inconvenience of having to find him instead of finding an agreeable dance partner.

If she was being honest with herself, there hadn't been anyone she'd been particularly interested in dancing with, even if there were some handsome fellows. Nix's brother, Lucian, was expressly beautiful but horribly unapproachable.

You've danced before, she remembered. *Under the stars.*

Then he'd ruined the experience.

There had to be other agreeable gentlemen to meet, she supposed, and decided she'd just have to dance with them all once she'd returned with Mattias. How was she to meet the love of her life without opening the door to possibility?

The sound of her new boots—dainty and unsuitable for the gravel roadway—echoed eerily in the darkness. "Tai," she called again, hiking up her skirts to keep them from dragging in the dust. She'd made it to the middle of the village where the dark meeting house stretched out across the street beyond the green. She could see the shadowed outline of the large tree in the green and turned to look over her shoulder at the inn, wondering if perhaps Mattias hadn't left. That this—venturing out alone—was careless.

A raven squawked.

No longer walking, Brinna stood at the center of the village and yelled for Mattias once more.

No answer. No Mattias.

Yes, it had been silly to venture out into the darkness by herself. There were so many places in the inn to check first.

She turned back.

The strange sound called her attention, and Brinna started and looked over her shoulder, heart pounding.

A man stood on the street illuminated by the faint light from the inn and the intermittent moonlight shining between the clouds. What little she could see was pale, his lips curled in what seemed a kind smile, though they were a disconcerting shade of red.

He smoothed his gloved hands over his dark wool of his jacket. "Hello?"

Her heartbeat quickened. He had a nice voice. How many times had she imagined meeting a handsome stranger in Sevens? Too many to count, though in her dreams, the faceless suitor hadn't been found in the dark, but often overwhelmed her with light. She squinted now, but not because of light—rather, a lack of.

"Greetings. There's a party?" The man started toward her, his steps nearly imperceptible over the roadway.

Brinna remained fixed to her spot but turned slightly toward him. "You're late for the party."

The man—without a hat, which seemed strange—smiled wider, and now that he was closer, she noticed his ink-black hair shimmered blue when he moved, like a crow in the sunshine. His skin also held a bluish hue, tinted by the shadows of the night.

"I'm afraid I'm lost. I was wondering if you might help me find my way?" he asked and smiled, his teeth bright behind his blood-red lip smile.

His voice was rather alluring, and despite her rational misgivings, the irrational seemed to be taking control. She tilted her head, considering him, feeling a strange sensation run the length of her spine, ending in her belly. It wasn't a pleasant sensation, and she took a step away from him, even if propriety insisted on hospitality.

With another glance over her shoulder at the inn, she considered leaving him to fend for himself, but she wasn't one to be rude. "The wedding is just that way," she said, gesturing. "I can show you."

Just a touch behind her last word, like an echo, another voice shouted, "Brinna! No! Run!"

She swiveled, staring at a shadow emerging from the darkness beneath the tree on the green. A man, moving too quickly to make him out but for the light he emitted.

Lucian.

Something hissed.

As if in slow motion, she turned back to the stranger, registering the change in his face, sharp and angular with sunken, hollowed eyes, the whites swallowed by darkness, the blood-red lips lined with sharp teeth.

"Mine," it hissed, no longer alluring, but terrifying, grating against her ears. The creature reached a clawed hand for her, cold enveloping her in its proximity.

She recoiled, opening her mouth to scream, when a wave of warmth hit her like a wall. A white-hot heat banded her waist and rush up her back, drawing her into its safety. A flash of a bright light followed.

Everything turned white around her, blinding her. Then everything disappeared.

In the Shadow of Dream
Coming 2024

ABOUT THE AUTHOR

Maci Aurora has been writing stories since she was a child. At eleven, she fell in love with reading Sunfire Historical Romances about girls who made a difference in their lives while falling in love. When she discovered Lavyrle Spencer and Judith McNaught, their novels cemented her own journey to tell stories about love. Since then, she's been forever lost between the pages of a book as both a reader and a writer. *In the Shadow of a Hoax* is her 2nd novel in the Fareview Fairytales series and her 9th novel overall (she writes contemporary romance as CL Walters). For the most up-to-date news about Maci's upcoming releases, fun extras, and behind-the-scenes bits, sign up for her newsletter on her website www.maciaurora.com.